Praise for

AMY HEYDENRYCH

'A devastating and totally unexpected twist, I devoured this in one sitting'
CHRIS WHITAKER

'Highly entertaining and brilliantly written'
JO SPAIN

'[Amy] writes with passion and ferocity'
JAMES CAROL

'Dark, original and thoroughly gripping'
T.M. LOGAN

'A dark enthralling novel packed with twist after twist'
WOMAN AND HOME

Amy Heydenrych is a writer and book blogger based in South Africa. She has been shortlisted twice for the acclaimed Miles Morland African Writing Scholarship. Her short stories and poems have published in multiple anthologies including *Brittle Paper*, *The Kalahari Review* and the *Short Sharp Stories* anthologies. When she is not writing her own fiction, she ghost-writes books and columns for global tech and financial companies.

Also by Amy Heydenrych

Shame on You

THE
PACT

AMY HEYDENRYCH

ZAFFRE

First published in Great Britain in 2019 by
ZAFFRE
80–81 Wimpole St, London W1G 9RE

A CIP catalogue record for this book is
available from the British Library.

ISBN: 978-1-78577-098-2

Also available as an ebook

1 3 5 7 9 10 8 6 4 2

Typeset by IDSUK (Data Connection) Ltd
Printed and bound in Great Britain by Clays Ltd, Elcograf S.p.A.

Zaffre is an imprint of Bonnier Books UK
www.bonnierbooks.co.uk

For Rhys

It was supposed to be a prank, a stupid mistake that evaporated the next day. She never meant for her to die. Truth be told, she didn't know exactly what she wanted. She hated herself while she did it and regretted it the second it was done. But later, beneath her begging and protestations, one fact remained: while she never meant for her to die, she did want to hurt her, just a little.

Chapter 1

What actually happened on the night Nicole died was vague as a rumor, caught through snippets of conversation behind closed doors. By the time the neighbors had guessed at what was really going on, it was too late.

Who could blame them? It didn't sound like death at first. A door creaked open. Her musical laugh suggested it was simply a friend stopping by. Nicole was well liked in the building, and always the first to offer a smile. Of course she would have friends over all the time! There were vague sounds – footsteps, clinking cutlery, the low hum of music through speakers. Nothing to cause alarm.

The apartments were packed like sardines, so the neighbors did what they always do. They turned the television up, they spoke a little louder, they put on music of their own. It was the usual competing cacophony that never got too loud or lasted after midnight.

But that night was different. The music got louder – the children in the building were unable to sleep. This was out of character for Nicole and inappropriate for a weeknight. The neighbors below her debated amongst themselves whether it was time to go upstairs and say something.

Every sentence of her conversation was shouted, the laughter raucous. Some heard the high-pitched shriek of a woman, others the low growl of a man. The neighbors tried not to focus on it, not to let each word aggravate them further, but it was all they could think about. They should call someone, report it, it was far too loud.

Suddenly, the laughter turned hysterical. It was out-of-control, hooting, belly-aching laughter, the kind that rips the breath out of your lungs.

A voice. *'What the hell?'* Then, a dull thud, like the sound of a bowling ball dropping to the ground. Something had shifted. It sounded strange, but not strange enough to investigate. The noise came to an abrupt end and all was silent. Palpable relief flooded the building. Soon, the neighbors forgot their irritation and the strange end to the evening, and drifted off to sleep, while the killer stepped out and paced past their doorways, while Nicole's blood spread like a halo around her, while she gasped her last breath.

Chapter 2

Isla
The morning after the murder

'You know what is at the heart of so many suburban murders? Politeness,' says Isla. She wrestles with her old Ford's dodgy steering to parallel-park it in front of an apartment building that seems too stylish to be a murder scene. It's one of those newly gentrified areas in San Francisco where every pedestrian looks ready to be snapped for a street style editorial. Isla barely misses the exposed shins of a hipster in rolled-up distressed denims and a thick, curly beard.

'Why do you say that?' says her best friend, Lizzie, on the other end of the phone. In the background she can hear the now-familiar sounds of early evening in London, the roar of motorcycles, the hooting of a bus, the buzz of commuters' voices. They haven't lived in the same city for years, but they speak on the phone every day when the time difference allows.

Lizzie is a graphic designer, worlds apart from Isla's extreme career choice.

'Well,' Isla says, leafing through her notebook while balancing the handset against her ear, 'in these cases bystanders always say the same thing.

"Murders just don't happen in this part of town."

"We're a very peaceful neighborhood."

"None of us saw this coming. The killer was an upstanding member of the community!"

'Sure.' Sarcasm burns fresh on her tongue.

Lizzie laughs down the line. 'You really are a ray of sunshine when you've just woken up.'

'I'm serious!'

If pressed for long enough, each neighbor can recall *something*. The night the abusive husband took it too far and the argument ended with smashing glass. The tall, burly men who kept lurking outside the door of the smartly dressed businessman in 12A who was rumored to have a gambling habit. Or maybe just a bad feeling that can't be shrugged off.

Isla fiddles with the buttons on the elevator, trying to recall the message that communicated which floor the crime scene is on. 'Listen, I better go. Good luck with your presentation today!'

'Good luck with your murder . . .'

Without the crutch of distraction, a deeper anxiety crawls under Isla's skin. The alert she received about today's case made the hair on the back of her neck stand on end. *A thirty-one-year-old woman* – the exact same age as her – *has been found brutally murdered, potentially by someone she knew.* The clipped police statement noted no signs of forced entry and the neighbors have insisted they didn't hear anything other than loud music, animated conversation and laughing. It brings back a memory of her own, a liquor-stumbling, stale-cigarette-kissed scene that she quickly pushes to the back of her mind. She's safe now, right here, on the other side of the police tape. As a reporter, she has the control to shape the story and take the power back. Yet the past is never too far away. This morning, it is on the other side of that door.

Isla flashes a media access card and steps into the apartment. Technically, she shouldn't be allowed near the crime scene until all the evidence has been collected, but in her time on this beat she has earned the trust of this division, especially Simon, the lead inspector on the case. Usually he allows her to slip in, undetected.

It's been ten years since Simon, then a rookie cop, called Isla and convinced her to reopen her sexual assault case. Nine years and six months since she looked into her ex-boyfriend's jeering face as they led him away in handcuffs at the end of a grueling trial. That moment still twists in her gut like a knife, the pain never dulls, no matter how many years pass. In many ways, she feels like the same vulnerable young woman she was all those years ago.

Simon, however, has been fortified by time – his limbs have thickened, and his stance strengthened. His dark hair is now shaved close to his head and today he's shrouded in a forensic suit. Anyone would think he would have shed his idealism and repressed his tenderness by now. But every time Isla approaches him at a crime scene, she is sure she sees the gentleness flash across his eyes, fleeting as a shadow.

She smiles at Simon briefly. The familiarity of him anchors her in the face of a new investigation. The body is in the bathroom – this is evident from the cluster of forensic suits outside – but there is also a *feeling* a place gets when something terrible happens. It's the leaden smell of blood, the chaos and mess that hint at the moments before, but it is also something spiritual. No matter how many crime scenes Isla visits, it still chills her to the bone.

She steers clear of the bathroom. To see the body first is too dehumanizing for the person inside. For many media accounts of a murder, it is about the gore. All empathy is stripped away before the story has even begun. She is more interested in the story behind the story, in who the person was before.

The apartment is small but decorated in a sleek, minimalist Scandinavian style. Every object appears purposeful and of a high quality. Easy, self-assured wealth. Isla takes note of the recycling bins in the kitchen and the thriving potted herb garden on the windowsill. Nicole Whittington was a woman who had her shit together.

Smaller details in the living room spark Isla's interest. There is a half-eaten bowl of roasted vegetable pasta on the coffee table, a romantic comedy on pause and a *Vogue* magazine on the couch, still in its plastic wrapping. A woman after my own heart, she thinks; a woman who was planning an evening alone. A few books stand out on the shelf: Marie Kondo's *Life-Changing Magic of Tidying Up*, Roxane Gay's *Difficult Women*, a frayed copy of Albert

Camus' *L'étranger* and an English – Japanese dictionary. In addition to the team spilling out the bathroom, she notices two people from forensics scanning the living room with a blue light. A picture starts sketching itself in Isla's mind.

She grits her teeth and pushes past the furniture and forensics to the bathroom in the corner of the apartment. The scene of the murder.

Simon steps in front of her.

'Sorry, Isla, this area is off limits. The forensics team is in the thick of gathering evidence.'

'Good morning to you, too, Simon.'

She's seen this look before – cases like these are hard on the police, as well as reporters like her. They're the kind that push you up close to the face of evil, and give you no option to look away. They set off a trauma that beats beneath your skin, long after the case is closed, the story is filed and the body is taken away.

Simon won't look her in the eye. 'The victim was battered to death with a bronze sculpture, and then propped up in the shower, like a doll.'

His gaze flits towards the bathroom door. Isla knows that Simon always struggles with cases where women are hurt. A few times, they have sat together in a coffee shop, Simon repeating the details of a case over and over, looping round the violence, processing it all. She always wonders, out of all the careers he could have followed, why he chose to be a cop? He turns back towards the scene, knocking over a perfectly nurtured orchid in the process. Clumps of soil scatter into the cream shag carpet. In the bulk of the forensic suit, his limbs have a mind of their own. Simon's clumsiness, in contrast to the seriousness of the crime scene, makes her want to lean forward and hug him.

'You need anything?' Isla reaches into her canvas messenger bag. She rummages amidst the plasters, headache pills, lip balm, hand sanitizer and pens.

'No thanks, unless you have a mini bottle of vodka in there and a pack of cigarettes. Listen, I'm going to need you to get out of here, right now. I'll send you the summary of the case when we're done.'

'But—'

'*Now*, Isla! Let's try and follow procedure for once!'

'Fine . . . sorry,' she says, heat creeping up her cheeks.

His eyes soften. 'It's nothing personal, OK? I promise we'll chat as soon as I'm done. Take care of yourself.'

It's a long walk to the door and an even longer wait for the elevator to reach the seventh floor. Isla can't help but feel a little disgraced, as if every official person buzzing about the scene knows that she is not meant to be there. She has stood at the frontlines alongside Simon reporting on gang violence, bank robberies and more. What about this case has made him wall it off so coldly?

Best to just go back to the newsroom, where she can forget this morning and the dread it has stirred within her.

She lurches the car into gear, eyes fiery with shame at the empty notebook on the passenger seat. Dammit! What a waste of a few hours. She'll have to come back and interview Nicole Whittington's neighbors later. Just as she accelerates, a young woman with thick brown hair pulled into a messy ponytail, and a pale, haunted face darts in front of the car.

'Jesus! Watch where you're going! You could have got yourself killed!' She wrestles with the gearstick of her car, and pushes her sunglasses on roughly, her eyes following the Lycra-clad figure as she sprints away.

She chugs across town, battling the traffic and the endless, steep uphills that make her clutch burn ominously. Her sunglasses are too smudged to see clearly – chocolate, she presumes. She turns on the radio, but cannot settle. The entire morning feels off, from the murder and Simon's reaction, to the strange expression of the woman who almost collided with her car.

There is no story without a beginning, no murder without a moment that incites it. Yet no woman asks for this, not ever. Something deeply unjust happened last night; the urgent question is, what?

Chapter 3

Freya
Three months before the murder

Freya takes a deep breath before ringing the buzzer.

'Play it cool,' she whispers to herself. 'This is only the biggest day of your life.'

She makes idle conversation with the security guard as she signs the register.

'You look happy,' he says, mirroring her wide smile.

'It's a big day for me,' she says. 'Possibly my biggest day yet.'

'Well, good luck! I'm sure you'll be amazing.'

She bounces from foot to foot in the lobby, waiting for the elevator to arrive. How many times had she dreamed of this moment? She worked hard, she tried her best, but never would she have believed that it would pay off one day. Who would expect that Freya, a foster child with a knack for computers, would end up working at the hottest tech company in San Francisco?

Freya remembers standing outside the Atypical offices one freezing January night, wrapped up in a thick coat and warming her hands on a takeaway coffee. She had been working punishing hours completing her Masters in software engineering while waitressing at an old Italian trattoria to pay for her final year of studies.

That night had been tougher than usual – mean-spirited customers, meager tips and an assignment that was far from done – so she had taken a detour past the modernized heritage building that housed Atypical's offices. It was the kind of startup that breathed life into the ideas that the rest of the world would be talking about in five years' time. In the three years since they launched, they had grown like a wildfire, and captured the imagination of Silicon Valley.

Back when Atypical was still working out of a garage, Elon Musk tried to buy the business, but the enigmatic founder and CEO, Julian Cox, flatly refused. Star computer science graduates from all the Ivy League colleges tried all manner of stunts to get hired, but the rumor on campus was that you had to be invited, usually after doing some time at one of the established tech giants. Freya spotted the lucky few who worked at Atypical sometimes, on the subway or at Whole Foods in the brief flash of a company hoodie bearing the now-familiar triangle logo. Yet she didn't actually *know* anybody who had ever succeeded in getting hired to work there. That night, she was so ragged from being overworked, so humiliated by the way customers had treated her in the restaurant, it felt like she would never amount to anything, let alone end up there. Looking back, there was beauty in her brokenness. She had put everything on the line to reshape herself into someone new.

It seemed impossible, but there was a fire that burned in her, even then. All she needed was one moment of grace, one foot in the door, and she would work the hardest of all. Sure, she had graduated with Summa Cum Laude, but when it came down to it, her real power was that she wanted it more than anybody else.

Now, a whirlwind year later, her heart pounds with excitement as the heavy copper door of the elevator slides open and she steps inside the offices. Her whole life has led up to this.

She sneaks a quick glance at her reflection in the mirror – minimal makeup, hair in a loose chignon and a slick of red lipstick to finish the look off – and runs her hands over the luxe finishings. Every detail thrills her. The past doesn't matter anymore. From this moment forward, she can become the person she was always meant to be. Maybe one day she may even reach the mythical status of Julian Cox.

Her fingers fumble for her notebook, where she has written some key facts to remember. Part genius, part Adonis, Julian is the newly crowned future of tech, a clean-cut savant who does not indulge in substances or inappropriate Twitter rants. In some ways, he is more famous than Atypical itself. He speaks ten languages fluently; he studied yoga with a guru in the Himalayas; he writes both forwards and backwards and was assumed deaf until his first year of school, simply because he was thinking so deeply. He is deliberately humble, and lived with his parents until his business got on its feet. Although

Atypical is not yet listed on the stock exchange and has no obligation to share information publicly, Julian still publishes the salaries of all his staff to promote equal pay.

The technology that has caused such a stir is a low-cost device that will bring free Wi-Fi to rural villages in Kenya and Tanzania. Through a combination of smart technology and GPS, Julian and his team at Atypical will introduce cheap medical technology that delivers much-needed supplies to those who do not have access to them. While the business is yet to break even, the hope and idealism keeps the investment pouring in. Freya can recite the ins and outs of the technology. She has read every article on it. And, although she's got the job already, she still has a fierce desire to prove herself.

As Julian approaches Freya, her breath catches in her throat. He is dressed in a simple gray T-shirt that exposes a sleeve of intricate tattoos. His dark, wavy hair falls just short of his shoulders. There is a mischievous glint in his eye, as if they are already complicit in something wonderful together. On a lesser man, the expression would pass off as sleazy, but on Julian it is simply warm.

'Freya! Welcome to the tribe.'

The word tribe conjures up trance concerts in the desert, and Shamans administering mind-opening psychedelic drugs inside hemp-woven teepees. While Julian is heading up one of Forbes' 'Top 10 multi-million-dollar businesses under five years old', there is something in his manner that suggests he'd be up for that as well.

'Right, let's take you on the grand tour!' The first thing that strikes Freya is how *easy* the office feels. An arrestingly beautiful woman with a natural afro and a septum piercing furrows her brow in concentration as she runs complex code on the screen before her. Identical twins are curled up on a sofa in the corner, having a heated discussion. A woman in a glamorous hijab and hoop earrings speaks animatedly into her phone. Every person radiates a sense of importance, a sense of being at home and stretching out confidently into the world. Just looking at them makes Freya stand a little taller.

There is a meditation room, yoga classes at lunchtime, a juicing station, fresh herbs growing off living walls, the latest MacBooks that only launched a few weeks before, and a room where you can draw on all the walls and floors. It is more of a paradise than an office.

While these perks are exciting, they aren't the reason Freya is here. She wants to be part of the boldest projects in data science and this is the place to do it. There are no rules, no limits and infinite opportunities for Freya to create amazing, life-changing work. Today, tech CEOs are our Greek gods, possessed with magical powers, their companies are where they practice their magic. She gets to use technology to elevate the lives of those less fortunate and make a real difference. She will be imbued with the power to work miracles. Her whole life is a miracle, an example of how the care of others can turn things around, so nothing could matter to her more.

Julian gestures to a desk that bears a charming, hand-written 'Welcome Freya' sign. There is a Mac in a box still sheathed in plastic, and a few gifts – a mug with a quote by Ayn Rand, Freya's favorite author; a packet of chamomile tea; and several slabs of Lindt white chocolate. These gifts are not random – they all happen to be her favorite things.

'Do you like it?' he asks, and she is flattered by how he searches her face for approval. 'We did our research to find out the things you love.' Freya smiles. These days, looking up a person online is alluded to so casually, so confidently. It has been stripped of shame and repackaged as the highest compliment. She expected this, long before she got the call. Which is why any picture of her doing anything she shouldn't have has been sanitized.

'It's perfect, thank you.' She pauses for a second, adds, 'I really appreciate it, so much.' Hopefully he can see how much she means it.

The day is a whirlwind of introductions. Freya smiles until her face is about to crack.

Later, when the copper doors of the elevator close behind her and she emerges, blinking, onto the city streets, she feels different. Like stepping into a movie, she is suddenly animated. The moment shines with importance, as she teeters on the brink of her future.

She runs through the conversations she had during the day and suddenly feels a little embarrassed at how keen she was. There were moments she thinks she said the wrong thing, where she came across as too excited, too awkward, too much. She walks home a little faster to outrun the feeling, instead focusing on the good. It's just growing pains, nothing more. This is a big step! She is living the dream, it's no wonder she feels a bit paranoid it will all be ripped away. But there is something else too, something that quickens her pulse and dries her mouth. Because while it was the perfect day in so many ways, after the joy there is a bitter aftertaste that lingers. The acrid, inexplicable taste of fear.

Chapter 4
Freya
The morning after the murder

The overwhelming sense of joy last night has settled into an uncomfortable jittery feeling that tugs at Freya. She throws on her Nike running gear and ties up the laces on her trainers.

Kate shakes her head. 'No matter how many years I have known you, I've never been able to understand how you can run on a hangover.'

'It's totally logical – you sweat out the toxins, and then the night before is forgotten,' she says.

Freya jiggles the key in the lock to let herself out the apartment. It's a muggy, humid day. The kind where fights break out for no reason. As she turns to go, Kate grabs her arm with surprising force. 'Be careful out there, OK?'

'Of course. I always am.'

As her steps fall into rhythm, she cannot escape her thoughts the way she usually does. She paces down streets she doesn't usually use, as if by running faster she will outrun her worries. She did something stupid last night. She played a juvenile, petty prank in the heat of the moment, and this morning she fears the consequences.

Her wandering takes her a few blocks away from Atypical, to Market Street, the location of the chic apartment blocks she could only aspire to live in. Maybe one day, when she earns enough to no longer have to share a house with Kate, Jasmin and Hattie. She chuckles. Who is she kidding – she will always want to live with them.

Sirens wail oppressively close to her, and she stops in her tracks as they speed past and park outside the building. Her mind goes somewhere else for a second, then she stops herself. No. Don't be stupid. It was only a prank. It couldn't have caused . . .

A message on her phone. A welcome distraction.

Hey, says an unknown number, *I'm so glad you said hi. I think you're cute too.*

It's innocuous enough, but this morning the message hits too close to home. It reminds her of the prank last night, and the grave mistake she has made. She wants it to be over, lost in the drunken memories of the night before, sweated out in this morning's run, but this message suggests she is wrong.

She can't think about this, not with the roar of sirens and the hiss of buses in traffic. She turns and almost collides with an old Ford, driven by a woman with scruffy auburn bangs.

'Jesus! Watch where you're going! You could have got yourself killed!' the woman shouts. Freya's heart is hammering in her chest, the adrenaline surges through her body.

She runs all the way back home, darting through the traffic, pushing past pedestrians, breath pounding in her chest, not once breaking her pace, never looking back. Her phone in her pocket, a functional object turned suddenly sinister.

Chapter 5

Freya
Five years before

Three a.m. The worst time of the morning. What one foster mother called 'the darkest hour of the soul'. Freya stretches in the cramped confines of her second-hand car. Her neck is so stiff, she can barely breathe and it feels like someone is hammering a large nail in the small of her back.

Everyone talks about saving for college, but nobody mentions the hidden costs, like textbooks, food and having a place to stay. Nobody remembers that the people sitting next to you in class will have the latest tech and wear $100 frayed denims with the attitude that they somehow deserve it, that they earned these privileges themselves. College is filled with people whose parents have money. Freya tries to push the resentment down and focus on the work, but some days are harder than others, especially when she can't even get a full night's sleep.

Quick footsteps, a knock on the window. 'Hey there, hey!'

Shit. Freya always tries to park far enough out of sight to not draw attention to herself, but close enough to campus security to be safe, but she must have slipped up tonight. She'd only got back to her car around midnight, after working in the computer labs, and probably wasn't as clear-headed as usual. She's not sure what would be worse – mockery or getting into some sort of trouble. Are you allowed to still study if, technically, you don't really have a place to live?

She pushes her hair out of her face and rubs the sleep out of her eyes before winding the window down. It's a manual window, not electric, and the process of opening it is awkwardly protracted. She stares into the bright, hazy eyes of Kate Jones, the only other girl in her computer science class.

'I thought it was you!' Kate laughs. 'You also had a rough night?'

'Uh . . . yeah.'

'I was supposed to go out for one drink after my assignment. But, you know how it goes. Suddenly wine turns into shots and shots into tequila and the next thing you're making out with a barman from Russia called Vlad who says he's here to get a modeling job.'

Freya is exhausted, but she musters up the energy to nod knowingly. Truth is, she hasn't had a relationship before. Romance is both something she has pushed aside in favor of her studies, and something she obsesses over. How would it feel to truly belong in another's arms. She resolves to keep talking until she wears Kate out. Perhaps then her secret will remain undetected.

Kate continues, 'Honestly, how did you find the assignment? I felt like I was reading Hebrew for most of it; I couldn't understand a thing! I think that's why I ended up going drinking afterwards, I felt like such a fool. If I fail another semester, my parents are going to kill me!'

Freya begins to respond, but then she sees Kate's gaze extend behind her, to the clump of clothes on the backseat. Her face twists in that all-familiar awkward grimace that someone makes when they are faced with poverty.

She speaks slowly, carefully. 'You live in your car?'

'Yes.'

She thinks for a moment.

'Isn't it cold?'

'Sometimes.' Freya can't believe that she hasn't made some excuse and driven off.

Kate simply keeps standing there, mouth agape. 'But you're the smartest person in our class!'

'Smart people can also be poor, Kate.'

She looks mortified. 'Fuck, sorry, I didn't mean it that way. I'm just shocked, that's all. Here I am with my own apartment and a monthly allowance from my parents, and I'm barely scraping by. You're amazing!'

'I'm not looking for pity, or awe for that matter.'

'I know, I know, maybe a cup of coffee and some early morning waffles will do? I'm starving. My treat.'

The connection is instant, like long-lost sisters. Breakfast turns into an impromptu study session, which turns into lunch, which turns into a friendship that leads to a deal. Freya can move into Kate's apartment, wear her clothes and eat her food on one condition. She has to help Kate pass college.

Chapter 6

Isla
Two days after the murder

Isla is accustomed to violence. Summarizing horrific acts into 300-word news snippets is part of her job. To work in a newsroom is to witness the dark side of human nature every day, and pretend that it doesn't hurt.

How often has her own mother whispered over the phone, anguish etched in her voice, 'Why did you have to choose a career that reminds you of all the pain in the world?' Isla's never been able to answer her, and has never doubted her profession. Until today.

Another woman's body, broken and defiled. A horror that becomes more familiar the more it takes place. It ignites a sense of urgency in Isla.

If she can break this story, really, truly blow the truth wide open, it would at least feel like her job means something. In reporting this murder truthfully and compassionately, she can find some sense of justice.

She has to act fast. The story is already being rewritten, online, by a thousand different authors. According to her research, Nicole Whittington worked for the white-hot tech startup, Atypical. Twitter, however, is already muddying the waters of her biography, with people publishing reckless hearsay. Was she black, white, or of mixed ethnicity? Was she beaten, found hanging, found after slitting her wrists? The claims and stories circle one another until there is barely a trace of Nicole left. What is the truth, and what isn't?

The answer begins with the case file, summarized and distributed to a selected group of journalists. The cause of death: extensive trauma to the head. Nicole was found with five blows to the skull, two hard enough to crack through. They were delivered by a bronze sculpture of a nude woman. Was the nudity of her body, and the weapon's a mere coincidence, or the work of a skilled murderer trying to communicate a message?

Isla does a reverse image search on the artwork. It's by an award-winning contemporary artist, and worth hundreds of dollars. In order to afford a piece like this, Nicole had a fair amount of disposable income. A quick glance at the company's public salary report confirms this.

There are other little details that intrigue her, the faint brushstrokes that, one by one, reveal the bigger picture. The perfect apartment. The dinner for one. The color-coordinated closet bearing only shades of black, white and beige. The absence of family photographs, but the abundance of high-end art. The spicy, musky scent of perfume floating out of the bathroom door. Apart from the meal, the bottle and the single glass, the place was immaculate. Attached to the abridged case file are some additional photographs of the crime scene. She zooms in on the medication on her bathroom counter: multivitamins, birth control, Topamax. Topamax – a powerful mood stabilizer used in the treatment of bipolar disorder. She minimizes the photo-graph on her computer to revisit later. Interesting.

She zooms in on a note on the fridge. It's a simple printout of a spreadsheet, a schedule. Why Nicole even bothered to print it out is anyone's guess, as every day looked exactly the same.

5.00 a.m: Wake up
5.30 a.m: Gym
7.00 a.m: Arrive at work
7.00 p.m.: Leave work
7.30 p.m. – 9.30 p.m.: Japanese lessons (Tuesdays and Thursdays) and French lessons (Mondays, Wednesdays and Sundays)

Usually, when you scratch the surface, you'll find that an ordinary person is not so ordinary after all. A shocking crime does not come out of the blue, it reveals the long, complex path the victim took to get there. It's more than the murder, or figuring out who was the last person the victim had contact with. The story comes before that.

Privilege or a good job does not render a person spotless. Isla has seen housewives running online fraud empires and CEOs smuggling drugs in business class. More often than not, women fall prey to the kind of everyday violence that nobody flags as abnormal. Stalking ex-lovers are dismissed as overzealous yet harmless. The evil bubbles below the surface, undetected, until the moment someone gets killed.

But this particular schedule leaves little room for any kind of evil to thrive. Nicole's social media feeds are spotless and earnest. Where would she have found the time to get mixed up in something sinister? If the printout on her fridge is to be believed, she spent most of her time at work. After going through it many times, Isla knows what she has to do. She pulls up the monochrome website of Atypical, finds the contact details at the bottom of the page, and makes the call.

'Atypical – how may I help you?' says a chirpy voice.

'Excuse me, can I set up a meeting with your CEO, Julian Cox?'

'What is it in connection with?'

'The murder of one of your employees, Nicole Whittington. I'm a journalist.'

A pause. 'How do you . . . ? Wait. Just a moment please—'

'I'll stay on the line.'

'He can see you tomorrow morning, at 10 a.m.'

In the time Isla has been a reporter she has learned one thing for sure. In order to get to the bottom of the story, you need to get to the people involved first.

According to Google Maps, Atypical is nestled in the heart of The Mission, close to Isla's favorite burrito joint. The restaurants look more polished than the last time she visited the suburb, and the pedestrians look cooler, but some things haven't changed. The street murals still bathe the area in a riot of color that takes her breath away. Isla's running late, but she stops for a moment to take a picture on her phone.

She spots a group of men wearing sleeveless puffa jackets, walking toward a Tesla that is tethered to a charging station.

'A flock of tech-bros,' she says to herself. 'I must be nearby.'

Discerning which San Francisco sub-culture a person is from is one of Isla's secret talents. Maybe it's because she deals with unsolved cases every day, but she likes to focus on the details people give away in their clothes, shoes and mannerisms.

Every person fits in somewhere, no matter how convinced they are of their uniqueness. That's her theory. Pity she hasn't figured out where she fits in just yet.

As Isla approaches the covert entrance to the building and signs in with security, she feels a ripple of embarrassment at her worn Converse All-Stars, frayed jeans and simple T-shirt. She's only just turned thirty-one – on the second of February, an Aquarian through and through – but these tech startups already make her feel dated. She believes in the smell of old books, the crisp, clean break of a new Sunday paper over coffee and croissants and small bookstores where you can run your fingers over all the potential stories. She is old enough to remember burning mix CDs on her computer, or asking the record store to import an obscure album from Iceland. She doesn't know how to fit in at a place like this, or even pretend to.

Atypical's receptionist shows her to Julian Cox's office.

'Good morning, you must be Isla. Come inside! Great sneakers by the way . . .' he says, in a voice so animated it would take Isla at least three coffees to match him.

'Thanks.'

Everything about him is accelerated. He barks an order for a matcha latte to his receptionist, asks his Google assistant to play some Jack Johnson, answers his mobile, approves a deal and hangs up again in seconds. His office, a glass-cube smelling of incense, makes Isla feel as if she is in a smoky fish tank, with everyone watching them.

He turns to face her, his bright green eyes burning intensely.

'I had Converse like that in Junior High. Took me months to save up for them. One day bullies spotted the clean white of new shoes on my feet. I lost my straight nose, and lost the sneakers too.'

It's a lot to share in the first five minutes of meeting someone. Isla doesn't quite trust it. 'I'm sorry. It's hard to imagine you being hurt that way now.'

'I know, but I'm proud of my past. It gave me the desire to be successful. Everything is a blessing in the end.' He's good. Guys like these, they're storytellers of the first degree. Isla needs to remember that, no matter how tempted she is to be drawn in.

He plays with the collection of shamanic rings on his fingers, his gaze somewhere in the distance. A punch from those ringed fingers could cause some serious damage, Isla thinks. 'You know, I still can't believe all of this is real. Just two days ago she was sitting exactly where you are, trying to wrangle more budget out of me for one our ambitious projects.'

The thought makes Isla squirm in her seat. The abandoned life of a person is far more haunting than their death could ever be. She scribbles in her notebook – *Nicole was strong, a go-getter.*

'Well, I really appreciate you taking the time to—'

'No,' he jumps in, 'I am so thankful that you came to us. You're the first journalist to call. Nicole has ... wait ... sorry.' He pauses and puts a hand over his eyes. They sit in awkward silence, waiting for the moment to pass. 'She *had* been with us from our inception three years ago and was part of the family. When a business gets so big so quickly, that feeling of community is everything. Everything you see around us, this so-called "success", is tough in its own way.'

The honesty is startling. Isn't this the new American dream that everyone hopes for? Learn to code, build an app, make billions? Nicole must have been ballsy to hold her own in a male-dominated industry like this one, and conjure such emotion in Atypical's charismatic leader.

'What was she like?'

'She was everything I could have hoped for in an employee, and a friend. Driven, dynamic, brilliantly intelligent.' He pauses. 'Are you getting this down? Driven ...'

'Dynamic—'

'Great, you've got it. Nicole could have had any job she wanted, but she chose to believe in Atypical. She even supported me when I said no to Elon Musk – I'm sure you've read all about that debacle. Anyway, she understood what we were building and was prepared to defend it. She was one of those women who really *stood* for something, you know?'

Isla remembers the recycling bins at Nicole's apartment, the fresh potted herbs, the bottle of locally sourced wine, the fair-trade linen, the sweet iron smell of old blood and the spicy, musky scent of perfume.

'What did she stand for?'

He gazes into the distance, smiling. 'Well, she wanted a fairer, more equal society. She was experimenting with ways of using technology to truly help others and bring people together.'

'How so?'

'Her passion project was working with governments and NGOs in East Africa, to bring underprivileged communities free access to Wi-Fi and medical services. The technology we are about to roll out in those countries is thanks to her ferocious idealism.'

Isla nods – she has read a bit about this story online. It's a big deal.

'Is there anybody who wouldn't support these developments? Telecommunications is a cutthroat industry and is highly regulated by the government, especially in Africa.

Maybe some local players weren't happy with your new technology?'

Julian shifts in his seat, and tenses his jaw. 'It can be tough entering new markets, sure, but Nicole had her contacts wrapped around her little finger. She was charming, and passionate about helping women in need. She'd go there and try out the food, drink at the local bars and even go dancing. Most importantly, she showed the authorities that our technology wasn't another empty gesture of aid, it would truly help.'

Isla makes a note to look further into this herself.

'She really seemed to work hard. Could she have possibly taken drugs to keep going?' From what she could gather from the crime, it had many of the qualities of a drug or gang-related murder. It was not pedestrian, but performed by someone who was comfortable with violence.

Julian looks shocked. 'Nicole was completely clean. She didn't drink, smoke, eat meat or gluten. Her system wouldn't even know how to react to an aspirin.'

Isla thinks back to the wine and the bowl of pasta. Julian clearly didn't know his employees as well as he thought he did.

'There was a bottle of Topamax visible in the crime-scene photographs. Were you aware she was being treated for a mood disorder?'

Julian is distracted by a message on his phone, but suddenly looks up. 'Oh. That? Yes she mentioned it briefly but I make a point in not interfering in the personal lives of my staff. Her bipolar disorder didn't affect her work in any way.'

Funny, Isla didn't name Nicole's mood disorder – she merely alluded to its existence. The left side of Julian's face spasms every now and then. A nervous tic. It always happens to the smartest types, the ones whose minds won't leave them alone. Isla can tell that he is used to having all the answers, or not hiding them. In the absence of the appropriate response he is on edge, wound up like a spring.

'Julian – could I possibly interview a few of your staff members, and get a feel for Nicole's life here?'

He hesitates, then his expression returns to its friendly mask. 'Yes, of course.' He points to a worried redhead rifling through papers in a nearby office. 'Just speak to Mathilda over there, and she will coordinate it for you.'

'Thank you, I really appreciate it.'

His cellphone flashes again. 'Sorry, I've got to take this,' he mumbles. Isla feels relieved to have a moment free of his intensity. She swivels her chair and takes some time to observe the office swimming around her.

It's shinier and more hopeful than the dire interior she is accustomed to at the *San Francisco Times*. She spots a tray of smoked salmon and cream cheese bagels in the open-plan kitchen, and her eyes linger on their Nespresso machine. It must be at least an hour since she had her last coffee! Atypical seems like a really great place, just like all the fawning news articles say.

Employees talk quietly among themselves, the cheerful office space awash with the hush of fresh grief. Isla shudders at her own memories of navigating the blank space that follows a trauma, that dreaded period where nobody knows what to say, and so nothing is said at all.

Then, she spots a familiar tousle of brown hair, a pale, haunted face. She's not doing anything to cause suspicion, simply struggling across the room with three mugs of coffee. But Isla *knows* her from somewhere. Has she seen her in an Atypical news story, maybe? Or has she been pushed against her in a tram? No, she knows those eyes, she looked right into them, held their gaze for long enough to recall their unique almond shape.

It hits her, heavy, sudden and sure. It's the same woman she almost ran over outside Nicole's apartment the day before. Close up, she notices her hunched shoulders, and grinding jaw.

Julian walks back into the room, smiling distractedly. His mind is already onto his next task. Isla is seconds into overstaying her welcome.

'You're OK to find your own way to Mathilda's office?'

'Yes, of course. Thank you for your time, Julian. It was an honor to meet you,' she says graciously. She turns to walk away, but a spark of intuition makes her turn around. 'And by the way, who is that young woman over there? The one handing out the coffees? I feel like I know her from somewhere.'

Julian looks up briefly from his MacBook. 'She joined us a few months ago. Lovely girl, sharp as a tack. Her name is Freya Matthews.'

Chapter 7

Freya
Two days after the murder

Freya stares at the message on the screen. Another message. Another number. She is beginning to suspect this is not one person behind the screen, but several. Her mouth is dry. Her pulse, racing.

Hey baby, your profile pic is hot. You don't have to be lonely anymore – I've got what you're looking for.

It shouldn't matter so much. She's used to getting online messages out of the blue. Like that so-called CEO from Kentucky who sent her a private message on LinkedIn to say he liked her profile picture. Or the message request on her Instagram account from a man in Italy who she has never met but thinks she should join his modeling agency. People float up from the ether all the time, only to disappear again. It is nothing to worry about, or take personally. Everybody lives their life online, in full view of strangers.

So why does she flip her phone over and bury her head in her hands? Why does the message follow her for the rest of the day, as if it is ink imprinted on her skin?

In the middle of the night, she wakes up groggy and panicked to the repetitive pinging of new messages coming through on her phone, one after the other. Every text is in response to something she allegedly said two nights ago. And the content of the messages hits far too close to home. It could be a misunderstanding, but Freya is afraid it's a cruel joke, played by someone who knows about the prank, someone who is intent on getting her back.

Chapter 8

Freya
Four years before

'She's running late.'

Freya looks up from the pamphlet she was reading into the open, fine-featured face of a young woman. She is around her age, with long, curly hair and a nose ring. She doesn't look half as nervous as Freya is.

'Excuse me?'

'The finance director. She's stuck in a meeting off campus. But they've told us to wait here for her.'

'Oh . . . thanks.' Freya turns back to her pamphlet, which lists all the amazing qualities of her college. Not that she needs a reminder, as she's been coming here for a year. But her money's run out faster than expected and she's going to need some help to stay.

A pause. 'I'm Jasmin.'

'Freya—'

'You're another financial aid student, right?'

Freya plays nervously with a loose strand of thread on her shirt. 'Is it that obvious?'

'Not really, don't worry! But I pride myself on having a talent for reading people. I'm on a scholarship for psychology. Well, partial scholarship.' She leans back and looks at her, smiling. 'So what's your story?'

'Uh, I've been studying computer science for a year. I didn't qualify for a scholarship when I joined here, but I'm hoping my marks will speak for themselves now.' Eighty percent for data structure and algorithms. Ninety-five percent for computer architecture. Top of the class for everything. It was a good innings, but would it be good enough? A degree from this university has the power to change her life.

There is something in Jasmin's eyes that makes Freya want to talk, and unwrap every fear, laying them on the table between them. It's no wonder she is training to be a psychologist. As she tells Jasmin her story, she feels her body relax and her breathing slows down. Sharing her burden with someone who understood has made every-thing feel OK again.

'Well, I think that you'll get the scholarship,' Jasmin says, her voice sure.

'You can't know that.'

'You work hard, Freya. This matters to you. And I believe good things happen to the people who deserve them.'

An optimist, of course. That's why she has that serene glow to her.

A tall, formidable woman strides in. 'Sorry I'm late, ladies. I'll be with you in a minute.'

THE PACT | 40

Freya sits on her shaking hands, and runs through her motivation one last time in her mind. This is either the end of the road, or the very beginning.

'Don't worry,' says Jasmin. 'You got this. And when your appointment is done, I'll be waiting outside for you. We'll go get the two-for-one burger special at the diner down the road, get to know each other and become great friends, you'll see!'

Freya smiles weakly. That sounds nice, more than nice. It sounds like a life she's not sure she deserves.

Chapter 9

Freya
Three months before the murder

Freya squints as she pulls a needle and thread over and over through the bright ruby fabric before her. The warm glow of sunrise both deepens the color and makes it difficult to get the stitching just right.

Her best friend, Kate, walks into the living room, rubbing her eyes. 'Freya, it's barely 6 a.m. What are you doing up? You know you've just started your dream job, right? It's OK if your hobbies take a backseat.'

She looks up briefly from her work. 'Sewing is more than a hobby to me. Coding crowds my mind with ideas. Sewing clears it.' Stitch by stitch, she is adjusting, growing, understanding who she is in this new life.

Jasmin and Hattie stumble through, clutching coffees. Freya smiles at the incongruous picture of her three roommates standing next to one another. Kate is strong and sharp, Jasmin gentle and willowy and Hattie unabashedly sexy in her every gesture. Their friendship doesn't make sense, but it has fueled Freya for over four years. This is her family.

'Maybe you'll meet someone.' Hattie winks. 'It must be a few months since your last boyfriend.'

Jasmin gives her a shove. 'Don't listen to her, Freya. It's inspiring that you have so many talents.'

'Exactly,' Freya says. 'Besides, Hattie, sewing my own clothing and wearing vintage is a radical act in a world of throwaway fast fashion. I'm too busy changing the world right now for a new boyfriend.'

'Well, isn't that a mouthful,' Kate laughs.

Freya bites her lip. She is not quite telling the truth. While she is all big talk in front of her friends, she actually wishes she had someone closer to share this particular life stage with, someone whose arms she could fold into and sleep, safe in the knowledge that her good fortune won't be taken away.

'How is the new job, anyway?' asks Kate.

'Better. Three days in and I'm starting to figure out where everything is, at least. I just can't wait to get stuck into more work.'

Jasmin gives her a hug. 'Good for you. Fight that urge to pick at your life and find something wrong with it. You have worked hard for this moment, and you deserve all the happiness it brings.'

'We know you,' says Hattie. 'You can never just relax, you're always looking for the catch. There's no catch this time. Life is simply good.'

Freya nods, but doesn't voice her disagreement. It is natural to feel nervous during the first few days of a new job, especially one with stakes as high as these. This is her dream – if she loses it, she will have failed herself, and shattered her own aspirations. But maybe the girls have a point, perhaps she just needs to be a bit gentler with herself. She is crossing the strange no man's land between her old and new life after all.

A reminder pops up on her phone.

'Dammit! I forgot I have an 8 a.m. meeting. I better get in the shower – stat.'

'Good luck!' her friends shout behind her, 'And remember to enjoy yourself!'

Freya bustles into the office and grabs her new tablet out its box. It's time for her first meeting.

There is an excited hum in the air as clusters of developers, marketers and strategists crowd together, passing trays of gluten-free donuts and talking among themselves. Everything is new, fresh, expensive. She pulls her sleeve over her scuffed vintage watch. Freya wonders who her friends will be, and what projects they will work on together, but for now she sits alone. She taps the tablet in front of her randomly, trying to look busy.

Julian struts in, hair pushed back, adrenaline pumping through his veins. 'OK, OK, order everybody! Before we begin I'd like to formally welcome our newest recruit – Freya Matthews. I have never felt so nervous about getting someone to sign a contract with us. This woman is the real deal.'

Freya looks into the sea of welcoming faces. This moment of belonging among kindred spirits is something she has always longed for. These people really *see* her. If the young student version of her could see this now, she would break down in tears.

A young man sits towards the back of the room. His posture catches her eye at first. While everyone leans forward, drinking in each word Julian says, he leans far back in his chair, surveying the room with a wry grin. He doesn't possess the overly groomed sheen common to most executives. Instead, he's a bit rough around the edges. Mussed-up dark hair, crooked teeth, a fraying leather jacket rolled up enough to expose muscular forearms. The only clue to his tech cred is the latest Apple Watch on his wrist. His brown eyes meet hers and don't look away.

The attraction is instant. It has the pulsing raw urgency of brushing against someone on the dancefloor. The sweet champagne frothiness of trying to sit near to a crush in class. The fleeting mysticism of spotting a handsome stranger on the train reading her favorite book. The feeling surprises her, and she is reminded of her conversation with the girls that morning. Maybe she will meet someone special. Maybe something wonderful is going to happen.

He smiles slowly, mischievously, and Freya tries to assume a poker face. Not many people get a shot at Atypical, now is not the time to be flirting. She tries desperately to avoid the corner where he is sitting, but her eyes are pulled there of their own accord. Whenever she finds herself looking at him, he is staring back at her.

Finally, she finds out his name as it's shouted across the room.

'What do you think, Jay?'

'You really want to know? Well, here it is—'

He is sarcastic and opinionated, smart and self-deprecating. In a few sentences he confirms everything she suspected about him. He is an industry bad boy, the kind of guy who doesn't give a shit that technology is the hot industry to be in right now. He is real, raw and, Freya concludes, here for the same reasons she is. It's not about the glory, but about the work and the process. It's about mastery, and using technology to do something *real*.

After the meeting is over, he comes to find her, coffee in hand.

'Hey, new girl, I thought I'd bring you a welcome cortado.'

'That happens to be my favorite. How did you know?' She wonders if Jay took the time to research her online like Julian did. Her Instagram feed is littered with images of fresh cortados positioned artfully next to her computer science assignments or sewing projects. Either way, it feels good not to lie to please a guy, or to act grateful for an unwanted gift. She'd started drinking cortados while working at the trattoria down by Fisherman's Wharf and has had a thing for them ever since.

'You just look like a woman with good taste. Nice tattoo by the way. Fractals are so romantic – a shape that has occurred in nature for centuries, yet expresses the core concept of coding.'

'Are you trying to mansplain my own tattoo to me?' She quips. Jay laughs in response.

She looks down at the Sierpinski Triangles on the inside of her wrist, illustrated in the lightest ink. To anyone outside of this room the image would simply be a great tattoo, but in here, it is imbued with rich meaning and marks her as one of the pack. Sometimes, the most important desires are expressed as symbols. She's impressed that he noticed.

'Thanks!'

She sways from one foot to the other, trying to think of something to say next. Just as she draws a breath to speak, a woman with a harsh black bob appears next to him and says crisply, 'Hi there, welcome to Atypical. I'm Nicole.'

She is all refined, smooth edges, expensive perfume and neat black nails. She's the kind of woman Freya imagines becoming one day: successful, smart, petrifyingly beautiful. An imagined future flashes in her mind of the two of them rushing to Soul Cycle after work, going to art gallery openings and poetry readings, cooking in each other's kitchens, toasting with tall champagne flutes to celebrate each other's promotion at work. But Nicole seems distracted.

'Sorry to break up the party, Jay, but we're late.' Her perfect hand clasps around his arm and lingers long enough for Freya to notice. She gets the feeling that she is making a nuisance of herself and it's time to go.

He rolls his eyes. 'Duty calls, but speak soon. I look forward to getting to know you.'

'Me too . . .'

It could be nothing, but then why does the air feel hot with the stares of other women? Why does his face keep flitting across her mind? How did he instinctively know what coffee to get her, and notice her tattoo? Freya's had her fair share of dating men where her imagination and optimism made up for everything they lacked. She should be careful. But a giddiness bubbles up in her, despite her reservations. Atypical was supposed to be about making her mark in her career, not about finding a guy. Maybe, just maybe, though, she has found both.

Chapter 10

Isla
Two days after the murder

Isla sits in the small meeting room that has been organized for her by Mathilda, who emphasizes that not all staff have given their statements to the police yet. Isla is to ask superficial questions only, questions that paint a picture of who Nicole was.

She asks to see Freya first. Isla is sure she saw her in the street outside Nicole's apartment the morning after the murder. She is certain she witnessed pure terror in her face. It makes her wonder if Freya knows something about the killer, and whether she is afraid they will strike again.

Freya hurries into the room, closes the door behind her and flashes Isla a smile that illuminates her small, fine-boned face. She is younger than Isla realized. Eager to please.

'Good morning, I'm Isla, a journalist from the *San Francisco Times*. I'm writing a piece on Nicole Whittington and am collecting some facts and anecdotes about her.'

Freya nods. 'That is a lovely thing to do.'

'Thank you. I'm trying my best. Nicole seemed to spend a lot of her time at work, so I thought I would start here.'

'She did,' Freya states. 'Work hard, that is. Nicole was an extremely hard worker.'

'Did you know her well?'

Freya hesitates, and focuses on the table between them.

'We worked together on a few projects, but I wouldn't say we were friends. I haven't been here very long, and Nicole had other friends, like Melanie!' She points vaguely to the open-plan space adjacent to the meeting room. 'She'll be able to tell you more personal details about Nicole.'

She is speaking carefully, enunciating slowly, as if every word is critical. Isla has seen this before in interviews with highly intelligent people, especially lawyers. They understand the heft of each word they use, its potential to build or to cause damage. These kinds of interviews take much longer. But then again, it could be the careful framing of a story to mask the truth. Better get to the point.

'If you weren't friends, how would you describe your relationship? Any problems? You were on the same team, and you seem like a likeable person—'

'Thank you, being very social doesn't come naturally to me actually. I'm a stereotypical coding nerd.'

'I think you're selling yourself short. You've been a great help to me and I've only just met you. Are you sure you didn't pick up anything about Nicole, especially since you worked together a lot?'

Freya shakes her head, an edge of cynicism creeps into her voice. 'This isn't school anymore. Nobody wins prizes for Prom Queen or Miss Congeniality. We are all here to do a job, and Nicole and I both did it well. We just kept our work and personal lives separate. I'm sorry but I don't think this is going to help your story.' She gestures again. 'Melanie can tell you everything you need to know.'

THE PACT | 50

Isla notices the bloom of pink beginning on Freya's cheeks. Her inability to sit still. She is flustered.

Isla leans forward, and hands Freya her business card. 'Thank you for your time. If you think of anything else that could be relevant to my story, please feel free to give me a call. Anything at all, even if it seems inconsequential.'

As she gets up to leave, her chair falls to the ground.

'Shit. Sorry. I'm such a clutz.'

'It's OK. Freya, one more thing if I may?'

She turns around to face her head-on, eyes flashing. 'Sure.'

Isla doesn't expect much, but it's worth a try to see her reaction alone. 'You know, I recognized you and have been battling to place you, but I think I have an idea now. When I left Nicole's apartment building, I almost ran my old Ford into a young woman wearing running gear. She had long, dark hair, just like yours. I'm almost sure it was you—'

Freya answers quickly. Her voice is sure. 'That's just not possible. I live on the other side of town. And besides, I'm sure I would have remembered you too.'

Yet there is something about the way that Freya looks over her shoulder as she walks to her desk, and something about the manner in which she digs frantically in her purse for her cellphone, scattering old till receipts all over the floor, that makes Isla wonder if Freya is telling the whole truth after all. Because, from where she is sitting, she looks like a woman with something to hide.

Chapter 11

Freya
Three months before the murder

It's been a little over a week and Freya's desk already feels like home. She sips her coffee out of her new mug, and scans through her emails. There is a new one from Jay.

Our first meeting is in half an hour. Looking forward to it.

She looks up from her screen, smiling, only to find he is watching her, waiting for a response.

Me too . . .

She replies, holding back adding a smiley face at the end. She wants to appear sophisticated, and professional. As much as she is looking forward to her first meeting with Jay, the sight of Nicole's name on the meeting request puts a dampener on things. Amidst everyone's warmth, Freya feels a disconcerting chill whenever she crosses Nicole's path. Is it her imagination, or does Nicole sigh heavily whenever Freya enters a room? Is she being paranoid, or has Nicole not once returned her greeting?

She smooths down the red skirt she finished sewing this morning and walks to one of the meeting pods, a conspicuous white egg that floats in the center of the office like an alien spaceship. For all her technical savvy, Freya has never been good with handles and switches and is already stressing about opening the damn thing. She tries to look casual as she runs her hands up and down the unyielding surface, getting more and more desperate.

Nicole pushes past her and holds up her access card. The door slides open with a curt 'beep'. Does Freya feel the slightest shove as Nicole leads the way inside? She takes a breath, and remembers the advice of her friends. Don't overthink things. Allow yourself to be happy. Let things be good.

They sit and wait for Jay, the final person expected at the meeting. This is the first project Freya is working on with him and she's nervous. He could be the office player, waiting to hit on her at the first opportunity, or he could be a genuinely good guy, who wants to get to know her. It would be nice if she had a female friend at work with whom to pick apart such small, superficial things, but she still eats her lunch alone. She looks awkwardly over at Nicole, who has not lifted her eyes from her cellphone once since she arrived.

Freya braces herself to speak. Nicole is probably just shy, as many people are.

'I love that necklace you're wearing,' Freya says, pointing to the intricate silver piece resting against Nicole's shirt.

Silence. The only indication Nicole heard her is the quizzical rise of her eyebrow. Freya feels a little bruised, but tries again anyway.

'Gosh, have you seen the weather report for today? I don't remember when we last had rain forecast like this! It's not normal in fall, even for San Francisco.' It doesn't make sense, and it's a little weak. She waits patiently. Silly as it is, surely Nicole will recognize this as an effort to make conversation?

She looks up from her phone briefly with flashing eyes. 'Do you mind just keeping quiet until Jay arrives? I'm playing a game on my phone and I'm kinda at a critical point here.'

Freya feels a clenching of irritation and shame in her chest. This is just blatantly rude! Nicole is throwing down a gauntlet, and Freya has no idea why.

There is nothing to do but sit with the silence and embarrassment itching under her skin, making herself look busy by answering emails. Such a strong reaction feels alien to her. Freya has always been the kind of person people warm to.

Once, at school, everyone in class was given a piece of paper to pass around. On it, they had to anonymously write a compliment for every person in the room. Freya was nervous. She hadn't been at this particular school for long and was worried that her sheet of paper would return blank. There were some superficial comments, of course, such as 'great hair', and 'good at math', but right at the bottom, someone else had written 'easy to make friends with'. Since then, she'd always hung on to that. It has been her way to survive and stand out in a world of constant change. That, and her skill in mathematics.

Jay breezes in, holding a laptop, a bundle of sketches and a chewed pencil. Old school. She likes that. Ideas feel clearer in pen and paper before they make their way into code. It's the way she brainstorms ideas too. He's wearing a worn Arcade Fire band shirt today. She nods her head. Great taste in music, too.

He sits across from them, oblivious to the tension souring the air around them. 'Good morning! Sorry I'm a bit late – had to make up my cardio count for the day, so I took the stairs. This Apple Watch is starting to run my life!' Jay's eyes linger on Freya and his lips curve into a smile. 'You look different today . . . Have you done something to your hair?' He noticed! The night before she had practiced doing it in an elaborate halo braid whilst watching a YouTube tutorial. Today, she has threaded a scarlet ribbon – an offcut from the skirt she made – through her hair. She feels more herself than she has in a long time.

'Thanks.' She blushes. 'I'm trying something different. To fit my new life here.'

'And what a life that promises to be,' he says, his voice as smooth as syrup.

Nicole throws Jay a simmering look. It's quick, but impossible to miss. 'Perhaps we can try to begin this meeting without commenting on a woman's appearance?'

'Relax, Nicole, it's just a harmless compliment. You have to agree that Freya looks lovely today. Really elegant.' It is a word that makes her push her shoulders back and forget the skulking figure of Nicole darkening the room. Elegant.

Freya soon gets lost in the work. She takes careful notes as Jay speaks, calculating and recalculating in her mind what the solution may be. She's learned to seek refuge in the cool facts of numbers, and to focus on her ability to make sense of them. Experience has taught her that people can often be disappointing. This is the only thing that is real.

'Coffee?' Jay asks as they all gather their things.

'Better not,' Freya says. 'I've got a lot of work to do.' Jay needs to understand that she has been hired at Atypical for a reason and will prove herself, no matter what.

He nods solemnly. 'Respect! Don't let me stand in your way. But can I ask you one question then?'

'Sure . . .'

'Can I have your number?'

Freya laughs. It only took one week of her being here to hit on her. 'You're an executive director here, you could just get it from my employee file.'

Jay's eyes crinkle. 'I could, but a gentleman prefers to ask.'

'Well, then, a gentleman can have it with pleasure.'

As he taps her number into his cellphone, Freya looks towards Nicole. For reasons she cannot name, she wants to impress her and win her over. But she has already huffed off, leaving a faint trail of Dior Poison in her wake.

'Don't worry about her,' says Jay. 'Nicole has gone through a lot lately, and her social skills were the first to bite the dust.'

They turn together and watch her pace between the desks, a shimmering ball of energy. Clusters of people part for her, so powerful is the force around her. But there is a split second where she turns around and looks back. She stares at Freya with eyes so wounded that for a long time afterward, Freya battles to feel at ease again.

Later, she receives an email from Nicole with no subject.

God, you should see how infatuated the new girl is with Jay. It's so embarrassing. She's practically gagging for it, poor thing.

It's just an opinion, it shouldn't matter. But her stomach twists all the same. Another email from Nicole, in quick succession. Freya winces as she opens it.

Oh silly me. I typed in the wrong address! Next time I will be more careful.

Everything that matters is said between the lines. What Nicole really means is that next time, Freya should be more careful too.

Chapter 12

Freya
Two days after the murder

Freya watches Isla pack up her things and leave the meeting room. There is something endearing about her scuffed sneakers and army surplus coat, and her unruly hair that keeps escaping her ponytail. Freya watched how Isla held eye contact with each person she interviewed, and the way she nodded her head softly, making notes every now and then. She seemed attentive, and kind, the sort of person who knows what to do in times like these.

She wanted to follow Isla out the door and say, free from prying eyes and prickling ears, 'I lied. I did know Nicole. She made it impossible for me to forget her. Every minute of every day, I was aware of Nicole's presence.'

That's why she played the prank on her. After months of ridicule, Freya wanted Nicole to feel what it was like when the joke was on her. But death was never meant to be the punch line, not at all. Someone saw what she did, what Jay did, and now fear crawls beneath her skin.

A hand clutches her shoulder. Freya gasps.

'It's just me.' Jay's grip is unsettlingly tight, but his expression is concerned.

'Did you say anything about our prank to the journalist?'

'No, there wasn't time. Did you?'

Jay shook his head. 'Definitely not. It's not relevant to her story. And if the police question you, it's not relevant to their investigation either. The murder was definitely the work of somebody with a real problem.'

Freya nods. She and Jay are just a normal couple who have made a mistake. The murder is just a terrible coincidence.

'But still,' she says thoughtfully, 'wouldn't it be best to clear the air? We have nothing to hide.'

Freya is sure she sees a flash of impatience in Jay's eyes, but before she can pin it down, it's gone. 'Think of how it would look, Freya. You and Nicole had an acrimonious relationship, and Nicole and I didn't exactly break up on good terms. If you or I say anything about the prank, it will unsettle the whole investigation. The police will start asking questions that they needn't.'

She nods. Jay is right. Of course he's right. Nobody in their right mind would want to prolong this ugliness. The mere presence of the police and the journalist in their offices has tainted the place.

Jay takes her hand in his. 'We won't breathe a word of what we did, OK?'

'No, we won't.'

'It doesn't matter.'

'It was just bad timing.'

'It's a pact,' he said, shaking her hand.

'Yes, a pact.' To keep the peace, to blend in, to forget this ever happened.

'We should probably confirm each other's alibis if we're questioned by the police.'

Jay says it so casually, but Freya can feel the pressure pushing behind his words. He is not asking her, as much as telling her. 'Sure. Kate was in the apartment when I got home – I will ask her to confirm that she saw you too.'

'She saw me the next morning, so it's not really a lie.'

He's right, she supposes, it's just an extension of the truth. Something to be clarified so that fingers don't point in the wrong direction. His hand slides from hers, and they peer out the window, watching Isla pull the car door shut and lurch away.

'Who do you think did it?' Freya asks, feeling depleted.

'I don't know,' Jay says somberly, 'but at least it wasn't us.'

Chapter 13

Isla
Three days after the murder

Dead or alive, it's always about the body. The picture of Nicole that has made the front page is not of her in a suit or doing her extensive volunteer work, but one of her standing next to a mountain bike in tight-fitting shorts. The smattering of early news updates have already mentioned how fit she was, how attractive. In the age of information overload and the daily assault of trauma after trauma, reporters have to find an angle to convince the world that she really matters.

Isla crumples the paper before her. She's wracked with a familiar feeling, a heart thudding, throat-closing discomfort. It floods her body whenever she sees a woman being raped in a television show to 'create a sense of how vicious the historical times were', or gratuitous descriptions of violence towards women in the thrillers she picks up on trips back home to visit her mom in Minnesota. Helplessness. She does the only thing she can do, and calls Simon to get an update on the case.

'Hello?' Simon's voice is barely audible above the clattering din.

'Are you somewhere you can talk?'

More banging. A long hiss. 'Yes! Sorry, I'm actually at the station. Every Friday I cook breakfast for the guys – eggs, mushrooms, cherry tomatoes, the works.'

'No bacon?'

'I'm Jewish, you know that,' he laughs. Isla forgets about Simon's religion, because he's not religious as such but his spirituality is evident in his kindness towards others, his reluctance to judge, and the thin red Kabbalah string dangling on his wrist.

'Does everyone do this?'

'No, just me. I cooked for the guys once and now they insist I do it once a week. I secretly love it, to be honest. How are you, Isla? Listening to that Spotify playlist I sent you, I hope?'

Simon is more of a music snob than Isla is, and recently shared a playlist with her called, 'Songs for murder'. It's a seething mix of Nick Cave, The Police, The Smiths with some Dr Dre thrown in. The raging spirit pulsing in the notes reminds Isla of the girl she was before.

'I have! It's pretty good actually.'

The background noise has disappeared. Isla can picture Simon pacing the small, leafy courtyard at the station, smiling.

'Don't sound so surprised,' he says. 'It's taken me years of trauma to put that collection together.'

Isla spots her boss on the other side of the room. Time to get to the point of the call.

'I wanted to ask if you have had any news on the autopsy yet?'

'No, it's still too soon. Again, you know this, Isla,' he chides.

'Sure, but I thought I'd try my luck.'

The smile Isla had at their earlier banter has faded. She wills herself to remain calm. It's just another crime story, with the same processes that are always followed. The paper has run an initial feature, outlining the bare bones. The case will be fleshed out, if she is patient.

'Have you examined the CCTV footage yet at the apartment building?' she adds. 'Or analyzed her phone records? And do you have any initial suspects yet?'

'Hey, hey, slow down! You can barely breathe, you're talking so fast! We're on it, Isla. All of it.' His voice changes then. 'This case is a big one for you, isn't it?'

It's not how a police officer usually speaks to a journalist, but their relationship is far from normal. He knows why the murder touches on her greatest hurt.

'I suppose. I want to give Nicole the dignity that I was never given by the press.' Her heart races as she remembers the images in the paper, and the words used that minimized the crime perpetrated against her, that made her out to be a liar. Even when she won the case and her boyfriend was charged, there were still questions, and snide remarks. For something that happened over ten years ago, some flashbacks still have the power to knock the breath out of her.

'I don't want to read another story about a broken woman. I want to hear about her strength, and who she was before.'

This isn't the first time they have had this discussion.

'If anyone can write a story like that, it's you. I've always believed in you, Isla. I'll send on the information when I get it. We will speak soon.'

Isla is quiet. The words *I believe in you* mean more than Simon could ever know.

Her eyes scan the report once again. She doesn't share her suspicion yet – that Nicole Whittington and Freya Matthews – the nervous woman she met at Atypical's offices – are somehow linked. She doesn't reveal that she worries for Freya's safety. Why else would Freya wall herself off so carefully? Yet instinct doesn't hold up in a conversation with an investigator. Only hard evidence will.

'Cut yourself some slack, OK?' he says.

'Yeah, Simon, got it.'

She takes a sip of coffee, so hot it scalds her mouth. She's meant to be tough, unflinching, objective. But here is another story about a woman reduced to two dimensions and black-and-white type, and it cuts deep through her every sinew, until the knife scrapes the bone.

Chapter 14

Freya
Three days after the murder

On the walk to work, Freya is absorbed by her cellphone, like so many other pedestrians. Some smile and tap happily as they respond to a funny meme, and others frown as they pre-emptively catch up on emails. Freya is the only one who stares at her phone with all color drained from her face.

The message she received on waking this morning made her blood run cold.

Good morning, beautiful – do you always sleep in such revealing clothes? You're trying to tease me, aren't you?

Freya was wearing an old, worn T-shirt from university. It was a soft, frayed secret comfort. Not the kind of thing she wore in front of her roommates, or Jay. It's not only because of its age and the hole on the left shoulder, but because it was practically transparent. The moment the message came through, she wrenched her curtains shut and threw on a bathrobe. Who was looking at her? And why?

She knew she shouldn't, but she replied. *Who are you, and how do you know where I live?*

The reply chilled her to the bone. *Sweetheart, you told me to come here.*

An invitation. An address. Didn't she and Jay write something similar as a joke the other night? The resemblance was too much to bear.

Now, although she tried to put it out of her mind, she rereads the message, as if by looking at it often enough, a clue will reveal itself.

Pushing against the warm bodies of strangers on the sidewalk, she feels every unwelcome touch, every pair of eyes that assesses her, and then looks away. Then, a body separates from the throng. Heavy, sharp footsteps approach swiftly behind her, their urgency pushing her like a current. She walks faster. It's OK, it's OK, she thinks. There are people everywhere, she won't get hurt. Yet people get pickpocketed, robbed, kidnapped and worse in public spaces. The perpetrators are professionals, who know how to blend in and dodge the interest of the innocent eye.

The faster she goes, the more she feels the presence behind her, closer, closer, closing in on her, breathing down her neck. She would cry out but she is suddenly mute. Panic has swallowed her voice. The presence behind her barrels towards her, it can't be stopped. This is it, he has followed her from her home and found her here.

Freya is pushed up against the wall, eyes shut and breath ragged. And then, the presence is gone. She is free.

She opens her eyes and watches as a tall, overweight businessman thunders down the sidewalk, absorbed in a phone call. The crowd flows on, too focused on their destination to notice Freya standing like a statue.

Is this how Nicole felt when she walked home a few nights ago? Did she read a reply to a message she hadn't sent, turn around, wondering if someone was waiting in the shadows? Did she close her door and sigh in relief when she made it home safely?

Freya is used to being alert, she knows how it feels to pre-empt the unthinkable and to imagine herself in the place of the assaulted women she reads about in the news every day. But this is different. Because something dark lies between the lines of the messages on her phone, something that makes her feel that the threat is imminent.

Chapter 15

Isla
Three days after the murder

An unsuccessful visit to the apartment block on Market Street. Five pages of bystander interviews, two hours spent drinking weak cups of tea in the various apartments on the edges of the murder scene. Everyone heard something, but what they heard is unclear. Was it a man's voice or woman's voice? There is an almost 50/50 split.

It is enough for Isla to consider Freya as a potential witness. Her presence outside the apartment that morning is too much of a coincidence. She calls Simon to run the theory past him.

'With all due respect, I don't think she saw anything.' He sounds weary this morning and in no mood to entertain Isla's outlandish theories. She persists anyway.

'I know I saw her outside the crime scene that morning, behaving erratically. I almost hit her with my car!'

'You can't pin someone down as a witness just because they happened to jog past a crime scene, hours after it happened,' says Simon.

Isla ignores his resigned tone. Every interview confirmed that Nicole had had company that night. It could have been Freya, or someone they both knew at work. Maybe even someone in power . . . someone stopping Freya from telling the whole truth.

Simon continues, 'The staff at Atypical are untouchable. We spent the last few days interviewing each one, including Freya. There was a big office party on the night of the murder, and everyone has an alibi.'

'Really?'

'Yes. Trust me, I would love that to be a lead as much as you do. But at Nicole's estimated time of death Julian posted live video updates of himself cracking open champagne on the company's Facebook page. There is video footage of Nicole's friends, Melanie and Anne, stumbling out of the Atypical building in the early hours of the morning. As for Freya, as a part of her statement she gave me the details of her three roommates, who have all confirmed that she left the party early and spent the remainder of the evening with them. There's footage on Freya's Instagram stories where she is drinking hot chocolate in her apartment with her housemate Kate, time-stamped at 1 a.m. that night.'

Isla's heart sinks, but she tries to sound upbeat. 'Have you had a look at the security-camera footage?'

'It's inconclusive,' he says. 'That night was one of the coldest this season. The camera is only angled towards the entrance of her corridor. Several people pass through, but their faces are shrouded in coats and hoods.'

'I'm sure I spotted a flash of brown hair in the stills, and half the bystanders I interviewed today thought they heard a female voice that night, a voice that sounded afraid.'

Simon is gentle with her. He listens when most police officers wouldn't and is often more yielding than required when offering classified information. His ability to see beyond the obvious is what makes him a great cop. But Isla has taken it too far, even for him.

'It could just be a coincidence, Isla. I spoke to her for over half an hour. She was upset that her colleague has been murdered but that was it. She didn't seem any more traumatized than anybody else in the office.'

'Then how do you explain the voices the neighbors heard that night? All accounts point to the probability that Nicole knew her killer.'

'People have the ability to tell themselves extraordinary stories. How would you feel if a murder took place a few feet from your doorstep? Wouldn't you try and make sense of it?'

'You think it's a false memory.'

'How could they be sure that it was even Nicole they heard laughing? I need witness statements and hard evidence in order to have a viable case. The murder looks like the work of a seasoned criminal, of which there are several operating in the area. I'd pin it on gang violence, or some random person.'

They are both silent as the information percolates between them.

'What if I could prove that there's a link between Nicole and someone she knew?'

'You can try. Not all violence needs to mean something. I'm afraid your theory just doesn't hold from an investigative or legal point of view. Remember, we're a strong force, with many resources you don't have access to.'

Isla recalls the fragility in Freya's eyes. She had seen something she shouldn't have, Isla is sure of it.

'The likelihood of you discovering something new about this case is almost impossible, Isla.'

Impossible. She's heard that before, many years ago. She staggered into a police station crying *help me, somebody please help me*. She had never felt so filthy, with her bare feet, torn clothes and the stickiness of blood on her thighs.

The officers on duty had rushed to her. The first, a thin, wily type with a thick mustache. The second, a thickset woman with a severe bun. They held her as she collapsed, comforted her as she shook. They let her cry as the now all-familiar panic inhabited her body for the first time, and took hold of her with the force of a spirit.

She was ushered into a corner office and wrapped in a warm blanket. The female officer – Mandy – had taken the pen from her to write her statement. Isla was shaking too much to write it herself. Saying the words out loud was excruciating, but necessary. It had the disgusting, satisfying pain of lancing a boil. But when she uttered what happened, she noticed the imperceptible change in the officer's expression, no matter how she tried to hide it. It was a mixture of disbelief and disappointment.

'Will you repeat that, please?' the officer had asked politely. Isla's shock started to catch up with her. The

muscles of her legs ached and pain prickled at the surface of where her flesh had broken. The fear that had
driven her to walk barefoot to the station in the cold
dead of night had given way to a crippling tiredness, a
will to sleep until the evening had assumed the texture
of a dream. But she repeated the course of events, slowly
and carefully, even though she could see the doubt in the
officer's eyes.

Impossible. Such evil can't be committed by young men
who play in indie bands and write songs with sweet, soulful lyrics and play the ukulele. Such crimes are reserved
for the nameless monsters that prowl the quiet streets after
dark. Poor men, bad men, the kind with rough skin, and
broken teeth who look more at home in prison cells than
in normal society.

Impossible. For so long, she had believed that too. She
had kept herself up at night analyzing what she had done to
provoke it, how her fragile memory had twisted the events
to rid herself of any blame. She shuddered when she saw the
scars on her feet, an unwelcome reminder of her guilt.

She hangs up. Glugs the rest of her cold coffee until her
hands stop shaking. She's worked hard to heal and reframe
the power of words. Impossible is no longer a simple word,
impossible is no longer an ending. She opens her notebook
and begins to write. Impossible is a challenge.

Chapter 16

Freya
Three days after the murder

A new message. A new number. A different person, again.

Hey . . .

She ignores it.

What are you doing tonight?

She remains silent. Eyes fixed on the cell. She thinks it will go away if she doesn't reply, but it doesn't stop.

I want to touch you, I want to taste you. I want to do all the things you asked for.

She digs her nails into her wrist until the scream surging within her disappears. But in its wake she feels empty and wrecked with worry. Whoever is behind these messages does not like her. They don't want a date, a casual fling, or even a one-night stand. Every come-on feels like an intrusion, an expression of power. Whoever is on the other side of the phone knows about her prank, and doesn't want her to forget.

Chapter 17

Freya
Three months before the murder

Freya glances quickly at her phone, and picks it up, feeling a warm rush. It's him.

Hey ☺

She can feel Jay watching her across the room.

Hey . . .

You free after work?

She pauses. Is this a good idea? She has a lot going on. There is work to take home, a dress that she was hoping to cut the pattern for. Her new life has expanded to fill every gap. But then she remembers that feeling she has sometimes late at night, that sting of loneliness, the yearning for comfort.

I can be, she types.

Meet me outside at five ;)

Freya turns around and smiles. The gray sky outside suddenly seems brooding and romantic, and the dreary task in front of her exciting. Something good is coming.

'Can you please stop smiling like an idiot, Freya!' hisses Nicole. 'Can't you see that Julian has investors in his office? You could at least pretend to be getting some work done.' She flips her hair and starts whispering something to Melanie. Freya's stomach turns. They keep glancing in her direction. It would feel less torturous if she could hear what they are saying. The unsaid hurts most of all.

The last hours of the afternoon stretch relentlessly under the heat of their attention. A few minutes before the end of the day, she can't take it anymore, and starts gathering her things. This way, she has a moment to go past the restroom to freshen up.

'You know we finish at five, right, Freya?' Nicole says.

'Yes, I do,' she answers, trying to smile.

Nicole won't quit. A smug smile tugs at the corners of her mouth. 'Well, on my watch it says it is five minutes to.'

Freya is about to say, maybe her watch is slow, maybe she should just give her a break, maybe she should just mind her own business, but she bites her tongue. She sits back down at her desk, ignoring the sniggering behind her, staring aimlessly at her email until long after the clock strikes five.

Jay is waiting outside. The clouds have parted, giving way to an incongruous golden light. In its glow, his features look even stronger.

'Phew, I was beginning to think you'd stood me up! My Apple Watch and I were going to take our walk all alone!' he says.

'Fair enough. Getting your daily steps in comes first.' Freya's laugh falls flat. She thinks of telling him about Nicole's comment, but it sounds too petty. Nobody likes a catfight. 'Sorry, I got held up. Where are we off to?'

He smiles in a way that gives her a glimpse into what he looked like as a young boy. Cheeky, bold, but eager to please. 'I hope you don't think it's cheesy.'

They pass the Zeitgeist beer garden and Freya breathes a sigh of relief. The easygoing bro and beer mix isn't her vibe, and she hopes it isn't Jay's.

As the sidewalk crowds with people walking home from work, she notices his hand lingering above the small of her back, not quite touching. Freya moves a bit closer.

'I like your style, Freya,' he says, pointing to her 1970s wrap blouse. 'I've never seen any other woman dress like you.'

'Thank you! I make my most of my clothes or I scrounge around in vintage stores for them, like these pants for example.'

'My jacket is vintage.'

'I thought so! They don't make clothes the way they used to.'

He takes her hand casually as they cross the street. The shift is palpable. His touch, a statement of intent. 'So it's a style statement for you?'

Nobody has ever been so interested in her sewing. Most people are more excited about her ability to code – it is a more twenty-first-century sensibility after all. 'It's a bit deeper than that. I don't want to create waste in the world by buying clothes that I just throw away next season. It seems so pointless! Besides, whenever I tack a pair of pants or mend a jacket, it's a reminder that anything broken can be repaired, which isn't that different to coding.'

'Or life,' says Jay. 'Either way, it's a beautiful belief to have.'

'It gives me some meaning, anyway.'

'We're almost there.'

Freya guesses the destination even before they reach it. She has walked this path many times before, as a teenager on field trips and later, as a student. No matter how many times she approaches the place, she is always filled with the same sense of anticipation and awe.

'You're taking me to the California Academy of Sciences?'

'Yup, and revealing myself to be the greatest nerd of all time.'

The sidewalk fills up as they get closer, tourists and schoolchildren jostling them on either side. Jay holds her hand tighter, and her heart flips. She doesn't know what this is yet, but there is definitely something.

They settle in front of the Mangrove Lagoon exhibit. Stingrays, mantas and fish swirl around them in a riot of color. Freya sighs. It feels good to relax.

Jay looks ahead. 'This place has that effect on me too. Whenever I'm feeling a bit low, I always end up here. Something about nature's endless possibility calms me.'

Freya touches her tattoo. 'Like patterns, repeated in different iterations. I love how, whenever I visit, I learn something new. I don't ever want to stand still, you know? Get bored with my life.'

He squeezes her leg, 'I don't think there's any possibility of that. If your approach to your job is anything to go by, you're going to live your life with more enthusiasm than most people ever muster.'

Freya covers her face. 'Ah, man, I'm so embarrassing, aren't I? I don't know how not to be excited. I just want to learn and experience and do it all.'

'Don't ever apologize for yourself,' he says, turning to face her. His eyes are a deep, soulful brown. 'Your energy is amazing.'

Perhaps it's the words he uses, or the way his gaze lingers on her face, but Freya realizes that Jay is more than a cute guy at work. He really *sees* her. He understands what she holds most important.

So she opens up, word by word, anecdote by anecdote. He shares funny stories about the first three years at Atypical, how initially Julian used to wear his hair in a ponytail and was once mistaken for an Uber driver by one of his own investors. She tells him about her first coding project, an online game dedicated to her favorite band at the time, Twenty-One Pilots. His eyes crinkle when he laughs. Her cheeks feel sore from smiling. The aquarium auditorium empties out, with only the fish left swimming silently around them.

'Gosh,' he says, 'we didn't manage to see any of the exhibits! Next time . . .'

'Yes, next time.'

There will be a next time. Freya feels light-headed. This is really happening. She waits for him to kiss her. Surely he will kiss her? The spark is there, crackling between them. He walks her home and stops at the door of her apartment building.

'Tonight was quite something. *You're* quite something.'

He leans forward, and her heart thuds. This is it. Instead, he plants a chaste kiss on her cheek.

As she walks to the door, she turns around, and as he lifts a hand to wave goodbye, she sees something in his eyes. He wants her, and although it may complicate her career and her already difficult relationship with Nicole, she wants him too.

Chapter 18

Freya
Four years before

She takes a deep drag on her cigarette, chokes, then crushes it with the heel of her shoe. Freya has never been able to inhale. But she needs something to take the edge off, something to stop her from going back into the club and causing a scene she'll regret.

He was supposed to be The One. Firmly built, fun-loving and the second smartest person in class next to her. Blond, sea-bleached hair, the quintessential California guy. She'd spent the night in his room a few times, and they'd watched movies on his laptop. He was a bit of a savant, the kind of alpha geek that played her his favorite movies with regular intervals for his long explanations on each scene. They'd fooled around, had sex. And she'd come back again and again for more movies and a lot more sex. She was under the impression that it had all meant something.

But tonight, she saw what a liar he was. He'd said he was staying in to study, but she had had a feeling he would be here, at the student bar, having a laugh with his friends. The bar was on her way home from the library, so she stopped by. Her mind was whirring from everything she had learned in her latest assignment and she was looking forward to a break. She didn't expect to see him with his arm snaked around a petite girl with a golden bob, kissing her hard, both hands firmly in the back pockets of her jeans. It was so crass. She thought he was better than that. She fled outside before he could see her. Now here she is, another rejected girl, sitting on the sidelines alone.

'Can I bum a smoke?'

The girl in question is wearing a mini-skirt, and a black top that has been unlaced down to her cleavage. Her ash-white hair has been cropped into a pixie-cut. Freya thinks she might be the sexiest woman she has ever seen.

'Yeah, sure.'

'I'm Hattie.' The girl inhales on her cigarette deeply, and holds out her hand for another one. Smokers, they always know how to spot those who are only smoking for show. She smacks her lips. 'Menthols? Seriously?'

Now she has definitely been outed as a fake smoker. 'I like the taste, I guess.'

'You're crazy. You out here to cool off?' She looks down at Freya's hands. 'Your fists are clenched so hard they're turning white.'

'Something like that. I just caught my boyfriend cheating on me.' It feels like a stretch calling him her boyfriend, but more embarrassing to admit the actual looseness of the arrangement.

'Bastard! I hope you slapped him across the face.'

'No,' Freya laughs wryly, 'but I wanted to.' There's an urgent despair behind her laugh, a silent scream. No matter how well she does at college, or how many friends she makes, she can't shake this desire to be loved, to be one person's only thought. Why does love keep slipping from her grasp? It is a serious thing, to love a person, to taste their skin and move in time with their body. To betray that trust sickens her, and awakens a deep-seated anger she didn't know she had.

Hattie arches her back as she sits down next to Freya. 'You should be more like me. I'm proud of my body and want to use it in as many ill-advised situations as I can. Nothing makes a man crazier than a woman that doesn't need him.'

'I don't know if I could ever do that,' says Freya, frowning. 'I'm far too serious.'

They sit for a moment, the music from the bar thrumming in the background, punctuating Hattie's conversation as she shares stories of her latest conquests. She's funny, smart and self-deprecating. Flickering between them is that spark she always feels when she makes a new female friend, that light pressing its way through the words. It feels like the beginning of something.

'I'm so glad I met you tonight. I was feeling so low. Seeing my boyfriend, well now *ex*-boyfriend, like that is a huge shock. I don't think it's really sunk in yet.'

'I'm glad I met you too.' Hattie smiles. 'But seriously, you should lighten up.' Her voice suddenly turns grave. 'Hold on to love less tightly. Desire will kill you, unless you kill it first.'

Chapter 19

Isla
Four days after the murder

'*You know, Barbara, the death of Nicole Whittington is yet another reminder that it is still unsafe to be a woman in America. You can lock your doors, but you're still at risk.*'

Isla picks at a bowl of instant noodles, hate-watching *The Circle*, America's number one female talk show. One of the five women huddled around the circular table, blowing gently over her black tea, is Tiffany, an old classmate. Isla remembers her as smart, determined, principled. It still shocks her to see her long, flamingo-pink fingernails drumming on the table, while spewing conservative vitriol.

The women titter over the papers spread in front of them. '*It's such a shame. She really was a beautiful girl, so full of potential.*'

Tiffany purses her lips before she speaks. '*We need to also look at the area she lived in. These young, cool girls want to live in neighborhoods that seem edgy, but in reality these places are still dangerous. They attract the homeless, drug dealers, and dead beats that live off the state. And let's not even get started on the safe injection sites popping up all over town . . .*'

Isla laughs darkly into her noodles as she watches the women nod sagely. 'Oh Jesus, I can't believe people actually buy in to this shit!'

She turns the television off and pushes her dinner to one side. In truth, it's not that funny, and it's turned her off her food. Conversations like these, innocuous as they may seem, plant seeds of prejudice. It's getting harder to laugh at the hatred edging its way into the media, and the insatiable trolls that feed off conflict online. She's beginning to question how healthy it is to be a journalist in this climate. Does she have any power at all to help others through the stories she tells?

Her phone flashes in front of her. It's Lizzie, FaceTiming her from London. She checks the time – it must be around three in the morning there.

'Hey, Liz! Everything OK?'

Lizzie is wearing pajama pants and a sparkly top. There is a glint in her eyes, and a glass of champagne in her hand.

'Yes! More than OK. I just had the best night with the most *delightful* man. We went for dinner and drinks at this tiny underground bar, but then left because the people were pretentious and boring. We ended back at his place watching YouTube videos of Lionel Richie! It was hilarious, Isla, I can't even begin to tell you.'

'You're drunk.' Isla smiles.

'Rubbish, I'm in love.'

'Lust, you mean . . .'

'Is there a difference? Both feel the same at first.'

Lizzie's accent has grown more and more English in her daily life, but when she slurs, it's a deep Southern drawl. 'Anyway, what the hell are you doing home on a Saturday night? And is that your college hoodie, I see?'

Isla sighs. They always have the same conversation, every weekend, and she always has the same reply. 'It's been a long week. I'm tired.'

Lizzie disappears out of the frame for a moment, and returns with her glass emptied and a tub of ice cream in hand. 'I worry about you. When is the last time you spoke to a man our age?'

'Simon is round about my age! I talk to him all the time.'

'That's cheating. He's a work colleague . . .' Lizzie arches an eyebrow. 'Isn't he?'

It's hard to explain. She only calls Simon for work, but she has started to look forward to their conversations, even when the topic is the latest crime she has to report on. He always seems to have great new music to share, or a funny anecdote about a crime scene. His sense of humor is a little odd, a little dry, the kind that not all people get, but *she* always gets his jokes. Her job is unrewarding at the best of times, but he makes it a little lighter.

'Yeah, yeah, you're right. But we talk about other things too.'

'Well, that's good! It's a start! And I suppose you two are close already because of—'

'The incident,' Isla finishes her sentence.

She can never bring herself to say the word. It sounds too violent, a word that doesn't quite belong to what took place that night.

Lizzie always plays along. She doesn't like to remind her either. 'Yes, the incident. You've known each other for years – no wonder you're close!'

'Don't look at me like that, Lizzie. I know that look . . . it's nothing. He's just a colleague. I don't look at him in that way.'

She laughs and winks into the camera. 'Well, darlin,' maybe you should.'

Chapter 20

Freya
Three months before the murder

Freya dishes out four plates of lasagna for herself and her roommates. It feels good to be back with her friends, celebrating the end of her second week in her new job. Life is much simpler here, and her friends' questions remind her how exciting things have become.

'Come on, spill everything!' says Hattie.

'I want to know it all. Are you settling into the job? And, most importantly, what's it like getting so much one-on-one time with that delicious boss of yours?'

Freya's cheeks grow warm. 'He's actually really approachable.'

Jasmin laughs. 'Oh, I'm *sure* he is.'

Freya pictures the cozy interior of Julian's office, the way he's always ready with a friendly handshake or a reassuring pat on the shoulder.

'It's not like that, honestly. I couldn't have asked for a better boss. So far, he has met with me every day to hear how I'm finding the work, and the company. And it's not just about me simply doing a job, he genuinely wants to hear my ideas on how to make his business better. It's really encouraging.'

There are small things that Julian does that make a difference. He's already left a pile of new books on her desk, which are related to her interests. It means the world that someone so admired at his job is taking her seriously.

'There is someone, however, who I think is really delicious,' she adds. Her friends move closer.

As she describes Jay, from his wild dark hair to his ability to write the most complex code, warmth spreads over her. This isn't like the childish crushes of the past. He is courting her.

'We went on one blissful date to the California Museum of Sciences two days ago . . .'

'Basically, a Freya dream date,' says Hattie.

'Can you let me finish?' Freya laughs. 'We went on one date and he asked me on a second yesterday. He didn't even play it cool and wait!'

Ever the cynic, Kate says, 'Don't you think it's a bit premature to be dating someone in your new job?'

'Not really. He's so similar to me, and it's not like he's made a move on me or anything.'

'A true gentleman, what a rare breed!' says Hattie.

'A modern-day mythological creature, an urban Loch Ness monster!' adds Jasmin.

Hattie says, 'It *is* possible for a guy to like a woman without trying to sleep with her on the first date. I mean, I haven't experienced it, but I've heard it happens.'

Kate looks at Freya carefully, an indecipherable expression on her face. 'Are you really that similar, or is this like the time where you fixated on Peter at college because you both liked The Weeknd?'

They all start laughing. 'I was such an idiot, at that point, *everyone* loved The Weeknd! No, it's in the subtle things. He doesn't like the exact same bands as me, but he loves vinyl and searching for forgotten albums at old music stores.' She gestures to the tweed dress she's wearing. 'And he appreciates my style. It's also in the way he is with me. He *sees* things about me that I'd always hoped someone would notice.'

'Like that overly romantic imagination of yours?'

She playfully slaps her friend. 'No, it's just this feeling that he was here waiting for me all along and I just needed to find him.'

Kate whistles, long and low. 'Easy there, tiger. Go on a few more dates first.'

Freya blushes, and her heart skips a beat.

'You have to admit there is potential. No hand-holding, no come-ons, just his smoldering stare and his whip-smart banter.'

Kate is getting distracted now, wanting to practice handstands against their grubby wall. Her muscular arms tense as she slowly balances her whole body in the air. The strength in her small frame always comes as a shock to Freya.

'Enjoy it,' says Hattie as they watch Kate. 'That feeling of lust building between the two of you, with no knowledge of when and where it's going to burst.'

Just the thought of it makes Freya sweat a little, despite the cool weather. 'So, you think it's going to happen, Jay and me?' she asks hopefully.

'Of course! It's a done deal,' says Jasmin. Freya's heart soars at the confirmation, but then she catches Kate's expression, which looks grave.

'It just sounds like it has the potential to get quite intense. I mean, I've known you when you were dating Chris for that brief period, and even Ian. You're passionate, hell, I remember some of your fights with them, but I've never seen you this – what's the word for it? – feverish.'

Jasmin nods between mouthfuls of lasagna. 'She's right, Freya, you look a bit whipped. I feel like Jay is pressing a button for you.'

Freya gathers the empty plates and storms into the kitchen. She hates it when Jasmin psychoanalyzes her, especially when she's right. Freya's crush on Jay *has* pushed a button for her, it has touched a suppressed longing to feel loved. While her friends have grown to become her family, they could never bring the intimacy of true love. She has wanted men before, but she has never needed to be close to anyone like this.

'I know I seem crazy, but it just feels special.' She catches her glassy-eyed reflection in the kitchen window. Her hair, while messy, looks glossy. There is a fresh sheen to her skin. In that split second, she can imagine how she looks through his eyes. Beautiful, wistful, *elegant*.

A look of doubt flashes across her friends' faces. Kate has a patronizing look that only makes the anger in Freya rise. She feels like she needs to defend herself.

'It's hard to explain if you haven't felt it before, Kate,' she says curtly.

Kate doesn't know, because she has gone from one doomed relationship to the next since before they became friends. Both women are accustomed to pacing through bars, eyes lowered like prey, pulsing with the fear of locking gazes with unwanted men, giving them the wrong idea. Liking someone usually means kissing them in a dark corner, bumping into them weekend after weekend until the hookup settled into an inevitability which may be called a relationship for a brief while. Online dating has been no different – the guys they really wanted disappeared while the desperate ones lingered. The attraction brewing between herself and Jay feels intentional, which adds to its meaning. Kate wouldn't understand that, and part of Freya wonders if her friend is jealous.

'You're right,' Kate says bitterly. 'I wouldn't know. My life is just one sorry, fragmented warning tale on how lonely it can be to surf the backwaters of Tinder.'

'That's not what I meant.' But Kate's arms are folded tightly, and she is pressing her lips together the way she always does when she is trying to keep her composure. Hattie and Jasmin glance at Freya in warning. This is about to turn into a fight. 'I'm just worried about you. You have more potential than all of us put together. I wouldn't want you to waste it on a guy.'

'Like my mother did?' It is a sore point and everyone knows it. Freya's mother put her up for adoption when she was a year old. According to the note she left with her at the orphanage, she was a promising engineering student who fell pregnant in her second year of college. She tried to take care of Freya by herself, but gave her up when she realized that no matter how hard she tried, she was too young to give Freya the life she deserved. As a result she grew up a cliché, a stray without a family, a new life that had robbed her mother of her own. 'I'm not stupid, Kate. I know what I'm doing.'

Tension bristles between them. Kate's voice softens and she pulls Freya into a hug. They've known each other too long to cling on to a disagreement.

'I know, and I love you, which is the only reason why I am concerned. You're standing at the edge of your new life and everything is so close. And unfortunately it still holds that a man can afford to make a few mistakes along the way. Tech isn't a friendly space for women to begin with. You need to be sure of who you want to be.'

Freya wants to be respected and a master of her craft, but most of all she wants to be remembered for making a difference. She wants to take her intuition for technology and use it to help women who don't have the power to help themselves. Whether that makes her successful or rich is beside the point. The work is her greatest inspiration, and her greatest healer.

They hold each other for a while, Kate stroking her hair. The others quietly leave the room. In moments like these, Freya feels the full force of their friendship, the protracted, tearful conversations, the vicious end-of-the-world fights that peter out in an hour, the shared secrets and clothes, the dancing, the music, the neon-lit midnight trips to McDonald's, the late nights spent studying, the joy and high-fives at their results. This is the home she has created for herself.

She always hoped to find a romantic love similar to the bond she shares with her friends. That's what makes her feel so good about Jay. The few times she has been in his company, alone or with her colleagues, she has felt carefree and fully herself. She hasn't had to dumb herself down for him. She stands firm in her ideas and feels colorful and interesting.

'I can't wait for you to meet him,' she says softly, imagining Kate, Hattie and Jasmin hitting it off with him, laughing at his jokes till they cry, grabbing her by the arm when he leaves the room to say, wow Freya, yes, we can see what you have been talking about, this man is something special.

'There is nothing to worry about, you know, I have everything under control.'

Chapter 21

Isla
Four days after the murder

What Isla needs is hard evidence. She will find out more about both Nicole and Freya, and see where their lives intersect. Were they simply work colleagues, or did they have something deeper in common? She searches Freya's name, and finds nothing but a smattering of achievements. There is Freya, looking not much younger than today, accepting an award for exceptional achievement in computer science. There is her radiant, smiling face staring out from her Facebook profile. Isla takes a look at her friends list. She recognizes some names – Jay, Julian, a product designer called Virginie – but Nicole is not among them.

While Nicole's neighbors and her colleagues only have nice things to say about her, a crop of unsupported statements from Nicole's so-called friends and family have begun to creep into the media. Isla spreads today's papers in front of her, and highlights them, one by one.

'She was unapproachable, and mostly kept to herself.'

'Nicole was addicted to work and never left the office.'

'I wouldn't be surprised if she had a secret life – she never revealed too much.'

'She had a history of mental illness.'

Each statement, each quickly drafted article is another weight on Isla's chest. The news is a cycle, temperamental as the weather, and the tide is about to turn. Nicole is about to go from a victim to a topic of cold debate, as people begin to wonder what she did to ask for it.

She takes another color and highlights passages about Atypical. In each piece, the company comes off perfectly, especially Julian. It is as if Nicole was privileged to work there, and not the other way around. Statements about her workaholic tendencies are punctuated by paragraphs about everything that the company has achieved. Isla has heard rumors that the tech industry has a dark side, where bright young hopefuls become entangled in sex parties, and CEOs indulge S&M fetishes. Simon was once tipped off about an anonymously opulent high-end hotel room, only to find underage sex workers draped over a man whose face had previously appeared in the *Financial Times*. Yet by reading the flattering statements on Atypical's noble vision, it would seem that the company was different, on the surface at least.

Her hands travel up to her neck subconsciously. Her shoulders feel as solid as concrete, her jaw tense. She should call Lizzie, or her mother, just to focus on something lighter and get out of her head for a while. They both say it's not good – this fixation on stories about women like her.

But Isla knows what happens next – the masses on Twitter will start to gain momentum and question

Nicole's character, her sanity. Soon, the trolls will find something – maybe her clothes that night, or the amount of makeup she was wearing – to say that she deserved it. Words like slut and bitch will be thrown around carelessly, without thought to the woman she was.

It's a strange aftershock that follows a crime.

Why? Because if horrible things happen to those that don't 'deserve' it, then nobody is safe.

Chapter 22

Freya
Five days after the murder

There is something alarmingly intrusive about seeing a stranger's message flash across your cellphone screen. It is immediate, intimate, as real as unwelcome hands running down your spine.

But, thinks Freya, it doesn't have to be this way. She has some control. She blocks a few of the numbers, but more messages keep popping up.

Hello, gorgeous.

I love your dirty mouth.

Are you free tonight? Now?

She shakes her head. She can't get upset about this any longer. She has a job to do, a boyfriend to love, and a pact to uphold.

She logs on to a website that offers reverse cellphone number searches. Maybe if she finds out who is doing this, she can put a stop to it herself. For an extra $5 she selects the option that reveals the location of the sender. She wonders if Nicole did the same, and if she felt the same panic she feels now.

One number is from Monte Sereno, the other from Albany and two from Palo Alto. Two of the messages have numbers that are intentionally blocked.

She buries her head in her hands. It's getting too late for this. She'll approach the problem with a clear head in the morning.

A loud bang breaks her thoughts with a jolt. A stone, she thinks, something hard, has hit her window. This is unusual – she lives on the second floor. A spider web crack unspools around the place of impact. Freya lowers herself to the floor, too scared to cry for help and looks down. It is too late for construction or any kind of activity that would fling stones about, and there is nobody in the street below her.

From across the room, she sees the reflection of her phone lighting up the wall. This is a message, a sign. Because while Freya cannot see anyone, someone wants her to know that she is not alone.

Chapter 23

Freya
Two months before the murder

Freya takes the long route to her desk. By weaving through the office in a certain path, she can make it all the way to her chair without feeling Nicole's eyes on her, or hearing her muffled laughter. She knows she's fooling herself, but there is a spark of hope that if she just keeps out of Nicole's way, she will stop being a target. Nicole may forget about her, and pick on someone else.

Today, her plan is foiled. Nicole is standing right next to her desk, talking to Melanie. She will be the bigger person, no matter how much it hurts.

'Good morning, Melanie. Good morning, Nicole,' she says through gritted teeth.

They look back at her with faces of stone. Freya is sure she spots a smirk creeping up on Nicole's face. The animosity towards her is thick and immutable.

She smiles as if it's normal, as if they simply didn't hear her, but tears threaten to spill from the corner of her eyes. If she can just hold out until she reaches the bathroom, then she can have a cry, just to release the tension. Right now she must stay strong. The way Nicole looks at her makes her feel unwelcome, hated. Feelings like that begin to stick to you, no matter how much you fight them. You start to treat them as your own.

'Nice jacket!' It's Virginie, a product designer who joined the company from Paris, only a month before Freya.

Freya blushes. She points to Virginie's worn-in white shirt, tucked effortlessly into a pair of high-waisted jeans. 'Thanks, I made it actually, well, part of it. And I love your shirt, by the way.'

Whispers. Just loud enough for Freya to hear them. It's Nicole.

'That jacket is ugly as fuck.'

Freya feels a rush of heat to her face, her stomach turns. She found this vintage jacket at one of the stores in the East Bay. She was immediately attracted to its worn black leather and knew exactly what would make it even more perfect. She rushed to the little haberdashery only frequented by old ladies and seamstresses in the know, and found two strips of intricate cream lace. It took a few nights to stitch the delicate lace into the cuffs of the jacket without breaking the handiwork. The result is a little bit romantic, and a little bit rock 'n' roll. This morning she had felt like she was wearing a piece of art, something that expressed her essence, now she just feels embarrassed.

Virginie clicks her tongue loudly in Nicole's direction. 'Don't listen to her. It's easy to seem stylish when you wear black all the time and spend hundreds of dollars on clothes directly from the mannequin. I prefer someone who takes a risk.'

The affirmation from another woman in the face of such animosity makes Freya want to weep with relief. Sometimes it's hard being the new girl.

'Thank you, that means a lot.'

'My pleasure! Don't let the cruel girls get you down, and find me at lunch, OK?'

Another relief. For the past few weeks, Freya has slunk to the fire escape, eating the same peanut butter sandwich surrounded by plumbing and worn, defaced walls, the secret, shameful exterior of Atypical's lush office space. She didn't want to give Nicole the satisfaction of seeing her alone, and while she has wanted to eat with Jay, their budding relationship is kept outside office walls for now. They have been on four dates so far, and even shared a kiss. She loves how their relationship is unfolding, and that they are doing things the proper way.

Bolstered by her interaction with Virginie, Freya flings the jacket over her chair, puts her headphones on and searches for a podcast to listen to. Every now and then, she spots the two women staring at her, talking intently. What now? she wonders. Does it ever end?

A hand on her shoulder. It's Julian.

'Good morning, Freya. Have you got a minute?'

They walk to his office, chatting idly about the latest Apple iPhone release. She's used to these meetings now, they have them almost every day. But this one feels different, because out the corner of her eye, she spots the women sniggering among themselves.

Julian's face twitches. 'How is the algorithm design going? I'm concerned that I got too excited and overloaded you with work. Are you coping?'

Freya looks up abruptly, 'Of course!'

Something about this conversation doesn't feel quite right, or quite friendly. He leans forward, into her space.

'I'm curious then, Freya. I've been hearing reports that you are spending your time here watching YouTube clips, scrolling Instagram and listening to podcasts. You know I have to take comments like this seriously, no matter how much I believe in you. Should I be challenging you more?'

Julian says it in a helpful way, but his face is weary with disappointment. He hired her in the faith that she had some-thing brilliant to offer, and he thinks she is falling short.

Nothing could make Freya feel worse. She is usually the person who always works the hardest, the one who shines with her resilience and commitment. She would give anything to succeed here, why would she waste her chance surfing the net on the job? She can do that all night when she gets home anyway! It's mortifying. She opens her mouth and tries to sound calm.

'I think there's been a misunderstanding. I listen to tech podcasts while I code but I don't watch YouTube or check social media. I need to focus. The work I do requires com-plete concentration.'

He puts an encouraging hand on her shoulder, massaging it slightly. The gesture is a little odd, a little out of place, but Freya knows he means well.

'I know,' he says, 'and this is exactly what I suspected but I sometimes have to check these things out for myself. Unfortunately we have some rumor mongers' – he flicks his head in Nicole's direction – 'who can get quite persistent in their claims. I have to honor all feedback.'

Their eyes meet and they both smile. Julian is on her side. He believes in her.

'You're a strong girl. Stand your ground and pay them no attention, you hear? Take it as a compliment.'

A compliment is all very well when you are Julian and get to sit in a protective glass box in the middle of the office. It is very different to the prospect of entering the fray day after day, and trying to be gracious in the face of passive aggression and the gossip. A compliment doesn't help when you have begun waking up at night, drenched in sweat, unable to stop your mind looping over what small torture will be inflicted on you the next day.

All she can do is smile and nod, then walk back to her desk. The air feels chillier now, the office space she was initially so enamored with, all hard edges. Fuck it, she is proud of her handiwork, she will wear the jacket. It doesn't matter what Nicole thinks.

She slips it on and gasps as a shock of cold slaps her back. Then she smells it. The dark, dirty scent of filter coffee, and the roughness of coffee grounds. Someone has poured coffee inside the cream satin lining of her new jacket. The brown stain runs along the inside of the jacket and into the lace cuffs she picked and stitched so meticulously. Freya fights back the tears. It's only an item of clothing. She has many more. But this one was her favorite. Come on, she wills herself, don't be unprofessional and cry at work! But this was more than just a jacket, it was a symbol of her old and new lives coming together.

'Come to think of it, I actually do like that jacket,' says Nicole, as she walks past with Melanie to have a cigarette. There is a depth of rage in her fake smile that makes Freya's stomach turn. How does Nicole have friends? And how do they stomach being around such toxicity? Why does nobody stop and help her? A fear tugs at her, threatening to unspool her completely. Her dream job is slowly turning hostile, all because one person is out to get her.

Chapter 24

Freya
Two months before the murder

Freya picks at the lace on her leather jacket, tearing it off strip by strip. Undoing her handiwork feels painful, unnatural. Tearing apart this project is worst of all. She sewed this jacket to fit in with her new life. It was a symbol of hope.

'What are you doing?' Kate, as usual, so attuned to the sound of Freya up and working at her sewing machine.

Freya holds up the jacket, a lump in her throat.

'Oh, Freya, I'm so sorry. You were so proud of that jacket. It feels like you only got it the other day! Is this because of Nicole?'

Kate gingerly picks up the lace and turns it in her hand. 'Shit. The stain has spread everywhere. It's ruined beyond repair.'

'It's so silly,' Freya says, trying to be strong. 'It's just a jacket and it will look just as good without the lace. I guess it's because . . .'

She doesn't have to finish her sentence. Her best friend knows. Kate takes the destroyed fabric out her hands and wraps her arms around Freya as she cries and cries.

Chapter 25

Isla
Six days after the murder

'So let me get this right, you're investigating a case of a woman who has been murdered, and you've had one of your hunches – this time that a woman who has no strong link to the victim has been involved?'

'You should run a true crime podcast, Mom. Your line of questioning is brutal! But yes, that's about right.'

Her familiar guffaw resounds over the phone, making the hundreds of miles between them feel inconsequential.

'Don't get me wrong, I trust you. I just can't believe this is your job.'

Isla has been studying the footage of the evening, frame by frame, social media post by social media post. She has printed out a blurry selfie of Freya and Jay Singh grinning maniacally into the camera at the office party, his hand tellingly low on her hip. And another video of Julian Cox cheering on Nicole Whittington as she twirled self-consciously on the center of the dancefloor. Every person that interacted with her that night could be a potential witness.

'What makes you so sure that Freya has seen something she shouldn't have?'

It's the question that has been keeping her up at night. 'Well, seeing her outside the apartment that day is too much of a coincidence. And then her demeanor during her interview. She seemed too careful, like she was consciously avoiding saying the wrong thing. She knows something, and she is trying desperately not to think about it.'

'Isla—'

'Yeah?'

'I can hear your breathing from here. Are you using your asthma pump at the moment?'

It's only when she focuses on it that Isla realizes that it feels as if she is breathing through a thin straw. 'My old one is around here somewhere.'

The feverish heat of her mother's worry beams through the phone. The woman has superpowers. 'As soon as I hang up, I want you to go straight to the doctor and get a new prescription, OK? You do not sound well, and I worry about you.'

Stress-induced asthma, where her anxiety grips its fingers around her throat and won't let go. Every time she reads the name Nicole Whittington in the news, or imagines how scared and lonely she felt that night, or the shock in her eyes when the first thud of her treasured artwork hit her skull, the grasp grows tighter and tighter. Whoever did it just left her lying there. After all these years, this is something that grinds at the back of her mind, that feeling of being discarded as if you are nothing, of being treated like trash.

'Are you having flashbacks again?'

'Kinda—' If you can count waking up in the middle of the night sobbing as a flashback and the constant jumpiness that plagues her. Post-Traumatic Stress has manifested in her life as a constant state of disease in the world. And then there is the remaining guilt that she cannot shake, no matter how irrational it is.

'Please go talk to someone, and for God's sake, eat something that doesn't contain chocolate or coffee! You'll give yourself an ulcer!'

Isla hides her packet of M&Ms underneath a cushion on the sofa, as if her mother can magically see them. 'My friend at the station, Simon, keeps telling me this too. He calls it my "battery acid diet".'

'He sounds like a wise guy. Maybe you'll listen to him, even if you willfully choose to ignore your mother.'

She laughs. 'I love you, Mom.'

As she sits alone, the silence still ringing with her mother's voice, sadness washes over her. What kind of person would she have been if she had chosen not to go out that night? Would she eat better, exercise more, have a few more friends, or maybe even a boyfriend? Would she have had the energy to fight for a place at a better newspaper, or the strength to host her own TV show and oppose her small-minded classmate, Tiffany?

Although Isla's wounds have healed, she doesn't quite feel whole. She walks around tentatively, as if she is missing something critical. A normal conversation becomes an effort, let alone a normal relationship, a normal life.

Isla looks at the time, 10 p.m. Still many hours left to research and avoid sleep. Perhaps if she can get to the bottom of the mystery surrounding Nicole's death, she will feel like she still has some power and agency against the depravity she sees on a daily basis in the news. If only she could write the real story, she would feel more at peace.

Chapter 26

Freya
Two months before the murder

When you move around a lot, you soon learn that it only takes one enemy to make your life a living hell. Just one person, like Nicole.

It's a Saturday morning and Freya should be sleeping. Instead, she is on her way to a volunteer coding center downtown, alone. Her attempts to drag Virginie along fell on deaf ears – 'I already waste five days of my life at work, why would I waste another?' she said. Jay is away for the weekend, visiting his parents in Boston, but has already sent her a cute picture of a kitten, wishing her a happy morning. She is up far too early, mind whirring with anticipation of the day, so she takes an extended walk through the Presidio to catch the pink blush of the sunrise over Golden Gate Bridge. Watching the cyclists and joggers in the glow of the morning makes her feel boundlessly positive. Today, she will spend the morning helping young women learn how to code with some of her colleagues.

This could be the day she finally feels worthy of the luck she has received. Her position at Atypical is a result of a few teachers nurturing her talent, lecturers giving her a chance and her college believing in her enough to sponsor her. Helping women in a similar situation to hers will make the cycle complete. Yet her mind is crowded with thoughts of Nicole. Freya keeps pushing herself to try harder, and be friendlier, in the hope that she will somehow earn Nicole's approval. Nicole is running the workshop today. Maybe if she's helpful enough, they will finally become civil.

The building is worn but functional. There are twenty computers set up on old wooden school desks. An urn hums at the back. Next to it, there is a tin of cheap instant coffee and some boxes of tea. She smells the peanut butter sandwiches before she sees them.

The desks are already filled with girls in their teens. The room is silent, save for the tapping of keyboards and the voice of the person lecturing up front. Freya smiles. It takes something special to hold the attention of so many young people. She felt that something the moment she sat in front of a computer for the first time: potential, ambition, the realization that she had the power to change her world if she wanted to.

A sigh comes over the mic. Freya rummages for her glasses and puts them on. Shit – she'd got carried away with her early morning walk and ended up late! Not only is she late, but it's Nicole's lecture. Not the smartest way to gain her approval.

She mouths an apology and sits in the back row.

'What you've got to realize,' booms Nicole, 'is that good coders understand human behavior as much as they do facts and figures. Coding is like weaving an intricate tapestry – on the back it may look complex but on the other side it looks pleasing to the human eye.'

The girls all nod in unison, rapt. She continues. 'There is no use making something just because it's cool or you've pulled off some impressive technical feat. I'm not interested in that. The Internet is a big place, filled with flashing lights and nonsense, and it's our job to make things a bit easier, to help it make sense. I want to see ways in which technology can be applied to the grittiest, most challenging parts of life. What if technology could educate those who cannot afford to go to school? Or what if it can be used to deliver clothes, food or medical supplies to people who lack these essentials? We don't need another clever app.'

The girls clap and beam at Nicole. Freya is a little jealous. She is still petrified of teenagers and it takes a lot of grit to stand up there and speak like that. As always, Nicole's style is effortless, her edgy office look replaced by perfectly cut jeans, a slim black polo neck and Givenchy ankle boots. The bitch has everything, style, career and confidence. It is impossible to imagine that this is the same person that constantly whispers behind her back.

When Nicole finishes, she walks around the room answering questions and helping some of the girls. The smattering of Atypical colleagues present do the same. But there is something in the way Nicole does it that shines like a beacon. She laughs raucously at their jokes and listens patiently to their concerns. Some hug her or give her a high five before she kneels down next to them. The love everyone feels for her is tangible. Freya pushes the thought out of her mind, but it comes nonetheless. *It's not fair.*

Freya weaves through the desks towards her, ignoring the way Nicole's face shuts down as she moves closer.

'Hi, I'm sorry I'm late. Traffic . . .'

She rifles through a stack of paper. 'It's fine. Here is what we're working on. If you can just go round the class and check how everyone is going, I would really appreciate it.' It's slightly forced and overly polite, but it's not an insult. A formidable start.

The girls are charming, hard-working and suck up every-thing she says like sponges. Freya's cheeks hurt from smil-ing. This is what her purpose is. She doesn't care about the new cellphone in her pocket or the boots she bought yester-day. She wants to see the face of someone without hope light up when they realize they are worth something, that they are smart, and that they have something to contribute after all. That is the silent killer of those who don't grow up with the privilege of money, stability or a happy home. They begin to think their voice is meaningless, that they are not worthy of a seat at the table. Freya knows this.

She looks up from helping a particularly promising young woman with a stutter and catches Nicole staring at her. Freya checks and triple checks to make sure she's advised her in the right way. Nicole meets her eye, and she spots the hint of a genuine smile.

The rest of the hours speed by, buoyed by a new hope-fulness. Freya always makes friends with everyone in the end, even the most stubborn enemies. All they needed was the right moment to bond and turn the situation around! Virginie was right – she didn't need to get so upset about Nicole.

The kids disperse, one after another, until it's only Atypical staff left. Nicole is buzzing. There is a swing in her hips, and lightness to her steps. Freya knows the feeling, there is nothing better than a job well done. It keeps her going for days, its own kind of fuel. A new energy enters Nicole's voice now, as she begins to round everything up.

'Great work today, everybody! Can you believe these kids? I can't even get my head around being so talented at that age. Now who's up for a quick bite to eat? Mel? Dave? Anne?'

Nicole goes around the room, asking each person by name. Freya looks up expectantly, ready to say 'yes', but her name is never said. Worst of all, not one of her colleagues calls Nicole out on it.

They walk away, a close-knit group laughing and joking, leaving her standing conspicuously outside. Freya tries not to feel upset, but the feeling infiltrates her whole body. It could have just been a mistake, she has been quite quiet, after all. She could follow them under the assumption that she was invited all along. But, in the distance, Nicole turns and smirks, holding eye contact with her for a few excruciating seconds. This was not a mistake, it was intentional, and it makes her want to scream.

Chapter 27

Freya
Six days after the murder

I need you, the message says. These are words she wanted to hear once, when she was younger, unconfident and alone.

I can't stop thinking about you.

It doesn't make sense. It must be a mistake. But if it is a mistake, why won't it stop?

You're a naughty girl, Freya. Why won't you send me that picture you've been teasing me about?

It's the kind of sexy banter she's had with the odd boyfriend, a thrilling game of tag, but this time, she screams into her pillow. She throws her phone on the floor. On impact, a crack snakes across the black screen.

'Who the hell are you?' she whispers, like a woman trapped, like a woman whose every move is being watched.

Chapter 28

Freya
Two months before the murder

Freya paces to the office, the wind howling at her neck. It's still dark and the streets are quiet. The solitude calms her. She turns the corner and spots Bean There, Done That, the coffee shop a few blocks from the office, and the strangest thing happens. Her stomach twists into an excruciating knot. She cries out, keels over and struggles to catch her breath.

This happened yesterday, and the day before. Always this terrible pain, and always the same spot. Freya thinks she knows why. As soon as she sees the coffee shop, her body realizes where it is going and revolts. The ache is her soul's way of saying *run*.

Another day lies ahead of Nicole belittling her, of Nicole questioning every decision she makes. It's like being hit with a thousand small stones. Each one is insignificant on its own, but fighting off a constant assault is exhausting. And through it all, she has to fake a smile and pretend this doesn't bother her.

'Pull yourself together,' she says as she walks into the office. She needs to act like an adult, and not be seen to be participating in cat fights. The silence of the empty space is intoxicating. She was like this at college too, shifting through libraries before everyone woke. These usually busy places take on a holy quality in the moments before they become animated with people. Or – in this case – before the office is darkened by Nicole's presence.

She checks her reflection in the window – she can't wait to show Virginie the sleek, fitted jumpsuit she's put together from a 1970s pattern she picked up at a vintage store. Matched with her bright maroon blazer, it's definitely a striking office look. Will it inspire Nicole's ridicule? Or will it be something else this time? Trying to prevent an attack is hopeless. Nicole will find a way to single her out. She always does.

Her hand feels for the light switch and the office is illuminated. On days like today she feels ashamed and a little immature. Why does this hurt so much? Why can't she take the everyday knocks of adult life? There is no doubt that she is smart enough to be here but is there something in the way she carries herself, in the way she acts, that has made her deserve this? That makes her an easy target, a victim?

The emails in her inbox make her feel better. Most begin with 'wow', 'great job', and 'I'm impressed'. A smile glows across her face. She knows she's doing better than anyone expected. Not that she would expect anything less from herself – coding is the language she feels most comfortable with, it's the complexities of human language she battles to understand.

The elevator doors open and her heart jumps in her chest. What if it's Nicole, and she is stranded in the office with her, alone? Free from her colleagues' eyes, would Nicole ever *physically* hurt Freya? There is something explosive behind her constant, aggressive verbal assault. Maybe she is being mad, irrational, and overly sensitive, but she keeps her house keys nearby, sharp side up, just in case. Her hands are trembling now. She busies herself by typing a note on her cell to buy a can of pepper spray.

But it's not Nicole, thank goodness. She can tell exactly who is approaching from the sound of his footsteps. Freya turns around, smiling.

'You walk like the Incredible Hulk, you know that?'

'Well, well, well – hello there!' he says. 'I quite like this habit of bumping into each other so early in the morning.' His hair is still wet from the shower, the warm musty cologne fresh on his skin. She has begun to picture his early morning routine, the water falling against his chest, him walking to his cupboard in his boxers, the song he hums to himself as the kettle boils. What does his private world look like? Will she ever be privy to it? By the way he lightly touches her hand, she hopes that she will, soon.

Jay throws his vintage leather jacket across his desk. Freya tried to explain to her roommates how cool it was after another giddy evening with him. She even searched online to try to show them something similar. But the jacket holds stories of its own that can't be replicated through a picture on the Internet. It's the kind of jacket a person has to live in to earn its faded effect. This fascinates her, the man he was before he met her, the intimation of a life well lived.

After starting up his computer, he walks toward her, and her mouth goes dry.

'Thanks for last night. I keep thinking about it.'

'Me too . . .'

It was a silly premise for a date, initially. There was a sale at her favorite fabric store and she wanted to go after work to buy something warm and cozy to make a winter coat. Jay asked if he could come too. She was nervous at first – how would he react to trawling through four floors and ream upon ream of fabric? She shouldn't have worried because he had a good eye, and charmed all the staff. Their conversation bloomed among the riot of color and pattern, and they kissed each other deeply, hidden behind curtains of rich maroon velvet.

'I particularly enjoyed that kiss,' she adds.

'Don't get me started! I didn't want last night to end. And that says a lot because I usually can't stand shopping. Please, come for a quick walk with me before work? We can grab a coffee.'

'I've just had one,' she says, hesitantly. She needs to work. Most importantly, she needs to be seen at her desk and working when Nicole walks in. She doesn't want to make things harder for herself than they already are.

'Come on, you could always use a little more. Besides, I want to talk to you about something.'

He must notice the wave of fear she feels, the ever-present pull towards her work. Freya keenly feels their imbalance of power: she has yet to prove herself, and he has proved himself already. He holds time in his hands like small change, time he has got to lose.

'You've earned it, everyone can see that,' he continues. 'There's a little gem around the corner that serves up my favorite croissants. You don't want to miss this.'

'Fine,' she says, 'but I can only spare half an hour.'

They walk in step, and she notices with a smile that they fit together perfectly. She in her vintage suit, and Jay in his smart jeans, classic loafers and chestnut leather jacket. The pavement has been washed clean by rain the night before and the sunrise has given the city an ethereal glow.

Slowly, through the course of several dates, late-night phone calls, shared laughs and gentle mornings like this, the distance between them has shrunk. Every now and then his hand brushes against hers and her heart skips a beat. Sex is close now, inevitable.

'*When are you two going to fuck already?*' Nicole had said the day before, mouth twisted in a sneer. It was a quiet afternoon in the office and Jay had come past her desk to discuss a new client. As always, Freya could feel the other women watching but she didn't care. She had solved a critical technical problem that morning and felt invincible. Jay started a silly argument about her endearing love for The Shins, calling them a 'weak Mummy's boy band'. She pushed him playfully and he pushed back. After years of strength training, she was tougher than he expected.

In the cold light of the new morning, Freya cringes. It was unbelievably childish, and so stupid. What kind of person finds themselves play-fighting with a colleague, a director no less, at their new job? She really needs to remember what is important. Most of the time she does – her work at Atypical consumes her every waking moment – but somehow being around Jay turns the smallest, most vulnerable screws loose in her mind. She becomes unhinged.

'*When are you two going to fuck already?*'

She said it as Jay was holding tightly on to Freya's wrists. People from other departments had started to stare. She couldn't angle her head enough to see through the glass walls of Julian's office, but she could feel his disapproving gaze. They looked like two hormone-crazed teenagers, looking for any excuse to touch one another. Freya was shame-faced, but a little proud, a little excited. Nicole had a point. Sex was definitely in the air between them.

Freya looks at him now, admiring his easy walk and assured smile. He is the kind of person who confidently occupies every inch of space in their world. She hasn't known him long but he already feels like a close friend. Everything between them is smooth and easy. Nicole's bitter face flashes in her memory, her rabid, harsh words. Why was she so insistently awful to Freya? The closeness of the morning has boosted her confidence. She decides to just come out and ask him.

'So, what's up with Nicole anyway?'

'What do you mean?' he says lazily, turning and picking something out of her hair. It's a tiny blossom, which he turns round and round in his hand.

'She doesn't seem to like me very much.' It was the understatement of the century. Just voicing it makes a lump swell in her throat. Freya looks across at him, fast enough to see a shadow creep over his face. He feels the tension as keenly as she does.

Jay is quiet for a moment. He takes her arm casually and leads her down a side street, towards the café. The world around her takes on a blurry quality. Maybe she needs that extra coffee after all.

Finally, he clears his throat. 'Can you blame her? You come in here, fresh out of college and hit the ground running. Everyone's talking about you. Nicole has worked for three years to get where she is today, and you're just swooping in and taking it all. There is nothing more dangerous, or toxic, than a jealous woman.'

She thinks of her clipped, work-related conversations with Nicole. She may be a bit bitchy but she is extremely intelligent. Besides, Atypical is expanding at such a fast pace. There is more than enough work to go round.

Jay moves a step ahead of her, muscling through the people at the counter, ordering two espressos and two pains au chocolat. The shop is packed with locals spreading out today's paper on red-and-white checked tablecloths. They find a corner of the café and sit down. It's the kind of perfect moment that would be a shame to ruin. She's soon buzzing on the caffeine, flaky pastry and smooth dark chocolate. Jay's thigh feels warm against her own. She could simply lean over and kiss him, right now and lose herself in him. Freya resists. The anxiety screams, urgent. She needs to know the truth first.

'Jay?'

'Mmm?'

Freya's heart pounds in her chest. Does she really want to know the answer?

'Were you and Nicole ever . . . you know . . . involved?'

A complicated look flashes across his face. 'I mean, it's OK if you were,' she says, 'I just thought I'd ask.' It's not really OK. The thought of them together makes her deeply uncomfortable, but she doesn't want to appear the kind of woman who can't take a bit of competition.

He sighs. 'I suppose it's obvious, isn't it? Yes, Nicole and I had a brief fling, over a year ago. I wouldn't call it a relationship. We'd both had one too many drinks one night and something happened. We were just two adults having a bit of fun.'

Of course. The man always calls it a bit of fun, doesn't he? He can shake it off with ease and forget about it the next day. For the woman, the intimacy, or the lack thereof, lingers.

He laughs incredulously. 'I don't know why she's so weird about it still. It was so long ago.'

'Maybe she liked you a bit more than you realized?' Freya feels bad for Nicole. She's been in that situation before where her genuine emotion has been misconstrued by a man as harmless fun. That's how she could write off most of her relationships. However, from what she has experienced so far, Nicole is cold, brittle and tense, quick to escalate a conversation to an argument. Freya can't imagine her laughing, tugging Jay's hand while removing her clothes in a champagne-bubble haze. She is a difficult woman, the kind that makes a man's heart stop when her number appears on his phone. She won't make the same mistake, she will be lighter, different.

'I mean, who wouldn't fall for you a little bit,' she says, more to herself.

Jay takes her hand in his. 'Touché, I could say the same for you. Which brings me to something important, which I really should have said yesterday.'

His skin is warm against hers, the attraction between them palpable. The past doesn't matter, does it? One woman's heartbreak can be another's true love. She sees Nicole's behavior with a new perspective. Her fighting words are those of a scorned woman, the one who didn't get the guy she wanted. Perhaps she was different back then, perhaps heartbreak changed her. Yet one glance at Jay confirms that he and Nicole could have never worked. He is far too rough around the edges. Nicole may have been a fling, but Freya was always going to be the one Jay chose.

'Yeah? I'm intrigued now.'

'I've made a big deal of this now, haven't I? I like you, Freya, a lot. I lose all sense of time when we are together, and when we're apart, I find myself wanting to tell you all the little things that happen in my day—'

'I do too,' she says. 'When something happens, I want to message you straight away. It's weird.'

'Right? I haven't felt this way before, to be so *in sync* with another person. Which is why I wanted to ask if you wanted to make this an official thing.'

She laughs. 'Of course! You didn't need to ask so formally!'

'I wanted to. A woman like you deserves it. You're different.'

She breathes in the scent of his recently smoked cigarette, and then tastes its bitterness on her tongue. His hand is soft as it rides ever so slightly up her shirt.

'What about work?' she asks, nervously. 'I'm worried about what Julian will think.'

'Let's give it a few months where we keep this just to ourselves, OK? Then, when we're ready, we can share the news at the office.' He takes her hand. 'For now it will be our little secret.'

As they walk back, the challenges inside don't seem as daunting anymore. After years of hard work and struggle, her path now seems to be greased with good fortune, careering to an inevitable happy ending. Nothing could possibly go wrong.

Chapter 29

Isla
Six days after the murder

Isla jumps when the phone rings. She really needs to ease up on the coffee.

'Hello?'

'Isla, it's Simon.' She smiles, despite herself. Simon sounds so abrupt over the phone, but what could easily be construed as unfriendliness is simply shyness. For someone who spends a large part of his job having difficult conversations on the phone, Simon is particularly averse to the communication method. In person his chats are meandering, and follow many tangents.

'How are you doing today?'

'Busy. I've just sent you the coroner's report that you requested.'

'Really? Thank you! Let me make sure it's come through.' She clicks through her emails with gritted teeth, stomach churning. Isla is best described as a person who lives in a constantly adrenalized state.

'How are you doing, by the way?' asks Simon.

There it is. An email titled, *Confidential: Coroner's report for Ms Nicole Whittington.* 'The usual,' she says, distractedly. 'Flirting with burnout, running on sugar and caffeine.'

'You really should invest in a multivitamin,' he laughs. 'I'm serious. You would feel like a new person on some Vitamin B12 and zinc.'

'Jeez, Simon, you really buck against the cop cliché, don't you?'

Beneath the intimidating brawn, Simon is a sensitive soul. Two years into his career as a cop, he was on the scene of a terrible crime and took a few months off afterwards. Ever since then, he has been diligent about self-care, from the fresh foods he grows in his back garden and his dedication to home-cooking, to the range of supplements he swears by. Although they discuss crimes, past and present, he has never mentioned what happened that day.

'I have my moments . . .' He slips back into his hurried demeanor. 'I've got to go. Did you receive all the information?'

'Yes – it says here that the UV light revealed hidden blood stains in the living room?'

'Correct, which means the murder might have taken place there, and the body moved into the bathroom.'

Isla's mind whirred. The attacker must have been strong enough to carry a body, in that case.

'Did you get the images as well?' asks Simon.

'Yes,' she says, a sense of trepidation creeping in as she considers opening the horrific pictures on her computer screen.

'Good. Shout if you have any questions.'

'Have a good day, Simon.'

'You too. Remember what I said about the vitamins.'

'Who was that?' asks Kenneth, the paper's new managing editor. After the paper was bought out by a faceless corporation the year before, Kenneth was brought on board to help 'streamline production', which was code for 'cut as many jobs as possible'. Isla and her colleagues call him 'The Grim Reaper'. For that reason, she walks a daily tightrope of smiling compliance and secret distrust. She and Kenneth don't exactly have the same ideas on what constitutes breaking news.

'Just Simon, one of the guys at the station. He's sent me a fascinating coroner's report on a recent murder.'

'The lawyer who was killed while dropping his kids off at school?'

'No, it's for Nicole Whittington.'

She can feel him behind her, his eyes scanning over her shoulder.

'This is the tech-industry girl!'

'Yup.' *And please, please move on*, she begs silently.

'I thought you covered that story the other day?'

Isla bites her tongue. 'It was a short, front-page article. I wouldn't call it a proper analysis.'

'So, what stands out for you in the report so far?' Kenneth doesn't usually pay her so much attention. Something about that makes Isla feel hopeful. This could be her chance to prove herself to Kenneth as a serious investigative reporter.

'The murder weapon, for one. She was battered to death with a small bronze statue, a piece that fetches a nice price at auction.'

'So . . .'

'So the police say the murder is too violent to be a crime of passion, but surely, if the person was a seasoned criminal, they would have taken the weapon, washed it off and tried to sell it?'

He moves in closer. 'Good point. Were any fingerprints found on the body?'

'None that are identifiable enough to be useful to the police. They have found clearer prints in the bedroom, and now the kitchen and the living room as well. The police haven't found any matches yet, but have taken the prints of those who have been identified as of interest to the case.'

'Was anything else taken?'

'Nothing, except for a gold necklace from Tiffany & Co that Nicole had registered on her insurance. It spelled out the letters of her name. It's quite a sentimental item for a person to take, but I'm guessing they would just melt the gold . . .' She feels more confident in his interest, adding, 'I'm thinking of interviewing some more people close to her. I've already spoken to some of her colleagues in the company she worked for, in order to create a clear profile.'

He chews something invisible. 'Mmm, is that what we really want to do, though? Where do we want to sit in the debate over this? I've read the reports that Nicole was medicated for bipolar disorder. There seems to be more than enough compelling evidence that Nicole was a bit . . . troubled . . .'

'What do you mean?'

'There's rumors that she used to go to those exclusive sex parties that the tech illuminati go to. Didn't you see the exposé in *The Daily News*? Several unnamed sources said that they'd seen her in compromising situations.'

Isla knew those would come up at some point. The angle was just too irresistible for some journalists to ignore. Swingers' parties where the cream of the crop in tech shake on billions of dollars worth of investment in steamy corners? Cocaine and playful bondage? What's not to love?

'Nobody can say for certain those parties exist.' She stops herself from adding, and if they do, there is no way to negotiate that environment as a woman and come away unscathed. It's a game of virgin versus whore, one that any woman is bound to lose.

'I wouldn't be so sure about that,' he sniggers. 'Before we know her full story, do we really want to be pointing fingers at everyone else?'

'It's called journalistic objectivity?' she says, trying not to let her sarcasm appear too bitter. Ever since Kenneth joined the paper, there is the constant shadow of the perennial question: what impact will certain stories have on the handful of businesses that still advertise in print?

His voice is higher, spiked with laughter. 'Now, now, no need to bash me with your out-of-print journalism textbook! All I'm saying is we don't report in a vacuum. We live in a context of Twitter, Facebook and online conversation. You need to check the tide of opinion.'

Isla flashes a smile, hating how easy it is to bury her rage, how easy it is to access the vacant, compliant person Kenneth wants her to be. 'You're so right, Kenneth. Thank you for reminding me.'

'That's what I'm here for.' he winks.

Her smile drops the instant he slouches back to his corner office.

'Asshole,' she mutters and turns her attention to the file.

An elderly neighbor discovered Nicole's body the morning after her death. Her door was ajar, which was unusual. She was friendly and always the first to smile, but at the same time very private, slipping in and out of her apartment at strange, moonlit hours, hardly making a sound on the stairs. The open wine bottle confirmed the source of the racket the night before, but otherwise the apartment was neat.

The bathroom was another story. Broken perfume bottles created a thick, heaving fog. The mirrors had been smashed into jagged shards. Nicole's stiffening body was propped up unnaturally in the shower, her wet hair plastered over her face. Blood had dried in a clotted circle around her. The weapon lay close by, sharp side pointed obscenely up in the air. The smell knocked the old man off his feet.

Isla stops reading the report for a moment. For her, the most chilling aspect of reading any police report is the stilted, matter-of-fact language of the witness statement. She can imagine the witness sitting there, shaking so hard that they cannot hold the pen and write the statement themselves. She can see the gentle face of Simon, guiding them through the process of living out their ordeal a second time, so soon after it happened. She sees herself, in her first year of college, sitting opposite the officer, trying her hardest to think in a straight line. These reports always state the violence so plainly, you cannot see the heartbreak pacing in circles around each word. She braces herself for the rest of it.

The autopsy reveals the worst of it. Nicole died from repetitive blows to the head, first in the center of her forehead, then three more times on the sides of her head, cracking her skull and sinew. Isla sits on her hands to stop them shaking. Ironically, the first blow to the temple would have been the one that killed her, the rest were gratuitous, the actions of somebody who could not stop, the kind of insatiable violence that doesn't know when to quit.

She was found almost naked, with a kimono falling over her shoulders, but her clothes were not removed in the bathroom. They were found strewn in various places across her bedroom. Nicole slept with someone less than an hour before her death. The coroner implemented a rape kit, which revealed slight bruising that was open to interpretation. No trace of any date rape drugs was found in her system. Yet what about the signs that the sex had become rough? Was Nicole into this sort of thing? Did she frequent sex parties like the rumors say? Or was it rape? The evidence is inconclusive.

'Sorry,' she whispers as she looks closer at the pictures of Nicole's body. There is such indignity in the fact that the images even have to exist at all.

Isla closes the document. Enough. Did Nicole know the man that slept with her that evening? Did she love him, and did he turn on her? Did Freya look so spooked the morning after because she saw something, or someone that she shouldn't have? On looking at the physical evidence of the crime, Isla can't believe that a female would have the physical strength, or stomach to pull off such a violent act.

This is too much for first thing in the morning. But Isla can't stand up. Her knees are weak, unstable. She's light-headed, ears ringing. There's something about this case that pulses under her skin. Ten years ago there was a report written with her name at the top, where all the evidence pointed to signs of rape. Yet still, she wasn't believed at first.

Isla has to find out the truth, she has to wring out the real story and emotion from the stagnant words before her. She needs to be the one to deliver the justice when Nicole can't fight for it herself. For now, that means listening keenly to her every instinct, even when it doesn't make sense. She considers her interest in Freya, and the images of the office party that took place the night of the murder, the way Jay's arm slid around her waist. Maybe Freya looked so nervous because she was protecting someone close to her, someone like Jay.

Chapter 30

Freya
Two months before the murder

Freya's done it, she's really, really done it. She slams her hands on her desk victoriously and taps her fingers to the beat pumping through the office speakers. Her days here have felt tough recently, but now everything around her is infused with color. She, Nicole and Jay have been working together on fixing this code for weeks. Every time they tried a new solution, the whole system would crash. But last night an idea came to her in a dream. She grabbed the pad of clothing sketches next to her bed, and between the pencil swirls of Fifties skirts and blouses, she wrote the whole thing down.

Usually she hates waking. Sleep is the only period where she is truly at peace. Every morning, as consciousness stirs within her, she grows nauseous at the thought of another day of being attacked by Nicole. But this morning, she pushed the feeling down. She rushed to work, her handmade jacket slung proudly across her shoulders, a bright new lipstick on, shimmering with invincibility. The hours at her computer felt so easy, passing like a speeding car, like the vista of a new, green countryside whizzing by.

Now here she is, problem solved. It is a fix that changes everything. She can't wait to see Jay and Julian's faces when she tells them the news. It confirms she is truly meant to be here! Unfortunately, the first person she sees is Nicole. As her voice scrapes across her brain, Freya shrinks into herself.

'Remember, we have a meeting at twelve to brainstorm a fix for the code we're working on. You think you can make it on time?'

Freya wracks her brain for the last time she was late. She is usually the first one in the room, but there is no point in arguing, no matter how much the accusation stings.

Nicole can barely meet Freya's eyes. She does, however, make a show of examining the organized chaos on Freya's desk. Oh, how Freya has fantasized about this moment, where she can confidently put her in her place.

'We won't be needing that meeting, Nicole. I just sorted it out.'

'Really? You just sorted it out, just like that? Like it's a printer that just needed its toner cartridge changed?' Her high-pitched laugh feels like the edge of a knife.

'Yes, and I'll show you exactly how I did it in the meeting later.'

Nicole stands firm. 'Show me now.'

Freya has noticed before how strong Nicole is. She doesn't dare say no.

Step by step, she explains her working out, Nicole's shadow looming over her and the heady stench of perfume catching in her throat.

'No.' Nicole purses her lips. 'No, no that's all wrong. Sorry, but you're completely on the wrong track here. Good effort though.'

Nicole is wrong, she must be! But she's starting to not trust herself anymore. The stress has begun to get to her, she can feel it burning an ulcer in the corner of her mouth and thickening the fog around her thoughts. She used to be a perfectionist, but she's weaker now, and capable of mistakes.

Freya walks over to Virginie's desk for some moral support.

'Care for a hot chocolate break?' said Freya.

Virginie smiles. 'Have I ever said no?'

In the kitchen, Freya watches as Virginie piles spoon after spoon of hot chocolate powder into an oversized mug.

'I'm no scientist, but the ratio of hot chocolate to water looks pretty steep there.'

'Speak for yourself. In Paris, I would be drinking this out of a soup bowl. You Americans deny yourself the simplest joys.' She laughs, then takes in Freya's frowning face. 'What's up?'

'I thought I'd solved a massive coding problem today. It's the one thing I'm really confident in, you know? I can get to the bottom of any coding issue, if I have the time and space to think about it. But Nicole just came past my desk and tore the whole thing apart.'

Freya knows she is grinding her teeth, and bouncing frenziedly from foot to foot, but she can't stop herself. Just talking about it releases a tide of anger.

'You can't let her get to you so much,' Virginie says carefully. 'You're making yourself miserable.'

'I know,' she says hopelessly. 'I'm trying to let it go, really I am. But every time I recover, she does something else. And nobody around me seems to care.'

'Have you told Julian?'

'How could I? It would sound so petty! This isn't high school, and no action on its own seems so terrible. It's the sum of all of it together.'

Virginie scrapes the chocolate sediment from the bottom of her cup, her eyes meeting Freya's. 'I think he's more understanding than you give him credit for. He would do anything to help you grow your career, Freya. You just need to remember how valued you are. Back yourself!'

She licks the spoon, and adds, 'How about this. Let Nicole think she's won, and then find your almost-lover and run the idea past him on your own? Focus on your success for now, and then explain your situation to Julian later. As you Americans say, it's a win-win situation.'

They share a smile. In the office, only Virginie knows that Freya and Jay are dating. Freya feels a little better, and slightly more hopeful. She runs through the solution one more time, just to make sure it's absolutely perfect. This is the turning point she has been waiting for.

'Freya! Freya, come look at this!'

Jay comes bounding towards her desk like a puppy. For all his cool, he can be irrepressibly geeky. Another reason she likes him.

'What!'

He grabs her hand and pulls her towards Julian's office. He's so thrilled, he's forgotten that this kind of touch reveals the closeness between them.

As they rush towards the glass door, Freya sees Nicole's black hair and Julian speaking to her with a grin that lights up his whole face. The warmth in the exchange is a warning. Rage and despair beat between her ears. Her heart knows what has happened, even though she can't move her tongue, or find the words to express what is happening just yet.

Jay can't stop smiling either. 'Check it out, Freya! You know that problem we've been struggling with for weeks now? Nicole just breezed into my meeting with Julian this morning and solved it. Just like that!'

Every muscle in Freya's body tenses up as she raises her eyes to the screen projected in front of her. There is her solution to the problem, down to each calculation she ran to reach her answer.

Nicole looks her in the eye for once, and smirks. Freya won't give her the reaction she is looking for, the one roiling in her veins. She refuses to.

'Isn't it amazing?' says Julian. 'And Nicole says it just came to her this morning!'

Can everyone hear her breathing? Every gulp of air Freya takes is so shallow, it seems like it is echoing through the whole room.

She pushes past Julian, past Jay, past a gloating Nicole. 'I'm so sorry, I – uh – I'm not feeling well at all.'

It's only 10.30 a.m. Usually, she wouldn't have dreamed of bursting out through the office doors at such an early hour, but not today. The cold slaps her face. She doesn't care that she left her coat inside. She runs, and runs, the icy air seizing her throat. As she breaks into a sprint, the wind whistles in her ears.

How dare Nicole take that away from her? What kind of woman doesn't want to see another succeed? What kind of woman deliberately sabotages one of her own?

She reaches an alleyway, wheezing and crying. Her whole body is shaking. She raises a quivering fist to the wall. She is so angry she could punch right through it. What relief it would be to see the blood, to feel the crack of her bones. Maybe it would open her tight, pain-wracked body up and the rage would spew forth. Just before her skin makes contact with the brick she freezes, and stops herself. What is she becoming? When did she turn into this hopeless, volatile person?

It ends now. She will be better. She will follow Virginie's advice and rise above this. She will tell Julian the truth. There will be more opportunities to show him what *she* can do. Most importantly, she will show Nicole that it will take more than bullying to bring her down. If anything, this will make her rise, more driven and powerful than before.

Chapter 31

Isla
Six days after the murder

The blackness swarms around her. Isla bashes on the light switch, and fumbles for her asthma inhaler. Rushes to the bathroom and gulps down water straight from the tap. She has no memory of the incident, but the terror still courses through her veins. A familiar face morphs into a demon. A field of daisies transforms into a pit of writhing snakes.

There's no point in going back to sleep now. The fear will only linger and transform into another horrific dream. She pours herself a glass of water, quietly applauding herself for resisting a cup of coffee at this ungodly hour. But best to make use of the empty hours ahead of her. She turns on her laptop and begins to dig for information on Atypical. Maybe she will find out something that allows her convictions to make sense, or will discover another suspect she has not considered before.

If the Internet is anything to go by, Atypical is close to godly. Simon's word comes to mind: 'untouchable'. Isla doesn't have to understand the ins and outs of technology to know that they are doing something really important.

The language used to describe Julian Cox in particular is cult-like.

Her eyes scan a piece by a writer at Inc.com.

Julian Cox: Tech maverick with heart
by Janet Holmes

It is barely 7 a.m., and Julian Cox is sitting fresh-faced and fervent at his desk.

'The early hours of the morning are the most productive for me,' he says. In his faded jeans and gray T-shirt, he looks more like a freelancer than the CEO of a multi-billion-dollar tech company.

Inspirational quotes are displayed discreetly on the walls, and the soothing tones of a Deepak Chopra podcast play through his speakers. Julian is a visionary and a maverick with spiritual depth. It's not all incense and big talk, however, because at barely thirty years old, he has rolled out some impressive projects.

His hands wave in the air as he speaks. 'Imagine you are a young woman going through her tenth hour of excruciating labor in a tiny village, which can only be accessed by a small dirt track. There are complications, and you start bleeding uncontrollably. Usually, this would be fatal, and your child would grow up without a mother, but we are now able to deliver medical supplies, and even blood, quickly and safely.'

Atypical is single-handedly disrupting and democratizing access to healthcare, both in the US and beyond. Julian is also working on a tool that takes a person's personal data

and analyzes it to help improve their lifestyle. 'We are working with companies to make healthy living attractive and fun.'

Much of Atypical's work focuses on empowering and serving women. At the mention of this, Julian softens.

'Sometimes I get branded as a feminist ally, which is a
great compliment, but I am simply doing the right thing.'

Yet for all the good it is doing, Atypical cannot avoid the
latest scandal, the murder of employee Nicole Whittington.
Julian's feelings on the matter are clear by his tortured
expression. He excuses himself for a minute to collect his
emotions.

'Sorry, the grief is still very fresh. Every person who works
for me is like an extended family member, so when something happens, it cuts to the bone.' There is also the matter
of the conversation around the murder, in which Nicole is
labeled as mentally unstable and accused of attending the
exclusive Silicon Valley sex parties.

'These accusations are completely unfounded. People
make up false rumors, they lie and attack the integrity of
my staff and my business. This is a terrible situation, which
will live with me for my whole life. I will never, ever get over
this. The media focus has made me and my company feel
personally victimized. Unfortunately, I fear that this story is
being used as a political tool to stop us doing good.'

If Julian Cox pulls this latest project off, he will be able to
get blood transfusions and medical supplies to women
dying in childbirth in rapid time, by using a sophisticated

GPS system and real-time data. The world is a little bit in love with him, and it's easy to see why.

Every person hired at Atypical is equally perfect: qualified to the hilt, speaks multiple languages and is depressingly fresh-faced. Isla's overtired mind spins hysterically. There is literally no dirt on any person in this company. Each one has an alibi for that night. Could the killer have come from outside its idyllic walls? Could Nicole's murder have been a malicious attack on the company itself, as the article she just read implies?

The masses on Twitter murmur that Nicole was unstable, sexually deviant, that she somehow attracted the kind of person that would slaughter her in her own home. Some theories make it sound as if it was a punishment meted out against her. An eye for an eye, a life for a life.

She scans the shining faces on Atypical's business website again. Her instincts are screaming, her mind in overdrive. Everybody is just too clean cut for comfort. Except . . . except for the whisperings of Nicole being spotted at those high-end sex parties. She doesn't seem like the kind of girl who would don a pair of handcuffs and a short skirt if it didn't boost her career. If Nicole was going to sex parties with the cream of the tech industry, her colleagues at Atypical might have been there too. And where there is illicit sex, there are illicit secrets.

All Isla needs to do is get an invite.

Chapter 32

Freya
Two months before the murder

It wasn't meant to be like this. She wasn't meant to cry. But here she is with a running nose and wet cheeks, staring into Julian's kind face. Visits to his office are usually reserved for serious matters, and she feels mortified that she has come to him with this.

'I'm sorry, I'm really so sorry. I didn't realize this was getting to me so much. I wouldn't come to you if I didn't think it was a real problem.' She glances over at Nicole, the familiar feeling of dread stabbing her in the gut. She is at Jay's desk, leaning too closely into him, her hand tapping the table too close to his hand. He doesn't back away, but moves closer.

Julian speaks slowly. 'So to be clear, you would like to formally report that Nicole is bullying you. Can you describe some of her actions?'

This is the part that Freya has been dreading. Just state every action as a fact, and be calm. She remembers what Virginie said to her, that she has a right to feel comfortable at work.

'Well . . .' the doubt creeps into her voice. 'It's the little things – she is always talking about me with her friends, and whispering behind my back. She takes any opportunity to criticize my work. In the company WhatsApp group she routinely ignores me or deliberately contradicts my comments.' It sounds so petty, she flushes with embarrassment. Maybe she came here too soon, maybe she should have tried a bit harder to resolve it on her own. Will she be victimized even more, now that she has proven to be the type of girl who goes and tells the big boss?

She can hear Jay's bold, infectious laugh outside, followed by Nicole's. The sound of it makes her stomach turn. She turns to Julian. 'I know these things sound small, but they all add up, you know? They begin to hurt.'

Julian leans forward, and nods reassuringly. 'Freya, it's OK. I believe you. We will fix this together, I promise. I can't afford to lose you. Unfortunately, I will have to spend a little time gathering my own evidence, but we will hold a discussion between the two of you with myself and HR present.'

'Thank you. Julian, I really appreciate your support,' she says, growing bold. 'And one more thing. She took credit for my work the other day. I think I can prove that—'

'Now that *is* a serious accusation,' Julian says, his expression darkening, 'but it's the type of concrete evidence HR would need to file a complaint. Bullying happens to the best of us, Freya. It happened to me. If what you are saying is correct, I am on your side and I will put a stop to this as quickly as I can.'

'Thank you, Julian, I hope we can fix this soon,' Freya says, her voice cracking. She bangs her elbow hard on the door as she stumbles out and whispers, *'Because I think that this is starting to drive me insane.'*

Chapter 33

Freya
Two months before the murder

'Oooh, another dinner date!' says Hattie. 'Things must be getting serious!'

Kate shakes her head. 'I'd still be wary, and watch my back if I were you. The few times he's come past the house, I've just got a funny feeling about him.'

Freya glares at Kate. 'How so? He has done nothing but greet you sweetly and then left?'

'I can't explain it. It's just something in his eyes, and the resting grimace on his face. As Jasmin would say, I just get "a vibe".'

Freya is too annoyed to respond. Kate doesn't understand the powerful connection she and Jay share. Not everyone is as *aggressive* as she is. She doesn't need someone adding to the chorus of insecurities in her head. Honestly, her best friend is closer to her, and more infuriating, than a sibling.

'Go easy on her,' says Jasmin. 'Let her get a little excited at least.' Dear, gentle Jasmin, always on her side.

'I am excited for her, I just want her to be careful, that's all.' Kate pulls a piece of lint off Freya's white T-shirt. She'd decided on a simple outfit with jeans and vintage red mules today, and some scarlet tassel earrings that she made with the offcuts from a sewing project last year. The outfit is nothing special, but she feels sexy in it. More and more, she wants to show Jay the stripped-down version of herself. With him, she feels bold.

'Anyway,' says Kate, 'you look beautiful. You could totally sell those earrings on Etsy if you had the time.'

They both look up to the sounds of enthusiastic hooting outside. Kate raises an eyebrow. There is no doubt that Jay has arrived.

'Stop it, I know what you're thinking!'

Kate smiles politely. 'I never said a word. Have a wonderful time with your Prince Charming, Freya. May he be everything you hope he is.'

It's the first time Freya has seen Jay driving his car. Before this date, they have always walked to places after work, or met each other out. She is surprised to see him behind the wheel of a BMW 1 Series. Judging by his style, she had expected him to turn up in a carefully restored MG.

'Where are we going?'

He kisses her hello, his lips lingering on hers a few delicious seconds before pulling away. 'It's a surprise, but I know you're going to love it.'

After a winding drive through hilly back streets, he pulls up outside a tatty-looking Indian place called 'The Dosa Hut'. Even though the lights are too bright and they are the only people there, the dosas – thin Indian pancakes – are crisp and delicious, with a warm, spicy filling.

'This is how I wish I could cook. Seriously, how amazing is this food!' Jay nods, his mouth too full to respond.

'Can I tell you a secret?' she says.

'Please . . .'

'I've never flown overseas, I haven't been able to afford to yet. But that doesn't stop me from obsessively planning international holidays. I imagine the flights I'm going to take, I plot itineraries and even research what restaurants I would go to.'

He looks at her with a level of interest she doesn't think she has ever received from anyone before. 'That's incredible. Weird, but incredible. You need to go traveling. I'm sure Julian will put you on a plane to one of the East African countries we're rolling out the project in to help with the pilot.'

'You think?'

'Yeah, definitely. He thinks so highly of you. So where do you dream of traveling to?'

Freya beams. 'Well, that's the thing! The most recent destination I've been plotting is Kerala, in the south of India. You can travel down the Alleppey Backwaters in a beautiful, intricately engraved wooden houseboat, stopping at small villages along the way. The local south Indian cuisine is exactly what we're eating now!'

'Now I feel like I am a really great date.' He smiles. The waiter brings over more dishes – a light curry with cumin-spiced rice, and a tray of idli with two small dishes of dipping sauces, one tart coconut and the other masala.

Freya dives in. She doesn't watch for his reaction when she breaks off pieces of dosa with her hands. 'Hell, this is good. You're so lucky – you probably get to eat this all the time.'

'Why? Because I'm Indian?'

'Uh—'

He laughs. 'Don't look so awkward! I find it hilarious, really. You white people always think whenever I go home my mother serves me curry and sambals in a full sari. I'm actually more of an In-N-Out burger man, myself.'

So his favorite food comes from a chain? She'd thought he was a foodie, someone obsessed with quality, especially after their conversation about fast fashion and big business two weeks before. But his eyes lock on to hers intensely, his hands graze her thighs as they talk. He doesn't moan about her choice of conversation topic, or say she is being too intellectual, or too complicated. When they leave the restaurant and walk down the street, his hand is wound tightly around her waist.

His glazed expression and giddy grin say it all. He really, really likes her.

Freya's apartment feels miles away. As they get into the car they kiss passionately. He pulls at the hem of her jeans, moves his hands over her.

'I can't take this,' he says hoarsely. 'Just come to my place. I'm a few minutes away.'

In his bedroom, he strips each item of clothing off her slowly, running his fingers over her newly exposed flesh.

When there is nothing left, he steps back and looks at her for a second, eyes bright.

'You're beautiful,' he whispers.

His lips graze the nape of her neck, linger at her breasts and settle between her legs. Freya arches her back, moaning, her nails digging into his muscly arms. When she can't take it anymore, she pushes him back onto the bed and rocks into him, back and forth, until she shudders.

Afterwards, he wraps himself around her, his breath slowing. The silence sticks in the air.

'What are you thinking about?'

He's quiet for a while, then says, 'How hard I am falling for you, Freya, and how good it feels . . .'

She smiles. 'I'm falling for you too.'

'I can't believe a woman like you exists. You're different, you know that?' It's the second time he's said that. It feels like an important compliment. Tell me how I'm different, she wants to say, tell me how I stand out.

He gets up, and the moonlight catches the silhouette of his strong, lean body. 'Ah man, I shouldn't be falling so hard for you. I'm almost ten years older! Look at you, so sweet, so innocent.'

She steps towards him and moves his hand between her legs. 'I'm not as innocent as you think . . .'

He teases her, his breath turning ragged, heavy, then his phone rings. His hand darts towards it before Freya can see who it is. 'Sorry, I've got to take this.'

She has to find a way to calm this fire, this sense that everything is about to blow up in her face. Jay is on the balcony, distractedly pulling at the leaves of a succulent as he talks. She pulls a sheet over her naked body and explores the rest of the apartment.

His home is stylish, and expensive, but strangely empty. Where are the old records he has spoken of so fondly? Or his father's record player? For someone so enthusiastic about cooking, the Le Creuset cookware looks quite untouched. Where are the fresh herbs? Or jars of spices? She finds one box of green tea in the cupboard. She brews it and lets the cup warm her hands.

It's eerily quiet here, like she is sitting on the set of a TV show. Her eyes scan the living room hopefully, looking for any hint to the enigma she has just slept with for the first time. A bookshelf would be first prize, as his reading taste would tell her everything she needs to know. Finally, her eyes rest on a frame that has been turned down. Freya looks behind her, chest thudding – Jay is still outside.

She creeps towards it, judging herself for being such a snoop. Why can't she help herself?

'Way to go, Freya,' she whispers, 'it only takes a few months of liking a guy for you to go a bit crazy.' She shouldn't get too clingy. Keep it loose. But first, she needs to see who exactly is in the picture.

It's hard to tell that it's Jay at first. His hair has been slicked back with every strand in place. He is wearing a perfectly cut suit and the kind of pointed formal shoes that she knows he wouldn't be caught dead in. They've discussed how much they both hate those shoes, for heaven's sake! But there is something else that unsettles her. There is a coolness to his gaze, a tightly spun confidence fit for the boardroom. Any of the devil-may-care attitude she loves so much about him has been reined in and scrubbed off.

Freya notices his hand on the woman, before the woman herself. There is that same lightness of touch that feels so charged with emotion when it is directed at her. Her eyes travel to the woman's face. Of course, she shouldn't be surprised. It's Nicole. They look perfect together, with their matching dark hair and sharp designer clothing that Freya wouldn't choose, even if she had the money. They look so comfortable, the path to each other worn-in like expensive denim. She looks so beautiful, with a bright white smile and eyes that laugh off to the left-hand side of the camera. She's never seen Nicole that happy, not once.

They look like the kind of couple Freya used to admire while working in the restaurant, the kind too busy with their conversation to look at the menu, despite her regular, pointed reminders. Maybe it would feel better if the woman were a stranger. Maybe it would hurt less if Jay hadn't understated – no, lied – about their relationship. This was no quick fling or drunken night together, this was love.

His hand falls heavily on her shoulder.

'What are you doing?'

She turns around quick enough to see a flash of rage in his eyes. But then, as soon as it appears, it is gone.

'Oh, I'm sorry, I got bored and was just . . .'

'Snooping around? Don't worry, I know what women are like.' His face is friendly but there is an edge of disappointment to his voice. What an idiot. She shouldn't have got up and poked around his home! She decides not to ask about the picture. Better to leave the past in the past.

'Never mind,' he adds. 'Let's not waste time out here when we could be back in bed.'

He grabs her face a little roughly, growls what he wants to do to her next. It's dark, and a little dirty, the kind of thing she's found herself furtively watching once or twice in porn clips online. She felt ashamed watching it then, but she wants it now.

As he sinks his teeth into her shoulder, she tugs at his boxer shorts, and her jealousy melts away. Who cares if he dated Nicole? What does it matter if they were serious? Freya is irresistible to him. She gives Jay something that nobody else could give. They move together fluidly and as she touches him she wonders, did Nicole ever do this? Or this? Or touch him like this? She's smarter, sexier, *younger*. Just you wait, she thinks, I'm going to make him love me more.

Chapter 34

Isla
Seven days after the murder

'This was a horrible idea,' says Isla, tugging at the leather shorts riding up her butt and pulling her red crop top over her exposed midriff. When Isla approached her ex-colleague, Rae, about getting an invite to a sex party, this was not the level of commitment to undercover work that she had in mind.

'Sit up straight and put your game face on,' says Rae. 'You'll look out of place if you appear too insecure. Remember, the whole point of these parties is that sex is not a big deal. Tech companies have disrupted everything about the way we live, from how we get around to where we stay when we're on holiday. Now, we're challenging conventional attitudes to sex as well.'

'How did you get an invite?' Isla asks.

'Let's just say that the host has a soft spot for girls like me.' She smiles.

The last time Isla saw Rae, she was a bright-eyed intern with her sights set on political journalism. Now, at barely twenty-seven and a PR manager at a social media platform, Rae seems to be imbibing all the propaganda Silicon Valley has to offer. But who is Isla to judge? Rae is rich, gorgeous and, from the looks of things, completely happy.

'Thank you for letting me tag along today, and for taking my call after all this time . . .'

'No problem! I always liked you, and I think your . . . energy . . . will appeal to the guys there. All the cookie cutter models become boring after a while, especially when you see them at every event. Andy will be happy to see I've brought someone different.'

Andy Higgs. The inventor of the hashtag and now, the proud owner of several idealistic startups with lofty goals that are difficult to explain. His open relationship with his partner, Sue, has been the subject of several think pieces and a toe-curlingly candid interview in *Vanity Fair*.

Isla's breath has shifted into an oppressive pant and anxiety moves in waves of static through her body. Just like when she has her flashbacks. The first time, she was too young to know how sex could turn so coldly to violence. She must be crazy to put herself in this situation today, where men outnumber women, where sex seems free, but is transactional. The dirtier you are, the more liberated you appear, but as a woman, there is always a price to pay. No female is ever completely anonymous.

The smell of sex follows her. Isla should wrench open the door of this Uber and run. But there's another part of her, battle-worn and muscular, that wants to walk back into the fire that burned her, and fight even harder than before.

The car pulls up outside a sprawling white mansion. Two Balinese cat sculptures frame the open door. Everything is plush cream, from the winding stairway, to the glinting tiled passage that leads them to the outdoor reception area. It is still technically winter, but thanks to an Indian summer's day, the smattering of guests are dressed in very little.

At first glance, there is nothing sinister about the setup. It feels more like an awkward barbeque held for work colleagues than an orgy. A couple in their fifties pick at a bowl of fruit skewers. A group of young women compare bedazzled manicures. An impatient man with a furrowed brow pounds his MacBook in the corner, a bizarre sight that contrasts his cheerful penguin-printed Bermuda shorts.

'Are you sure we're in the right place?' she whispers to Rae.

'Shhh . . . give it some time. Want a drink? I spot some frozen rosé.'

'Yeah, sure.'

Then, she sees it. The stainless-steel champagne bucket next to the swimming pool, overflowing with condoms. A table in the corner, boasting an array of vibrators, lubricants and anal beads tastefully displayed beneath an opulent arrangement of blush-pink peonies. The awkwardness in the air, a mix of social anxiety and expectation. Isla leans against the wall, head spinning. It's not right that she is here. Her entire body revolts against it.

A short, bald man in a tight turtleneck and even tighter black jeans walks towards her, a whitened smile plastered on his face. 'How are you doing? Anything I can do to make you more comfortable?'

He is barefoot, and has the over-buffed sheen of the super wealthy. Isla recognizes him from his pictures in the paper, which appear to have been taken before his latest round of Botox. It's Andy Higgs.

Isla is too nervous to speak, but she has to be strong and get into character. This is her chance to discover something the police do not yet know.

'It is my first time here,' she says carefully. Andy raises an eyebrow and subtly appraises her outfit. 'In fact, I am quite new to The Bay and I'm looking to connect with some influential people, if you know what I mean.'

He laughs, pulls her in for a hug and her stomach turns. 'First of all, you need to know that nobody from San Francisco calls it *The Bay*. But you are in the right place if you want to network. Only the most elite are invited to these soirées.'

She blinks in a way that she hopes looks doe-like, and naïve.

'Like people from Google?'

'On your left, next to the toy table,' he whispers.

'Tesla?'

'Let's just say that those guys are forward thinking about more than just cars.'

Andy leans into her, the stretchy fabric of his jeans rubbing against her legs. She wants to scream, push him into the swimming pool, hold down his head, and run. Instead she smiles. These events are meant to be shrouded in secrecy, so Andy's pride at his guest list is a startling stroke of luck.

'You know, I'd love to meet someone from Atypical. Julian Cox seems pretty free-spirited.'

'No, he's not the type to show up here – he's far too concerned about his personal brand. But we have had a few of their team here, on occasion.'

Rae slides past Isla, passes her a drink and slips away with a wink. Isla hasn't had a sip of alcohol since the incident, but this situation calls for some fortification.

'Like Nicole? I've been following the Twitter storm, and it sounds like she came here often.'

A shadow passes over Andy's face, and he leans in closer. His breath is sour, and hot. 'Actually, she was pretty tame. She only visited my place once or twice, and only with her boyfriend at the time.'

Isla's heart beats faster. She glugs more of the drink than intended. It goes straight to her head. 'Was he one of the Google guys?'

'No, he was from Atypical as well, and very high up too. You may have heard of him – Jay Singh.'

Jay Singh. Isla recalls the photograph of his hand clasped around Freya's waist. Of course! The link she was looking for was right in front of her this whole time!

'But anyway,' Andy continues, 'they didn't fit in here. Nicole was sexy enough for me to want her to keep coming back, but I had to have Jay physically removed from the premises. I've made it clear several times that he is no longer welcome here.'

The patio fills up. The conversation grows louder as guests drink their wine in the sun. But all Isla can focus on is Andy's voice. She tries to keep her expression blank, and hide her anticipation.

'Did he hurt one of the women here?' she asks.

He shakes his head. 'Nothing like that. He got into a fight with one of the CEOs from LinkedIn, which happens, especially at parties like these. Some men think they are into free love, but in practice they get jealous. But I had to draw a line after that.'

'Why?'

'Because Jay broke the cardinal rule. No weapons on my premises. He was carrying a gun, and in the scuffle, it went off.'

This changes everything. Nicole had a love interest, and a violent one at that. A person that was photographed close to Freya on the night of the murder. A person who – while high-achieving and saccharine in his interview with Isla, and evidently the police as well – was prone to jealousy and carried a weapon.

Andy squeezes her arm. 'Lovely talking to you, but I think I better go mingle with my guests. You should do the same.' He winks at her. 'Good luck.'

Isla scans the crowd, suddenly feeling unmoored. What if one of these men hits on her, or invites her to their 'cuddle puddle'? Are people formally invited, or do these situations just manifest after everyone's had enough to drink?

Then, she sees someone familiar. He's wearing a sleeveless vest printed with hibiscus flowers, and long, skater-style shorts. The relaxed outfit is undermined by his muscular, crossed arms and downward gaze. Poor Simon – this looks like the last place in the world he wants to be. When he sees Isla, his mouth makes a perfect 'o'.

'What are you doing here?' he says.

'Just letting off steam, the way I do every weekend.'

He frowns in concern, and Isla remembers that she hasn't shared much about her current personal life – or lack thereof – with him. She knows that he has a big, dramatic, hilarious muddle of a family that take up whole chunks of his weekend with barbeques and Bar Mitzvahs and that his mother keeps on unsuccessfully setting him up with a series of unsuitable Jewish women. She adores the stories of his nephews begging him to hand over his detective's badge so they can play cops and robbers. However, when it comes to her own life, she has mentioned very little, probably because there is not much to say.

'Relax, I'm only kidding. That shirt, on the other hand, is no joke.'

Simon's cheeks flush. The ridiculous shirt shows a great deal of his skin. Isla tries not to let her gaze fall over the swell of his biceps, and the outline of his chest. All that weight training and healthy living has been paying off.

'I'm playing the part,' he says. Isla notices that he reserves comment on her own skimpy outfit, which makes her feel a complicated kind of warmth towards him.

'Great minds think alike,' she says. 'I spoke to Andy, the guy that organizes these parties, and he said Nicole came here a few times.'

'I suspected that. What I'm trying to find out is who she got mixed up with.'

'That's the thing, she didn't really mix with anyone. She came with her boyfriend at the time, who happened to work with her at Atypical. Do you know who I'm talking about?'

He smiles, and seems to finally relax into himself. 'I don't, but you're going to tell me.'

'Jay Singh. And what's more, he was aggressive, and brought a gun.' She scrolls through her emails on her phone, quickly pulling up the case file. 'And look, this picture shows him with his arm around Freya the night of the murder. My hunch wasn't too far off, now was it?'

Suddenly, music starts blaring. Simon and Isla turn to look at the crowd. Two waitresses-slash-models in Daisy Dukes hand out shooters. One of the older execs leans forward and cops a feel of one of them. The alcohol races through Isla's system, fierce and urgent.

Simon notices her discomfort. 'Come on, Isla, let's get out of here. I think this is a dead end.'

'But what about Jay? If that's not a motive then I don't know what is. The majority of violence against women is inflicted by someone they know, and mostly their partners.'

'I agree, and I wish it was as simple as that, but Jay has an airtight alibi.'

Isla tries to hide her frustration. 'And who exactly has vouched for him?'

As his lips move, Isla's mind whirs into gear. The pieces she was searching for fall into place. She can see in his eyes that he gets the connection too.

'Freya Matthews.'

Chapter 35

Freya
One month before the murder

A little bit of heaven is always laced with a little bit of hell.

Freya sits at her desk, lips bitten red, hair mussed up, skin flushed pink. Now that they've slept together, Jay's mark is all over her body. There is a confidence that comes from knowing that, as night falls, she will be in bed with him again, being worshipped. It makes her move differently. Freya feels languid and wanted. It almost masks her nausea as she walks into the office and sees Nicole's face. *Almost.*

Her inbox is filled with a barrage of Nicole's blunt emails. Every report Freya writes screams red with corrections. In the right-hand column, there is comment after sarcastic comment.

This is messy! Fix it!!!

A child could code better than this.

How many times do I have to repeat this?

She clutches her coffee mug to steady her shaking hands. Fires an email to Julian.

Hi, Julian,

Sorry to bother you but I just wanted to follow up on that meeting with HR? I would love to resolve this as soon as possible!

She won't let this get to her. She will try harder, shine brighter, and let her work speak for her.

Freya also hopes that by doing well, she may finally fit in and no longer be a target. There are ways in which she is still precarious, marginal. Her shoes are cheap Chanel knock-offs. Her iPhone is three releases behind. She wishes she could be like Nicole, with her unchipped nail polish and smooth hair that smells like vanilla. Will there ever be anyone as perfect as the ex of a woman's new partner? The weakest part of her imagines Jay holding Nicole's hand in some secret high-concept gin bar, laughing amid fairy lights, succulents and ferns. Jay and Nicole's past intimacy is revealed in the absence of words between them and it sets her mind ablaze. What did she and Jay share that makes Nicole hate her so intently? Their love must have been something special to make her clutch on to it.

Jay doesn't notice Nicole's hatred the way Freya does. In fact, she observes with a stab of bitterness, they still seem to be friends. He plays it down, but she sees the way Nicole finishes his sentences, the way his eyes flick up when she walks into a room. She digs her nails into her arm. Every offence has added up. This has become more than a feud. It feels as if the world she worked towards entering for so long is rejecting her.

Her mind whirs around each slight, fresh humiliation stinging her every time. When Freya says something in a meeting, Nicole and her friends whisper loudly to one another. She feels their eyes on her, watching, assessing, waiting for her to mess up. They talk about her in the bath-room when they know she is in one of the stalls.

Freya keeps refreshing her email. Why hasn't Julian responded about the meeting yet? She is ready to list these actions individually, no matter how petty they may sound. There is a poison that hangs in the air, violent in its potency, as visceral as Nicole's perfume. Some days, it feels like she cannot breathe. Freya shuts down her computer for the day and gathers her things, hyper-aware of the hiss of insults that follow her out the door and all the way home. One day there will be justice.

For the first time in weeks, Freya is home in time for din-ner. Hattie is frying up tuna fishcakes, while Jasmin is throwing together a green salad with homegrown spinach and bean sprouts. Kate is in charge of the wine, but hasn't got past filling anyone's glass but her own.

She runs her hand over Freya's jutting shoulder blades. 'Hell, but you're looking skinny.' The statement hangs in the air awkwardly. Freya is exhausted. She just wants one even-ing free of anybody's criticism, is that too much to ask?

'I'm not trying to lose weight or anything. You should see the spread the office lays out for us every day!' she deflects. The truth is that she is hardly ever hungry anymore. She's either hyped up on desire and conversation with Jay, or she's avoiding the kitchen for fear of bumping into Nicole or one of her friends. When she tries to swallow her food, it sticks in her throat.

Jasmin takes her aside as the others continue to potter in the kitchen. 'Are you sure you're OK?'

'Yes, why wouldn't I be?' She who has everything, she who is so young and full of promise. She who has met the man of her dreams.

'I don't know but there's an aura about you that feels –' she waves her hands vaguely – 'dark.' Jasmin is prone to oversensitivity and quick to spiritualize the everyday, but she has a point. Freya doesn't feel herself. In fact, she feels angry. She has done everything right, from getting good enough grades to stand out among her peers, to working several jobs to put herself through college in the first place. She is at work early every day, committed to her job and a loyal partner to her new boyfriend. She doesn't deserve this steady vitriol, nobody does.

After they've finish two bottles of wine, she finally finds the courage to say it.

'I'm being bullied at work.' The words feel alien on her tongue and are instantly followed by shame. Even though these women are her closest friends, she wonders if they will secretly think she has done something to provoke the bullying, or that she is imagining things. It's common to hear about bullying at school, but she is an adult! Surely she should know how to defend herself by now? Freya has always prided herself on being strong, tough, able to face anything. She's not the kind of person that gets bullied. She reminds herself that Julian believes her – that must count for something, right?

'What?' says Hattie. 'That's horrible! Tell us everything!'

As she lists every slight, and every insult, she sees the shock in her friends' faces and feels vindicated. This is real and it's goddamn awful. The hurt that has been building up for months is thick in her throat.

'Why didn't you tell us sooner?' says Jasmin.

'I felt ashamed and a bit guilty too. I am so lucky to work at Atypical straight out of college. You have all supported me so much and lived my dream as much as I have. I didn't want you to think I wasn't grateful.'

Hattie's face crumbles. 'Oh no, we would never think that.'

'I'm so fucking angry,' adds Kate, fists clenched.

Freya tells them about Nicole, about her perfect makeup, her apartment on the gentrified side of town, the French classes she attends at Alliance Française that seem to give her license to smatter her insults with pretentious, chic-sounding French phrases. It feels good to dissect Nicole with her friends, as they fill and refill their wine glasses. Their living room takes on a blurry quality, as Freya grows steadily more drunk.

'And the worst part is, Julian isn't doing anything about it!' she adds. 'It makes me wonder if he believes me in the first place.'

'I'm sure he does,' says Jasmin. 'HR processes sometimes take time, that's all! He needs to find a space in his diary to attend the meeting himself. She's being really terrible to you – it deserves their attention!'

'You know what the problem with Nicole is?' Freya slurs. 'She's a jealous bitch! She had her chance with Jay and I'll be the first to admit they would have made a hot couple but obviously it didn't work for some reason. And what's more, you can see that she totally made him change for her. He dressed like a different person when they were together.'

'She can't bear to see you happy and she can't take him being himself with you.' Hattie nods.

Kate adds, 'And the worst part is that you're so good at your job, you know? Look at you – you're so young, and smart, you can be anything you want to be, and you can take everything she has in a second.'

Freya feels a rush of love for her friends and a sudden welling of tears.

'It hurts, though, you know? I can't go one day without her looking at me and targeting me. I'm trying to be the bigger person but this feels like torture!' The last word comes out choked.

'It's so unfair,' says Kate. 'Without her, you have it all! The job, the boyfriend . . . you deserve it all but she's just trying to destroy it, all because she didn't get the guy!'

'Imagine if she got a job at one of the other tech companies, then all your problems would be solved,' says Jasmin.

'Or ran off with some Australian stud and went to live in the Outback,' laughs Hattie.

'Imagine her in the Outback!' says Freya. 'Her perfect hair all frizzed up in the heat and her Louboutin pumps covered in dirt!'

They're laughing hysterically for no reason. It feels good, to just get it all out, this ill-feeling shape-shifting into something light and pliable. Tears prick the corners of her eyes. Her stomach cramps. It's not even funny, but she laughs anyway.

'Or imagine,' shrieks Kate, eyes ablaze, hand resting companionably on Freya's shoulder, 'if somebody just killed her.'

Chapter 36

Freya
The morning after the murder

Freya pulls her wet hair into a bun. Her run took longer than she expected and now she's late. She paces past the newsstand, the donut truck and the vegan smoothie bar with its clinging scent of ginger. The elevator takes too long, so she takes the stairs up to the office, two at a time. Sits at her desk, legs aching. It's OK. She's here now.

She feels safe within these four walls, as if the stranger that sent her a message when she was on her run can't get to her. She looks over her shoulder. She shouldn't have worried about being late. There is nobody around yet except the office cleaners, who are still clearing away the debris from last night's celebration – beer bottles, an abandoned pack of cigarettes, the end of a joint. The faint smell of stale wine makes her even queasier than usual.

She taps her cell.

Opens the message again. Scans it again and again. Either it is a horrible coincidence, or somebody knows about the prank. It was just a joke, a little slice of revenge, but the single line of text stokes fear in her. She should have known this would get out of hand.

People start trickling into the office, sheepishly trading stories from the night before. Freya smiles at developers she has hardly worked with, and laughs at an anecdote with one of the women from the marketing team. The buzz of the client win, and the abundance of alcohol has brought everyone closer.

Everyone except Nicole. Freya recalls how rude she was last night, the toxic words she spat in her face with a tongue loosened by champagne.

When her desk remains empty, all she feels is relief.

Jay appears in front of her, two coffees in hand.

'You left early this morning,' he says.

'I gave you a kiss goodbye, but you were lights out. I needed a run before work, just to clear my head. Last night was—'

'A triumph. You really knocked it out of the park. I was such a proud boyfriend.'

She smiles. It still feels good to hear him say that – boyfriend. He is hers, and hers alone. Nicole can't reach him anymore.

'Thank you, it means so much that you believe in me.'

Freya's phone flashes. She covers the screen with her hand.

'Everything OK?' Jay asks.

'Yeah, just got a weird message this morning. It's set me on edge.' Freya searches his face for a reaction, but it remains blank.

'What kind of message?'

'Someone responding to a dating advert that I never posted,' she says, pointedly. Jay frowns.

'What did it say?'

'I don't know yet, that's the problem!'

He shakes his head. 'This is not good, Freya. This is not good at all. I don't like the thought of a bunch of men out there, looking at pictures of you.'

'I don't either.'

'Keep an eye on it, OK? I'll help you sort it out if these guys keep bothering you.' He lowers his voice. 'By the way, have you seen Nicole today?'

'No,' Freya says. 'I've been enjoying the calm before the storm.' More than that, she has been savoring the simple pleasure of easing into the day without her whole body clenched in fearful anticipation.

But worry cuts through his voice. 'Funny, she hasn't called in sick, and we have a meeting scheduled for now. She's not the type to go AWOL with no explanation.'

'I'm sure she will show up eventually.' Freya shrugs, and tries to sound relaxed, but panic is rising in her throat.

What if?

No.

It's too awful to even think about. It was just a prank, propelled by rage. Nothing could have gone wrong. She squeezes Jay's hand, turns to her emails and stubs out the flicker of fear.

Chapter 37

Isla
Seven days after the murder

'You want a ride home?' Simon gestures towards an inconspicuous station wagon, parked at the end of Andy Higgs' winding driveway.

'Sure,' says Isla. 'I've found out all I need to know.'

Simon's car is spotless and smells of cherry car freshener. He feels so close to her in this small space, close enough to touch. As the car whirs out of the gate and the glowering mansions blend into one, Isla grows light-headed. This evening had been painful, the cloying desire in the air unsettling. She held it together for the sake of capturing the story, but now the bolts and screws inside her are straining, coming unhinged. Too much time in this car, sitting exposed to Simon's quiet kindness, and she may just fall apart.

She swallows. Clears her throat. Fills the blank space with words.

'Do you ever wonder what goes on in these big houses?'

Simon smiles. 'Of course, but I've been working in San Francisco far too long to think that high walls and expensive fittings keep evil out.'

He goes quiet, and slows down before a towering modular house with outside walls painted a deep shade of gray.

'This place looks like a prison,' she says. Always filling up the silence.

'It was once far worse than that.' Simon bites his thumbnail. Isla remembers seeing him do the same thing at Nicole's crime scene.

'What happened?'

'I'd only been a cop for a year, and was still working my way up, doing odd jobs and sometimes going to the scene of petty crimes, break-ins and whatnot. But then one day, we got a call. There was a crime scene here, at this house, and they needed numbers.'

A security guard lopes to the gate, and Simon pulls the car away.

'So it was bad, then?' Isla prompts. This is the story, the one he has never told her before.

Simon seems lost, somewhere in the past. 'There were six bodies. Can you imagine what that looked like? Six bodies, all hacked to death with an axe. I'll never forget the white fur carpet in the entrance hall – it was soaked through with the blood of the mother. That really got me, the mother clawing her way to the door, trying to get help. My own mom would have done the same.'

She draws a deep breath. It is too horrible to imagine. 'I think I remember this story from the news . . . It was the son who did it, wasn't it?'

'He denied it throughout the court case, but all evidence pointed to him. When we got there, we barged into the house and found him sitting alone in his bedroom, unharmed, laughing hysterically and covered in blood.' He shakes out his shoulders. 'Man, I'm so sorry, I don't know why I'm telling you this. I think seeing the place again, and being in this suburb brought it all back to me. Funny, how places can do that.'

'Were you treated for PTSD afterwards?'

'There's a program they run for cops, but I went on anti-depressants for some time after. It helped. I think the senselessness of it all got to me. If that depth of darkness exists in the world, what is the point?'

It echoes Isla's own feeling that she's been having lately, every time she reads another case report or logs on to Twitter. It's too overwhelming to process. The volume of tragedy so powerful, it's impossible to know where to start. Sometime in their conversation, they have left the suburbs and reentered the humid, urban city that she knows so well.

'Do you see it now?'

'What?'

'The point?'

'No. The violence is still as senseless as before. But I feel more comforted in the power I have to fight it.'

'Like in Nicole's case . . . It was interesting to hear what Andy Higgs said today, about Jay being aggressive, and that he owns a gun.'

They're outside her apartment now. Simon sighs as he turns the engine off. 'Many men own a gun, Isla. I have a bad feeling about him, and the fact that he has a criminal record is extremely convenient but I need more than that.'

'He has a criminal record?'

'Yes, but not for murder. And it's irrelevant if I can't place him at the crime scene.'

Isla's mind is spinning – to place him at the crime scene, he would need to disprove Jay's alibi, which would mean challenging Freya's statement, and getting to the heart of the unease Isla witnessed when she interviewed her.

'Well, here we are,' he says. 'Are you OK?'

Isla fumbles in the tiny patent leather handbag she matched to her garish outfit.

'Yeah, I'm just looking for my house keys.'

'No, I mean are you OK after today? It couldn't have been easy going into an environment like that . . .'

The hinges threaten to snap open. No. She can't do it. She shuts down, the walls go up once again. She doesn't need a savior. She has carried her past just fine on her own until now. Looking down, she pushes the car door open.

'Thank you for asking, Simon, but I'm fine.'

Chapter 38

Freya
One month before the murder

'Want to grab dinner tonight?' Jay murmurs in her ear, as he leans over her shoulder and pretends to read the work on her screen. Sometimes, the clandestine nature of their office romance is thrilling – their own perfect secret that simmers between them, but then she looks up and sees Nicole watching with narrowed eyes.

'I can't, I've got to finish this project by tomorrow morning.'

Jay leans over and types on her keyboard, pressing against her. 'Come finish it at my place. I have wine.'

While the dinners and fancy drinks have been glamorous, Freya has always dreamed of an evening like this, where she and Jay happily coexist in his private world. There is only one thing that makes everything perfect.

She knocks on the door of Julian's office.

'Hey, Julian, I just wanted to check if you've managed to set up that time with HR yet?'

He looks mortified. 'Oh shit, sorry, Freya! I don't seem to have enough hours in the day at the moment, what with this big client deadline coming up and all. I'm going to set a reminder to do it just after I've finished replying to these emails.'

'Thanks, Julian. I really appreciate it,' she says, but as she walks away, she somehow feels less hopeful than before.

Two hours later, she kicks off her shoes and curls up on the couch while Jay speaks a command into his Apple Watch.

'Siri, put on some soul music.'

The room swells with the sounds of Otis Redding. Jay passes Freya a glass of red wine. Apart from the playlist, the only sound is the tapping on their respective laptops, and Freya's occasional sigh when she corrects a mistake. They sit on opposite ends of the couch, feet touching.

The wine makes her giddy at first, but then the second bottle makes her thoughtful. The laptops slip onto the ground as they curl around each other, discussing global warming, music, art, poetry and the ethics of artificial intelligence. Freya talks until her lips are dry, and laughs until her throat is hoarse. At some point she realizes she hasn't checked her cellphone all evening. In fact, she doesn't even know where it is.

The wine has made her drowsy. A lazy Dusty Springfield song now plays in the background. As if reading her mind Jay says, 'Want to get in bed and watch a film? I've got a box of chocolates that aren't going to eat themselves.' He takes Freya's hand and leads her into his bedroom. She still can't get over how different it is to what she imagined. Instead of cozy and quirky, it's gray and obsessively neat. 'Siri – find and play the movie *Hackers*,' He says. His Apple TV obliges.

As the opening credits roll, Freya's eyelids grow heavy and she leans her head on Jay's shoulder. He whispers something under his breath.

'What'd you say?' she mumbles.

'Freya,' he says, slightly louder, 'I think I'm falling in love with you.'

'Me too,' she says, holding him tighter. 'Me too.'

He tickles her back. 'You don't seem yourself tonight, though. I feel like you're not one hundred percent here with me.' His touch instantly calms her. 'Talk to me . . . is there anything wrong? Anything I can help you with?'

Her eyes well with tears. 'No, I wish you could. But I am completely alone in this. There is no way out.'

'Are you talking about Nicole? She's harmless. Her bark is much bigger than her bite.'

'It doesn't feel that way.'

Jay looks at her intently, his jaw resolute. 'We need to change that then. What is the one thing you think could stop this?'

Freya furrows her brow. It's a difficult question. Nicole's bullying started for no reason, so there is no reasonable way to end it. How do you fight something that makes no sense? Then she remembers the look Nicole gave Freya the first day they met, the constellation of hurt and rage swimming in her eyes. Callous as she appears, Nicole must be able to feel *something*.

'I want her to understand that I am a person too. I'm not an anonymous stranger that she can terrorize. I want her to know how *desperate* she makes me feel, targeting me day after day.' Freya holds Jay's hand tightly. She doesn't mention that, on bad days, she wishes she never started working at her dream job. She doesn't want to share with him the depths of her despair and scare him. Some days, she even scares herself.

Jay speaks slowly, and calmly. His voice alone is enough to kindle the hope that maybe this nightmare will be over soon. 'I think it's time you confront her. You are smart, beautiful and strong. You deserve happiness and her issues shouldn't stand in your way. I bet that as soon as you confront her, she will shrink away and never bother you again.'

'You think so?'

'Definitely. I know Nicole better than you do, and she is half the woman that you are.'

Hopefulness and despair beat through Freya's body. She kisses Jay on the cheek, but her jaw is clenched.

'I don't know about that. On bad days, I want her to feel the rollercoaster of emotions she has made me feel. I want her to also be petrified to step foot into the office and to feel nauseous every time she overhears me speak her name. On the worst days, I don't want to fix this at all. I want revenge.'

Chapter 39

Freya
Seven days after the murder

Where are you, babe?

You told me you'd meet me here?

I'm at the table in the corner, just like you said.

Hope you're wearing the lace thong you promised to put on for me.

Why aren't you answering my messages?

Why aren't you here?

Did you forget? Are you with someone else?

Slut.

Chapter 40

Freya
Three weeks before the murder

Where are you, babe? Can't wait to see you xx

A message from Jay. No matter how punctual Freya is, he always seems to be early. Another thing she loves about him.

She checks and rechecks the address on her maps app. Surely she's typed it in wrong? It's too late and too dark to be on an abandoned street in an industrial part of town. There are body shops, tile stores and the flashing sign of a strip club with one letter that has exploded, but no sign of the kind of place Julian would host tonight's company dinner.

She looks down at her new black heels and adjusts her red wrap dress. She was meant to feel a little French, sexy, but in the absence of an audience, she just feels silly. With a sharp pang of fear, she wonders if Nicole tampered with her invite, if the whole company is laughing and chattering elsewhere while she stands here, alone.

A homeless person lurches towards her. 'A dollar, ma'am, please!' She scratches around for some change, heart pounding. She hates what a life of looking over her shoulder has done to her compassion. Before she sees someone, she assesses whether or not they are a threat.

Another set of footsteps approaches. It's Jay, looking dazzling in a white collared shirt. He shoos the beggar away with an aggressive wave of his arms.

'You didn't have to do that, Jay. He was just asking for help.'

'Of course I did. This place is such a dodgy part of town, I'm glad I came out and tried to find you. I hate to think of my girlfriend being scared.'

'I thought I'd got the directions wrong!'

He smiles and squeezes her hand. 'I think most of us did. Julian has taken us to somewhere so cool it's not on the map yet.'

They walk through a barely noticeable yellow door and down a flight of stairs. Freya begins to hear music, and something else, a humming rising to a roar. They descend into a room with a long table, surrounded by the bright silver of exposed machinery. Virginie is already seated at the end, deep in conversation with one of the developers she fancies, who is toying with the feather on her hat. The evening is so far removed from her reality, it feels like a steam punk fever dream.

'This place is wild!' she gasps.

'It's a functioning brewery,' says Jay. 'Which Julian happens to own. He likes to experiment with brewing craft beer in his spare time.'

'And kombucha – it's great for the gut!' says Julian, appearing beside them. Out of the office, he is loosened, happier, the kind of guy who gets the party started. His hand snakes around her waist and lingers there. It feels a little inappropriate, but Freya just slips out of his grip. Better than making a scene.

Nicole arrives in a tight dress, which also happens to be red. She doesn't look Freya or Jay in the eye, but Freya can tell by the way she moves that she wants them to notice her. The jealousy is as sudden as a reflex. She has the kind of body Freya imagines men fantasize over, all sweeping curves with a small, delicate waist, small wrists. An image flashes in her mind of Jay pinning them down, and tying them up with a scarlet ribbon.

Freya acts nonchalant as each dish of the tasting menu is presented, in a grand display of steam and foam. She pretends she is always this cool, that this level of luxury is normal. Her façade only slips when she tries to help clear the cutlery for the waiters and waitresses. It can't be easy working such a big table. The whole company is here, which is over fifty of them. It's the kind of night that makes her feel part of something exciting and important. They are today's great minds, the chosen few, and anything is possible. If only Nicole would stop watching her.

She sits down next to Jay, and focuses on the conversation at hand. He exhales heavily before speaking, and Freya realizes he is drunk. In the flurry of firsts that characterize a new relationship, this is a big one. He's always cocky but now there's a hint of sexy rebellion thrown in as well.

'Here's my theory,' he says. 'Women don't want nice guys. They want a mirror. It's so easy to get a woman to fall in love with you – you just have to pretend to like the same things they do.'

One of the tech guys, Rod, high-fives him across the table. 'Preach, buddy!' Freya shifts uncomfortably, her dress riding up her thighs.

Jay continues, 'Women say we are the superficial ones, that we focus too much on looks, but girls just want someone to fit into their fantasy. As long as they have someone sitting opposite them at brunch who agrees with everything they say, who cares what he is like?'

The music is suddenly too loud, the room too hot. Freya clutches on to Jay's arm, harder than she intended to, and pulls him away from the table.

'You didn't mean that whole speech, did you? You know I see more to love than the things we have in common, right?'

She meets his chestnut eyes and is overcome by their warmth. Something happens when they look at each other, a spark, something that can't be explained away by his silly theories.

'Of course not, I was just stirring the pot a little. Sure, I got my heart broken in the past and felt that way about women, but it has all changed since I met you.'

Their hands find each other, and the spark courses through her, calming her unease. He leans into her and whispers, 'We have something special, and I plan to make you feel like the most loved woman in the whole of California.'

'Just California?' she laughs.

'Fine, the entire universe as theorized by Stephen Hawking. Now come, let me buy you a beer.'

Freya sways awkwardly from foot to foot on the dance-floor. Suddenly, there is a bump on her shoulder.

'You have something on your dress,' Nicole says.

Freya pulls at her dress in the dark, looking for the stain. In her hurry, she exposes her bra, just long enough for Nicole to notice, and giggle behind her hand.

Jay steps forward. 'Leave her alone. You know there's nothing there.'

'The tag is hanging out,' she continues, smirking. Dammit, that part is true. Freya had bought the dress in a rush that afternoon. 'God, Julian, why do you have to hire children who can barely dress themselves? Or who can barely afford the clothes they wear so they keep the tag on. That was the plan, right, Freya? To take your dress back to the store tomorrow?'

'Don't be jealous,' Jay says. 'You had an ass like that once.'

Everybody laughs, but Freya feels uncomfortable. Nicole needed to be called out, and she's glad that Jay has come to her defense, but the comment makes her feel like both of them are pieces of meat.

She watches Nicole strut to the bathroom, lithe and powerful. She couldn't look more beautiful in that moment, despite the men chuckling like boys behind her.

The lights are dim, and everybody is bathed in a blue-green glow. Freya can hardly see the food in front of her. But she is sure she spots Julian and Jay share a glance. She is certain Jay's hand snaps forward and grabs the salt cellar, pouring its contents into Nicole's glass of wine.

'A toast!' they cry, as Nicole sits down. 'Pick up your drinks everybody!'

Nicole's face contorts, and she spits her wine out, deep red dribbling onto her dress, dark as blood.

As the men snigger into their hands, Nicole's composure breaks and she runs from the table. Freya looks away. The pieces don't fit together, what she just witnessed doesn't make sense. Julian is the CEO, he would never stoop so low, and Jay is a man who is not only smart, but principled. She tells herself she was mistaken, she erases it from her mind, it is just a moment among moments during a surreal night, a detail that disappears by morning.

Chapter 41

Freya
Two weeks before the murder

Judging by the cool, blue light it is almost dawn. Freya stretches languidly across her bed. The sheets still smell of him and are freshly rumpled from his recent departure. She doesn't mind, more room to herself. And she gets it. Better for him to shower at his own place and walk to work alone. They have decided to announce their relationship to Julian when they have been dating for nine months. That's a solid time period. He can't argue that it's just a fling. Until then, they play it safe.

Jay loves her, and that is enough for now. The sex is good – she obsesses over it during the day and craves it like a drug – and so is the conversation. She loves how Jay pushes her boundaries, and then gives her a chivalrous little kiss on the forehead and tells her she looks pretty. Sometimes, though, he pushes a little hard. Their light S&M turns into him a little too dominant. She can't help feeling exposed when he's gone, like she's given away something she can't get back.

She doesn't have the words for this yet, and hasn't said anything to her friends. As soon as she steps out of her bedroom door in her rumpled pajamas, they start nagging her for details.

'Don't think I didn't see Jay slouching out of here with his hoodie hiding his face this morning. You two still going strong?' says Kate. She mutters something under her breath.

'What the hell was that?'

'Just a little French insult – it means "brute" in English. Just my way of saying that I think you're too good for him.'

Jasmin stretches her arms high in the air. While the three of them are just waking up, she has already been practicing Ashtanga yoga for the past two hours.

'Easy, Kate. The only two people who know a relationship are those inside it,' she says.

Hattie laughs. 'And those who happen to be trying to sleep in the room next door, separated only by a *very* thin wall.'

Kate shakes her head. 'Just remember what a fucking catch you are, OK? If he puts a foot wrong, if he affects your career in any way, he'll be so sorry . . . The same goes for that bitch Nicole. I'm waiting for her to go one step too far. Sometimes I wonder if she hasn't done so already.'

'I don't need you to swoop in and save me, Kate. I'm a big girl now.' No matter how hard she tries, she still feels like that poor girl living under Kate's roof. 'In fact, I don't need your scrutiny either.'

'OK, if you insist.' She mock-punches the air. 'But I'm here if you need me.'

Truthfully, Freya is not coping. She has ulcers in her mouth and an ache in her stomach whenever she thinks of walking into the office. Before every meeting with Nicole, she has to run and be sick. Sometimes, when she's at her lowest, she tortures herself with the reminder that they were together. And while Jay says and does all the right things, and she has never felt so comfortable with another person, a throwaway comment he made last night worries her. Her mind picks at it. They were lying draped over each other, their bodies entwined. Jay was unusually quiet, coiling and uncoiling a strand of her hair around his finger.

'What are you thinking about?' she asked, hating herself for it. No matter how many times they have had sex, his silence afterwards still unnerved her.

'Not much . . .'

A pause. She rolled closer towards him. He ran his fingers over her collarbone.

'That's not much of an answer.'

He flashed his winning smile. 'Well, what is it you want to know?'

'Something about the real you.'

Jay nuzzled into her neck. 'You know the real me! I have never been more real with a woman than I am with you. But OK, let's be open and tell each other the worst thing we have ever done.'

She laughed. 'Well, that's a weird one, but it's a start, I suppose.'

'It's just a bit of fun . . . you tell me yours, then I'll share mine.'

'OK, well . . . ' She had to think hard. Freya wasn't a 'bad girl'. She liked rules and structure. It gave her a sense of control. 'One time I bunked a whole day of high school to go to the beach. It was so obvious I had done it, because I got really sunburned. My foster parents nearly killed me!' She laughed at the memory. It was a good day, hot and sticky, sweet with soft serve and the scent of coconut tanning oil.

'We better call the police on this one! We've got a real fugitive here!'

'Stop it, I dare you to come up with something better.' What she really wanted to say was that someone like her didn't have the privilege of being bad. Her entire existence was precarious . . . a misstep would have flung her back into the nothingness from which she came. Jay hadn't shared much about his upbringing, but his sense of ease in the world spoke for itself.

'I was very bad back in the day.' He said it slowly, pointedly, as if he wanted her to know.

'Really?'

'Yeah, I even spent some time in a juvenile detention facility, you know, to iron some of the wildness out.' He spoke without shame, as if it was just another milestone on his journey to adulthood.

She didn't want to ask, but she heard her voice anyway. 'What did you do?'

He whispered in her ear. No, it couldn't be true. How could the person lying naked next to her have been so reckless? Or so cruel?

'Why?' she said softly. He had everything going for him. Wealth, looks, a good education, supportive parents. There was no need to turn to crime.

He laughed then, but it sounded dark, dirty, and rusted around the edges.

'I suppose I did it because I could, because there was something inside me, an urge, that wanted to destroy. You ever feel that way? This feeling of emotional vertigo where everything is perfect, your head starts spinning, you get bored with it all and want to tear it apart?'

No statement could have been further from Freya's beliefs. She was grateful for everything that came into her life, and spent most of her time agonizing over losing it. At college she was constantly afraid of being kicked out, no matter how many distinctions she got. At her new job, she keeps wondering when they will dismiss her or decide not to renew her contract, no matter how hard she works. To hear these words come out of Jay's mouth was an insult. It felt as if she had just slept with a stranger. She couldn't say anything so she kissed him instead, hoping the electricity between them would stun her into forgetting.

Now, it's morning. She has her cup of coffee and a bowl of warm oats. The sun shines weakly through the window and everything doesn't feel so bad anymore. Apart from what he said last night, Jay is perfect. No guy has understood her like this before or encouraged her to shine. She's so used to men shrinking the moment she gets technical about her work, or worse, competing and trying to explain concepts that she knows she has a better handle on. With Jay she doesn't have to fake her laugh or say, wow, thank you for explaining that to me, I didn't understand. She doesn't have to hold in a scream at the end of the day as a man explains the mind-numbing minutiae of his day at work, without caring to ask about her own. She can be herself and more, stretching higher into the future with him by her side. She understands those articles about marriage now, where they say a good relationship is like a partnership.

Every partnership comes with healthy disagreement, she assures herself, it is just one flint that causes the spark. Every person comes with baggage. So what if he's done something wrong . . . it makes him worldly, someone who has *lived* their life. And he turned it all around to become the person he is today.

She straightens out the rumpled sheets, erasing the signs of his departure. It's a new day, bristling with promise. Soon she will be at her desk, lost in the excitement of her work, and it will all be forgotten.

Chapter 42

Freya
The day after the murder

Hours pass, achingly slow. Freya wishes she could just go home, eat pizza and forget. She goes to Virginie's desk for a break.

'It's a bit strange, no?' Virginie says. 'Nicole never misses a day at work, not if she can help it. What could be so important that she would pass up another opportunity to torture you?'

'You're right, what could compete with breaking my self-esteem one chunk at a time?' Freya smiles. 'I guess she had a big night. Remember how she was hugging everybody?'

'Everybody except you . . .'

'And those dance moves she broke out to Iggy Pop? I didn't know her hips were capable of that! It would take a day for her to recover from that at least.'

'Or maybe she hooked up with someone from the office. I'm sure I saw Leonard from Research and Development checking her out. Wouldn't that be a relief for all of us! I still believe her personality will change if she just had some great sex. Oh. Hi, Jay.'

Jay looks uncomfortable, and nods in Virginie's direction. 'Virginie. Good to see you.' His foot taps the ground. His shoes make a scratching noise on the carpet.

'Every call to Nicole's cell has gone unanswered, and she hasn't looked at WhatsApp. According to WhatsApp, she was last online before midnight yesterday and it's now past 2 p.m. I think something is very wrong.'

The smile drops from Freya's face. Trepidation crawls on her skin. This is not good at all.

'I'm going to go check on her,' Jay says, throwing on his jacket.

But there is no time. The police stand in a solemn line at reception.

It happens in slow motion. Julian greets the police and escorts them to his office. Freya holds her breath as the scene plays out within the glass walls. Julian stumbles backwards onto his seat. He holds his head in his hands. His secretary runs to the kitchen to get him a glass of water.

Something terrible has happened.

Freya picks up her phone, ignores Jay's advice and replies to the message:

What do you want from me?

Chapter 43

Isla
Eight days after the murder

Isla is at the station again, attending a press briefing on the coroner's report. As the lead on the case, Simon is addressing the room of journalists. He looks much more formal than when she last saw him, but the image of him in that silly vest still dances in her mind. That, and what was beneath it . . . She opens her notebook and turns her attention to his presentation.

Simon gestures to the projected slide behind him. 'As you can see by the angle of the injury on Nicole Whittington's skull, the impact came from the right-hand side. The person we are looking for is most probably right-handed.'

A journalist from *The Times* shoots up her hand. 'Surely that doesn't narrow it down too much? Most of the world is right-handed.'

Simon pauses. Chews his thumbnail. After an extended silence, he says, 'You would be surprised. The people who have been linked to Nicole Whittington all share different dominant hands.'

So this might have a bearing on the case. Isla recalls a moment where Julian mentioned he was ambidextrous. 'Of course he is,' she whispers to herself.

Simon continues. 'I cannot divulge who is on our list of suspects at this time, but I will say that some new information has come to light recently, which has shifted our focus to someone new. We are still in the early stages of gathering evidence, but the suspect has both a motive and a criminal record.'

She knew it! Simon suspected Jay as much as Isla did. She wonders if he has found a way to prove it?

The presentation ends, and the group of journalists herd out of the room. Isla stays put, making a few notes while the ideas are still fresh in her mind. Isla is not sure how she is going to pull it off, but she has an idea of how to confirm whether Jay and Nicole interacted more than Jay has let on in his police statement. Because if Jay has hidden the fact that he and Nicole dated, he could be hiding a lot more.

She gets up to leave. But then she hears Simon's footsteps behind her, and smells the fresh wave of his cologne.

'Isla – wait!'

'Great conference, Simon.'

'Thanks, I was hoping I was going to see you this morning. I brought something for you.' He rustles through his bag. Several notebooks fall to the ground, as well as a protein bar, and a pair of handcuffs.

'Your bag is almost as interesting as mine,' she laughs.

His hand finally emerges, clutching a bright green bottle. 'Yes! This is what I was looking for! These are really great vitamins. They have everything, see? Vitamin B12, calcium, magnesium, all your omegas. You gotta have those omegas.'

Isla stares at him in disbelief, and he blushes. 'I'm sorry if this is out of turn or anything. I was just in the pharmacy and remembered our discussion about you not feeling so great. You work really hard and I . . . oh, I don't know . . . I thought I could help.'

She looks around to see if any of the other cops are watching, then leans forward and gives him a hug. His arms squeeze around her tight. A fierce, independent part of her wants to push him away, to reject his help. But then, there is another part that appreciates his open-hearted gestures. Today, she will try a bit harder to be nice.

'It is not out of turn at all, Simon. It was a lovely thing to do. Thank you.'

Still, her heart feels heavy. This isn't anything, and it could never work. He is a cop, she is a crime journalist. They are colleagues who work together or are pitted against one another, depending on the story. And besides, he knows far too much about her past. This is not the way romances start, if she was interested in romance in the first place. But his arms feel warm, and the gift was more than lovely – it was the kindest thing anyone has done for her in a very long time.

Chapter 44

Freya
Eight days after the murder

The police came again to extract DNA from every staff member who was at the party that night. One by one, they are led into a meeting room where an officer uses a swab to gather reference DNA from the inside of their cheeks. It's an unnerving reminder to Freya that there is a criminal investigation underway, and of the uncomfortable pact she and Jay made.

It was such a small thing, as Jay assured her. It probably didn't matter. But regret itches at the edges of her thoughts. Would it look strange if she ran in and asked the police if she could add to the statement, even though she had sworn that the previous statement was the whole truth?

Her phone vibrates in her pocket. She also failed to mention the barrage of messages she has received over the past few days. How could she possibly explain them without seeming paranoid, and delusional?

Freya can't afford to make mistakes. She has no safety net. There is no money, no extra padding. Her parents are not in the picture, there is no childhood bedroom for her to camp out in while she gathers her thoughts. If she gets a black mark against her name in the industry, she has squandered her one chance to ever make something of herself. The money she could do without, she has before, but to not be able to use her talent would kill her. If she can't work anymore, she stands to lose everything.

She glances nervously at Julian, who has just walked out of the meeting room with wild hair and dark circles under his eyes. His police statement took the longest. He can't find out what she and Jay did. If he does, it's all over. Her heart thuds as he makes his way towards her. This is it – he's coming for her.

'Freya, can I talk to you for a minute?' There is no sentence more dreaded than this one, nothing worse to Freya than the gentle breaking of terrible news.

Can I talk to you for a minute, said the social worker when yet another foster family hadn't worked out.

Can I talk to you for a minute, said her computer science teacher when her first-year scholarship application hadn't gone through, leaving her with the sinking realization that she would have to pay every cent of her tuition herself.

In these cases, all that was required was to follow meekly and accept the harsh fate gracefully without putting up a fight. Make the best of the worst situation. Freya can do that today. After all, she's been through worse.

'How are you doing?'

She wants to cry. She wants to scream with frustration at herself and the stupid thing she did, all for a guy. That's what it boiled down to in the end. The animosity between her and Nicole began with Jay, and Freya's rash actions the other night ended with him. Her temper wouldn't have flared the way it did if she didn't care about him so much, if she wasn't protecting what they have. She remembers Kate's words of warning, now a prophecy. *Men can get away with such indiscretions. The women always end up taking the fall.*

Multiple calculations run through her head: If Julian fires her right now, how long does she have to pack up her things and exit the building before security forcefully marches her out? How long will this discussion have to go on in Julian's office for until people start to notice?

She takes a moment to compose herself and looks at the CEO's disheveled appearance. He is wearing the same shirt as the day before, and keeps picking up objects from his desk and putting them down again, as if searching for something that he has lost. Why has he not taken a few days' compassionate leave to recover, like everyone else close to Nicole? She was one of the first to work at Atypical, and didn't draw a salary for the first year after they set up the business. She was an integral part of designing the company's social mission. Freya can only imagine how terrible Julian must feel.

'I'm OK, considering . . .'

'Yes, it's been a big shock to us all. Nicole was part of the spirit of this organization – she fulfilled a critical role.' He pauses and seems to gather himself, 'Freya, I've been watching you—'

Here it comes. Her ears start ringing and she feels light-headed. Does he suspect that she and Jay are together? It's not explicitly against company policy but what if Julian felt it was affecting her focus? The strange messages have all been received on her personal cell, not a company device – but does he somehow have enough access to see her message history over the past three days? She recalls a clause in her contract saying that her devices may be surveilled during company hours, but surely that is for work devices only?

And then, her greatest fear of all – does he somehow know about the prank? She knows that Julian is advised by a team of tech lawyers. Posting a message as someone else could easily be construed as harassment, or worse still, doxing.

'Yes?'

A hint of a smile, so out of context, Freya wonders if it is a nervous tic. It makes her feel uncomfortable but she can't put her finger on why.

'I've been watching and I can't begin to tell you how impressed I am. You have been steadfast and diligent through the horrible announcement of Nicole's death, and have a sense of calm that I could only aspire to. You have something different to any new recruit that has started here, and I think the word for it is *genius*. I can teach someone to code, but I can't teach them instinct, what lies between the lines.'

A hot, uncontrollable blush belies Freya's sense of pride. Julian has noticed something that she has always found hard to explain. It started in the math classroom, when she figured out the answer to a problem but could not explain how she got there. It continued when she began learning code. The language itself fell away and revealed its meaning to her. She never even had to try. It has always been a private dialogue between Freya and the symbols in front of her, until now.

'Thank you, Julian – the fact that you have noticed shows I'm working in the right place.'

'I mean it. Talent like yours is hard to come by, which is why I wanted to see you today.' He coughs. 'Nicole has left a gaping hole in our hearts, but we now also face the practical issue of how it affects our team. I need to know that my outreach project in East Africa is in safe hands. We have to deliver it in a month and we are behind. This project will benefit so many women. There is no time to lose. I need a strong, smart person like you to drive it. It will stretch you, but I know you're up for the challenge.'

It doesn't make sense. Freya thought she was about to get fired or enter a disciplinary process, not get a promotion! This is the opportunity she had dreamed of while studying, the chance to make a name for herself. And while she has not wanted to offend Julian, her current projects have been too easy. It would be great to have something to really sink her teeth into, something with genuine significance. She hesitates.

'I'm sorry this puts you in an awkward position, given your history with her. I really feel terrible now about not setting up that meeting.'

'It's OK, Julian. And of course I will do the job.'

'Fantastic! I'll send you all the details shortly.'

Julian moves in to hug her. This doesn't quite feel appropriate for an office, but Atypical isn't a normal office, is it? It has built a business on not being *typical*. But her jaw clenches as his arms wrap around her. Although she didn't say no, she didn't ask for this lingering embrace, the skin-crawling sensation of his arms curling around her, the brief contact of his hand with her butt. There is a hint of force behind the interaction, an imbalance of power. A sense that he has thrown her a bone, and now she owes him something in return.

Chapter 45

Isla
Eight days after the murder

Jay Singh. It is a clue, a pathway leading somewhere, but Isla needs more information for it to make sense. It's time to get back to basics. She takes out the sketch she drew of the murder timeline, back when she read the case file for the first time. This is the best way to make sense of a story. If she can map out the sequence of events that night, and the role of every person involved, something may spark a fresh idea.

Nicole Whittington left the office at 8.30 p.m., after a few drinks at the office party. They had completed a tough assignment and were celebrating meeting the deadline. Her neighbors heard her let someone in 'around 9.30 p.m.' According to Simon, Freya mentioned in her original statement that Jay walked her home. This adds up, as the security-camera footage in the abridged case file shows the two of them leaving the building together at 9.15 p.m. But what happened in the hours between 9.15 and 1.30 a.m.? Does Freya know where Jay went after that? He could have gone to Nicole's apartment. As Jay and Nicole reportedly dated for a while, he might not have had a problem bluffing his way through the security at the apartment's entrance.

She breaks off a square of chocolate, cracks her neck. Perhaps she is more antisocial than most but there are very few people Isla would welcome so eagerly after 9.30 p.m. at night, especially not an ex-boyfriend. But maybe Nicole was different, and was happy to welcome late-night guests who didn't call in advance.

Unless. Unless the person *did* call ... Her heart beats faster and her mouth goes dry, as if she can physically see the core of the story and she is reaching, stretching towards it. A few flicks through the contacts on her phone to find Simon's number. After what feels like endless ringing, he answers.

'Simon here.'

'Hey, Simon, it's Isla.'

'Hi! How are you doing? Taking your vitamins, I hope?' His voice is gentle and welcoming. The idea of him fretting over her health makes her smile, despite herself.

'Listen, have you checked Nicole's phone records leading up to her death?'

'Of course.'

'And?'

A long silence – Isla quickly checks the line to see if it's still connected. 'We haven't had the resources to follow up on anything in detail, to be honest. There was a call earlier that evening, but it was around the time she was leaving work or still at the office party. But I've been instructed to focus on other leads right now.'

Isla is a little annoyed. The suspect Simon hinted at during the press conference fitted Jay's profile exactly. Why can't he just confide in her? This is why they could never get closer than they are now – his profession requires him to conceal the truth while he pursues justice, while hers is to reveal the truth to the court of the public eye. Simon uncovers the truth slowly and deliberately, while Isla tries to think five steps ahead, in order to preempt what the big story might be.

'Can I follow it up?'

'Yeah, sure, but I wouldn't get my hopes up. We would have looked into it if we thought it was a deal-breaker for the case.'

A fast, furious panic beats beneath Isla's skin. This may be a waste of time, an unnecessary distraction to the other five stories she has to file for Kenneth this week. But there is something in here worth following.

Simon whispers the number over the phone. Isla jots it down and slips it into the pocket of her yellow parka. Finally, the prospect of some hard evidence.

Chapter 46

Freya
The night of the murder

Something in the air makes Freya's chest clench. It's the kind of night where either something terrible or something wonderful is about to happen.

The stakes are higher tonight. Everyone feels it. Just two more hours left to make the seven o'clock deadline. The whole Atypical office is working together to create a new algorithm for a top-secret client. People are divided into teams, coding against the clock. Everyone apart from Julian, that is, who is pacing up and down the open-plan office, his hair pulled up in a warrior-like knot on the top of his head. Amid all the excitement, Freya feels heavy with disappointment. It's been several weeks and Julian has still made no move to resolve her conflict with Nicole. And worse, he has thrust her, Nicole and Jay together to check the code for glitches. Doesn't he understand how much Nicole's bullying has hurt her?

At first, she takes a deep breath and zooms in on the work in front of her, lost in the challenge. Jay disconnects and overrides the tension with his usual breeziness. Every now and then, Jay and Freya's arms brush against each other, and they smile. The thrill of sitting so close together, of being so in love with one another without the rest of the office knowing yet, is electric. Nicole is determined to make every second of the interaction difficult.

'I know what you did, bitch,' she whispers, loud enough for everyone working around them to hear.

'Excuse me?' Freya's hands begin to sweat. What is it now? She has tried so hard to keep out of Nicole's way.

Nicole flashes a picture on her cellphone. It's her shiny red Honda Civic, with a big gash across the left-hand door. She shakes the image in Freya's face.

'You scratched my car, I know you did!' People around them start to look uncomfortable. Virginie spots the drama from her side of the office and dashes forward.

'Don't make a scene, Nicole,' she says.

'Don't make a scene, Neek-hole,' she mimics, with an exaggerated parody of Virginie's accent.

'You're crazy, you know that?' Virginie says. 'You probably scratched your own car just to get some attention.'

Jay breaks up the group of women with an impatient wave of his hand. 'For God's sake, Nicole, keep your shit together! We're all on the same side, remember?'

She huffs off and sulks at her desk, and Jay follows her. From a distance, with Nicole's waving, passionate gestures and Jay's calm hands on her shoulders, it looks like a conversation between lovers.

This is exactly what Nicole wanted. Freya simmers, and while she is now able to work in peace, she can't help feel a little dirty, a little less confident than before. She checks and rechecks the work she has just completed. There is a fragile, quivering part of her mind that always wonders if Nicole singled her out because she is truly not good enough to be here. The bullying has chipped at her confidence, piece by piece.

Half an hour to go. The mood has grown hysterical, silly. Julian is pumping the latest hip-hop track and handing out shots of freshly juiced wheatgrass and ginger, laced with ginseng. The whole room whoops and does a limp-limbed Mexican wave every time a task is closed off. It reminds Freya of those early freshman parties, where the air was thick and heady with risk. Everyone laughed and shouted, but underneath the mirth was a sinister undercurrent, a feeling like it could all turn violent in seconds.

The cheering grows louder.

Five!

Four!

Three!

Two!

One!

Seven p.m. Julian sends off the document, and swaps the juice for champagne. There is toasting, laughter, more music. Everybody is too buzzed to go home.

Freya strays from the excited crowd and sits alone at her desk, emotionally spent. She checks her work again, petrified that somehow she missed something, that the client will email Julian with a list of mistakes that all turn out to be her fault. It's irrational but she always doubts herself.

The champagne sparkles in her hand. She takes a tentative sip. It tastes expensive, like another universe where everything is light and easy. Up until now, she has been the kind of woman to drink the house wine. Her drinks of choice always tasted bitter and severe, like compromise.

An arm wraps around her shoulder. Jay. They have agreed not to be affectionate during office hours, but the evening's victory has made his gestures loose and his eyes warm.

'This is quite the sad, lonely sight. Why aren't you with the rest of us celebrating?'

'I just feel drained, I suppose.'

He sits next to her and grabs her hand. 'What you did out there was brilliant, OK? Don't let Nicole take that away from you.'

'I just don't understand,' she says, her voice desperate. 'Why would she accuse me of doing something as awful as vandalizing her car? I don't even know what it looks like!'

'Listen, you can't expect to argue rationally with someone like her,' he says calmly, as if the accusation was nothing at all. He slips a bottle of champagne out from under his jacket. 'Now, let's celebrate you.'

Freya downs two glasses in quick succession, letting a delicious giddiness fizz around her thoughts.

'Atta girl,' says Jay.

But Freya's hands won't stop trembling. 'I can't let it go, Jay . . . I'm sorry. I think Nicole is a fucking bully. I'm young and new here, she couldn't have picked an easier target. I have wracked my brain countless times over what it is I could have done to offend her so much, and it just doesn't make sense. I know you guys dated, but still, does your romantic history warrant this sort of abuse?'

'I've noticed the way she acts around you, especially lately,' he concedes. 'She's like a pit bull grabbing the neck of a rabbit, shaking it and refusing to let go. She's complicated, but this is getting out of hand, even for her.'

She feels bolder now.

'Tonight she made me feel like I'm some sort of low-life criminal. Do you know how that feels? I have to watch my back all the fucking time, Jay. I overanalyze every single thing I do. I feel like I'm going crazy!'

Freya doesn't usually talk like this, all sweary and slurry. Yet tonight it is freeing, as if she is breaking something within her wide open. In the distance, the music reverberates through the speakers. Her favorite song.

'Jay, *Jay!* I need to go dance to this, right now!' She tugs his hand and leads him around their cluster of desks, past Nicole's. Her computer screen is unlocked, and Freya's eyes unconsciously flit to its contents. She stops abruptly.

There is no code up on the screen, no work. There are several adverts up, all showcasing apartments nearby. While she was trying to taint Freya's name in front of the whole office, she was *apartment hunting?* The rage hits her so hard she almost loses her balance.

'Oh my God. Jay!' she whispers.

'What. The. Fuck?' he gasps, and swiftly clicks into her search history. It feels like a step too far, but she is also curious to know the truth. Jay pulls up a long list of the pages she has visited: apartment listings, news sites, Facebook, Pinterest and a Finnish street style blog.

'She wasn't even working tonight.'

'She shouldn't get away with it,' says Jay, his voice brittle. 'Enough is enough.'

Freya never wanted to fight back for fear of seeming petty or rash. But her anger feels justified now.

As the party escalates in the distance, as the sound swells, they click through Nicole's web browser. Jay is working quickly, like a pro. Before Freya can say anything, he is on an online dating website.

'Jay! What are you doing?'

'Just trust me,' he says. 'It will be funny.'

Freya watches Jay create an online dating profile for Nicole, pulling in a picture from her Facebook account, which is a breeze as she was logged in and had the page open anyway. They're laughing, whispering, wild and angry. Let's play a little joke, let's teach her a lesson. They're not even sure what the lesson is anymore. Typing furiously, they take turns. Freya forgets what she has said as soon as she writes it but it's dirty, sexy, a little bit twisted. It's the kind of daring sex she has had only once or twice when she was really drunk or experimented with drugs, the kind of sex she is having more often with Jay. He one-ups her and they giggle into their hands like naughty teenagers. 'Maybe if Nicole gets laid she will leave us all alone.' On some level, she believes it. His hand feels for her thigh. At the end they have a personal advert that reveals Nicole's full name, phone number and residential address. Its title, 'Looking for no-strings-attached sex tonight.'

Chapter 47

Isla
Nine days after the murder

Isla can tell it's going to be a rough day by the way Kenneth minces towards her. She's done something wrong again – this much is clear – and he is utterly triumphant as a result.

So what if this story isn't the big one that puts her on the map? There will be other opportunities. Every day she stays in this shitty newsroom, her don't-give-a-fuck attitude reaches new heights.

With such a tiny team, many of the journalists simply loot the flood of press releases for the day, edit them slightly and pass off marketing copy as a story. She may seem cantankerous, but this is not what she signed up for when she studied for her journalism degree.

And she certainly didn't sign up for a clueless boss like Kenneth.

'Isla, Islaaa!' he huffs. 'You have hardly been in the office. Where the hell were you this morning?'

Jeez, here we go. His head bobs furiously and the pitch of his voice gets higher and higher.

'I was attending the press briefing on Nicole Whittington's murder. You know, just doing my job.'

'I told you that we've reported enough on that case. There is nothing more to say. There are seven other stories

I have emailed you to follow up on, and you haven't replied to one of my messages.'

'With all due respect, Kenneth, I disagree with you on the Nicole Whittington case. I want to keep going.'

Kenneth staggers back. 'Is that how you're going to play this? Well, that smile on your face is going to fall very quickly when I tell you that we're scheduling a disciplinary hearing for you. Your old editor may have tolerated this disrespect, but it's not going to happen on my watch.'

Sweet old Bernard Labonowski. The mention of Isla's old editor imbues the scene with a feeling of sadness. Bernard was a rough-around-the-edges old newshound who looked far more intimidating than he actually was. He was of the old journalistic guard, the kind that prized the rustle of in-depth news in a print newspaper over the easily digestible and forgettable news summaries of today. He let his stories prove like a good dough over several days or weeks, until the final result was a joy to consume. He let his journalists find their feet through their own risks and mistakes, gently guiding them away from the edge of career suicide when necessary. He had been let go during the restructure, a bombshell he faced with quiet dignity and the promise to work on his great novel. Bernard, the man who showed her how to correctly use an Oxford comma and where to find the best meatball sandwich on Dutch crunch bread. He sent her three-page, handwritten letters every few months with updates on his life and his new adventure of running a bookstore. They read like poetry.

It's a crying shame this clown has taken his place. Word on the street was that Kenneth had only ever edited corporate magazines, which doesn't surprise Isla in the slightest.

'Be my guest, I'll be at my disciplinary hearing – with bells on.' The sinking feeling in her stomach betrays her false bravado. It will be OK. She'll get a job at a PR agency or start writing shiny propaganda for a corporate company. It won't look that different to what Kenneth wants her to do now. The money will come. She will find a way. Even if she has to go back home and live with her mom for a while, it wouldn't be the worst thing that could happen. Surely anything would be better than this!

As he storms off he says, 'And don't you dare think of leaving this office. From now on I am doubling the number of stories due from you each day.'

Chapter 48

Freya
Nine days after the murder

You want to play, baby?

Someone has posted an advert in Freya's name, just like she and Jay did the night Nicole died. She's sure of it. Messages have been flooding Freya's phone ever since.

Every message sexual. Every come-on a response to something Freya seems to have said. This is not random, every one of these different men thinks they are responding to something that she has allegedly written.

She looks over her shoulder, taking in the row of developers seated close to her. Is one of them behind this? Did they see what she and Jay did? Her stomach churns. The whole disaster looks that much more disrespectful, now that Nicole is dead.

Then, there is her sudden career development. No matter how insulting Nicole was to Freya in the past, Nicole remains another woman who built a powerful reputation for herself in a man's world. It is shamefully low to raid her legacy so soon after her death, especially after sending out the words she wrote in Nicole's name. Yes, it was a random act, a prank, but everyone in this industry knows that nobody respects the opinion of a woman who has been labeled a 'slut', even someone as smart as Nicole. A smutty personal ad, in conjunction with the whisperings of her showing up at several sex parties, would have been enough to poison her flourishing career.

Freya paces to Jay's desk. Her whisper grazes her throat.

'We need to talk!'

'About what, babe?' He's never called her babe before and the casual way he drawls the word makes her think it isn't a compliment. Freya is confused. Where is the man who makes her laugh until her belly aches? Her boyfriend, who she can turn to with all her troubles?

About what. Where does she even begin? Her phone hums again in her pocket.

'You know what!'

He purses his lips. 'Let's go outside.'

The walk is silent. His hand doesn't search for hers. There is no electricity pulsing between them. Did she do something wrong? Has her promotion offended him? Or has she misremembered the events of that fateful night?

They stand face to face in a foul alleyway filled with bags of rotting rubbish. A rat scurries across the wet paving. Jay lights a cigarette and avoids eye contact with her. His gestures are boyish, defiant. Someone needs to be tough in this situation. Freya realizes it has to be her. She starts with the obvious, the most hurtful of all.

'You haven't been replying to my messages.'

'Your messages haven't warranted a reply.' His tough-guy act softens and she spots his eyes welling up a little.

'This has been a rough time for all of us. I don't think I realized how hard it would hit me, you know? I'm sorry if I've come over the wrong way. I've been so overwhelmed and have coped by going into my shell. This doesn't change our relationship at all. I love you, I really do. But this is something I need to go through on my own.'

A thread of doubt winds its way through Freya's mind. Maybe she should be more understanding, and give Jay the space he needs. That's what a good girlfriend would do, surely? But she can't shake the possible link between their prank and Nicole's murder.

'Fine, but can we talk about it now? I have a bad feeling about the other night.' They had both been so drunk. Freya, more drunk than she realized. Adding fuel to the fire was her anger, a hot urgent rage that needed to be sated. They made a petty decision in the moment that neither of them would have made in their right minds.

'Let it go, Freya. It was a prank, that's all. It's a coincidence that she passed on the same day. You don't just summon a murderer to someone's house, like an Uber.' Passed, as if she willingly stepped out of this life into another place, as concrete as a neighboring room. Passed, as if she remained whole and her battered body wasn't found the next day. He takes her hand and squeezes it tightly. 'Remember, we have a pact. We promised not to tell anyone what we did.'

'Jay, I'm not freaking out for no reason here.' She digs for her cell. 'There is something else. Remember the messages I showed you the other day?'

She pulls up her message history, and he scrolls through them, his thick eyebrows deepening into a frown.

'Shit.'

'It's a bit more than shit, *babe*.' The word tastes bitter.

'I don't know what to say . . . I'm stumped. This is really shocking.'

Freya takes the cell from his hands and opens her mail app.

'And there is something else. This email here says that a new device signed into my Gmail account this morning, and it definitely wasn't mine. Someone is watching me, Jay.'

'I think that is just a coincidence. You know how hackers are. They're always trying to get into people's Gmail accounts. I would just click on the icon that lets you report it to Google. At least that's one thing we can fix.' He moves toward her and holds her tightly.

After the nightmare of the past few days, and the latest torrent of messages, all she needs is this. To be held, enclosed, protected from herself, to remember that she is loved, and to be told that everything is going to be OK. 'Listen here,' he says softly, 'I get it, OK? It's hard enough when a person dies. The fact that this is someone you didn't like adds a whole new complexity to the situation. But you can't blame yourself. I can't blame myself either. My feelings towards Nicole are . . . complicated. She was a fucking nightmare, but she didn't deserve the way I dumped her, and she definitely didn't deserve the way she died. We made a silly mistake, Freya, but we had nothing to do with her murder.'

'But what about these messages, then? What if these people messaging me know who killed her? Or,' she says, voice lowering, 'what if the same person is out to get me?'

'I don't know how to explain that,' he whispers, and her heart falls. Everything is different now. Their relationship feels tainted and her promotion feels unfairly won. The whole situation makes her feel sick with guilt. She pulls away from him.

'Come on, let's break this ridiculous pact. We can tell Julian! What harm will it do? Maybe it will give the police a lead?'

A shadow passes over his face but then sharply disappears.

'Let's not cause a scene, Freya. We can't let our emotions or our guilt get in the way of the investigation. We wouldn't want to waste police time, would we? As for Julian, he has other things on his mind.'

'What about the messages? They're getting perverted, Jay . . . I'm starting to worry. Surely this counts as sexual harassment?'

'I'm not sure, but how about this – I'll do some research and see if I can figure out the source myself? Both you and I have better tech skills than the police, I can assure you of that. And you wouldn't want to go to them with a false accusation, would you?'

'No . . .' But Freya feels empty. Another day of harassment. Nicole's torment has been replaced by a gang of faceless strangers.

'Come, let's go back to the office. A few hours on your new project and you will forget those assholes exist in the first place.'

Jay starts to walk back and begins to whistle. The tune is familiar. Freya realizes with a start that it is from a Christmas carol.

The thing that first attracted Freya to Jay was his breeziness, his perennial ability to appear cool in the face of any challenge. It was in direct contrast to her compulsion to pick every situation apart. She craved some of that easiness with a hunger akin to lust, as if in the act of pushing their bodies together some of his nonchalance would rub off. Now she wonders if what she thought was a carefree nature was, in fact, cowardice.

As she falls in step with him, he slings his arm around her waist, drawing her closer. 'Come on, Freya, can't you see that everything's perfect? Don't let that super-smart head of yours ruin it all.' In that moment, listening to his funny, lyrical chatter, walking in her rare 1920s Ferragamo pumps, bought when her first salary hit her bank account, going back to a place where she is wanted and appreciated, it feels good. But there is an edge to the feeling, sharp and cold to the touch. It whispers *RUN. Run, while you still can.*

Chapter 49

Isla
Nine days after the murder

Armed with a phone number, Isla feels invincible. There is nothing to push a story forward like cold, hard facts. Simon wanted new information, now here it is! She blushes, even though nobody is looking at her. For some reason, she wants to impress him. She logs in to her paid public database service. It may be onerous and difficult to navigate, but it gives her access to any publicly available records. Truth be told, she finds nothing better than wading through the muck, panning for gold.

Now, just to select a soundtrack that reflects the electricity in the air. She selects a Rage Against the Machine album. The relentless rhythm of the funk-guitar and snare drums leaves her breathless, transported to a street corner outside a club once more, sharing her headphones and a cigarette with Him, the handsome stranger that would become her boyfriend, who would become her rapist. *'Wait for this part, Isla, wait for it, YES, can you feel that?'* She pushes the thought away. He can't take the love of music from her, nobody can.

It's fine, eagle-eyed work. Time begins to flow differently. Isla squints at the database before her, breaks once to deliver platitudes to a hovering Kenneth, and twice for a cup of coffee, filter, cold. It starts to feel tedious, the continuous running numbers make her eyes water. Did she write the number down incorrectly? Did Simon deliberately lead her down the wrong path? Just when she's about to give up and admit defeat, there is a match, an identity number listed next to the phone number. She cross-references this with other public information, including property ownership listing, and a company registration for Atypical, where he is listed as one of the founding executive management team.

She can't help but laugh. The proof she needed, shimmering in black and white. Her hunch manifested into reality.

Jay Singh.

There was a call between them the night Nicole died that lasted over nine minutes. Isla can only just bear speaking to Lizzie or her mother for over nine minutes! Simon mentioned they wrote off Jay as a suspect because he had an alibi, but what if he was lying? If he was innocent, surely he would have mentioned the phone call in police interviews, and in his brief chat with Isla? Surely he would mention Nicole's last words to him? There is only one reason a person hides information, and that's because it leads to a place they don't want anyone else to know about.

Chapter 50

Freya
Nine days after the murder

Freya has always believed there is no problem too complicated to fix. As a little girl, she had a silver bracelet, a sympathy gift from a nice family that couldn't keep her for longer than a few months. She treated it like a treasure but it couldn't have cost that much, as the silver wore off and the chain kept getting tangled. She would chide herself for not cleaning it enough, or being more careful with it and spend hours undoing the knots. No matter how impossible it seemed, she would always find a way.

Now she stares at the computer screen in front of her, trying to figure out the issue with the code she has just written. Usually the answer would reveal itself with little struggle, but today she can't focus, not since that journalist, Isla, paid her a visit. She knows something, Freya is sure of it. The thought makes her light-headed.

An irrational part of her pictures the headlines, the double-page exposé: *Young software engineer pranks colleague just before her death.*

Freya is not the kind of person to live in the shadows, burying away her secrets. She's a rock to her friends, the kind of person they turn to for advice. Just like the way she can spot the source of a problem in coding, she can clearly discern between right and wrong. Wasn't she the person that Hattie turned to for advice when she found out that the man she thought was a commerce major was actually fifteen years older than her, and married? Didn't she help Jasmin make a list of pros and cons when she was agonizing over whether or not to not open a professional practice with her Masters in Clinical Psychology, or pursue a career in alternative healing?

She closes the project she's working on. She needs to tell someone, her heartbeat won't slow and her breathing will stay ragged until she does. Jay is busy on a call – she is breaking their pact, and he's going to hate her for it – but it feels like the right thing to do.

Her legs threaten to give way beneath her as she walks toward Julian's office.

He is alone, teetering in a headstand. Loud, chanting music resonates in the room.

'Sorry to bother . . .'

'Oh hi, Freya! That's OK, I'm just processing a lot right now and taking some time to regroup. Did you know that inversions can help with focus and brain function?'

'I didn't . . .'

'I hope you are cultivating your own yoga practice, or something similar to help disconnect from the workplace. This industry is tough, and you need to look after yourself.'

Is it really going to be as easy as this? Is she really going to throw away her job and, most probably, her relationship, while her boss stands before her red-faced, panting and smelling of sandalwood incense?

'I need to discuss something serious . . . uh . . . I'm not quite sure where to start.'

His brow furrows. 'I owe you an apology, don't I? We never did get to have that discussion with you and Nicole about her behavior towards you. That probably would have given you the closure you needed in this terrible situation, am I right?'

'Well . . . that kinda has something to do with it, but not really.'

'Oh no, please don't tell me you're unhappy here, or that you want to leave. That's the last thing I can deal with right now.'

Freya's cheeks grow hot. His anger at her would be easier to take than his disappointment.

'Oh no, it's nothing like that. I am so happy here Julian, really I am.' And while it's hard to admit, her job has become even easier since Nicole died, the landscape of her day no longer fraught with dread. There is a sense of excitement and purpose that came the moment she was promoted as lead on the East Africa project. Things would be perfect, if only she could shake this feeling of guilt. If only she could look at her phone without the fear that someone was after her, too.

'OK, is everyone treating you well here? You and Jay seem pretty . . . close.' A pointed gaze, a turning upwards of the corners of his mouth. His eyes move over her differently. It's the first time she's noticed him do this, and she doesn't like it.

At the mention of Jay's name, her eyes dart across the room. He is still busy on a call but watching her. Usually her skin tingles under his focused attention but today it makes her worry.

'We get on very well as colleagues,' she says curtly, 'but I have a confession that involves him.'

Julian's grin widens. 'You don't have to keep up pretenses on my behalf. If you two want to cuddle up in obscure coffee shops and go on ambling walks together, it's fine by me. Your work speaks for itself.'

Freya is puzzled. She doesn't remember bumping into Julian when she was outside the office with Jay. Maybe she just didn't see him.

'No, no, it's about Nicole . . . I did something stupid the night she died, and I think you have a right to know.' This is it. No turning back now. She recalls the trust glistening in Jay's eyes as they shook hands, as they made their promise. She could turn and run now, but this is a risk she has to take.

Julian's face shuts abruptly, as starkly as shutters slamming closed.

'Go on . . .'

Freya speaks so softly that Julian has to lean towards her. He is close enough for her to smell his spicy aftershave. She minimizes Jay's involvement. If she has chosen to ignore their pact, she may as well be decent enough not to drag him down with her.

He listens carefully, then turns thoughtful. 'I see. Well, this is not very good. It's not good at all.'

The tears come, no matter how much she tries to will them away. 'I'm so, so sorry! I don't know what came over me! It's no excuse but Nicole and I had been clashing quite a bit and, man, I feel so stupid! I would do anything to take it back.'

Freya expects Julian to call the police. Instead, his face crumbles.

'Freya, *I* am so sorry. We had some . . . problems . . . with Nicole in the past and I should have seen just how seriously she was targeting you. I should have made the time to hold that damn meeting with HR. It was my job as CEO to protect you and I failed in that. Please accept my apology.'

The room feels brighter, and Freya isn't so scared anymore. Julian is a good, principled man. Like a true CEO, he is able to pick apart a situation and see what the problem is. For him to acknowledge her pain makes her whole soul flood with light. The constant stress of the past few months begins to release. Everything is going to be OK now. Julian understands her. He's on her side.

She stands to leave and he holds his arms open. 'Come over here, you can't leave without a hug.'

'I don't know what to do next,' she says, a little desperate. 'This is the worst thing I have ever done.'

'You are too hard on yourself. By not talking to anybody, you've built it up into this big thing in your head. It's just an unfortunate coincidence.' They are hugging so tightly that his stubble rubs against her skin.

'But she's gone now,' she whispers.

'Don't worry, we're going to fix this together. Don't go reporting it to the police or anything just yet. They have enough on their plate as it is.'

She feels it before she realizes what it is. His hand incrementally lower down on her waist than it should be, yet again. A new look in his eyes. Freya is light-headed, the world swimming around her, a thick blur of office chatter, the boiling kettle, the grind and growl of the coffee machine.

Then, as quickly as it transpired, the spell is broken. Julian steps away from her, sits back down and types furiously in response to an email.

'Looks like we have a few more investors on board for our East African project!' He smiles. 'Can you imagine the hundreds of women's lives we are about to save? I get shivers just thinking about it.'

Freya forces a smile in response. She floats out from the close confines of the room, back into the office, back to work, back to Virginie filling her in on the latest news coverage of Nicole's case.

Maybe she imagined it. Yes, she probably imagined it. He probably just made an honest mistake. She is in enough trouble as it is. She can't afford to make a scene now. Julian is a good man, she's sure of it. She is so desperate to believe it, that she'll chant it, over and over, until it feels right again.

Chapter 51

Freya
Nine days after the murder

After her interaction with Julian, she feels emboldened. She will not cow-tail to Jay's pact, or even Julian's advice. She trusts her own conscience, and it is telling her to report her side of the story to the police.

Walking through the door makes her shudder. Even though her report is small in relation to everything else that probably passes through this station, she can't shake the paranoia that she could easily be arrested.

'Hi there,' she says to a ruddy-cheeked young woman at reception. 'I'd like to report – wait a second—' She makes it to the bathroom just in time to be sick.

She hears footsteps outside. A gentle rap on the door. The woman's soft voice. 'You OK?'

'Yes.' She wipes her mouth clean. Opens the door. 'Nerves just got the better of me, I think.'

'Don't worry, it happens to many people who come in here. Trauma, you know? Are you here to open a case?'

Her mouth goes dry. Just tell them about the prank. It's so simple.

'No, I'm here to add to a statement I made?' Her tone is weak, her sentence sounding like a question.

'No problem,' the young woman says, swiveling her chair closer to the computer screen in front of her. 'I just need the name of the key person in the case and then I can call up the lead investigator.'

'Nicole Whittington.' The name alone still has the power to flood her body with raw terror. 'And my name is Freya Matthews.'

She recognizes him the moment he walks through the doors and turns towards her. He has a kind, open face that is emphasized by his shaved head. Her panic slows. Maybe a man like this will understand.

'Detective Simon Cohen,' he says, 'and you are Miss Freya Matthews? I remember taking your statement the other day.'

'You remembered my name.'

'It's a talent of mine.' He smiles.

He walks Freya to an interview room alone.

'So, how can I help?'

'I'm here to add to my statement.'

His expression looks puzzled. He holds a pen poised in his left hand. 'Sure . . . go on.'

She spills the whole story faster than he can write it down. Every time she repeats it, she feels more and more stupid. It is hard to capture the fire that blazed in her chest that night, the humiliation that needed to be released once and for all.

He taps his pen on his notebook. 'So both you and Jay Singh wrote the advertisement?' His face flushes red. Not a promiscuous sort, then.

'Yes . . .'

'And whose idea was it to do this?'

Jay grabbing the laptop, typing in the name of a dating site, writing the first sentence.

'It was both our idea. It just evolved after the conversation we were having.' This doesn't feel right. She wanted to keep Jay out of this.

'About Nicole Whittington being difficult that night?' Simon's eyes have narrowed.

'Yes. She'd been bullying me for some time, and that night she accused me of keying her car. The situation had grown out of hand.'

It doesn't follow logically from her last statement, but Simon asks, 'Did they have a romantic history at all?'

The picture at Jay's house. The hurt in Nicole's eyes.

'Yes, they did. But it was over long before I started at Atypical. I think it played a role in her rage towards me, but she was a complicated person with a few mental health issues, as I'm sure you have discovered.'

Simon looks away too quickly.

'And Jay Singh was with you the whole time?'

'Yes!' The obsessive focus on Jay makes Freya uncomfortable. They were both equally at fault. They took turns at writing those filthy words. Yet it was her own decision to report her role that night. This feels wrong, as if she is accusing Jay of something without meaning to. She isn't even sure if word has got to him yet that she has broken his trust. 'Uh, I think he should come here and speak for himself.'

Jay had been with her since that first bottle of champagne, and had walked her home. Although, he didn't walk her all the way home, did he? As soon as they reached the beginning of her well-lit street, he mumbled an excuse about leaving something at the office, kissed her and walked away. She didn't think much of it, as they often met at each other's houses, out of sight of their colleagues.

Simon meets her eyes intensely and lowers his voice. 'Ms Matthews, I'm going to ask you something now and I would like you to answer with complete honesty.'

Freya's whole body begins to quake. 'Yes?'

'Did you delay sharing this information with me because you felt intimidated in some way?'

'I don't know what you mean . . .'

'Let me be specific. Did someone tell you not to share this information with the police? Jay, for example?'

Freya thinks back to her and Jay's conversation. Easy, breezy Jay telling her to relax and not waste police time. To mention this now would feel like a betrayal. Love forgives the little things. Love protects. Love is supposed to keep its promises.

'No. I just, well, I didn't want to waste your time with a petty story. I was embarrassed.'

He softens. 'Don't be embarrassed. People make mistakes, and do things for all sorts of crazy reasons. You wouldn't believe the cases we see in here that are a result of bullying. Kids as young as six pushed to the edge by it.

Unfortunately, bullying plays a role in too many suicides as well.' He closes the case file.

'Thank you for coming to me. Every little piece of information helps my investigation. And if you would like some counseling for bullying, please take some of the helpful flyers at reception.'

'Thank you.'

'It's a pleasure – I can't recommend counseling enough.'

Freya makes to leave. 'Wait, one more thing before you go. Do you maybe remember what you wrote in the advert?'

Freya is mortified at the thought of reading her drunken words out loud. He clicks idly through the dating site. Nicole's profile still exists, but the advert is gone. Simon swears under his breath.

'It would have helped to read, word for word, what was said.'

'I'm sorry, I don't remember.'

Freya runs over the elusive contours of the message in her mind, like a word that is at the tip of her tongue. Of course she remembers, how can she forget? But to say it out loud would feel too extreme, too incriminating. Besides, in her pocket, her phone displays one new message. It is sexual, dark and dirty. It is presumptuous, brazen and clear in its desire. And it is the exact same message Jay and Freya wrote that night.

Chapter 52

Freya
Nine days after the murder

A tall woman with long, platinum hair walks purposefully towards Julian. She ignores the turning heads, and sheds her thick white coat to reveal a white pantsuit beneath it. The only hint of color is her lipstick, which is as dark as clotted blood. The atmosphere in the office shifts. Whoever she is, her power ripples over every person here. She darkens the door of Julian's office, and Freya is certain she sees him shrink in his seat.

'Who is *that*?' she whispers to Virginie.

'It's Atypical's silent partner, the brains behind this operation. Ruth Johnson.'

As if she hears the women mentioning her name, Ruth turns to face both of them. Julian joins her and gestures for Freya to come to his office.

Her stomach lurches. Ever since their encounter the other day, Freya has been avoiding Julian.

'Freya! Lovely to see you. There is someone who has come to join us who I really want you to meet.'

Why now? Why so soon after a member of the Atypical team has been murdered? Something doesn't feel quite right about this. But then, Freya meets Ruth's gray-blue eyes that focus on her, bright and warm. Every gesture she makes is slow and assured. Her authority announces herself in the in-between spaces, in what she doesn't have to say.

'Allow me to introduce you to my co-CEO, Ruth Johnson,' adds Julian, now looking a bit weaker.

'Hello, Freya,' she says in a soft, low voice that vibrates with warmth. 'I am Ruth, one of Atypical's founding partners. I've been traveling for the past two years, but Julian needs all hands on deck for this East African project, so I have come back. This kind of work really inspires me.' The new development illuminates a spark of hope. Atypical could live up to being the company she dreamed about after all.

There is an ease in how Ruth moves around Julian, brushing carelessly against him, leaving no space between them. Freya wonders if they were lovers once, or close friends.

'Ruth has been so looking forward to meeting you,' says Julian. 'I've been harping on and on about how special you are. I'm going to leave you two to get to know each other better.'

She feels it coming on despite her misgivings ... the glow. Julian still thinks she is special, even after what she did. They value her here. She is safe.

Her mind whirs at a breakneck pace. Say something, *anything*, she thinks.

Thankfully, Ruth speaks for her. 'I was so excited when Julian told me you had started here. I'm assuming he didn't mention this when you joined but I have been tracking your achievements for quite some time and insisted that we make you an offer.'

Freya can't look her in the eye – the praise is too much to process. To think that during all those years of striving, during all the extra hours waiting tables, during all the small wins, the broken shoes she couldn't afford to replace, those desperate moments where she feared she would amount to nothing, there was someone looking out for her, someone who recognized her potential. She never expected this feeling, how much it hurts to be appreciated.

'Ruth . . . I . . .'

'You know, Julian thinks we hired you for your talent, but to me you're worth so much more. You have something he couldn't even see, because he wouldn't know what to look for. I know the kind of hunger that pushes you to come in early, stay late and take on extra projects, that fear you'll never quite be good enough.'

Freya feels as if Ruth can see right through her. Every day she comes into work, she fears that this is the day she is found out for being insufficient, a fraud.

Ruth continues, 'I know because I've been there, and I've come from nothing too. We're just the same, you and me.'

Freya sees it then – under the platinum dye, perfect blow-dry and airbrushed makeup – a softness masquerading as toughness, a vulnerability faking at strength. Ruth will know what to do, how to make this right. Maybe she can mentor Freya. People are always sent into your life at the perfect moment. This is the lifeline that she was looking for. At that moment, despite all the despair and fear of the past few weeks, Freya feels a little more positive. Ruth is someone to be trusted.

Chapter 53

Isla
Nine days after the murder

Isla is sprawled on the couch with a large bag of peanut butter M&Ms, a bowl of popcorn and a blissful three hours ahead of interior design show reruns. Her mother is miles away, watching on a sofa of her own while talking to her on the phone.

'You know how funny it is that you're addicted to home décor shows but you can't bring yourself to buy anything other than the bare essentials?' She laughs.

'Just you wait and see, Mom. One day I'll have one of those homes with perfectly seamless indoor and outdoor space, with floor-to-ceiling glass and cream lounge sets that have never seen the face of a grubby butt cheek.'

She cackles over the line and Isla can just imagine her expression. 'My girl, I've raised you better than that.' Tonight, like many nights, Isla misses the mismatched furniture of her family home, the walls covered in photographs and her scrawled pre-school art. She aches for the familiar smell of roast chicken and her mom's unparalleled crispy potatoes cooking in the oven, the hours spent leaning against the kitchen counter drinking wine and laughing. She hasn't found any place quite like it in San Francisco. She doesn't know where to start.

'How's that story going?'

Her heart sinks. The story. It hasn't been going anywhere at all. After sourcing the identity of the phone number, she sent the lead to Simon, but she's unsure if he did anything with it. He was distracted on the call, talking at a hundred miles an hour. Either way, it felt like the honest thing to do. If Jay Singh is truly involved, the police can pursue the lead and release the information to the press.

A beeping noise interrupts the call. 'Wait, Mom, I think someone is trying to get through on the other line. Let's talk later . . . Hello?'

Silence. A faint voice. 'Isla, is that you? This line is really bad.'

'Simon?'

'I've been trying to get hold of you all afternoon. There's been a new development, which we are confirming in the media shortly. I wanted to talk to you first though. Turns out you were on to something with the phone number.'

Isla's hands shake as she rifles in her bag of M&Ms and shoves a handful in her mouth. Several fall out the pack and onto the carpet.

'You were right. It's Jay Singh.' It feels so obvious now. During her interview with him he was too smooth to be innocent.

'Some physical evidence has been discovered on the body, and we have got the results back. It is a dead-on match for Jay's DNA sample that we collected at the office.

Then, as luck would have it, Freya came into the station and added to her statement. The information painted Jay in a very suspicious light, giving me a concrete reason to follow the lead.'

Isla's heart starts to pound. Her instinct about Freya was right – she was protecting Jay! She wants to say something, but Simon is speaking too quickly.

'Along with his iPhone, we took in his Apple Watch as evidence this morning. The call history confirms that he spoke to Nicole that night, and, here's the interesting bit, the data on his Apple Watch shows he walked exactly 1.5 miles at 10 p.m., just a few hours before Nicole's time of death.'

'So?'

'We went and measured the distance between Atypical's offices and Nicole's apartment and it didn't match. But then I recalled Freya's statement about Jay walking her home. The distance between Freya's and Nicole's apartments is 1.5 miles, which matches the distance captured on the watch. This is the kind of data that will really help us in court.'

'Amazing! Do you think you will be able to pull the actual GPS locations as well?'

'If we're lucky, but we're hoping for a confession before that.'

Simon takes a sharp breath. There's more. 'We're going to his house in the next hour to make an official arrest. Thank you for everything you shared with us, Isla. I think this is it, I really do.'

'So,' she says, 'what is your theory of what happened that night?'

'I really shouldn't be throwing theories around, but I would hazard a guess that this is a crime of passion. If Jay killed Nicole, it's because he didn't have the self-control to stop. That fits in with the picture Andy Higgs painted of him too.'

Self-control, it's a word Isla scoffs at now. Hardly any man has it in her experience, especially under the influence. It's the reason Isla feels sick to her stomach when she passes a nightclub. The potential for violence is coiled in the beat of the music. It's why she swapped her punk, checkered skirts and Doc Martens for gray sagging jeans that hide her legs. Hide your body, hide your weapon and you'll always be protected.

Nicole's crime-scene pictures looked chaotic – even in the static photographs Isla could feel a frantic, menacing energy bouncing around the room. Yet for all the blood and mess, the injuries themselves were efficient. She will have to go back and check, but she's almost certain that it only took a few minutes for Nicole to die.

Isla thinks back to the first morning she went to ask questions at Atypical. The bright lights, the expensive computers, the free food and the edgy music. She was blinded by the brilliance of it all. During his interview Jay was good-looking, yes, but also funny and charming. He made Isla laugh in a way that felt genuine. Could he have killed Nicole? And if Jay had left the office and walked Freya home, could Freya have known where he was headed to next? Or did she perhaps follow him and see something she shouldn't have?

It wouldn't be the first time a man hurt a woman, but it all seems too simple.

Chapter 54

Freya
Ten days after the murder

Freya's phone buzzes continuously in her pocket.

Hey, baby . . .

Hi

Nice to meet you, Freya

Hello, Freya

Whaddup, cutie

Hey, wanna chat?

What are you wearing?

She switches her phone to silent. She needs a break from thinking about this, just for a moment.

Her head and body ache, but her drive has pushed her out of bed. Today, she will sort her life out. She will start by confronting Jay. He has been avoiding her ever since he said he would try to figure out the source of the messages. If he can't do it, she will simply do it herself. All she wants is for everything to feel normal again, to feel the warmth and security of his affection like she did before. As she closes the front door behind her, her gaze flicks left, and then right, looking, assessing, wondering if there is someone waiting for her in the shadows.

She paces to the office, cappuccino and croissant in one hand, navigating the steep, winding roads without having to check the street names. The route feels part of her now, natural. Despite the drama tightening its grip around her, she is starting to feel like she is a hotshot young programmer working for a kickass startup, and not an imposter.

The bustle of her commute can't take her mind off Jay. She has a feeling he doesn't want to see her, and she can't understand why. She felt this acutely the day before.

She was sick yesterday and tired to the bone. The police visit and the chilling text messages hadn't helped matters, either. By 2 p.m. her eyes were streaming when she tried to focus on her screen.

It was probably the cumulative exhaustion of the past few days, and the constant reminder of Nicole's empty desk. Her head kept on slumping forward as she typed and she kept on forgetting what she was meant to be working on.

Jay was in a meeting, so she sent him a message,

Feeling ill. Going home x

Hours later, the lethargy that had crawled into her bones was still hanging on. Every inch of Freya's body ached as she forced down some cereal for dinner. She'd never had a mother to dote on her when she was sick, never had a special meal she ate but it didn't stop her longing for that feeling of being a child again. Stupidly, she thought Jay may have read the desperation between the lines of her message and surprise her with an unexpected visit. Kate would be shocked if she knew this, but Jay already had his own set of keys to their place. She kept checking her phone, and looking towards her bedroom door, but both remained motionless.

Finally, as if on cue, her cell lit up the darkness of her bedroom. It was a message from another unknown number.

Hi . . .

Through the fog of her fatigue, she started to feel strange. Perhaps it was best to ignore the message. But the stranger continued.

I want to do things to you, the things that you wrote about in your advert. Why did this keep happening? She wanted answers.

What things? she texted.

Another message. *I want to tie you up, I want to make you scream.*

Her blood turned cold. This was no longer an annoying coincidence, it was something that struck fear deep in her heart.

What advert? she replied, suddenly wide awake.

Don't play coy, you little tease. You know what, bitch? Forget about it. You're not that hot anyway.

Freya's nausea intensified and she threw the phone across the room. Isn't this what they did to Nicole? Someone out there was making a point. They knew what she and Jay had done, and wanted to punish her.

She fell into a fitful sleep, taunted by the message and hurt by Jay's silence.

But today was a new morning, crisp and sunny. She was going to toughen up and tell Jay that she informed the police of their prank, and confront him on his change of behavior. Even if the prank had nothing to do with Nicole's death, she needed to do the right thing. If they are meant to be together, he will be principled enough to understand why this is so important to her.

She walks straight to his desk. Better to do it early before she chickens out. Yet even though it is past 9 a.m., he is not there. Her colleagues are fretting around the office, visibly upset. Through the glass windows of Julian's office, she can see him on the phone, running his fingers through his unruly mop of hair.

Julian pushes open the door to his office. 'Everybody! Stand-up meeting! Now!'

His uncharacteristic show of aggression scares her. A memory of his body pressing against her flashes through her mind. With Julian, who is the myth and who is the man?

He pushes open the door of his office.

Freya walks to the main meeting room, and Virginie falls in step with her.

'Here we go again. Is there no end to the drama in this place?'

Freya clenches her fists. 'I'm nervous. What's happened now?'

They squeeze into the crowded room and find a space at the back. Freya makes the mistake of looking down at her phone. Fifty new messages. Shit. She has got to do something, today.

'People, hi, can we have some quiet please!'

Everyone shushes around the room manically.

He continues, 'Great, thank you. I wanted to take the time to speak to you all in person so you hear the news from me and not in the press. Unfortunately, Jay Singh, a highly valued and respected member of our team, was taken into police custody in relation to Nicole's death late last night. It would appear there is some new evidence that links him to the scene of the crime.'

The room is silent. Freya can't breathe. Her cheeks flush as she avoids the curious eyes of colleagues.

Dear God, it's her fault. She remembers the detective, Simon's, interest in her story about the prank, and the way he kept on focusing on Jay. She has implicated her own boyfriend, the person she loves. In her rush to confess, she remembers the detective's interest.

Her mind spins. Freya listed Kate as her alibi, and Jay listed Freya as his. Even though Kate had not seen Jay that night, she had begrudgingly agreed to confirm that Jay was at their house. Because it was clear that he was – his boxer shorts were lying on the floor of her bedroom and his jacket was strewn across the sofa the next morning. If, or when, there is a trial, she will have to take a stand, and relay the events of that evening under oath. Her testimony could send him to prison.

The acrid smell of Julian's sweat fills the meeting room. 'Stunts like these are common in murder investigations, but because of the high-profile nature of our company, this particular nugget of information is bound to get a lot of press. Remember that Jay is innocent until proven guilty. There must be a reasonable explanation for this. Please, everyone, I want you to stay calm, and –' he looks at them each in turn, and Freya is almost certain his gaze lingers on her a few seconds longer than everybody else – 'under no circumstances, say a word to the media.'

Virginie pulls her aside as everybody walks solemnly out the meeting room. 'Are you all right?'

'Of course not! I don't understand what is happening! Jay didn't murder Nicole. He slept in my bed that night!' She doesn't mention the hours before, when they were apart, Freya with Kate, and Jay someplace unknown.

'That's the thing with men,' Virginie says. 'They think of themselves first, and often that thought process is driven by little more than sex. Try not to be too upset. You can do so much better.' Freya had always suspected Virginie disapproved of Jay. They never seemed to speak to one another directly. Still, this is not the time for I-told-you-so's.

'Thanks for that, but I need some space. I'm going to the restroom.'

As soon as she locks the door, Freya goes on to Twitter to get the real story. A search for the hashtag Nicole Whittington reveals the sordid details of her worst nightmares. A source has shared that DNA evidence has been found on Nicole's body, and it matches Jay's sample. She doesn't have to dig much further to discover the truth: it wasn't just any DNA. It was Jay's semen.

She remembers their long kiss goodnight at the top of her street, the way Jay squeezed her ass and said, 'Wish I could come home with you right now.' He gave her his coat then, which she wrapped tightly around herself to ward off the winter chill.

Tears scorch her cheeks and a hot rash breaks out on her neck. Freya forces her mind to go there: Jay unhooking the clasp of Nicole's bra with the same deftness of touch, his lips grazing her neck, his eyes focusing on her, and in that moment, wanting nothing more. Knowing it happened in the past stung, but the fact that he wanted Nicole when Freya was so willing to give him everything sears the most vulnerable part of her. He told Freya he loved her, for goodness' sake! It's too much to take – she dry heaves over the toilet bowl.

As the hours creep on, her sadness turns into anger. How dare he share a bed and a secret romance with the woman who bullied her? How little respect did he have for her that he could make her look like such a fool? It's the deceit that kicks her in the guts, the sheer level of planning that would have gone into it. Why pretend to side with Freya in the first place? Why play that stupid prank at all? What kind of sick, sadistic relationship did they have?

She was such an *idiot* to trust him. Just a stupid graduate, fresh out of college who doesn't yet know the ways of the world. Her hands shake. She wants to stand up at her desk and shout, 'How many of you fuckers knew this was going on? How many of you laughed at my expense?'

She wants to throw her brand new cellphone and watch the screen shatter beneath the point of her ill-fitting high heels, breaking all those unwelcome messages into tiny little pieces. She has never felt more powerless.

She rustles through the mess of papers on her desk until she finds the business card. She needs to tell her story, start to finish, to someone who will listen without judgment, someone who will order her thoughts. She needs to set the record straight. So she does the only thing she can do, the one thing she is not supposed to do.

She calls the journalist.

Chapter 55

Isla
Ten days after the murder

Isla shouldn't be here. This coffee shop is a forty-minute trip from the office and Freya is already ten minutes late. Kenneth warned her not to leave her desk and gave her strict instructions to only transcribe soft-news PR pieces in the office, but this was the only time Freya wanted to meet. Witnesses like her get jumpy at the slightest obstacle or change in plan, often viewing it as a sign they shouldn't talk. Isla was not about to take that risk.

So she sits and waits, her left leg bouncing up and down, waiting for an acceptable amount of time between her first espresso and her second, purposefully not checking her phone. Twitter is alive with theories on Nicole's death.

@JamesGray Jay is Julian's prodigy and has his whole career ahead of him. Why would he sabotage that for a woman? This smacks of a political smear campaign.

@PeterSmithers Why is nobody focusing on Nicole's history of mental health issues? This is not a cut-and-dried murder case. She must have done something to provoke the attack.

@AllyBarnes Can we all just acknowledge the fact that she had sex with the guy? What if he had nothing to do with her death and she killed herself in a really brutal way? She was disturbed.

Her phone rings. It's Kyle, the news editor. One bored afternoon of bonding over emo-punk of the late 2000s and their favorite graphic novels has resulted in over seven years of easy friendship.

'What!'

'Isla, where the hell are you? Kenneth has come to check on you at your desk and he is *pissed*.'

'I'm busy, out on an errand.'

'It isn't a story, is it? Kenneth says you're not allowed to be out on a story. Isla, Isla?' He was always a bit of a prude deep down, despite his hardcore punk front. She hangs up and shoves her phone in her bag. Kyle can improvise and she'll buy him a rare comic book to make up for it. Right now, she can see Freya arching her neck and searching for her.

She looks worse than the first time Isla met her – pale-lipped and bristling with nervous energy. Her face seems puffy, as if she has spent the past few days drinking. She has, however, made an effort, which Isla can tell from the new clothes she is wearing.

'Nice dress.'

'Thank you, I made it from an old pattern I found.'

'Wow! I would never have guessed. Coffee?'

'Oh, no thank you. I can't seem to stomach the stuff this week.' Isla nods understandingly. She can't picture being so stressed that she would go off coffee. Something must really be eating at her.

She looks up at the clock as she really needs to get back in the next hour, but Freya looks too fragile to jump straight in to things. Isla takes a deep breath and focuses in on her. 'So tell me a bit about yourself.'

Freya trots out a neat story about always being interested in computers, which culminated in her being accepted into the College of California to study a Bachelor of Computer Science. She was active on campus, with skills that made her stand out. This led to her being headhunted by Atypical. It's the kind of dry narrative delivered in the stock-standard animated tech startup tone that she hears every day in this city, but Isla can tell by the fire in Freya's eyes that she truly believes it.

'That's your career history, not your story.'

Freya looks uncomfortable, which is exactly what Isla expected. She is still in the heat of her twenties, when a career is seen to define a person. While Isla wouldn't exactly call herself the glowing symbol of work-life balance, she does know that the late nights, hurried meals and emails on holiday don't amount to as much as you'd hope.

Freya steels herself to speak again. 'OK, my mother fell pregnant with me when she was nineteen, and in her freshman year of college. She tried to look after me for one year but it was too much for her, she didn't have the resources to do it. Eventually I was placed in foster care. While some families were lovely, it never worked out for one reason or another. I bounced from family to family, home to home. The fact that I managed to do well at anything at school, let alone get accepted into the top coding college and be headhunted by Atypical, feels like a miracle. I guess that's why I emphasized it so much.' She's smart, Isla will give her that.

Her phone is vibrating in her coat again. It keeps going on and on until she can't ignore it a moment longer. 'Excuse me, Freya . . . Hello! What is it?'

'It's me, Kyle, again, your only friend left in the office? Isla, you have to get back right now. Kenneth is moving your desk!'

'What? To where?'

'Um, you don't want to know. Just get back here from whatever it is you're doing, OK?'

Isla really hopes there is a reason Freya brought her out here. She swirls the espresso on her tongue – it's a damn good one, she should buy some beans before she leaves – and tries once again.

'You mentioned when you called that you had something to tell me about that night?'

Freya leans forward. 'I was sleeping with Jay.' It's the kind of secret shared between friends and, if Isla is honest, doesn't bear much weight on her story. It also doesn't explain why she would look so guilty.

'*Too*,' she corrects herself. 'I was sleeping with Jay too.'

'I'm sorry, you must feel awful.' She adds carefully, 'Did you love him?'

With that, a seal is broken and Freya's story begins to flow. Of course she loved him. They met on her first day of work, and the attraction was instant. She wasn't looking for love, but what do you do when you find it anyway, say no? She thought it was going somewhere special. They dated for a few weeks and were officially boyfriend and girlfriend after a month. He told her that he loved her. They had started to make plans together. Never once did Freya imagine that there was someone else, let alone Nicole.

'I find it impossible to believe he was there at her house,' she says.

Ah man, if Isla had a penny for every time a woman didn't believe her man could have committed a crime, she could have retired from journalism and opened her dream home décor boutique years ago.

'Freya, I know it's hard to stomach, but sometimes men cheat, and the ones who are really good at it know how to get away with it. I don't know if you're aware but there was evidence of semen found on Nicole's body.'

She visibly shudders. 'Yeah, I know.'

Isla's phone starts buzzing again, so she picks it up and cancels the call. This is where the true story is, buried somewhere in the timeline.

Freya continues. 'I can accept that they had sex, and that he was cheating on me, but murder? It doesn't make sense.'

'Why?' asks Isla.

'Because, even though there was a part of the evening after he kissed me goodbye that we weren't together, later in the night he let himself into my apartment and slept in my bed. He came home to me. His alibi is true. I think it was someone else.'

'Why is that?'

The noisy café fades into the background. Isla can only hear Freya's raspy voice.

'I added to my statement the other day. There was something I wasn't truthful about. That night, Jay and I pulled a stupid prank. We wrote a dating advert in Nicole's name and posted it online. I didn't expect anything to come of it. I just thought that a few guys would send her messages and she would feel annoyed and embarrassed.'

'I don't understand . . . why would you do that?'

'Nicole had been bullying me at work. Badly. It all added up and I wasn't thinking straight anymore. In a crazy way, I thought that making her feel as ashamed as she made me feel would somehow get her back.'

'You didn't expect she would be killed.'

'Of course not. But now I'm so scared the two incidents are related.' She reaches into her handbag, and pulls out her cellphone.

'Look at this message.'

I know you like it rough, baby. I'm going to give you everything you asked for, and when you scream, I won't stop.

Isla turns cold. 'Freya, that could be classified as a rape threat. You must take that to the police, immediately.'

Freya looks away. 'But I'm getting hundreds of these messages a day. Each time I block a number, a new one comes up. They all seem to be responding to a fake dating advert, just like the one Jay and I wrote.'

The next words Freya utters make Isla's blood turn cold. 'I think someone knows what Jay and I did. I think this person murdered Nicole, and that I am next.'

Chapter 56

Freya
Thirteen days after the murder

'What a cheating, lying, disrespectful prick!' Kate says. She paces up and down their small kitchen, making the space feel tinier than it already is.

Freya holds her head in her hands. Her face is raw from crying. If she slept at all the past few nights, she doesn't remember it. Scenes from her relationship with Jay kept flashing through her mind – the secret coffees, the hours in bed, the philosophical discussions. How could it all have been a lie? The police must be mistaken, there must be some sort of catch. She recalls her last police statement with a cold sense of dread. This is all her fault. Why couldn't she have just kept her mouth shut?

'I should have known the police were zoning in on Jay. When I spoke to the lead detective on the case, he kept on turning the conversation back to Jay. He didn't care about our prank.'

Kate stops dead. 'And is that such a bad thing? The man is toxic, Freya. This is your proof.'

'I just feel so helpless, you know? Like this whole thing is spinning out of control. I met with one of the journalists – Isla – and I told her all about the prank. I showed her something else too, something that scares me the most.'

The kettle is whistling, and the microwave moans as it heats up her instant oats. The cacophony of sounds and the rage flashing in Kate's eyes make her breathing ragged. Freya reaches onto the kitchen counter, where her phone flashes repeatedly.

Kate scans the messages, her brow furrowing. 'What is this?'

She takes a deep breath. 'It's something that I haven't told you, or told anyone but Jay, and now Isla. Ever since Nicole was murdered, I've received hundreds of messages from men responding to a personal advert I allegedly published somewhere on the Internet. There are men asking me for the nudes I promised, men waiting to meet me at restaurants across the city, and men sending me pictures of their dicks. Now, the messages are starting to turn violent, threatening.'

Kate drums her fingers on the kitchen counter, lost in thought.

Freya adds, 'I tried to trace the numbers but they are all from different locations. As soon as I block a number, another appears. Jay tried to figure out the source of the messages, but I don't think he got anywhere. My advert must have been posted on a secure platform. Nothing has worked. I am exhausted, I can't think straight and I don't know what to do.'

Kate's fingers stop. 'Right. This is what you are going to do. You are going to ask directly what platform they found your advert on.'

'But—'

'I know it's traumatic, but you have to do it. You will then figure out where the advert has been posted. Then you can just get hold of the people who own the website, and they will remove it!'

Freya nods, the muscles in her body relaxing. 'I've been too scared to do that. What if I encourage them by talking to them? What if they see it as a come-on?'

'We will deal with that if it comes to it,' Kate says. 'And I've changed my mind about the journalist. I'm glad you spoke to her. Whoever is behind the messages knows what you and Jay did that night. Maybe a little press exposé will give them the scare they need.'

'I feel like someone is attacking me, over and over again. I need to do something. I need to fight back.' Freya can feel the fury shift beneath her skin, fierce, alien. She has to release it somehow. 'I'm going to find out where that dating advert is posted a bit later. Right now, I'm going for a run.'

'But, Freya, it's pouring with rain outside!'

'I don't care.'

Kate looks worried. 'Please be safe, OK? And take my North Face jacket. You don't need to get sick on top of everything else.'

The rain against Freya's face feels like a baptism. Cleansing. A new start. She takes the same route she always does, a scenic run through Golden Gate Park, which shows the best of the city and the Pacific Ocean. She quickens her pace, and the trees pass by in a green blur.

She is painfully aware of her body today. Her breasts feel too big and noticeable in their crop top, her running leggings too tight. Her phone vibrates in her pocket. It could be a Strava notification – she always logs her runs – but she has a feeling that it is something else, another message. She glances at it.

Hello, Freya, I've got us a table at Souvla. Can't wait for you to blow me under it, like you said x

She has to keep running, keep moving forward. Who, besides Jay, knew about the prank? Who would be able to mimic the message word-for-word? Jay isn't that twisted, surely? An image of him in bed with Nicole, his neck still sweet with the scent of Freya's perfume. Maybe they were the ones who laughed at her in the end.

The park is too quiet. Freya veers into John F. Kennedy drive. Her breathing has become labored, which is unusual. She can usually handle three miles before needing to rest. She pushes forward, even though her limbs are aching and tiredness is overtaking her body.

Past the tourist traps and the shops, and into a part of town nobody knows she goes. She added it to her route two weeks into working at Atypical, telling herself she wanted to clock the extra distance, fooling herself that she preferred the gritty urban landscape to her previous pleasant amble along the coastline.

Finally, when her legs can't move any further, she stops, red-faced. She glances across the road at her daily landmark. It looks innocuous enough. People thread in and out, hauling shopping bags and children, busy with their days, rushing through the rain. Nobody would ever guess that Nicole was murdered there just eleven days ago. Nobody would guess that, weeks before that, Nicole would casually walk in and out of those doors each day, dressed in sharp-angled monochrome, not a hair out of place, eyes locked on her cellphone. And all the while, Freya was watching.

Chapter 57

Isla
Fourteen days after the murder

Isla picks up a giant slab of dark chocolate on the way to the office. The meeting with Freya has raised more questions than answers, but there is a more urgent issue at hand. One doesn't have to be an investigative journalist to figure out that the next few hours are not going to be pleasant.

Her piece-of-shit phone died in the hour of traffic back to the office and she can feel the heat of the incensed missed calls and unread messages burning a hole in her coat pocket. She tells herself she couldn't care less, and that she is more a rebel than a do-gooder anyway, but a part of her feels a sting of shame. All she ever wanted was to do the thing she loved most, and make a difference.

As she trudges up the stairs, she hopes that everybody remembers that she isn't just rebellious. She is good. She can get to the core of a story like no other, because she truly *cares*. Surely, even in this new age of digital publishing, that counts for something? There is a disarming ringing in her ears as she pushes the doors open.

She walks into the newsroom, wincing in anticipation of Kenneth's rant. Instead, there is silence. The other journalists look up blankly. Kyle catches her eyes and mouths, 'I'm sorry.' Nobody makes a sound.

Isla is briefly buoyed by the faint, irrational hope that perhaps she got away with it this time. Maybe she can just walk quietly to wherever her new desk is, head held high, and pretend nothing ever happened. She has enough information to lie low for a little while. She will stay in the office for the next week or so to keep the peace.

Her desk. Oh shit, her desk. It's not where it has been for the past ten years, just as Kyle warned her. All that is left in its place is an empty space and a tangle of computer cables. She scans the room desperately, trying to keep calm, trying to keep up the appearance of being unmoved. But the sniggers behind her are sharp as knives.

Then she sees it. Her entire desk has been lifted up and shoved awkwardly against Kenneth's. All her cherished notebooks, stored in chronological order and including a Moleskine gifted to her from Bernard, have been dumped in an untidy pile on the floor next to it. Her personal possessions – chocolates, more chocolates, and a collection of chewed pens – have been placed carelessly next to her computer for all to view. Seeing her inner world laid bare like this makes her feel a little broken, a little less important than before. Her fists clench. That was probably Kenneth's intention with this whole exercise. She holds her head up high and walks toward her desk as if it has been located here all along.

'Good afternoon, Kenneth.'

'Afternoon, Isla.' He nods. 'Like your new office space?'

She moves languidly towards the chair and settles in it, holding his gaze. Never break eye contact, and never cry. He mustn't sense her weakness.

'It's just lovely, thank you. Here with you, right at the bold, beating heart of the news. I'm so – what's the word – lucky.'

He scoffs, 'Damn right you're lucky. If employment rights weren't so heavily skewed in your favor, I would have had you out of here months ago. But for now you get the pleasure of sitting right in front of me, where I can keep an eye on you.'

It's not a coincidence that the only paper lying on her desk is a rival, breaking the news that Jay has been arrested. She curses herself for throwing it all away. The lead was hot in her hands, but she didn't believe in herself enough to follow through with the story.

Isla plugs in her cellphone to charge and watches it flash back to life. Was it all necessary? Did she have to go so far beyond the call of duty that she may never work a crime story again?

But there is a thrill drumming in her fingertips, a hum at the back of her mind as the pieces of the story fall together, and a new audio file, recorded on her phone, shows that there is far more to this story than anybody could imagine.

Chapter 58

Isla
Fifteen days after the murder

'Hey, Simon! I saw this and I thought immediately of you.'

'Simon, this was on the bookshelf and it had your name on it.'

'Hi! I was in the area and thought . . .'

No, no, all options sound wrong. This was a stupid idea. It seemed so natural yesterday. Isla was browsing the shelves of a bookshop close to the office, and saw a copy of the latest Ottolenghi cookbook. Simon loves it when his mother cooks Middle Eastern flavors and speaks fondly of long, heaving tables of food at Friday Shabbat dinners. Isla flipped through Ottolenghi's recipes for latkes, hummus, tabbouleh. It seemed like a dead match. So she bought the thing. She even had it gift-wrapped.

Today, the present feels too ostentatious, and too heavy in her hands. It feels like a statement that she cannot confirm or deny. But the station looms in front of her, so she may as well drop it off and check on the status of Jay's arrest at the same time.

'Is Simon in?' she asks the woman up front.

'Detective Simon Cohen?' she corrects Isla, a little too frostily for her liking.

'Yes.'

'No. He just went out. Do you want to leave a message for him?'

Maybe it's for the best. It would be so embarrassing if Simon didn't like the gift, or if he took Isla's generosity to heart.

She pushes the parcel across the desk. 'Yes, I'd like to leave this for him, please.'

The woman frowns, looks pained. 'Sure, but I will need you to write down your full details on this slip, please, and go to security over there and get it scanned. We need to know there is nothing dangerous inside.'

Oh God, this was just meant to be a small, casual gesture, and now it's turning into a full-blown scene. Isla flushes, and offers the gift in its bright yellow wrapping to the guard.

'Heavy,' he says.

'Yes,' she apologizes.

The scanner is situated at the entrance of the station, where both the waiting area and a sliver of the holding cells are in view. Isla spots a flash of jet-black hair. He is a bit scruffy and worse for wear, but Isla recognizes him instantly. Next to him is a man in a gray, well-cut suit filling out paperwork. His brightly polished shoes stand out against the sticky linoleum floor. Together, the men turn to leave.

The first rubs his eyes, and when his hands move away, they meet Isla's.

Jay Singh. Tired and angry, but free to go.

Chapter 59

Freya
Fifteen days after the murder

Hey there, Freya.

It's on. Freya takes a deep breath and begins to type. Every word makes her feel complicit in this dirty game, but she has to know.

Hey . . . how did you find me?

A pause. The man on the other end is typing, is typing. Then nothing. *Is typing.* Finally, a message.

What do you mean?

Be bold. Don't lose him.

Where did you see my profile?

He is bold too.

And if I tell you, what will I get in return?

It's OK. She has flirted like this before. How many times has she humored a guy's come-ons because she felt too polite to reject him outright?

You'll have to tell me, to find out . . .

'*TheSpark.com, where else?*'

Yes! Finally. Freya opens her MacBook. Now she is armed with an address of the dating site responsible for all of this. It's different to the one she and Jay used, a fresh app that promises 'a match in your area, in seconds'. Everyone knows this is code for a no-strings-attached hookup. Her phone lights up. Another message, another guy.

I am sitting in this restaurant all alone. It's the first time I have ever been stood up for a date. The least you could do is fucking reply. TEASE.

Freya pushes it out of sight. This ordeal will be over tonight. Then she can turn her attention to her career again, and getting over Jay. This is to be expected, given he hasn't had access to his phone, but she craves a feeling of closure, and the opportunity to ask him, why?

'Ready for dinner?' Kate calls from the kitchen.

'Just a sec, I found the online dating site where my advert has been posted!'

'Amazing! Take your time then.'

'I'm hoping it will only be a few minutes.'

'I'll pour us each a glass of wine. To commiserate, and hopefully celebrate.'

Her phone flashes again – she can fucking see it, even though she has put it on silent.

'You know, you should change your number. In fact, you should have done that ages ago!'

'Why should male harassment be my responsibility? Besides, I haven't had the time,' she snaps.

'I can do it for you?' says Kate.

Freya ignores Kate. She ignores the phone too. Soon the buzzing will stop, and she will be able to breathe.

'Dammit!'

'What's wrong?' Kate asks.

'My computer's started running updates!'

'Try calling them from your phone? Not all social contact has to be initiated through a computer screen.'

Freya feels sick as she reaches for her phone again. She needs to be proactive about this.

'Good call.'

She scrolls up and down the mobile site, looking for a contact number. Each page is beautifully designed, with softly lit images of happy couples. What a damn lie, she thinks. This website says nothing. It doesn't tell her how to reach another human being, it doesn't explain how another person could simply go online and pose as her, for days on end.

Finally, she finds a tiny, innocuous icon in the bottom right-hand corner. *Contact us.*

She calls the number with shaking hands, preparing what she is about to say.

Someone used my personal details, and the photos from my Facebook account, and is posing as me. I don't understand how this has happened, because my account is set to private.

She swallows the guilt sticking in her throat. Braces herself to explain the situation out loud.

But the moment doesn't come. An enthusiastic recorded voice greets her on the other end of the line.

'Welcome to Spark, where we light up your match! Our operators can't come to the phone right now, but you can reach us at any time of day via our simple online help center.'

Freya hangs up firmly and throws her phone across the couch.

'Wine?' offers Kate.

'Thanks.'

A few moments later, she cradles the glass in her hand, full, thick and red.

Kate looks over, her brow furrowed. 'You're sure putting the booze away these days, Freya . . .'

'Not lately – the past few weeks I can only stomach one glass!'

'Before that, you were having almost a bottle a night.'

'That's only because of the situation with Nicole. I still don't feel quite like myself again.'

Her computer screen lights up. 'Finally!' Freya sighs. She bashes out a firm email to the faceless, probably soulless, people behind Spark.

To whom this may concern,

Someone has created a fake account in my name and has been matching with, and messaging people on Spark. I have received an avalanche of unwanted messages and images.

A lump swells in her throat as she types the last sentence: *I am starting to feel unsafe, and I need help.*

There is a reassuring ping as the message is sent. She takes a sip of wine, enjoying the warm fire slip down her throat. Across the couch, she can see her phone repeatedly lighting up.

'Maybe I should start a drinking game where I have to take a sip of wine every time I get a message?' she wonders, more to herself than to Kate.

A new email from Spark takes the edge off her despair. This is it. They will ask her a few security questions, she will authorize for the account to be shut down and this nightmare will be over.

The contents punch the breath out of her.

Hi there, Freya,

We are sorry to hear you've been having some trouble with Spark. We love what we do, and love that we have matched over 600,000 couples in the few years that we have been online.

Spark works through a secure online system that protects the account holder's privacy at all times. That's why we are password free. Every person that sets up an account with us does so using their own Facebook account. This is why your images have pulled through to our website.

If you want to shut the Spark account down, you need to contact Facebook or trace the person who set up the account in the first place. We're sorry, but our hands are tied. We can't help you.

Chapter 60

Isla
Fifteen days after the murder

When Simon's number flashes as an incoming call, Isla almost doesn't answer. Just thinking about the debacle of dropping off his gift at the station makes her cringe. What if she got him in trouble? In retrospect, a gift to any member of the police from a journalist does not look good: it smacks of a bribe.

'Wow, that cookbook was such a great surprise when I got back to the office this morning!' She can hear him smiling over the phone. Despite her embarrassment, she smiles too.

'Really?'

'Yeah! I've only discovered Ottolenghi recently but I think I'm his biggest fan. If I ever get to London one day, I'm going to eat at one of his cafés. My mom made his apple and olive oil cake for my dad's birthday this year.'

'I wasn't sure if I was off the mark . . .'

'You were spot on. Thank you for the wonderful gift.'

He doesn't ask why she spontaneously bought him a present, and she doesn't say. Mainly because she is not sure why herself. She changes the subject.

'I saw Jay Singh at the station. It looked like he was about to leave?'

Given her last conversation with Freya, Isla is not surprised. The killer is still out there. Jay's alibi was, in fact, correct. Freya's constant harassment only adds fuel to the fire.

Simon's voice goes quiet. 'That happened this morning. The prosecutor said we didn't have enough concrete evidence for a trial. Can you believe it? His smart watch literally placed him at the murder scene! But he holds that the evidence of sleeping with someone isn't enough to accuse Jay of murder. And with the best lawyer in San Francisco on his side, there was no way that Jay was going to stay behind bars.'

'I'm sorry, Simon, you seemed so sure.'

'I think I was hoping that we had enough to draw a confession out of him, but he pushed back during the entire questioning.'

'What are you going to do?'

'Not sure. While I may not be able to prove that Jay is guilty just yet, the whole encounter with him made my skin crawl. One thing is for sure, he is definitely not innocent.'

Chapter 61

Freya
Sixteen days after the murder

Freya runs into the office. She's late for a meeting. She bursts through the doors. The table before her is already strewn with sketches. Julian and Ruth are both standing at a whiteboard, battling it out over a minor issue. This world seemed so unattainable a few months ago. Now the distractions outside these four walls have her battling to remain present. She takes a seat and smiles at Ruth. While her relationship with Julian may feel strained, at least she has one mentor who seems to understand her and have her back.

Her head is ringing and her body aches. She hasn't been sleeping as well as she used to.

A big red number seventeen flashes and nags on her cell phone. Seventeen unread messages.

I'm standing outside your house.

I saw you walking into work today – you were so close I could almost taste you.

You can't ignore me forever, one day I'm going to break the door down and take what I deserve.

The messages are becoming impatient, violent. Something sinister crackles between each word.

You better watch your back, Freya.

She forces herself to read each one. If Spark can't help her, she will have to face her fears and report it to the police. Two weeks of this torture is long enough. But the thought of reporting it makes her want to faint.

The last message is from Jay. For a moment, time stops.

My lawyer got me out. The police were wrong. I owe you an apology and I know I have some explaining to you. Please can I see you? I have a few days off and then I'm back at work on Tuesday. I don't want to do this in the office.

He's out? Freya can't bear the thought of seeing him. She wants to both hit him, and run into his arms, begging for confirmation that this was all a terrible misunderstanding.

Jay still cares. It's the longest message he has ever sent her. Freya can feel the worry pressing on his words. But she puts the phone down, and does not reply. He slept with the woman who made her life hell. And later that same evening, he got into her bed. She was drunk, turned on, and in love. As she stripped his clothes off, she didn't smell Nicole on him. Perhaps she didn't want to. But the betrayal fouls the air now.

She sends Virginie an email from her phone. *Jay's out. I don't know how to feel. The cops think he did it, but if Jay killed Nicole, wouldn't I know deep down? How much can you trust the one you love?*

Her reply, instant. *You can't trust him anymore. You shouldn't have trusted him in the first place. Je suis desolée, mon amie, I should have been a better friend and warned you.*

Warned me? What do you mean? Freya is confused. Sweet, light Virginie who never looks ruffled by office politics? Who always has the perfect comeback? Why would she be so ruffled by Jay?

Nothing. I've just always had a bad feeling about him, that's all.

Freya wants to press her for more information but she is interrupted by fingers grazing her neck and digging into her shoulders.

'Freya, why are you so tense? These neck muscles are hard as a rock.' Julian's voice frays at the word hard, and it brings back that uncomfortable incident in his office. Did she imagine that? She looks to Ruth desperately, but she is focused on the presentation in front of her.

'Freya, you have done an amazing job running with Nicole's project. Somehow, despite all the trauma you have endured over the past few months, you have put the project back on schedule and within budget. As we get closer to deadline, we want to give you every opportunity to focus' – Ruth's usual composure is replaced with the bubbly excitement of a young girl. She can't hold it in much longer – 'which is why we are giving you your own office!'

'Excuse me?' Freya finds this information hard to process. She's been working through a fog, pushing through all the anxieties crowding her mind. If she managed to come up with anything great, it must have been by fluke. Her mind, body and heart has never been so compromised.

Julian wraps his arms around her. 'You heard right. Today, we're going to turn your experience of Atypical around.'

Freya untangles herself from Julian's grip. 'Sorry, I need a minute to process this.' An office is nice, but it would have been nicer if they had listened to Freya the minute she informed Julian of Nicole's bullying. It would have been better if he had set up the meeting with HR, had acknowledged Nicole's aggressive tendencies and protected Freya.

'Are you OK, Freya? You look a bit strange . . .' says Ruth.

'I do?'

'Yes, you look as if you're being hunted.'

If only Ruth could see the incessant trickle of messages on her phone. Or the selection of nude photographs of herself that she received yesterday. In the pictures, she is angling the phone so that her nipples are visible, and her hand flicking her shaved crotch. In the background, she can recognize the blue spine of her second-year computer programming textbook. The images are not recent, they were taken while she was at college and was not streetwise enough to crop her face out of her sexts. The only way somebody could have accessed them, is if they hacked into her personal phone.

She turns away from Ruth and sends another message, to Kate this time.

Sometimes, I worry that I willed Nicole's death into being.

There is a boiling hot rage within her, a foreign feeling she has never quite experienced with such intensity before.

It's strange, because it's not as if she hasn't experienced adversity before. Her four years of study were filled with the minor and major challenges that make up a life. However, every little snag in her path felt as if it had a purpose, as if she was moving towards something bigger than she could comprehend. The drama of the past few months – while punctuated by more success than she could have hoped for – just feels pointless.

She takes a deep breath and forces a smile. She will be more grateful, she will stop allowing the negativity to bring her down and do her very best at her job. At least the code before her always makes sense.

'I'm just overwhelmed,' she says. 'This is the best news I have heard all day.'

Julian smiles. 'I'm glad we can make you so happy. We want to do everything we can to help you focus on your job. We hope you feel safe here.'

They all sit, smiling at one another. Freya feels many things, but safe is not one of them.

'Well, go on then!' says Ruth. 'Pack up your desk and move, right now!'

Freya walks carefully back to her desk, feeling dizzy. This is all happening so much faster than she expected. She knew deep down that she was good, but after so many years of struggle, she thought that success would take a little longer. It's only been four months!

Four months, and her desk looks like it survived a recent earthquake. Papers and notebooks are strewn everywhere. The succulent Julian gave her as a welcome gift has shriveled and died. She shakes her head at herself. If she is going to become a tech maven one day, she is going to have to keep a tidier space. How she will manage this, she's not sure. She is not the kind of person to think in a straight line.

Four months and she has one picture up. It's of her and the girls at a Cuban-themed restaurant on the beach. There are fairy lights everywhere and they are laughing about something. Freya's wearing a red, off-the-shoulder dress she designed herself, and can still remember how light and feminine it made her feel. Her skin still burned from her fresh tattoo. The triangles. It's a great memory, of a time when everything was pure, and everything was possible. It's also from before she started at Atypical. After all this time, she never got the courage to put up a picture of her and Jay. He asked her to be his girlfriend, he said he loved her, but according to the display on her desk she was always alone. A petty part of her seethes. *Nicole* probably had a picture of Jay on her desk.

She opens her drawer. Its contents have been untouched since her first day at Atypical, so it is much neater. The collection resembles the hopeful desk of a schoolgirl at the beginning of term: lip-gloss, chewing gum, vanilla-scented hand cream and a box of tampons. Four months, and the box of tampons has remained unopened. She turns it around, over and over, in her hands, fingers growing numb. The world around her is drained of color and sound. Her only focus on the plastic seal, still intact. No, no, it can't be. She could have brought some from home, or borrowed from a friend. She hasn't felt . . . she can't say the word . . . surely she'd know it if she was? There are *signs*, for God's sake. Symptoms. They were careful, weren't they?

There was one night where the sex was a blur, where Freya danced the line between comfort and discomfort, pleasure and pain. It felt dangerous, risky and passionate. They'd got caught up in the moment and . . .

Now, sitting in this unnerving stillness, she can't remember the last time she craved chocolate or felt bloated. When last did she feel that never-ending hunger? When last did she wake up to the shock of blood?

Later, she buys a test and struggles to pee on the stick in the small Starbucks bathroom next to the pharmacy. She knows the result in her heart before she looks down.

A new crisis, a new curveball, a new future quivering with uncertainty.

A question and an answer that stares back at her, bold and unwavering.

Chapter 62

Freya
Seventeen days after the murder

Freya drums her fingers on the table in front of her, waiting for the call. Yesterday, she called up her doctor, secured his last appointment for the day and took a blood test. He said it would take up to twenty-four hours. It is now hour twenty-two.

She tries to focus on the sewing project in front of her, a sweeping satin kimono made of sari fabric. It's very loud and bohemian. Very San Francisco. And if the blood test result is what she suspects, it will be just the ticket.

Her phone rings. An unknown number. Usually she wouldn't pick it up, but she's expecting the doctor to call any minute now.

'Hello?'

Silence, save for the sharp intake and exhale of breath.

Anxiety hums in her ears, a swarm of bees.

'I said, hello? Who is there?'

A cough, a whisper, 'Freya . . .'

'Who the fuck is this?'

'Don't swear,' says the voice, 'it's unbecoming for someone so beautiful.'

A tear rolls down her cheek. Freya doesn't dare make a sound, doesn't dare move. 'Where are you?'

'I'm watching you sew. I love the way your fingers move.'

'Please tell me who you are,' she asks, trying to mask the pleading from her voice.

'But you know who I am? You asked me to watch you. You said it turns you on. Oops, your nightdress has slipped over your shoulder . . .'

'Leave me alone,' she hisses, and hangs up the phone. That's it. She will change her number today, just as soon as the doctor calls.

Another ring. 'What the hell do you want from me?' she shouts.

'Uh, Freya Matthews? It's Dr Fraser speaking. I have your blood test results in front of me.'

'Dr Fraser! Shit, I'm so sorry. I thought you were—'

'No problem. So your HCG levels are through the roof. This means the outcome of your test is very clear.' Dr Fraser is prone to speaking in science jargon, as opposed to English.

'Which means?'

'Freya, you're five weeks pregnant.'

Chapter 63

Isla
Eighteen days after the murder

A soft, rapping on the door. Probably a delivery guy with some random décor item Isla has forgotten she ordered off the Internet. Purchasing throw pillows out of loneliness has become an unfortunate habit lately.

But there he stands before her, strong, sheepish and clutching a shopping bag.

'Simon, hi?'

'Hey, uh, sorry to bother you,' he stutters, sweat glistening on his brow.

Isla's not sure what to say. 'Have you had another break-through on the case?'

'No . . . sorry. We're still working on it. I was just in the area and thought I could drop this off for you. There was a book sale at the station and this one was written for you, I think.'

He thrusts it towards her, an offering. It is a thick, hard-back encyclopedia of criminology. Her heart soars as she fingers the navy, gold-embossed cover. It's beautiful. It's also a message. A book for a book. His way of returning her gesture. She needn't have felt nervous about giving him a present.

'Wow, thanks . . .'

'You're really good at your job, Isla. You've got a great investigative eye. You should work on that, nurture it so it doesn't go to waste.'

Today, of all days, Isla needed to hear these words. She has been feeling deflated, and unsure what to do next. There is something else about the gift, and Simon's face when he hands it to her, that makes her throat swell with emotion. It feels good and uncomfortable all at once.

'This is incredible,' she says, forcing cheer into her voice. 'I'm going to use it a lot!'

He smiles broadly.

She wants to invite him in, and page through the book together. She wants to pour them each a coffee and argue over their theories about America's most chilling cold cases. She wants to spend the day in his positive, hopeful company, instead of whiling away the time alone. But yet, she can't stop herself.

'Listen, Simon, I'm sorry but I've got a thing I need to get to. It's Saturday, you know. Super social day for me.'

He looks down, disappointed. 'Yeah, of course. Me too, lots going on. My family beckons.'

He turns to leave and Isla watches him out of the window as he lingers a bit, finally turning left and pausing at a newsstand. She could have hugged him, at least. But the gift presses on a wound that makes her whole body heat up. To be lonely hurts, but moments like this make her remember that opening herself up hurts even more.

Chapter 64

Freya
One year before

She lies curled on her bed, a thin, pale comma.

'I can't do it,' she whispers. Her belly churns and aches, her body shakes with the chills. It's a nasty bout of gastro, and although she has an antibiotic, it doesn't help that she has a final computer systems analysis exam tomorrow.

Jasmin strokes her head. She, Hattie and Kate have been taking turns to sit by her side since she fell ill. Her best friends, so different that together they work seamlessly as a foursome. 'Let me make you some peppermint tea. That should soothe the cramps.'

'I don't think I can stomach anything right now.'

Hattie walks in with a tray of chicken broth and hot toast. 'You may think that, but I promise that you will feel better once you have something lining your stomach. Trust me, I'm a WebMD-qualified hypochondriac.'

They watch her in silence as she tries to force down a slice of toast.

'Jeez, guys, be creepy why don't you!'

'Sorry,' Jasmin laughs. 'We're just so worried. You have worked so hard for this day. Remember when you thought you wouldn't get the funding to stay at college after your first year, but then after looking at your results you got through?

Or when you spent the entire summer break going to extra classes that you paid for from your waitressing job, just so you could get ahead? You deserve this, Freya. You're almost there!'

Their heads turn as the door opens. It's Kate.

'What am I missing out on over here?'

'We're just trying to help the patient gather strength to get to her last exam tomorrow,' says Hattie. 'But she's battling.'

'I am not!' Freya protests.

'You are super depressed,' says Jasmin, 'I can see it in your eyes.'

'Wait. I have an idea.' Kate walks back into the room with armfuls of pillows, and on the next trip lugs in the Smart TV her parents got her over Christmas. Then, half an hour later, she arrives with a tray of steaming banana fritters and a can of whipped cream. 'To help with those cramps,' she says, as if it's the most logical solution. 'Is everyone ready for some Netflix?'

Freya knows they all have other places to be. Jasmin also has an exam coming up in the next few days, Hattie usually goes to spin class on Wednesdays, and Kate was supposed to be spending the night with her new sort-of boyfriend. Instead, they cuddle up on Freya's bed that is hot with fever. They select one show, then another, and another. Jasmin's head lulls onto her shoulder as she falls asleep. Beneath the queasiness, an unexpected feeling of joy rises up, uncomplicated and whole. These are her best friends, her family, her source of strength when hers is lacking. How lucky she is to have a group of women who know what she needs, before she has the courage to say the words herself.

Chapter 65

Isla
Eighteen days after the murder

Isla scans the morning's papers. More information on Nicole is starting to seep through. Alleged old boyfriends have come out the woodwork, calling her loaded names. Her family is from Zimbabwe, and cannot be reached for comment, but the information frames her firmly as an immigrant, someone taking a high-profile job on American soil. Nothing is said out loud, but Isla can feel the sympathy for Nicole waning. The words no longer paint her as vulnerable, or worthy of compassion.

In the first paper is a feature with a large photograph of Julian in a suit looking both handsome and troubled. The headline, 'Is Atypical under attack?'

Atypical is the tech company on everyone's lips. No other business has made such a tangible impact on the world's poor with cutting-edge technology. Julian Cox, still a decade shy of forty, has built a name for himself as an industry maverick, a role model who shows that you can combine care with commercial success. But, after the murder of one of his staff members, it is feared that this wholesome business is under attack. There is no doubt that when billions of dollars of investment are involved, a crime perpetrated against the company, or an employee, is purely political.

Isla wipes her eyes roughly. Soon, nobody will even remember Nicole's name. Men like Julian and Jay will be forgotten too, left free to move on and live another treacherous, hypocritical day, still pulsing with promise, and with life.

Chapter 66

Freya
Eighteen days after the murder

It's the weekend, and Freya finally has the time to brave the queues at the cellphone store. Now, she has a new phone number. It took an hour of queuing and what felt like hundreds of forms, and at the end she felt light-headed, but she did it. If Spark can't help her, and if she can't get to the bottom of the technology herself, this is the next best thing. She breathes in the fresh, rain-soaked air. Sweet freedom. At least one of her problems solved.

There is still the matter of seeing Jay for the first time in the office on Tuesday morning. Her mind is already spinning. Will everyone just pretend the arrest didn't happen? That they haven't read the tweets and news stories about the proof that he slept with Nicole the night she died? Thank God she has her own office now, a space to hide. No matter how angry she is, as soon as she looks into his eyes, all she will feel is hurt. He is still the man she loved a few weeks ago, and that love doesn't just dissolve into thin air.

And then there is her pregnancy, a fact that fills her with shame. She was meant to be the girl who was careful, the girl who was good. She shudders. If Kate finds out that she has wasted her one shot like this . . . well . . . she's not sure what she will do. Five weeks is early. She can hide any early signs with her newly made kimono, and can quickly sew a few other items that deliberately shroud her stomach. Good tailoring can cover up a multitude of sins.

She checks her email.

A new device has just signed into your Gmail account.

Strange. Must be because she just changed her phone number.

Then, a phone call.

Wait.

A phone call?

She hasn't given her number to anyone yet. Not Kate, not Jasmin, not Hattie.

An unknown number. It's probably the cellphone store confirming the line for her new number is active.

'Hello?'

A thin, reed of a voice, both needy and sinister: 'Freya, why are you trying to hide from me?'

Chapter 67

Isla
Eighteen days after the murder

Pacific Heights is not Isla's kind of place. The picture-perfect, dollhouse-like buildings fill her with a sense of unease, as do the scrubbed-clean families running with strollers, or the super-rich kids vaping in two-hour queues for Saturday morning brunch. One of the immaculate masses is her old friend Kirsty.

Isla and Kirsty met back when they were scene kids, swaying in the front row of underground gigs with mussed-up hair and scuffed sneakers. When the attack happened, Kirsty was the only one who came over with small offerings of comfort like graphic novels, cigarettes, and the new album from her then-favorite band, System of a Down. Back then, Kirsty was the one who knew which party to go to every night and who was dealing the purest drugs. Now, Kirsty knows the best place for a Vitamin IV and which Montessori school the Zuckerberg kids are going to next fall. Isla tries not to feel jealous at the shiny aura of comfort she exudes, especially when she's not sure if she'll be able to afford her meal at the expensive restaurant they're meeting at.

'Isla sweetie, it's so divine to see you. You're looking so well!' Isla smiles weakly. This falsity is the heartbeat that keeps their friendship alive. They care about each other, and hope that if they fake a rapport for long enough, their relationship will return to what it once was.

'Nice place!' she says, taking in the edgy, monochrome fittings and the menu, featuring several different iterations of avocado on toast.

'This old place? It's just my local. The kids and I come here every day before the school run.' Kirsty runs her fingers through her caramel hair. She launches into a story about the second one, whose name Isla always forgets. It's something exotic. Peony? Carnelia? Isla tries to focus but a familiar silhouette catches her eye.

She would recognize that patronizing mince anywhere. It struts through her worst nightmares. He looks slightly awkward in his active wear, his hair shower-slicked and clinging to the nape of his neck.

'Oh shit, my boss, Kenneth, is here.'

'Is that a bad thing?' Kirsty says, turning around and craning her neck to get a glimpse of him.

'Yes! Yes, oh my God, don't turn to look at him! Jeez, Kirsty! I don't want him to see me.'

'Sorry,' she says, laughing. 'Anyway, what were we talking about?' Kirsty continues her story, and Isla tries to be a good friend and reach between the divide of who they were then and who they have become. She doesn't value the same things Kirsty does, and her new crop of Lululemon-legging-wearing mom friends seem like another species entirely, but they've shared too much for her to just let go. Apart from Lizzie, Kirsty was there for her when nobody else was, and there's not enough money that can erase that.

Every now and then, Isla looks over to the corner table where Kenneth is sitting, nursing a cup of tea and poring over the latest edition of their paper. He must live here, and if that is the case, he earns more than she thought. Her heart pounds at the prospect of him humiliating her in front of her successful friend.

Someone slips into the booth next to him. He's wearing a beanie, sunglasses and puffa jacket, so she doesn't recognize him at first. The designer yoga mat curled under his arm though gives it away. Julian Cox.

She knew it! Last time she saw him, there was something off about him that she couldn't place. Isla is not sure what this means just yet, but it is too much of a coincidence to not be important. The two look around furtively. Isla hunches so as not to be seen. They shake hands and huddle closely together, speaking softly. A third man joins them, short and squat. He has the weathered skin and quick, nervous gait of a soldier who has been in service.

'And then Lisa was like, "I asked for the tiles in duck-egg blue, not Santorini blue!"'

Isla holds up a hand to Kirsty to stop her story for a second. She reaches for her phone and takes a picture. She doesn't know what business Kenneth and Julian have together, or who the man is with them. Yet one thing draws at least two of them together: the murder of Nicole Whittington.

Chapter 68

Freya
Nineteen days after the murder

Sunday evening is supposed to be quiet, but the city has a particularly menacing edge tonight. The voice keeps replaying in Freya's mind. How did he get her number?

She runs the phone over in her hands, and tries to pull it apart as she rushes home. The pedestrians around her feel aggressive and impatient, pushing at her from all angles. There must be a tracking device in here, or something. A message comes through. A close-up shot of a penis.

'I think I'm going to be sick,' she mutters to herself. Her blood sugar is dropping. She steps out of the flow of pedestrians and holds on to a railing, breathing heavily. The pang in her stomach reminds her that she hasn't eaten all day.

She is drawn in by the sharp tang of barbeque pulled pork at a nearby deli. She pushes to the front and orders a large sandwich with extra coleslaw and dressing. There is nowhere to sit so she slumps on the ground outside, eating quickly and downing a Coke to get her strength back. She should call Kate, and get a ride home, but she can't stomach another glance at her screen.

Pull yourself together, Freya.

She thought it was bad a month before, walking into the office with the sickening sense of dread over what abuse Nicole would subject her to. The pain, while fresh, was a continuation of the sense of unease she has always felt in the world. She could have never expected how much she would long for the simplicity of that dread now.

A block away from her home, she reaches a pedestrian crossing and stands swaying on her feet as she waits for her turn to walk. All she can think about is washing the day off her and lying, warm and clean, under the covers.

'Rough day, huh?' says a quiet, male voice.

Freya turns towards him. He is small and thin, with a bike propped next to him. His cycling shirt emphasizes his reediness, as does the helmet that teeters precariously on top of his head. He doesn't look dangerous, just an average guy making conversation. She doesn't have it in her to be nice, but she tries anyway.

She sighs. 'You can say that again.' She turns to face the road. Why is the light taking so long to change? The man is silent, but she can feel that he is searching for something else to say.

'Bet you can't wait to go home, open a bottle of wine and just release the pressure.' It's a bit too personal, but strange men crossing boundaries in conversation is nothing new to her. When she was a waitress in college, men used to ask openly about her relationship status and her bra size.

Finally, the light changes. She offers a thin smile in his direction and walks towards home. Not long now until she can close her eyes and forget. Just a few weeks ago, she was rushing back to meet Jay, to close the door behind them and tangle together, to get lost in the unique tenderness they shared. But now she knows it wasn't unique, it was standard B-grade lust, laced with the lazy platitudes of a man who is accustomed to juggling more than one woman at a time. Her fists clench.

Lost in the haze of her own thoughts, she doesn't register the whir of bicycle wheels beside her. It's the cyclist again.

'Nearly there!' he says brightly, swerving his bike closer. The street is quiet, the only sound his wet wheezing.

Freya is not one for small talk, especially tonight. Had her closed arms and quick walk not given him the message? She shouldn't have smiled.

His tone becomes more desperate, jeering. 'You don't have to be so coy, Freya!'

She stops dead.

Run.

She scrambles to find something in her bag that she can use as a weapon.

Run, run, run.

All she has is a nail file, but if she aims it towards his eyes . . .

'Leave me alone, please!' she pleads.

'You weren't so unfriendly online . . . you sounded up for anything.'

Something unconscious in her knows already. It bubbles beneath the surface. Somehow, she has called him here. Or someone pretending to be her.

'You're mistaken, I have a boyfriend. I'm not interested.'

Letting a man down is like handling a loaded gun. You have to be tentative, slow-moving, but quick-witted. A simple 'no' could be registered as an invitation to attack.

He thrusts his phone in her face, for proof. There are lines of messages between them, some extremely graphic. There are pictures of her, taken years before. 'You little tease,' he sneers, pushing his bike aside and edging towards her.

He is stronger than his small frame suggests. His arms wind around her and pull her close to him. He pinches her arm, hard, hisses, 'I know you live right here. You are going to unlock it, and invite me inside.'

'No,' she screams, hoping someone, anyone will hear. With a jolt of terror she remembers that it is Sunday night. Kate is at her French class, Jasmin is teaching yoga and Hattie is away for the weekend. There is nobody here to help her.

He shoves her against the wall, so hard that she loses her breath. 'Get your fucking keys out right now, bitch!'

Freya is doubled over, wheezing and crying. She watches his foot, clad in a spiked cycling shoe, rise up to kick her.

The door opens. Relief floods Freya's body. It's Kate. She must have skipped French class.

'What the hell is going on here?'

'Stay out of it,' the man shouts.

'Look, see this phone in my hand? I'm calling 911. You better run.'

'Fuck you!'

Kate rushes at him, shoves and sends him sprawling. As he gets up and runs to his bike, she wraps her arms around Freya.

'Get AWAY!' Freya screams, long after he has cycled away into the night. *'Get away, get away, GET AWAY!'*

Chapter 69

Isla
Nineteen days after the murder

'I guess my question is, do women have no responsibility at all when they are attacked? If a woman dresses in revealing clothing or makes herself sexually available, are we just supposed to ignore these factors when she is attacked? Why is it politically incorrect to say that a woman may have been asking for it?'

A picture of Nicole dressed up for Halloween as Wonder Woman flashes on the giant screen behind the circle of women. The tight Lycra emphasizes her muscular thighs. She smiles coyly into the camera, as if she trusted the person taking the image. Now it is looping on daytime television, telling a lie in her name.

Why aren't they focusing on the murderer? The scene from yesterday morning replays in her mind. Julian, Kenneth and the mysterious man in the coffee shop. Could squeaky-clean Julian be behind this? And could he be the one harassing Freya? Out of everyone at Atypical, he is the one most likely to have access to her contact details, and he would have the ability to see what took place on his network that fateful night. Maybe he knew that Freya and Jay played that prank on Nicole, and the harassment is his way of punishing Freya? But then what motive would he have to kill Nicole? Isla chews one of her fingernails and turns her attention to her phone call with Lizzie.

'Isla! What is that racket in the background? Are you hate-watching that talk show again?'

Isla turns down the volume. 'No . . .'

'Please, I could recognize that high-pitched, grating voice anywhere. Come on, it's Sunday evening where you are. Go out there and do something good for yourself!'

She feels a surge of panic. 'I don't know what to do.'

'Think of something, and find someone to do it with. I love you, Isla, but you're exhausting! Now, I've got to get some sleep, it's almost fucking Monday and I think I'm still drunk.'

Out of everything from her old life, Isla misses dancing, she misses hearing new music, and being right at the front with the music so loud that it blends with her heartbeat.

Before she can stop herself, she finds Simon's number and calls him.

'Hey, Isla! It's so good to hear from you! Is everything OK?'

Her heart thuds in her chest. This could be really embarrassing. He'll probably say no, and she should prepare herself for that.

'Funny question, but are you doing anything now?'

'You want to talk about the case?'

'No, no, nothing like that. There's this new band playing at Alamo Square and I've read amazing things about them. My . . . uh . . . friend Lizzie suddenly can't make it, so I have an extra ticket.' She flushes at the white lie, but knows Lizzie would support it.

There is muffled conversation on the other end of the phone, and the sound of Simon furiously clicking his pen. 'That sounds really nice. I've almost finished my shift. I can come straight from the station, and pick you up on the way?'

'Perfect, but I'm not, like, asking you out or anything!' she blurts out. 'I just don't want to waste the ticket.'

Ugh, why did she say that! It makes it even more embarrassing.

The golden light catches the pastel Painted Ladies on Steiner Street, Isla's favorite homes in all of San Francisco. The band grinds through its sound check. She and Simon settle on her Indian block-printed picnic blanket, another impulse buy from Anthropologie that she hasn't yet had a chance to use. She thought it would feel awkward sitting with him in a setting so far-removed from work, but it feels like a continuation of their usual easy relationship.

'Thanks for this, Isla,' says Simon, passing her a bottle of cider. 'I've been so tied up with Nicole's case, it feels good to get out.'

'Tell me about it. Any new leads?'

'None that I can talk about yet,' he says quickly. 'But, let's not talk shop tonight. Why would we want to with a sunset like this?'

'Oh look, the band's about to start playing.'

A trio of dewy-faced men with mussed-up hair and neon yellow bomber jackets strum distractedly at their guitars. The lead singer grabs the mic, and begins to croon in high-pitched falsetto.

Simon coughs. 'So, where did you hear about these guys again?'

'I read about them on Pitchfork.com. They were listed as one of the acts to watch in 2018.'

'They're awful!' he laughs.

'I know, right? Appalling!' Isla snorts. 'How can this whole crowd pretend to like it? We're getting too old for this, Simon.'

But even though the music is terrible, the fading light is perfect and the cider is warming. They stray into one of those meandering conversations where the content fades, but the feeling lingers. If it wasn't starting to get late, and if a chill wasn't creeping into the air, Isla could spend many more hours talking to him. Simon looks over at her mid-laugh, and though they are just friends, and though she sometimes feels damaged beyond repair, tonight feels just right. For a moment, everything is wonderful.

Chapter 70

Freya
Four years before

'Run, Freya, run!' Kate screams, wild and breathless.

Her legs are shaking, her feet clumsily pushing in front of the other. She has an awful feeling she can't go on for much longer.

'Faster! For fuck's sake!'

They should have never taken the shortcut through the park. But it was late and they were exhausted after five hours of teetering on spiked high heels, serving cocktails and smiling for tips. It was a tough gig, one that Freya did for the money and Kate endured to prove to her rich father that she could make an honest living. The arches of Freya's feet had gone into spasm, and her legs were numb from the rapid succession of tequilas she and Kate had thrown back at the end of their shift. Every mile was agony, so they took a risk. Freya had her key in her hand, sharp side facing out. They felt prepared for anything.

The park was well lit but eerie. They walked fast, quietly exchanging stories about the evening, self-consciously pulling down their short skirts. Freya despised the dirty pick-up lines and seedy glances, but the tips were better than a week of waitressing. They had both made over $100 that evening, and Freya was already imagining the sewing paraphernalia she was going to spend the money on.

Outside the blue glow of the club, Freya was too aware of her bare thighs prickling in the cold air. Just a few more blocks and they would be safe and sound, wrapped up in blankets and eating grilled cheese sandwiches.

The men came out of nowhere. Freya felt their cold hands on her, before registering their balaclava-clad faces. Pushing, pulling, tugging her to the ground. Her whole body froze as hands groped under the hem of her skirt.

An animal-like scream in the distance, which only after a few seconds Freya realized was her own. '*Help! Somebody help!*'

She bucked and twisted as she wrestled one hand free and pulled out her wallet. 'Here! Take this! And my watch, please, just let me go.' A fair trade, a few material possessions for her dignity, her life. Miraculously, it worked.

'Freya, *no*!' Kate cried, a fierce rage on her face. They both knew it was the only money she had.

The attacker's grip loosened as he moved to grab the wallet where she'd tossed it to the side and she used his momentum to push him off her and broke free.

'Fuck this shit. Freya, run, *now*!' Kate screamed, the other attacker still holding her pinned from behind, as she kicked at him with her heel.

'What?'

'RUN! And don't look back.'

Shock, fear, and something primal made her turn and run. Kate was always the stronger one, the leader. She had to have a plan.

Shouts echoed through the trees. What the fuck are they doing to her? She remembered her phone in her pocket and dialed 911 with a shaking finger.

'Excuse me, hi, we have an emergency. We were attacked in the park, my friend is still there . . . yes, sorry, I will slow down . . .'

As she spoke, the shouting ceased. The park fell silent. She heard the staggered sound of the men fumbling out the park, the one giving a final shout, '*You crazy fucking bitch!*'

Then, footsteps behind her.

'Hang up the phone!' Kate said, breathing heavily. There was mud all over her face and her skirt was torn.

'But?'

'It's fine, I took care of it.' The words sounded so casual, even though there were tears streaming down her face.

'Kate –' she suddenly felt very ill – 'what did you do?'

She glanced down at Kate's hands then, white-cold fingers gripping her shoes. Those treacherous cheap patent black stilettos that looked more like torture devices. The heel of one was covered in blood.

'I fought back.'

Chapter 71

Freya
The night of the murder

The street before her winds and tumbles. Freya laughs hysterically as she trips up the stairs and struggles with the keys into her apartment. How much champagne did she have to drink, one bottle, two? The tartness of scallion lingers on her tongue from the tray of cold snacks on the boardroom table. She felt hungrier than she had in a long time and had polished off a plate to herself.

She barely makes it to the bathroom before she is sick. Scenes flash behind her eyes. Jay grabbing her waist and pulling her to him, a dance-off, her strangled karaoke rendition of Katy Perry's 'Firework'. She thought she could handle her alcohol, but she was wrong.

She thrashes under the covers, exhausted but unable to go to sleep. The light of the occasional car driving by dances on the ceiling. She hurls herself towards her phone, sends Jay a dirty message saying all the things she wants to do to him. It's not her, she's playing a role, but maybe it's a woman she wants to be one day, a woman she is becoming. Something about tonight – the thrill of the deadline, the wanting in Jay's eyes – makes her feel bold, powerful.

She gets up and goes to the kitchen. Maybe a glass of water will help the mania crawling under her skin.

Kate appears by her side, rubbing her eyes. 'Christ, you sure know how to make a racket when you're tipsy.'

'Sorry, I'm a bit wound up.'

The positive mood that overcame her has been replaced by a dark, uneasy sense that she went too far tonight, and revealed too much of herself. The reality of Nicole's hatred for her feels unbearable and immovable. She has a hopeless sense that no matter how much time and training Julian invests in her, she will never go far in the company with Nicole constantly tripping her up.

She tells Kate about Nicole's antics, the computer screen, the advert, the sick, provocative words. It felt so logical at the time, the only solution to get her revenge. It has been an excruciatingly hard few months. Her breakdown, inevitable.

Kate nods, quietly. 'I understand why you did it. Nicole deserves payback.'

Suddenly, Freya can't quite breathe. 'But if someone shows up at her house, and Nicole finds out I was involved, my future at Atypical is over! Even if I'm not fired, she will make my life a living hell.'

They stand in silence, listening to Freya loudly gulp the last of her water. Kate looks deep in thought. Out of the two of them, she is always the calmest.

'Hang on a minute,' she says, grabbing Freya's cellphone. 'I have an idea.'

Chapter 72

Freya
Twenty days after the murder

Pregnant. The word has looped in her mind the past few days, the secret scorching her tongue. No word could be more definitive. The everyday early evening sounds play out in the next room. Hattie is swearing because she put too much smoked paprika in the chili con carne and she can hear Kate blustering through the door. The smell wafting through the room makes her sick with hunger. It's the type of scene that Freya assumed would play out, undisturbed, for many years to come.

Her hands are shaky, her thoughts unhinged as they churn over the information. She had a plan for her life, a sequence of events that she had followed diligently up until this point. Study, do well, get a great job. She worked hard and wanted to reap the benefits. She has always believed that the world opens up to the hard workers, not necessarily the ones blessed with talent. Sure, she wanted love, in whatever form that took, but she imagined settling down in her mid-thirties. She dreamed of being a company director by then, with the money and reputation to take time off. She had always tried to do everything in her power not to repeat her mother's past.

Pregnant, with the child of a cheat, and a man who has been accused of murder, and who has subsequently been released. Pregnant, while someone out there knows where she lives, and has begun to follow her. Is the man who tried to push her into her own house and attack her, the same one who has her new number? And how exactly did he get it? There are only two people who she knows that are smart enough to install a tracking device on a cellphone, Jay or Julian. Jay keeps on begging her for a meeting, so it can't be him, so could it be Julian? Lately she has noticed a darker side to him, one that makes her nervous.

She terrorizes herself by reading research studies on the cost of motherhood on a woman's career. Her mind runs the sums. As good as her current salary is, she wouldn't be able to pay for daycare, rent and support a child on her own.

The feeling of arriving before your time never goes away. You never quite feel welcome. You never exhale and settle into your skin. There is an urgency pushing you forward, a desperation to prove yourself worthy of your place. All she has ever wanted is to feel truly accepted. That was Freya's burden to bear. While she has always wanted a child, she hoped she would have figured out more of her own life before that child came.

Her phone flashes. It's another message from an unknown number.

I'm standing on the sidewalk looking at your apartment. There are condoms in my pocket – and a knife.

'Fuck. Off!' she screams, throwing the phone across her bedroom. She buries her head in her pillow, screaming continuously, the screams catching in her throat, becoming sobs.

All three of her friends burst into the room. Jasmin grips her fighting body, with arms that are much stronger than they let on.

'Freya honey, what's wrong? Talk to us, please!'

How did she get here? Will her testimony help convict the man she loved and future father of her child? Does she keep this baby and risk a life of never quite giving it enough, or does she make it all go away?

She first shows her friends the message. 'It's another message. The guy is outside right now. I think it's the same one from yesterday.'

Kate pulls out her phone. 'We're calling the police, right now.' She shouts out the window. 'You hear that! I'm calling the fucking cops!'

Freya looks at the worried faces of her friends. 'Someone out there knows what I did.'

Hattie, ever the practical one, asks, 'Could someone have read Nicole's advert online and copied it?'

'But how would they have guessed that Jay and I were behind it? And the other day, when the cop went online he couldn't find the thing. I didn't delete it, and I don't think Jay did either. He wasn't nearly as worried as I was.'

Freya starts crying again.

'Her death wasn't your fault,' says Jasmin, gently.

'How do you know that?'

She gives her a hug. 'Because I know you're a good soul, Freya. You've just got tangled in a really awful, complicated situation.'

Hattie says calmly, 'Do you want us to come with you when you submit these messages to the police tonight? You have enough evidence to show that this advert is a risk to your safety.'

Freya runs her hands over her belly, still flat, still innocent. Dries her eyes.

'There's something else . . .' The friends look down in the direction of her hands.

Hattie's eyes widen. 'No!'

Jasmin holds her hand, 'Oh, Freya . . . is it Jay's?'

'Of course it's Jay's!'

Smoke wafts around them. The chilli is burning. Nobody stands up to turn it off, nobody moves.

'Fuck. *Fuck!*' Kate says, her voice now cold.

Freya sighs. 'The last thing I need is you saying I told you so.'

'We'll fix it, OK? I'll take time off work and we can go to the clinic together.'

Freya can't imagine waking up, getting dressed and filling in a form at an abortion clinic. There is still time, she assures herself, she doesn't need to make a decision just yet.

Her friends trickle out of the room and she lies on the bed with her new, exhausted body. A mother. A target.

Her phone flashes again. Who is it now? But it's only that journalist Isla, asking her for coffee again.

Freya manages a smile, despite herself. This is just what she needs. A new friend, an ally, someone more qualified to get to the bottom of this constant assault of attention. Maybe if they work together, one aspect of her life will start to make sense.

A cold panic grips Freya as she enters the station.

'Hi there, Freya, isn't it?'

She recognizes the burly cop's face instantly. 'Detective Cohen? We spoke the last time I came in?'

He reads between the lines. 'It feels like I'm always here,' he laughs. 'How can I help you this evening?'

His assured presence calms her. She shouldn't have worried.

'I'm going to start at the beginning,' she says.

Freya hands over her phone, and flips through the screenshots of each message.

He looks at her, confused.

'You don't know any of these guys?'

Freya shakes her head. She watches his face for a reaction.

'Bastards,' he mumbles under his breath, 'they don't understand the word no. Can you email all of these to me so I can print them and get them on file? We'll open a new statement.'

Freya then pulls up the new crop of messages. 'These latest messages have become threatening. The number is hidden, but I think it's the same person. There's a man, too, who keeps appearing outside my house.'

'That's harassment, pure and simple. Can you describe him to me?'

'Tall, mousey-brown hair, caucasian and quite thin. The last time, he arrived and left on a bike.'

'And the nature of his threats?'

'Physical. Sexual. Like the men in the messages before, he seems to think I asked for it.'

'I'm going to organize an officer to patrol the area around your apartment until we get to the bottom of this.'

I'm outside your door, when are you going to let me in?

I can see you through the window. Great ass you got, even better than the pictures.

I see you left your window open for me. I'm going to climb inside while you are sleeping.

Her hands travel to her belly.

'Please, I have no idea what he is going to do next.'

Chapter 73

Isla
Twenty days after the murder

If Isla has one thing going for her, it's persistence. From the time she was a little girl, her mother used to grip her shoulders and say, 'Us Davis women are not quitters.' It helped her conquer her Attention Deficit Disorder enough to excel in English at school, and, when things got really dark after *the incident*, it kept her going to the end of her journalism degree. Sometimes, when nothing seems to be working, you just need to push a little harder.

Isla searches Julian's name online again. Seven pages in, and still nothing. Ten pages, twelve. Amid the chorus of praise, she finds one odd note, buried deep. She would have missed it if she hadn't obsessively visited every single page that featured Julian's name. It appears on a poorly designed personal blog with a stock-standard header and type that reads a bit too big. The site is called, 'My Startup Life'. The article, is titled, 'Why I am filing a sexual harassment charge against Atypical, and Julian Cox.'

The article begins with a paragraph that makes Isla shiver: 'I have no vested interest in reporting a sexual harassment incident. If anything, this could ruin my promising career. But I have made peace with the consequences. My peace of mind is far more important.'

The story is emotional and jumps around. Isla can feel the heat rising from the words. They are taut, muscular, sweat-stained, ready to fight. This was a woman who had decided to stand her ground. In between the ranting phrases, a story starts to take shape. The young woman, Jess, started out at Atypical as an intern. Atypical was the ideal company, and Julian was the dream boss. He was a bit physical sometimes, a bit of a hugger, but there was nothing she could put her finger on at first. After a few months of working there, Julian invited her into his office at the end of a long day to discuss career opportunities. He offered to give her a massage, which she turned down. He said he had trained in tantric massage, and she refused again. Finally, he suggested that, if they were to have sex that night, her career would benefit in return. When she said no, he harassed her over text message repeatedly, and with slurring phone calls in the middle of the night.

Isla wraps her arms around herself, as she reads the same two sentences over and over.

'I know nobody will believe me. Julian is perfect, a phi-lanthropist and I am barely out of college, but I have to put this out there. I don't care what happens, but if I can warn one woman, then I will feel like something good came out of all of this.'

The comments are brutal. The online trolls found the blog post and showed no mercy.

You're delusional – you wish Julian was interested in you.

What makes you think you have the right to drag Julian Cox's name through the mud? You are nothing, and after this, you will continue to be nothing.

There is also the more subtle:

Are you sure you didn't do anything to make him think you were interested? A man doesn't just hit on a woman out of nowhere.

Isla laughs out loud at that one. She has been hit on in the doctor's waiting room, in the grocery store, while taking out the trash and at a late-night pizza joint. Men are experts at hitting on women out of nowhere.

She clicks on the 'About Me' page. The woman's name is Jess Fisher. She describes herself as an 'Internet junkie, cupcake addict and general busybody'. Her earlier blog posts are excited reviews of new online gaming products and coding trends. General wide-eyed, innocent geekery. This was an enthusiast, someone who took pleasure in working hard and toeing the line, unless something forced her not to.

Isla opens a new search window. Types in the name Jess Fisher. The website was last updated three years ago, at the time of her sexual harassment post. A part of her hopes that Jess has excelled since then, and risen through the ranks at another tech company. Hell, she needs a good news story right now. Hopefully, Isla can pay her a visit and hear the truth about Julian firsthand. But, as she clicks through page after page, another fear in her is confirmed.

Apart from the old entries on her blog, there is no other mention of Jess. According to the Internet, she no longer exists.

Chapter 74

Freya
Twenty-one days after the murder

Tuesday morning and Jay is back, walking around the office as if nothing has happened at all. Freya can't look at him, but she can hear his voice bellowing a greeting to others. At least she has her own office to protect her. But sometime in the near future she is going to have to face him, and explain why she hasn't replied to any of his messages.

Virginie knocks on the door. 'Want a cookie?' Ever since she warned Freya about Jay, she has been overly sweet, as if trying to make up for her strong words about him. Even though Freya pressed her further, she still doesn't quite understand the animosity she feels toward Jay. 'I made them myself last night. I may have put too many choc chips inside.'

'You say that like it wasn't intentional.'

'You know me too well, Freya.' She holds a cookie in her direction. 'So, would you like one?' The sugar grazes the inside of Freya's nostrils, she's unable to bear the smell of it.

'No thanks, I'm fine at the moment.'

Virginie cocks her head in the direction of the board-room. 'And are you fine about Jay being back?'

'Of course not, but I'm trying to just focus on my work and stay out of his way.'

'After what he's done, he should stay out of *my* way,' Virginie says.

Freya swallows slowly and turns her focus back to her screen. She doesn't have morning sickness as such, but more an all-day queasiness. She can't stomach anything solid. Even if she wanted to deny the fact that she is pregnant, her body won't let her forget.

Kate hasn't eased up on her campaign to 'take care of it'. She has found every opportunity to confront her. 'It's the wrong time, Freya, and it's definitely the wrong guy. Who knows, you probably conceived the same night he slept with Nicole.'

The final jibe was humiliating and unnecessary. Freya bristles just thinking about it. She thought that nothing could come between her and Kate, but the atmosphere in the house is prickly. They now share their meals in loaded silence.

Jasmin's assurances, slightly softer, circle her thoughts too. 'You will be an incredible mother, when you are ready. But there is nothing wrong with opting out of a future you are not prepared for. It is OK to say, "not yet".'

But she can't bring herself to leave the office and take the bus to the clinic. There is a strange comfort in not deciding, in being caught between two worlds.

She paces quickly through the office to the bathroom, and splashes her face with water. Anything to feel a little less queasy. She applies and reapplies her lip-gloss in the mirror, wondering if anyone can see in her face that she is keeping a secret.

'You're hiding from him, aren't you?' It's Melanie, Nicole's closest friend. Since Nicole's death, she has spent most of her working days staring Freya down. This is the longest sentence she has ever spoken to her, and it catches Freya off guard.

'Uh . . . excuse me?'

For the first time, Freya notices that Melanie is showing signs of strain. Her lips are chapped, and a tight, strained bun draws attention to her bloodshot eyes. There is a fragility present that Freya has never encountered before.

Melanie reaches out and touches her arm. 'It's OK. You must be really hurting right now. You're *so* young – how were you to know that Jay was such a cheat?'

It's not rational, but Freya feels angry. After all these women have done to her and now they try and reach out? Melanie stood back and watched every day while Nicole victimized her, she is just as guilty as Nicole was. She has no time for her smugness disguised as empathy.

'I'm a big girl, I'll be fine,' she says bitterly. 'I don't need anyone's pity.'

Melanie doesn't look shocked or surprised, but calm. Kind even. 'This is not pity, Freya. It's simply one woman reaching out to another.'

Freya can't hold it in anymore. 'Well, I could have used that a few months ago when Nicole made every moment of my time here a living hell.' She's surprised at how ragged her voice sounds.

'Listen, I'm sorry about all of that, OK? Nicole was so, so angry at Jay, and we were angry too. How would you feel if someone screwed over one of your best friends so much that they were never the same afterwards?'

Freya thinks back to that time Jasmin was so in love with a man who turned out to be sleeping with a woman working the bar at their local club. They called her a man-eater behind her back, and listed with vitriol all the ways she had lured him into her bed. That was easier, somehow, than admitting that he had never truly loved Jasmin all along.

'I get that. But it doesn't mean it wasn't wrong, or it didn't hurt. I'm a good person, Melanie. I'd only been here a few minutes before she decided to bully me.'

Melanie moves closer to Freya now, close enough for her to smell the sweetness of chamomile tea on her breath.

'I know it's hard to see right now, but Nicole was a good person too, the best. You two were quite similar, and might have been friends in another life. What she did to you was completely out of character and it spun out of control. You know what that feels like, surely?'

The last sentence catches at Freya like a sharp thorn.

'Did she love him?' she asks, voice shaking.

Melanie looks at her frankly. 'More than she ever loved anyone. They shared a deep relationship and a workplace. She was convinced that she had met her soulmate. There was a *plan*, you know? When they broke up after two years together, she couldn't get a hold of herself again, she was devastated.'

Freya does the math. Nicole worked at Atypical for three years, Jay, just under two and a half. If they were together for two years, it means that Freya arrived on the scene mere months after their breakup.

The lights in the bathroom suddenly seem too bright, the smell of disinfectant harsh. Here she thought that the dinners, long-winding walks and impassioned discussions were adding up to something. Naïvely, she imagined herself to be the protagonist in this story, the great love that Jay had been looking for all along. Nicole was supposed to be the other woman, the unfortunate diversion before he met the real thing. But Kate had been right about him.

Shame wracks her like a fever as she remembers how self-righteous she'd felt, how justified she'd thought she was in meddling with Nicole's life that night.

Then, she recalls meeting Jay's eyes after they played the prank. They were wild with the adrenaline of a man who had just pulled the trigger, excited at the chain reaction that had been set off. What kind of man would deliberately hurt the woman he had once loved, and still have sex with her after he had done it? Did the betrayal turn him on?

Her phone buzzes inside her coat.

I want to push you down, and make you scream.

Chapter 75

Freya
Twenty-two days after the murder

A slim, discreet black box tied with a red ribbon is delivered to her office.

'Someone got lucky,' the spectacled receptionist quips. Freya turns to see if Jay is watching her. Of course he is watching her. Ever since he returned to the office, he won't stop emailing her and asking her to meet.

Freya goes to the quiet of her desk. She feels his gaze follow her. She tugs the ribbon loose, and unpeels the wrapping paper. Inside the cardboard box is a set of handcuffs, a velvet blindfold and something she can't quite identify. She calls Virginie to her desk. 'What are these?'

'They're nipple clamps, what else!' she says, 'Ooh la la, Freya, I like this new side of you. I'm glad you're moving on from Jay and getting the attention you deserve.'

'I . . .' She pauses, and decides not to voice the thought pounding at the edge of her skull. 'I've decided to experiment with my sexuality.'

'Good for you!' But she never ordered anything of the sort. There is no new boyfriend who has bought the gift for her. There was only a note that said, *You think you can stop us from being together, but you can't* attached to the box.

Then, another message on her cellphone: *I'm standing outside the window of your office waiting to see your reaction. Hope you like them xx*

She runs to the fire escape, her phone pressed hot against her cheek. She needs the privacy for this.

'Detective Cohen? I've received a package at work now.'

'OK. Who other than you has handled it?'

'Just me and our receptionist.'

'Don't touch it again, I may be able to pull some prints. I'll be at your office shortly to collect it.'

No place is safe. She now knows that the messages are coming from one anonymous man only, a man who knows where she works. When Detective Cohen arrives to collect the package she feel's Ruth's eyes on her.

'Everything OK?' she asks.

'Yes,' Freya says. 'It is now. I've been having some trouble with harassment, but the police are looking into it.'

'That's good to hear. You really have had a rough time lately, haven't you?'

Ruth is right. She's being stalked by a stranger, and the place where she works is swimming with sharks. If Jay closing in on her wasn't enough, Julian's behavior has only got more odd. She needs help.

The Head of HR, Mathilda, has bright red hair and the constantly flushed cheeks of someone under relentless stress. This is further accentuated by the unlikely pop of neon pink lipstick. Her child-like voice and gentle demeanor make her seem on the verge of reaching across and hugging Freya, or bursting into tears.

'I'm glad things are going better for you here. I heard that Nicole made your life a bit of a misery when you started a few months ago.'

It doesn't seem right to harp on about that now. 'Yes, I suppose she did.' She still bears the scars – a raised heartbeat whenever she sees Nicole's desk, a relentless number of mouth ulcers and a cynicism she didn't have six months ago.

Mathilda plays with the Hello Kitty stress ball on her desk. 'If anything like that happens again, please tell me, OK? Every person should feel comfortable here. This is *so* important to me.'

'Well, there is actually something I came to speak to you about. I've been having some trouble . . .'

What if Mathilda judges her, and asks how she got in this situation? But it could work out for the best. Mathilda could have some solutions. If Detective Cohen is working on the outside and Mathilda from the inside, she may finally feel safe.

'Go on. I'm here for you, Freya.'

A sigh of relief. 'Gosh, this is so awkward. I sometimes feel as if Julian gets a bit too close for comfort? I love how friendly he is and I appreciate our management structure, but there have been a few occasions where I have felt uncomfortable.'

The atmosphere in the room changes. Mathilda's eyes harden. 'Julian? Are you sure?'

'Yes. Listen, I don't want this to be true as much as you do.'

'Julian is a feminist. He fights for women's rights! Explain to me a bit about what happened.'

It is embarrassing to say it out loud. She explains his hand travelling below her waist, and the lingering hugs. The unasked-for massage in the boardroom.

Mathilda leans forward and gives her a hug. 'Freya, it has been such a hard time for you. From Nicole's bullying, to her death, to Jay's arrest. You have been working yourself to the bone as well. I honestly think your mind is playing tricks on you. He didn't force himself on you, did he?'

'I know what I felt . . .'

'A sexual assault allegation is *very* serious, Freya.'

She feels terrible. This is not how the conversation was meant to go. 'I just needed to tell someone . . .'

'Nobody else has complained about this the entire time Atypical has been in operation, but these things do happen. I'll make a formal note of it. Will you promise to report any more incidents directly to me, as soon as they happen?'

'Yes . . .'

'For now, go home and rest, Freya. Give yourself some time to recuperate. You are too hard on yourself.'

'But—'

And with that, the door is shut. But her unease around Julian has not been resolved, Jay walks free in the office, the messages keep lighting up her phone, and she can feel Mathilda's eyes watching her closely, carefully, as she packs up for the day and goes home.

Chapter 76

Isla
Twenty-three days after the murder

Everybody is innocent, everybody is guilty. Something has got to break through the cracks.

Freya has agreed to meet again. Her striking jacket detracts from the dark circles under her eyes.

'Nice jacket.'

'Thanks!'

'I think I've seen you in something similar before?'

She fiddles with the sleeves. 'It's the same one. I had sewed some lace in here before, but then I had to pick it out after an incident with Nicole. That's why there is some loose stitching still. The lace was ruined beyond repair.'

'Well, it looks great on you, brings out the color of your eyes.'

'Thank you.'

'How are you feeling about the case?'

'I don't know what to believe anymore,' she says, pouring various sauces over a large toasted burrito.

'You're still certain it wasn't Jay?'

'Yes, but some days I second-guess myself.' She crosses her arms and hugs herself protectively. 'You should have seen his face after we played that prank. He got off on it.

But then my mind goes back to him lying in bed with me in the early hours of the next morning. It had to have been someone else.'

'Like the person sending you those messages . . .'

'He has been coming to my house, and now my office. The threats have got violent. Since I changed my number, I don't think there's a lot of men still responding to this advert; I think it is one man who is stalking me.'

'Have you told the police?'

'Yes,' says Freya, between bites of her burrito, 'I reported it to Detective Cohen, and gave him a package that was dropped off at my office. He's hoping to pull some finger-prints off it.'

Isla touches her hair, self-consciously. 'I know him. He's one of the good guys.'

'He's been great, so helpful.' She says it with a neutral expression, as if this is simply a fact. But Isla's heart won't stop pounding at the mention of his name.

Focus on the story. Could a murderer be summoned from the depths of the Internet and kill for no reason at all? Isla doesn't mention the details she has seen in the case file, or the witness accounts of that night and Nicole's laughter. The man Freya is describing sounds too strange to elicit that sort of reaction from Nicole, so late at night. She returns to the sequence of events, in order to make sense of things.

'How do you think Jay managed to sleep with Nicole that night?'

Freya looks close to tears. 'I have no idea. He came to find me at the office party, we drank together and he walked me home but dropped me around the corner, saying he had left something at the office, so he must have gone straight to Nicole's then. Later on, he returned to mine.'

Isla thinks back to ten years before, to the shock of waking up, bruised and covered in her own blood, reaching desperately for lost time. She was a party girl then, she was used to getting blackout drunk. But the feeling after the attack was different. While it took a few months for all the memories to return, she was consumed with an animal-like agony and unnamed despair, the sense that something terrible had happened.

'Freya, do you think you have had any memory loss? Could you have been drugged?'

She turns pale. 'No, no definitely not. I remember everything. Clearly.'

Maybe she had too much hanging on her hunch about what Freya witnessed, maybe this was all a waste of time. She tries a different tack.

'What about your boss, Julian? Besides the IT support team, he is the only person who would have access to your work computer and your phone number,' she suggests.

Freya stops eating, and looks her dead in the eye. 'Do you know something?'

Isla looks down at Freya's hands. They're shaking. 'No . . . but tell me what you mean?'

'It's not my fault!' she says, her voice rising enough that the patrons look over curiously. 'And I swear, I am not imagining things. Julian has touched me a few times, in a way that was definitely intended to be sexual. I can't stop thinking about it.'

'Freya, this is big. If he did that to you in the workplace, surely he could take it a step further, hiding behind an anonymous number?'

'So you believe me? It's so hard to say this about Julian, because everybody thinks he is perfect.' Her voice quivers, on the verge of tears.

'Of course I believe you!'

'Mathilda, the head of HR, says I've just gone through a hard time and I'm imagining things. I started to wonder this myself. Julian is really affectionate, and such a placid person. He does yoga, and he's a card-carrying Buddhist.' She starts laughing. 'He literally has a card with his Buddhist membership number on it in his wallet.'

Isla thinks back to the enthusiastic article she read in the very paper she works for. It crowned Julian as the kind-hearted savior the tech-industry needs. There are no gods in this town, only mortals. Julian and Kenneth are up to something, that meeting they had in the restaurant confirms it. And a sexual predator doesn't strike only once. Could there be more sexual harassment cases that they are trying to squash? Could Nicole have been one of them, one that took a deadly turn? And what of Jess, the young woman who shared her story three years ago and has now seemingly disappeared off the face of the earth? This is more than a random incident, it is a pathology.

'This may be an insensitive question to ask after all you have been through, but are you friends with anyone who was close with Nicole?'

Freya smiles weakly. 'I couldn't have answered that a few weeks ago, but I have actually started talking to Melanie, one of Nicole's best friends. She's much nicer than I imagined! I wouldn't call us friends, but we have begun to chat every now and then.'

'Next time you see her, could you ask her if Nicole ever mentioned Julian making any sexual advances on her?'

Freya shifts in her seat. 'I don't think I like where you're going with this. He didn't try to rape to me, or anything. It was just a moment, a few seconds where I felt he went too far. It was probably nothing. I can't afford to be making any false accusations right now . . .'

It's heartbreakingly typical. After an initial moment of boldness, Freya has talked herself out of her predicament and is denying her instincts. Isla wishes she could grip her by the shoulders and say, hold on! Stop beating yourself up for no reason. One day, you will get past all of this, and it will be better than you ever imagined. Instead, she asks for the check and watches her walk away.

Isla steels herself for a long afternoon ahead in the office under the watchful eye of her boss. Then, she has an idea . . .

Chapter 77

Freya
Twenty-four days after the murder

Friday afternoon, 3 p.m. Freya can't focus.

Another picture from an unknown number. It is of an empty, four-poster bed, covered in plastic sheeting with a set of handcuffs attached to each corner. Along with it, a message saying, *I've got some surprises in store for you. I'm going to do all the things you told me about.*

Freya sends the screenshots to Detective Cohen, along with the message, *Please find him.*

She can't get comfortable in her office chair. It is as if someone is twisting a knife at the base of her spine. Old muscle cramps from the days of sleeping in her car are aching back to life. She refuses to research anything about pregnancy and body changes – it would make the situation more real – but she's pretty sure the baby is the reason.

Melanie catches her eye through the glass partition of her office and they share a 'can this day end' smile. This budding friendship still feels alien to Freya, she keeps looking over her shoulder expecting to meet Nicole's angry gaze.

'Hey, Melanie?'

'Call me Mel,' she says, buffing her nails with a polka dot nail file.

'Would you like to go for a drink after work? There's a new cocktail bar that's opened in Valencia Street. It's got a mid-century glam feel about it, apparently.'

Freya can see that, with her retro-styled shift dress and pinup hairdo, this is music to Mel's ears.

'Give me a second and I'll pack my things. Nobody's gonna notice if we slip out early.'

At the bar, Mel orders a Beehive, an aromatic cocktail of botanist gin, honey, lemon and salt.

'God, this is sublime. Do you want a taste?'

Freya tries to calm herself and keep a poker face. Would Mel judge her if she knew that she was pregnant? Would she be shocked to know that Freya is contemplating keeping the baby?

'No, you enjoy it. I'm going to stick with my vodka, soda, lime here,' she says, swirling her glass of lemonade.

The menu has a selection of fondues on offer, and they order the one with aged cheddar cheese and bites of sourdough bread. The food is comforting, and the act of sharing it makes it easier to open up.

Mel is giggly and warm, the kind of social drunk who hugs after every sentence. She tries to match her new friend's exuberance, while not letting on that she is still completely sober.

'Freya, you are so much fun! I wish we had become friends before.'

Me too, Freya thinks. Me too.

'I know, right? Working at Atypical is crazy. I could have done with the moral support!' She darts around the main reason she needed moral support in the first place. Nicole.

'Moral support is definitely required in this office! From the socially awkward development guys who can't look you in the eye, to Jay, it really is a minefield out there.'

'Tell me about it.' Freya pauses. 'By the way, Mel, have you ever experienced any weird behavior from Julian? Like, has he ever felt a little close for comfort?'

She pushes her red lips into a grimace. 'Hah, now you are officially part of the Atypical team. It's shocking when it first happens, isn't it?'

'It's happened to you?'

'Of course, and Nicole, and many other women who work here. Nobody says anything because it's hard for the mind to process, I guess. He is the perfect boss until . . . his eyes linger on you a bit longer than is comfortable, or his hand moves onto your waist, or your ass. But I can't really speak for the other women, as I didn't get the worst of it.'

'What do you mean?' she says, heart pounding.

'Well, it was an open secret that Julian had a thing for Nicole. He would message her relentlessly, and then abruptly block her number. Once, on a funding trip, he followed her back to her hotel room. You know, standard pestering horny boss stuff.'

Freya suddenly feels dizzy.

'I think that "standard pestering" should be renamed "sexual harassment". Why didn't she say anything?'

'She tried, but HR just slotted her into this long reporting process which took ages to resolve. Nicole told me once that she believed that HR thought she was lying. She was going through some personal issues at the time of her complaint, and a bipolar diagnosis doesn't exactly add to one's credibility.'

Mel looks different now, her face is pale. An unspoken realization takes shape between them.

Freya grabs her hands. 'He did something to me too. It wasn't a coincidence. Neither of you were imagining things.' A new understanding falls into place. She recalls those early conversations in Julian's office, where he tilted his head suggestively toward Nicole, when he uttered the word 'gossip-monger'. By pitting smart women against each other, they were unable to work together. Which was perfect for Julian, as they couldn't compare notes.

'HR told Julian, you know. He did not react well to the accusations at all – he called it a character attack,' Mel adds. 'After that, I couldn't help but notice that he knew every little thing about Nicole, from her favorite food to which Soul Cycle classes she attended on the weekend. It was like he was spying on her.'

The information jolts Freya to attention. Julian has always known a little too much, from the moment he welcomed her to Atypical with her personalized gifts. Could he have been spying on her too? And could he have known the exact moment when she changed her phone number, and what she changed it to?

Will she share this new development with Isla? Or – dare she imagine it – with Detective Cohen? Will she become the woman who makes a scene, with all the risk that it involves? It could ruin Julian's career, and his revolutionary technology may never make it to the women who need it most. Is she really prepared for the consequences that come with sharing her discomfort?

But then, beneath the flashing neon bar sign and the All-American retro décor, Mel leans forward and whispers, 'I know at least five other women who have stories too, and I think they'll finally be ready to talk.'

Chapter 78

Isla
Twenty-seven days after the murder

Isla pages through yesterday's paper, only to find another article on Julian Cox, written by her colleague, Lauren Chambers.

'So it's OK for Lauren to visit Atypical, but not me?' she mutters to herself. But then, she sees why.

Julian Cox – My private agony
by Lauren Chambers

In this interview, I go behind the scenes with Julian Cox, founder and CEO of Atypical. What I discovered was the unexpected fragility of one of San Francisco's most respected businessmen.

How is Atypical going, Julian? Any news to share?

Yes! We are about to launch our ground-breaking technology across villages in Kenya and Tanzania. Soon, underprivileged women will have instant access to medical supplies and professional help.

The plight of women is a particular concern for you. Is there any reason for this?

Well, with so much inequality and violence towards women, it is the duty of men to use their skills and do all in their power to raise them up.

This violence has occurred quite close to home recently, hasn't it?

Unfortunately, yes. One of our treasured staff members was sadly attacked in her own home, resulting in fatality. Obviously situations like these are out of my control, but it does make my mission all the more personal.

Had you experienced violence against women before in your own life?

(Wipes a tear from his cheek.) Yes, and it shaped my entire life path. My stepfather was extremely physically abusive to my mother, and sometimes to me as well. He once beat her so badly that she was hospitalized for a week to heal from her injuries. In that week, he did things to me that are . . . uh . . . very hard to discuss. Once you are violated in a certain way, it changes you. Either you shrink into yourself completely, or you get out there and try and help others where you can.

So the abuse in your past played a role in founding Atypical?

Absolutely. If I can ensure that one person gets well thanks to my technology, and that all mothers and future mothers get access to the appropriate care they need, then I will feel as if I have done something important with my life, however broken it may be. Deep down, I think I am trying to do right by my own mother.

Do you think your critics will be surprised at this informa-tion?

I'm not sure, but I hope they will be moved. No matter what anyone thinks of my actions or the recent tragedy that has befallen my company, I hope that they see that Atypi-cal is essentially just the manifestation of a dream, and that dream sprang from my own pain and vulnerability.

For more on Atypical's mission statement and their latest project, you can access their YouTube channel here.

The positive profile seems a little too convenient. It smacks of a pre-emptive defense strategy.

It wouldn't be the first time that a corporate magnate was accused of sexual harassment. Looking back on her inter-actions with Julian, she can see the signs now. The overly familiar manner, the incessant flattery, the small, casual omission of information. Julian edited his life to inspire others and build himself into a brand. He made Isla – and every other woman he encountered – feel special, and cho-sen. This false sense of trust was the perfect opportunity to cross the line.

It's been a few days since she saw Freya last. She won-ders if she has managed to speak to her colleague yet. She doesn't want to harass her, but she picks up the phone anyway.

No reply. Strange, she normally answers Isla immedi-ately. After her last conversation about that stranger circling her house, she hopes Freya is safe.

She tries Simon.

'Hey, Simon! Any news on Nicole's case?'

'No can do, I've been taken off it.'

Isla's frustration arches and shifts into desperation. 'What, why?'

'My boss didn't say. But it seems like an investigator from another district wanted to get involved. I'm focusing on Freya now. It turns out I was able to pull some prints from the gift she received at the office.'

'And?'

'They match a suspect who has been charged before with three separate incidents of stalking and harassment.' It conflicts with Isla's current theory, but it makes sense nonetheless.

'Has he ever . . .'

'Killed anyone? No. But he uses personal adverts to find his victims. Once he has made contact he ramps it up, sending gifts, calling at strange hours and sending threatening messages.'

Could he have used the same method to find Nicole as well? But who posed as Freya in the first place?

'So he didn't post the advert?'

'No, it doesn't look like it. Besides, our tech team has found the personal advert written in Freya's name on TheSpark.com. They traced the posting to an IP address within the Atypical building.'

Within the building. So it *could* be someone who knew what Freya and Jay did, and someone who was perhaps a little angry at their blossoming relationship. It could be someone like Julian.

'I can't believe it!' she says.

'Crazy, right? We don't know whose it is yet, though.'

'Can I ask you one more favor? Do you have access to Nicole's computer records from the night?'

'I do, but you know that it has been marked as classified information in the case file. I'm not allowed to share it with the press.'

'Why?'

'We discovered some unusual activity, something that the team has reported on and is still looking into. I can't share such a sensitive, active element of the investigation, especially now that I have been taken off the case.'

'Please, Simon, it's just a formality. What could she possibly have to hide? She was the victim! It's not like the whole case will come crashing down.'

She hears Simon biting his thumbnail. 'It's illegal. Remember, I work in law enforcement, Isla.'

'Only if you tell.' She feels guilty exploiting Simon's friendship and a small part of her feels a bit dirty for pushing his limits like this, but she's too far into chasing this story now. She will do anything to get to the bottom of it.

'Fine, pick up a flash drive from me this afternoon. I'll be waiting outside.'

When she sputters past the station in her car, Isla ignores Simon's loaded look and she takes the flash drive out of his hands. She doesn't let the ache in her heart spread as his hand lingers on hers.

She ignores the alarm bells ringing in her ears when she inserts it into her office laptop in the early evening, hours after Kenneth has packed up and gone home. The drive to find what she is searching for is too great.

She picks The Smashing Pumpkins as her soundtrack and starts trawling through the information. Isla is always amazed at how many websites a person touches in an average day. Minute by minute, we leave our grubby fingerprints all over the Internet, drawing a winding path for ourselves based on the slightest whims. On that day alone, Nicole had interrupted her workload to look up the lyrics to a song, and searched for 'the perfect basil and tomato pasta sauce'.

Heartbreakingly, she had also Googled 'what to do when you are still in love with your ex'. Jay really had sunk his claws into Freya and Nicole. Both deserved better.

Then, as Freya mentioned, she sees the URL for the dating site in the search history some time later. This must have been when Nicole had left her desk, and was enjoying herself at the office party. Next in the history, a page entitled 'New Advert'. In black and white, it all looks so innocuous. It is hard to imagine Freya and Jay hopping behind her unmanned laptop, pretending to be a darker, dirtier version of Nicole.

Isla looks for a copy of the advert itself – she wants to confirm what it says. Maybe she takes the act of writing too seriously, but she's hoping that she will find a clue in the wording that will lead her to the truth of what happened that night. Instead, she finds something more definitive.

She rereads the page several times to be sure she has understood it correctly. If this is really true, then everything changes. 'Advert not published. Cellphone authorization not granted.'

This particular page is highlighted in the corresponding police report, with a reference back to Freya's second statement and an action item to call her and inform her that the advert was never sent.

Of course! You can't simply publish anything online these days. There are checks and balances, hoops to jump through. Before publishing, the website automatically sent through a text message to confirm Nicole's identity, a test that Freya and Jay could never have passed because it would have been sent directly to her cellphone. It also means that on the night, Nicole would have known that somebody was trying to pose as her online.

Freya had been torturing herself for no reason, because no advert was ever published in Nicole's name. The only person who could have known what they were trying to do enough to mimic it would have had to have been someone on the inside.

Chapter 79

Freya
Twenty-seven days after the murder

The riot of red flowers on Freya's doorstep is as shocking as a splatter of fresh blood. Her throat closes. She approaches them tentatively. If they are from the man who has been circling her, he may be nearby.

Her hands feel for the pepper spray she now carries in her purse. As she picks the flowers up and smells them, silence. No fingers suddenly clasping around her neck. No heavy breathing. She is alone.

The flowers have been wrapped in delicate layers of tissue paper and tied with a satin bow. There must be three dozen in here. The effect is elegant. When she opens it, she realizes the card has been bought from the California Museum of Sciences with an illustration of the cosmos on the front. Jay.

She pauses for a second and closes her eyes, letting the warm sunlight caress her face. These small moments in nature are the only thing able to calm her. She is no closer to feeling safe, even though Detective Cohen is doing his best to track her stalker. Work is not going well either. Over the past week, Ruth's patience with her has begun to wear thin. Between comments such as 'You look so tired', and

'Are you sure everything is OK?' she's beginning to wonder if Ruth can instinctively sense the secret brewing within her. She's coming up to six weeks – no risk of showing, but she fears that everything that matters shows in her face.

A voice behind her that she recognizes instantly.

'You can't keep running from me forever, Freya.'

She's heard that line before. Then she sees him, head bowed, but a familiar face. Adrenaline pulses through her veins.

'Jay . . .'

'Glad to see your habits haven't changed. A run around the park, a smoothie at Jenny's Health Foods and then a shower at home,' he says, glossing over the situation with his trademark cockiness.

Those soulful eyes that once captivated Freya now appear jaded. His casual demeanor now seems subversive.

'You should go.' She puts the pepper spray away, turns and starts unlocking the door. This morning's run was a bit too far, and her legs are starting to shake.

He steps in front of her. 'Please, just join me for breakfast. Please? You could hear my side of the story at least?'

It's the words *at least* that tug at her. She could listen to him. She is carrying his child after all. Her statement alerted him to the police in the first place. There is also a part of her that, after everything that has happened, wants to see him beg. Maybe then she'll stop crying at night, maybe then she'll stop missing him. Stronger than her pride is the need to know that he is hurting as much as she is.

'Fine, but I'm only staying for a juice.' It's the only physical sign she is pregnant so far, this insatiable craving for orange juice. She wonders if her mother craved the same thing, if in an alternative universe she would watch Freya drinking glass after glass and know her secret without her saying a word.

They walk to the café and sit awkwardly opposite one another. Jay is the first to break the silence.

'Freya – you've got to believe me when I say this is all a terrible misunderstanding.'

'I'm battling to see how physical evidence of you having sex with Nicole could be a misunderstanding,' she says, feeling a bit proud at her comeback. She wants to fast forward to the moment she tells Hattie, Kate and Jasmin how this all played out. She might redeem herself in Kate's eyes. This would be a welcome development as they are still, technically, not speaking.

'Tell me what really happened that night.'

'You really want to know?'

'Every sordid detail.'

He plays with the sachets of sugar in front of him, arranging them in a straight line. 'Nicole hadn't been well for a while. Psychologically, there were some challenges. You of all people know how imbalanced she was . . .'

It feels like another lifetime – the pointed stares, the whispered insults, the feeling of always being on edge. There was a sense of menace to Nicole's every move that made it difficult for Freya to breathe. It was more than office bitchiness, it pressed on a hurt deep within her. Sometimes she still wakes up in the middle of the night, composing a comeback to an argument with Nicole, finding the right words to express to her the breadth of her pain.

'That makes what you did even more disgusting.' The word sticks in her throat. 'You *knew* how she hurt me.'

His eyes soften. 'I do. And it killed me. But in a way, Nicole was suffering more. She spent some time in an institution to try and treat her borderline personality and bipolar disorder, but even that didn't help.' The waitress brings their drinks, and he waits until she is out of earshot. 'She was threatening to *kill* herself,' he whispers. 'Every day she would send me messages saying that, without me, she may as well die.' It doesn't fit. Strong, powerful Nicole on her knees for a man? But Freya cannot make assumptions. She knows what love can do.

'So that night was a sympathy fuck?' She doesn't like the acid that sears her voice, and the place of need that it bubbles from. Dammit, he mattered to her. He mattered so much! And now he's gone and ruined it all.

He looks to the floor. 'There was a lot going on that night. You were blazing bright like a sun and it got to her, Freya. Hell, it got to me. She was begging me to fuck her and there was this crazy, stupid, drunk part of me that wanted to.'

It's a cold fact that rests between them, ugly and unwanted. It was so ugly, she had no doubt it was true. Freya tries to stay strong and stop her voice from shaking. 'You needed to feel like a man again . . .'

'I'm not proud of it. Do you know how sexy you were that night? You were completely in your power, doing shit that men double your age could never understand. You are an electric current, Freya, and I get to go home with you and know you in ways nobody else will.' His eyes tug at her, pull her in deeper.

'Please, look at me. I was filled with this disgusting sense of self-sabotage that night. I think deep down, I didn't believe I deserved you. So I did the only thing I knew how. I consciously destroyed it.'

She pushes away the compliment. 'How did it feel, to fuck her?' This language isn't Freya, it's too hard. But the shock of the past few weeks has turned her to steel.

Jay takes her hand in his. Her heart starts beating loudly in her ears. She doesn't take it away. 'It felt lonely and sad. I kept picturing you.'

'And then you had the gall to come home to me . . .'

'The guilt hit me as soon as we finished. I thought that if I just lay in your arms long enough, my stupid mistake would be erased.'

His fingers lightly stroke the inside of her wrist. It hurts, and she knows it's wrong, but Freya can feel the fist of her rage unclenching. 'Did you do anything to Nicole?' she says. 'Anything . . . violent?'

'Of course not! You can't really think I killed her. I was simply in the wrong place at the wrong time. I deserve for you to hate me for what I did, but I didn't hurt Nicole.'

His hand moves to her cheek. It feels good, better than Freya expected. It wouldn't hurt to be lost in his love again, and it wouldn't hurt to feel safe.

She draws closer to him, feeling that familiar smooth skin, melting into the irresistibility of him. Her mouth opens and she lets in all of it, the chaos, the anger, the betrayal, the fear, the love. This crazy, cursed love. It's dangerous, vile, and will be her undoing. Nobody will understand. Not her friends, not Julian, not Ruth, not Isla. But she can help it no more than a plastic bag caught and dragged into the undertow of the sea.

Chapter 80

Isla
Twenty-eight days after the murder

'Morning, Kenneth.'

'Good morning, Isla. Glad to see you at work so early.'

'I am your ever-dedicated servant, my lord.' He gives her a sideways glance. She pushed it a bit too far, then. He carries on shuffling aimlessly around his desk and Isla smiles, continuing her mindless transcription of press releases. It doesn't feel so sickening faking friendliness these days, now that she knows she is on to something explosive.

A crazed stalker on the brink of arrest, a sex scandal, a potential murder suspect, justice all round. As soon as she finds enough sources to come forward, she is taking the sexual assault allegations straight to Simon. She can't wait to see his face! For now, she lives breathlessly for the day that all the pieces come together, and she rises up victorious. Kenneth's slimy brand of mediocrity that he calls journalism won't go unchallenged for long.

Kenneth's meeting with Julian was no coincidence. They are involved somehow, and they are covering something up. The picture she snapped of them together is an answer, all she has to do is confirm what the question is.

Her only door to that night is Freya, yet now she knows that the email she and Jay wrote together was never sent. No psychopath was called to Nicole's home as a result of it. Isla wants to tell Freya, and hear the relief in her voice. She also wants to revisit the incident that sparked her suspicions in the first place. She was not imagining things that morning. Now that she has met Freya a few times, held her eyes in conversation and observed the contours of her face, she is certain that she is the same woman she almost ran over the morning after Nicole was murdered. If that is truly the case, then what spooked Freya so much, that she felt the need to lie?

Yet all calls to her new number have gone unanswered. Messages are delivered, but not read.

Simon mentioned that there was an officer regularly patrolling the area around Freya's apartment, but what if the attacker slipped in while he was grabbing a coffee or in the restroom? Freya could be in danger and Simon would be none the wiser. What if he finally hurts her this time?

Isla has been distracted the past few days, with stories and the latest information in her investigation. How long has it been since she and Freya spoke? Three days? Four? Maybe even five?

She feels Kenneth's eyes on her and begins to type furiously. She must have been more lost in thought than she realized. Freya has to know about Isla's latest findings, whether she answers her phone or not. She opens up an email and types out a quick few paragraphs, listing everything she knows and how she found out. She attaches the police file, wincing briefly and the label 'classified evidence' and all it entails. Presses send. There, at least she has done something today. Hopefully Freya will call her when she gets the message.

She taps her pen on the desk in front of her. Isla can't explain why it feels like everything is riding on this, or why she needs to speak to Freya. Nothing feels more urgent, but all she can do is wait.

Chapter 81

Isla
One month after the murder

The home décor store is brightly foreboding. The potential of every item makes Isla feel panicked. How can she, with her limited budget, buy one piece that will both give her lounge an uplift and be easy to assemble? She thought this would be a good way to spend her Saturday morning, the kind of homely thing a real grown-up would do, but it's only made her more depressed. She is a thirty-one-year-old stifled journalist who can't let go of a dead-end story and spends her days sitting opposite her boss's desk. Lizzie and Mom are her closest confidantes, but they live thousands of miles away. On weekends she wafts through the city, alone.

Sometimes she wishes she had a partner to look at mundane things like desks with, or someone to share the thoughts racing through her mind. Her mind strays to the concert she saw with Simon. No, that was nothing, just two friends on the same case blowing off steam. He is probably running laps around the park with someone as fit and balanced as he is.

She has always considered herself independent, with no need for distractions like love, but her beliefs don't seem to fit her like they used to.

She walks out with nothing, as usual. Another fruitless shopping trip where she was blinded by the choice on offer.

She checks her phone, smiling at a silly meme of an alpaca in a police cap from Simon and a picture from Lizzie of the dress she's wearing to a wedding that weekend. She is introducing her Lionel Richie fan to friends and family there – it's getting serious! No messages from Freya yet. It's only 10 a.m. The day still stretches before her, tedious and empty.

Then, she sees them. His hand rests over her shoulders protectively. She looks smaller, diminished in his presence. There is a sort of love between them, but it is fragile and tentative. He kisses her with gusto and, while she returns the affection, Isla is sure she sees her pull away just a moment too soon. They could be any couple out on a fraught suburban shopping trip, trying to be happy, but they are not. Because it is Jay, playing at being a couple with another woman, and that woman is Freya.

A familiar sadness washes over her, like hearing the strains of a long-forgotten song. So that is why Freya hasn't been returning her calls or messages. She has forgiven him, after his despicable betrayal. Seeing them together is chilling.

She knows what it's like to desperately pretend everything is normal, in the hope that one day it will be. She understands the need to cling on to stability, no matter how fragile it might be.

Isla was exactly the same, once. Despite her shame, despite her reporting the rape, she dropped the case at first. She pushed away her flashbacks, convinced herself that she was hysterical, drunk or both. She swallowed the pain and let it fester. More painful than the crime itself, was the effort of trying to pretend it didn't happen. Her betrayal of herself was the worst betrayal of all.

Anyway, she was too fearful to test the truth – until Simon convinced her otherwise a year later.

She wishes she could go back and be stronger, and that it didn't take an outsider's intervention to make her finally go to court. She wishes she had hit back at the senseless, ill-informed early news coverage that accused her of crying wolf, and fought back. In many ways, she's spent her life fighting back ever since.

Freya and Jay walk on, and Isla lets them. Because she knows what it's like to love someone who consumes you, who scrambles your moral compass until you forget what is right or wrong. If you survive it, your entire world is shattered. It is impossible to trust in the magic of love the way you did before. It's no wonder she spends every Sunday by herself, and her evenings on the couch watching reality TV. The debris of hurt stays put for decades.

Isla starts typing a message to Freya, then saves it in her drafts folder. She will wait until the next morning when the emotion has dried from her words. Now Freya is not only being circled by a stranger, but a boyfriend with a history of assault and aggression as well. This case has become more than solving the mystery of Nicole's murder, it's now become about saving Freya too.

Chapter 82

Freya
Six weeks after the murder

The baby is nine weeks old today, according to her app. 'Congratulations,' it says gleefully. 'Your baby is now the size of a cherry.' She doesn't know why she has the app, it makes her look at her phone more than she should. But Freya still likes to keep track, just in case.

Ruth and Julian know. She's sure of it. An awareness beats beneath her skin. Just this morning, she noticed how they shared a look when she had to use the bathroom during her presentation. Pregnancy is full of little physical indignities that render you slightly less human, or rather, too human to function in normal places, like a workplace. Her constant low-level nausea makes it difficult to walk past the kitchen, or stomach the incense wafting out of Julian's office. She is forever sneezing, and searching through her handbag for Kleenex. Such physicality interrupts her workday, and theirs. She can see it in their eyes – the way they have started to believe in what she has to say a little bit less.

Jay, on the other hand, is none the wiser. They are at his house. In the week since they got back together, he has overcompensated in his efforts to show that she is welcome. There is a place at the sink for her toothbrush and beauty products, and a drawer in the bedroom for her clothes. She dreamed about this the first time they dated, but now it seems premature, and too much.

She doesn't like how his fingers lightly hold the back of her neck when they walk together.

He is in the kitchen making dinner, while she sits in the coolness of his open-plan living room.

'What are you so absorbed in?' he asks.

'Nothing of interest. Just scrolling through Instagram, the usual.' She tucks her phone into the pocket of her dress.

The salty, slightly burnt tang of the chorizo sizzling in the pan makes her mouth water. Her pulse slows, she tucks her phone away and tries to forget. No need to go making any proclamations just yet. This may be an imperfect reunion, but the presence of Jay in her life makes her feel at home for the first time. He brings over two steaming bowls of pea and chorizo risotto.

'Wine?'

'No thanks, I want to savor this masterpiece.'

He looks deep into her eyes. 'Come on, relax a little. A glass won't kill you. Where's my party girl gone?'

Freya changes the subject. 'How come you eat pork anyway, isn't it against your religion or something?'

'I'm Sikh, not Muslim,' he sighs, 'and besides, I'm not practicing. My religion is code. And bacon.'

Jay flicks through his Apple TV and selects a series she has been looking forward to for months.

'I didn't know you were a hardcore sci-fi fan,' she says.

He looks up. 'I'm the most hardcore. I was reading Ted Chiang short stories long before they turned his short piece "The Story of Your Life" into the movie *Arrival*.'

'It's very impressive that you know that . . .'

She nestles into him as the theme song begins to play. The more she stays by his side, the less opportunities there are for her to walk the streets alone. Those men can't touch her now.

He has apologized for slipping up with Nicole countless times, and assured her that he left her apartment long before anything happened. Freya has started to believe that it was simply a case of drunken bad judgment. Nicole was very persuasive, even she experienced this a few times. Freya received an email from Isla a few days ago, showing her evidence from Nicole's computer that shows, without a doubt, that the advert that haunted her was never even sent. A police officer called her and informed her of the same thing. Even Julian has been relatively well behaved, apart from the occasional lingering hand on her shoulder while she works. There is no need to make any sudden moves. For the first time in ages, all is relatively well.

So what about being here tonight, is making her feel on edge?

Jay's hand slips under her T-shirt and over her breasts. 'Gosh, you feel amazing. You're getting sexier by the day . . .'

There are signs if one looks for them. The slightest softening of her belly, a widening of her hips. Her body is slowly breaking free of its old shape and refashioning into something new. Freya really should tell him, before it's too late, before the news tells itself, but something is stopping her. Maybe she is addicted to the possibility of two different paths. As soon as she utters the word 'pregnant' to Jay, it becomes a decision to be faced as a couple.

She wishes she could ask her mother, 'Was it easy? Were you forced to keep me because you didn't have a choice? Or did you feel the kindling of something that you couldn't let go of? Did you spend weeks agonizing over it, paralyzed with fear, or was the answer always yes?'

Freya has a right to her twenties, to a decade of learning, experimentation and overwork. She has a right to spend her paychecks on shoes and handbags, or boozy brunches of overpriced smashed avocado toast. She has a right to pay back her student loans effortlessly and put money aside for a pension fund. She has a right to travel, and to follow her talent as far as it goes. A baby feels like a sentence, an abrupt end to the carefree life she had planned. She's seen the articles on motherhood shared on social media – she knows what a challenge it can be. Freya looks towards Jay – would he help her with the same enthusiasm he is courting her now, or would he simply disappear?

He presses pause. 'Got to go to the bathroom quickly.'

The risotto, while lovingly prepared, is far too salty. Freya grabs the chance to throw it in the bin. Pregnancy has reduced any tolerance for forcing food down. She glances around the kitchen – she'll never get over how clean it is. Even though Jay has just made a complex meal, the counter tops are spotless. So spotless, that a notepad sticks out.

She really shouldn't look, not after last time. But an innocent part of her thinks it is a recipe book. There is something revealing about the recipes a person jots down, it's a window into their secret comforts. And she is right, there is the recipe for pea and chorizo risotto scrawled on the page.

Maybe it's boredom, maybe it's instinct, but she turns the page. There is her name, Freya, and a list beneath it.

- Bob Dylan
- Vinyl
- Spicy food
- Italian food
- Sci-fi TV series
- Travel to exotic places
- India
- Receiving small gifts
- Vintage clothing
- Sewing

It goes on and on, until a scream starts surging in her chest. It's a list of every little thing she likes, a written representation of her quirks on paper. There is something clinical about it, chilling. Freya wraps her arms around herself.

'I really didn't take you for one of those nosy girlfriends.' Jay comes up behind her and wraps his arms tightly across her chest. She can't move. She has to get out of here, now.

Try to sound calm, back away gently. 'I'm sorry, Jay, I was just looking at the recipe for that gorgeous risotto you made for me.'

'You mean, the risotto you just put in the bin?' The rage burns around his words. She has to leave, right now.

He grabs her by the wrists and pulls her close, so close she can smell the alcohol on his breath. 'You're an ungrateful bitch, you know that?' There is something wild in his eyes. It shocks her. Where did all the care of a few moments before go? Where has this apparent hatred come from?

'Do you honestly think I like Bob Dylan? Or cooking? Or this filthy vintage leather jacket? Or the clothes you sew that make you look like a Junior High drama teacher?'

'Jay, I don't understand . . . we're the same. We get each other.'

'You will never, ever understand what it's like to be me,' he smirks. 'Do you know what it's like to enter a room and have your appearance announce itself before you even utter your name? To be assumed as less American because of your surname? Your sob story is very charming, Freya, but to call it the same as mine would be an insult.'

Her thoughts turn to the baby. Is shock bad for her? *Her*. It feels like a girl. Will this make her sick? Could Freya lose her? A strength rises up in her, enough to push him away and feel for the pepper spray in her pocket.

'Get away from me!'

He grabs her arms and begins to shake her. 'What do I need to do to make you trust me? Huh? How much more do I have to bend over backwards?'

The words bubble out of her mouth, like poison. 'Maybe you could start by not being such a fucking creep,' she says, gesturing to the notepad. 'I'm starting to wonder whether Nicole was the crazy one in your relationship, or if *you* were.'

His eyes flash. She's crossed a line. Time slows as he raises his hand, his rings glint as she flinches in preparation of bone meeting skin. Her knees buckle and she collapses to the floor. Is that blood she tastes in her mouth? Or fear? She shrinks her body into a ball, instinctively protective. She will survive this, she will fight, she will tell the story that Nicole couldn't.

Within the chaos she realizes what she knew all along.

She wants to keep her baby.

Chapter 83

Isla
Six weeks after the murder

When she sees a tall, burly silhouette hovering near her desk, Isla thinks with an irrational leap in her chest that it is Simon. Maybe he has found Freya's stalker. Or he could just be in the area and decided to stop for a visit – she wouldn't mind that either. As she moves closer, she realizes she really should get glasses. The man is actually shorter than Simon, with the curve of a belly straining the buttons of his shirt.

'May I help you?'

'I am Officer White. Are you Isla Davis?' His eyes barely meet hers.

'Yes . . .'

'Is this your computer, ma'am?'

'Yes.'

Isla looks around her. Is this another stunt Kenneth has pulled? All she sees are the eyes of the other reporters on her. She sighs. Surprise, surprise, she is the rogue journalist in trouble again. Bet they all want to see how this story unfolds.

He steps in front of her with unnecessary sass, she thinks. 'I'm going to need you to step aside while I search your computer.'

'I don't think so. Until you present a warrant, I have a right to privacy.'

He flashes a piece of paper bearing the letterhead she knows all too well. For the first time, her name is on the front.

'Enough for ya?' His mouth has too many teeth. It gives the impression that he is snarling.

'I don't understand.'

'Please step aside, ma'am, this will only take a second.'

Isla enters her username and password, then steps away as the officer clicks randomly, with narrowed eyes and the occasional grunt. It's a strange sensation standing next to her own desk while someone goes through her folders.

Isla steps back again and seethes. Just wait until she tells Simon about this. Where the hell is Kenneth? Surely this counts as police harassment?

The officer looks at her for a long time. 'Thank you, Isla. I've seen all I need to see here. You will be hearing more from me soon.'

He walks off, with a lopsided swagger. It's all so strange, Isla feels like she dreamed it up. Why would he come into her office unannounced and search through her computer? What was he looking for, who reported her, and what was the alleged crime?

She tries to settle into her morning by mucking around on Facebook and clicking through photos from Kirsty's latest skiing holiday to Val d'Isère. She writes an affirming comment on one or two of the photographs. Takes a sip of lukewarm coffee, which does nothing to help her racing heart. Runs through the past couple of weeks in her mind.

She hasn't done anything to justify interest from the police, or has she?

Chapter 84

Freya
One year ago

Graduation night, the moment Freya has been working toward her whole life. It took less than a minute to walk across the stage, to shake the Dean's hand and to accept her degree, but already she feels different. Life will be better from here on out, she can step boldly into her future.

Hattie, Jasmin and Kate are waiting outside the hall after the ceremony. They crowd her in a hug, a tangle of four black graduation gowns.

'You did it, you really did it!'

'And you made the Dean's List as well! You can do anything now!'

Some of her classmates shake her hand and congratulate her. To them, she is just another smart girl, but her friends understand the impossibility of this achievement.

Kate turns toward the door. 'Right, girls, are you ready to throw off your robes and take these gorgeous dresses out and celebrate?'

Kate's parents had booked a private booth at an expensive steakhouse. Hattie and Kate chatter happily, while Jasmin scans the menu for vegetarian options. Freya handles everything from the menu to the salt cellars with the greatest of care.

Kate's father is a portly, jolly man, with a relaxed demeanor who never appears to work too hard. He raises his glass of wine. 'A toast, to all four of you lovely ladies and your future – the world is yours!'

Their glasses clink loudly, and they burst into laughter.

'Now,' he says, 'order anything you like.'

Kate's mother, petite and blonde, adds, 'Wait! A special toast to the genius responsible for our Kate passing her degree: here's to Freya!'

Freya can't bear to have all eyes on the table focusing on her like this. She blushes furiously. 'I just helped Kate a little bit every now and then. She passed all on her own.'

Kate breaks a hot loaf of bread and butters it, passing a slice to Freya. 'That's not true, and you know it,' she whispers.

She's right. Although Freya intended to only help Kate every now and then, it was clear from early on that Kate battled to learn. No matter how many tutors or special resources her rich family threw at her, she seemed destined to fail. Year after year, Freya pushed forward in her studies, and dragged her best friend along with her, one ghostwritten assignment at a time.

As they toast and laugh and enjoy course after course, it dawns on Freya that the night is an entrée into a new society. Kate's money could get her so far, but a degree will get her further. Without Freya's help, she would have been an embarrassment to her family, a privileged but untethered soul destined to chip into the family trust fund as she floundered to find herself.

Kate, with purple lips and wine-stained teeth pulls her closer, and whispers in her ear.

'You will never understand how much your help means to me, how much it means that you sacrificed your time, year after year. One day, I will do something just as big for you. Wait and see. You deserve the world, Freya, and I will do anything to help you get it. *Anything.*'

Chapter 85

Freya
Six weeks after the murder

Her jaw aches from the impact of his fist, and a light violet bruise blooms on the left-hand side of her face. It's bad, but it could have been worse. In this room, a darker bruise would have helped.

'Julian, you have got to believe me. Jay was about to seriously injure me last night.' She doesn't add the most important bit, *and I am nine weeks pregnant.*

Jay didn't know who he was messing with. Being a woman alone for much of her life, Freya knew how to defend herself. She'd screamed in his face to distract him, then used the rage coiled inside her to deliver a powerful kick to his balls. As he doubled over in agony, she held her jacket over her face and pushed on the pepper spray, hard. Fighting through the fog, and coughing through her makeshift mask, she wrenched his front door open and ran all the way home until she was safely locked in her room, wheezing and stomach churning. Jasmin, the only one home, rushed her to the ER, where they checked that she and the baby were OK.

There were things she left behind last night: her special silver bracelet, the only bra that fits her right now. But she will not ask for these things back. She is far too angry.

Julian's eyes crease in concern. 'Freya, I'm so sorry to see you like this. Have you seen anyone about that bruise? Do you need some time off?'

'Yes, I went to the ER last night. They took my case very seriously.' The attending doctor wrote a note, booking her off for two days, stating a trauma and early pregnancy as a reason. She also stated that her injuries appeared to be the result of physical abuse. But if Freya had taken the time off, and shown Julian the note, Julian would then know her secret.

Freya's voice grows shrill. 'Did you hear what I just said?'

He sips his green tea slowly. 'I've heard arnica works miracles. You rub it in gently and then – bam – it's gone the next day. I have a great homeopath, if you'd like an appointment with him. He's usually booked for months in advance.'

Why won't he acknowledge what she just said? She changes tack.

'Julian . . . I have taken photographs of my face, and I intend to report Jay Singh to the police for assault.'

He leans across the table. 'Whoa! Easy there! This is a personal matter between you and Jay.'

Freya is trembling. Julian didn't see Jay's face last night and the way it contorted with rage. If she hadn't acted quickly, who knows what could have happened.

'I wouldn't come to you unless it was important. I honestly believe that Jay is a danger to me, and the rest of my female colleagues.' There has to be justice, some sense of accountability.

Julian looks out of his office, taps his fingers on the side of his mug.

'Don't you trust me?' she asks, her voice shaking.

Julian looks up and speaks slowly, as if she is a child. 'Let me put this in perspective for you. I have a director who has been with the company for two and a half years and has been directly responsible for our massive growth in the market. Then, I have a young woman who has just joined the company who starts making baseless accusations against him, after they have been romantically involved. And yes, I do know that you two were romantically involved, Freya. I know everything that happens here. This is the same woman who has reported *me* to HR for alleged sexual harassment. What would you do in my shoes?'

'My accusations are not baseless,' she says, but she has already begun to feel overpowered.

'Jay came into my office this morning to say that you lashed out at *him* last night. You were so intoxicated, apparently, that you fell as you attempted to punch him. He looks terrible – his eyes are red and swollen.' From the pepper spray, Freya realizes.

Julian continues, anger edging into his sing-song voice, 'You don't see him pressing charges, do you?'

Freya is so shocked, she cannot speak.

He sighs. 'This is the problem with hiring millennials. You are too young to understand how to be in the world yet. Breakups happen, Freya, and it's hard, but I'm not here to coach you out of it, and you can't let it affect your work. Not everyone gets promoted as quickly as you were – I only did that because I trusted you. I did *you* a favor. Now, I'm not so sure.'

'You know how hard I have worked, Julian, especially in the last few weeks.'

'Hmmm . . . have you, though? Just in the last week you have taken time off for' – he holds his fingers in exaggerated quotation marks – 'being sick and have run randomly out of meetings with no explanation.'

It's not fair, she wants to shout. What about all the late nights and early mornings? Or the weekends spent obsessing over getting the project just right? The light of his office is cold, his expression confrontational. It feels like her every effort has been forgotten.

'This job means everything to me.' She can feel her throat constrict as she utters the words. Freya has become used to being the top of the class. To be told her efforts have fallen short feels alien, wrong. Her cheeks are aflame.

Julian's eyes seem to soften. 'I know, which is why this behavior is so out of character for you. Storming in here and accusing one of my directors of assault? This is not the Freya I know.'

Freya feels so lonely, it's as if it is burning into every inch of her skin.

He continues, 'Tell me, Freya, what's *really* going on here?'

She plays awkwardly with the button on her shirt. Legally, she does not have to tell him she is pregnant yet, right?

But as he stares at her, mouth half upturned in a patronizing smile, she gets the feeling that somehow, he is no longer on her side.

Chapter 86

Isla
Six weeks after the murder

Isla sits and waits for the disciplinary hearing to assemble. Two coffees down and she's got more than a fleeting rush of jitters. The adrenaline and her are one, a flickering channel of light trying to occupy the space on the hard office seat.

What is going on here?

When she got the summons for the hearing, the text on the note vaguely said, *breach of confidentiality*. She may not respect her boss, but she respects her sources. If a source tells her something off the record, she honors this.

Kenneth strides into the room, chest puffed out. Behind him trails Sandy, the worn-out HR manager, someone in a police uniform, and a stern woman in plain clothes, who Isla assumes is their legal representative. She could have brought in a witness of her own, but Isla is a proud person. She would rather endure the humiliation alone. She hasn't even told Lizzie about this, and she definitely hasn't told her mother.

The room titters with false politeness, whispered greetings and comments on the weather. It is spectacularly rainy outside, the sheer volume of water rattles the windowpanes.

Kenneth clears his throat. 'Thank you for your uncharacteristic timekeeping this morning, Isla. It really pains
me to have to sit across the table from you under these
circumstances.' His mouth twitches in an almost-smile.
'It has come to our attention that you are in possession of
classified information, and have used this information to
tamper with persons of interest during a police investigation.'

Isla has played it close to the edge before, but she has
never broken the law for a story. That goes against all her
training. Bernard would never have stood for it. It would
break her heart to disappoint him.

Still, fair is fair. If there is a valid case against her, she will
take responsibility for her actions. If only she could figure
out what they are referring to. She hasn't been allowed to
report on any cases since the drama with Nicole's story, and
Freya still hasn't responded to her calls, or her email.

But then there is the email, the classified police report
that details the information on Nicole's computer, information that was specifically not shared with the press. Shit.

The police officer cuts in. 'The information you possess
is of direct interest to the state. It involves one individual
we questioned recently, and another person we may have
reason to bring in for further questioning.'

Isla's blood runs cold.

'Your possession of such information and your dissemination of it poses a threat to an active investigation,' he
continues.

Blood rises in her cheeks. Isla is mortified. What a stupid rookie error! A handwritten letter would have been simpler, and more efficient. Now they probably have an email trail that tells them everything.

Kenneth slaps a stack of paper on the table in front of them. The sheet on top is Isla's email to Freya, with each incriminating sentence highlighted. The pages that follow are printouts of the information she shared. Her sins exposed, in black and white.

The officer present adds, 'We also have evidence that you have recently given a gift to a member of the police force.'

The Ottolenghi cookbook. Shit.

Kenneth says, 'Giving a gift to a police officer in exchange for information is akin to bribery, Isla.'

'It's not what it—' Her eyes scan the room. She doesn't continue. She can see there is no point.

How did they know to go through her emails? Or what to look for? The answer hits her like a cannonball. No, no, it can't be! But there is no other explanation. Simon. Something inside her shatters. She should have known he wasn't the good guy he made himself out to be. They never are. Joke's on her – she shouldn't have trusted him.

The assault on her integrity is not finished. Sandy purses her lips. 'We did a general check on your email communication and were shocked to discover that you write long emails to friends and family every day on company time.'

Isla's heart sinks. With Lizzie in London, and her mother in a different state, she ends up emailing them a lot. A phone conversation never quite expresses what's in her heart – words are the truest form of communication she has. It's lonely in the city, when the people that care about those everyday things – like what you had for dinner or what series you're watching – are so far away. She may have given herself too much leeway and got carried away, making these small comforts a daily habit.

Kenneth says, 'We ran a word count on your daily emails and compared it to your daily output and well ... the results don't look good.'

Isla reaches for the glass of water in front of her and takes a long sip. Her mother always told her this is an effective trick to stop the tears from coming. Today, she thinks she may need a little bit more.

'We have summed up the complaints being held against you: the dissemination of classified information, bribery of a police officer, interference in an active police investigation and the abuse of company resources and time. Now, you have the opportunity to counter the charges ...' says the legal representative, with dead eyes. She must have sat through hundreds of these conversations in her career. Isla starts imagining the stories she could tell, and weaving it together in a feature article. She can't help herself, the journalist in her will not be extinguished.

The room is silent, save for Kenneth clicking his pen. Waiting.

Isla knows what she has to do. This disciplinary hearing is unpleasant, especially Kenneth's joy in the entire proceedings, but, for the most part, it happens to be fair.

'I accept all charges, except the one for bribery. The gift was simply meant to be a kind gesture, and the officer in question gave me the information willingly.'

Willingly is a strong word, but Simon definitely didn't put his job on the line for a cookbook. Which makes her wonder, why exactly did he say yes in the first place?

Sandy looks up. 'You understand the impact this could have on your career, Isla? You may never be able to write again.'

That part is rubbish. Her words cannot be contained, and will always find a place to belong, even if she doesn't. Still, she is heartbroken. What will her mother say? She has always been so proud of Isla and supported her path as a journalist, along with the risk and insecurity that came with it.

'Well,' says Kenneth, 'that was simple enough. Isla has admitted to her indiscretions and we are left with no choice but to take disciplinary action.'

The jury of three convenes and a decision is made. Isla is suspended until further notice, and will have to go into the police station to deliver a formal statement. Following this, the matter may be taken to court if the police deem her interference serious enough.

As she bundles a few of her most cherished items from her desk into her rucksack, a few stray tears drop onto her pile of notebooks. This shitty place wasn't the best paper in the world, but it was all she had. Somewhere, among the countless coffees, last-minute deadlines and editorial meetings she became a real journalist. She developed an instinct for a good story, she honed her powers of deduction and the research skills to prove them. For nearly a decade, she has been defined by what happened within these walls.

She rushes outside, without a word to her colleagues, as if she is only stepping out for a second, as if she has somewhere important to be. A formal goodbye is too embarrassing.

Isla blinks as the late-afternoon sun reflects against the buildings around her. It is not the paper it used to be. She doesn't belong in there anymore. It is only when the shame subsides and her sadness settles that she realizes something important. Kenneth has actually done her a favor. He has set her free.

Chapter 87

Freya
Six weeks after the murder

Freya tries to retain her focus. She puts the final touches on the plan for the East African technology rollout. Thankfully, Julian has only given her a warning and not removed her from the project completely. There are enough finicky details on the screen before her to keep her happily occupied for hours. This is the kind of challenging and involved work she signed up for.

'Pretty impressive black eye you have there,' says Chris, one of the developers.

'You should see the other guy,' she quips. He chuckles, and walks away. This seems to satisfy everyone in the office who has asked. It makes Freya's skin crawl, because it happens to be true. The other guy is walking among them, giving them orders, and nobody knows. Nobody except Julian, and Jay himself.

Yet the almost-attack she survived that night may as well not have happened at all. Jay is innocent until proven guilty. All she has is the outrage grinding in her chest, yet his outrage at her accusation holds center stage in Julian's mind.

His shoulders seem broader, his manner even more cocky than usual. He is a man who has won. Every now and then, he throws a smiling glance in her direction that makes her blood boil.

She can't believe she thought she was special, that they both really valued her. It was a phase, and now that she has started to bring up some inconvenient truths, she is distasteful, unwanted. Both she and Nicole are fading into the distance, yesterday's news.

A new girl has just joined, and Freya knows what is about to happen, even if she can't bring herself to confront it just yet. She can feel the possibility bubbling in the room. Her name is Bobbie, and she is breathtaking.

Bright blue braids contrast her dark skin. She has an unstudied edginess to her. An oversize denim jacket with a full moon hand-painted on the back shrouds her lean body. Freya tries not to look at her the way Jay surely is, eyes following the path of each curve and resting on her lips.

She tries not to notice the path that's set in motion, as Jay shows her around the office, laughing and joking. Bobbie leans towards him and shows him a video on her cell. There is something haunting about how close they seem, so quickly, and how Jay is wearing an oversized denim jacket as well, with a Run DMC logo spray-painted on the back. They are both wearing Adidas Stan Smiths, like twins. Should she pull Bobbie aside and warn her, or keep out of trouble? Jay was so awful to her, so why does it still hurt so badly?

Ruth catches her staring at the man she so recently loved.

'Freya! Your face . . .'

'You should see the—'

'You don't have to joke about it with me. That looks really awful. Let's catch up over a quick coffee and a walk?'

She still has a lot of work to do, but the invite makes Freya feels a little bit lighter. Ruth is a powerful woman, an ally she feels lucky to have on her side. Ruth has spent the past two weeks traveling and meeting with investors, so they haven't had a chance to speak. Freya has a feeling that Ruth may have the answers, and help her decide on what to do next.

'Yes, please!'

She follows her out the office and onto the busy side-walk. Freya is a little taken aback when Ruth lights a ciga-rette. 'I didn't know you smoked?'

'Retro, isn't it? Doesn't everybody have a vice?' She flings Freya a knowing look.

The rain has finally cleared, and a sliver of sunlight warms them as they walk. 'It's great to see you again, Ruth. I've been meaning to take you up on your offer for guidance.'

'This doesn't surprise me.' The comment is more abrupt than Freya is used to. 'You don't seem yourself at the moment, Freya, and I know Julian has expressed this to you as well.'

Freya tenses as she thinks of Julian's cold, snake-like eyes cruising her body – his come-ons a shocking contrast to the quotes on serenity and prayer flags posted around him. 'He did, yes.'

'He means well. As you know, Nicole suffered from a mental illness. I'm not saying that led to her death, but we are concerned about the wellbeing of our staff and want to help where we can. That way things are less likely to . . . spiral out of control.'

Freya thinks of how much it hurt to see Jay with the new girl this morning. The surging pregnancy hormones don't help matters. Imagine experiencing those feelings through the lens of bipolar disorder? No matter how vicious Nicole was towards her, Freya wishes she could go back in time and say, I'm sorry, I understand now.

'I'm having some trouble with Jay,' she says, searching Ruth's eyes for an inkling of recognition. 'With Julian as well. I am feeling harassed in the office.'

Ruth thinks for a moment, 'Do you have any proof of this?'

She points to the bruise, silent.

'All right. Freya, I am going to be frank with you because you deserve someone who will tell it to you straight. This is not beginning to look too good. You accuse Nicole of harassing you, and then Julian and an alleged group of men sending you messages. And now Jay's next? Don't you think that's a lot of attacks directed at one person?'

Freya is silent. Ruth has a point. It didn't look so good when listed one after the other. Still, she was certain what she had experienced was true.

'When I encounter times of trial, I use it as an opportunity to look inward. We are the masters of our reactions.'

The platitudes stoke her anger, but Freya nods cooperatively. 'You're right, Ruth.'

'Are you sure there isn't anything personal going on that is prompting this? Anything physical?'

As if in response, Freya feels a painful twinge on her left side. Numerous online searches have assured her that this pain is simply her abdominal muscles stretching, preparing to make room for the baby, but it still unsettles her. The pains have been coming on stronger lately, especially when she is stressed.

She believed that out of everyone at the office, Ruth would be the one to understand. Remember how she headhunted you, Freya thinks to herself. Remember how pleased she was to welcome you to the team! Yet something makes her throat close up. She just can't get the words out.

Ruth continues, determined to lead the conversation in a certain direction. 'As a woman, I consider myself both intelligent and intuitive. I've been noticing some signs that have been giving me cause to wonder that something' – she gestures vaguely in the direction of Freya's midriff – 'may be afoot.'

Freya can't slow the beating of her heart. She wonders if the answer to Ruth's question is written all over her face. This is her personal business, and in her opinion, has had no impact on her productivity in the workplace.

'Are you trying to say I've gained weight, Ruth?' Best to use humor to ease the question away.

'Not at all, you are as lovely as ever. But accidents happen, especially at your young age.'

Freya is affronted at the generalization. 'I'm very careful, Ruth, and have been caring for myself for a long time.'

'I have no doubt about that. You're an incredible woman, which is why I wanted to remind you that if you ever fell pregnant, it would be your right to choose to have an abortion if you needed to.'

The hairs on Freya's arm stand on end. This conversation is beginning to feel pointed, ominous.

'I know. I've always felt passionate about a woman's right to choose.' She doesn't add, *including the right to choose to keep the baby if she wants to.*

They have already looped around the block without her realizing. Ruth seems distracted, her thoughts already back at her desk. 'Well,' she says, 'this was a good talk, Freya. I look forward to seeing your stellar performance as we launch in the next two weeks.'

She laughs a biting, hollow laugh. 'I, for one, am relieved you're not pregnant. That would have made things quite difficult for you here. You have too much potential, and your work means too much to us.'

Ruth smiles, her perfectly applied wine-colored lipstick arching in a snarl. The words sound friendly, but everything in Freya screams that this is not a compliment, but a threat.

As she walks away, a message comes through on her phone.

'Ms Matthews. Detective Cohen here. I have an update on your harassment complaint. We found a young man trying to break in to your home this morning, and have taken him into custody. His prints match those found on the gift you turned in as evidence. Would you be available to identify him in a lineup?'

Finally, some good news.

Chapter 88

Isla
Six and a half weeks after the murder

The old green door creaks open and Isla breathes in the intoxicating smell of books. The place is quite something. A flood of books spills over every surface. They tower in tall, unsorted piles along the rickety staircase. They jostle for space along the floor-to-ceiling shelves. Crime, history, romance, religion, sex, cookery, music, Antarctic exploration, occultism, and philosophy. It is all here, every important and inane thought recorded. A fluffy ginger cat tiptoes over the literature, its tail fanning against the spines.

It's not the neat, ordered kind of place where you'd expect to find the hottest new releases. It's a store for long-time appreciators of books, people who may be looking for something rare and particular, or may just want to stay here a while, among the history and potential of all the pages.

He walks down the stairs, looking a little older than when Isla saw him last. His sunken eyes, framed by a mane of wild white curls, light up.

'Isla! Look at you, all grown up!'

'Bernard' – she smiles – 'I love what you've done with the place.' Many journalists foster an idealistic dream of owning a bookstore, but Bernard actually did it. The world of newspapers may have moved on without him but here, time has stood still.

They retreat into his office, which smells of sweet cigars and fresh coffee. Isla settles into a suede armchair and scans the photographs on the wall of all the authors that have visited.

'So, Isla, has some fantastic paper snapped you up as an editor yet? I can remember your gifted turn of phrase like it was yesterday. You always had this way of describing the world so that others could really see it.'

The compliment chokes Isla up. It's been a while since someone told her what a great writer she is. The story pours out of her, starting from the morning after Nicole's murder and ending with her disciplinary hearing.

'I have been floating around the city all morning, unsure of what to do next or where to go. I hated working there, but now I'm starting to feel like an idiot. Did I throw my career away, just to break a story? Did I let my personal motives interfere with my integrity as a reporter?'

Bernard removes his glasses, deep in thought.

'Hmm, this is a strange case. Are you sure that the crime is confined to this one murder?'

'Why do you ask?'

He rustles through a stack of unsorted files. He pulls out one with 'media law' scrawled on the spine. 'Because, if you take a look here, you will see that a journalist has a right to be in possession of classified information, especially if they can prove it is in the public interest. Your new editor should be supporting you in developing this story, not penalizing you for how you obtain your information.'

Isla's spirit lifts. She knew Bernard would somehow make her feel better. 'I suppose so.'

He is excited now, pacing the small space, 'Think about it. The only way we journalists break a story is through treading the fine line between what is public and what is classified. There has been no recent case in media history where a journalist has been arrested based on information in their possession.'

She knows where this is going, but she needs him to say it. 'What are you suggesting?'

'That now is not the time to back down, but to put into practice everything I taught you. Someone out there is trying to scare you, which makes me think that you are on to something big. Who did you say you saw at the café again?'

Isla finds the image of the phone of the three men gathered. Each one connected. Each one guilty, she's sure of it.

'There they are. That's Kenneth, as you know, and that's Julian. I just can't figure out who the third man is.'

Bernard pulls the phone towards him for a closer look. 'I'm sure I know that guy. I think he might be a lawyer, or a member of the public prosecution, maybe even the police! But I'm certain that they are trying to stop you from uncovering something. You just have to figure out what.'

Chapter 89

Freya
Six and a half weeks after the murder

The men stand in a row, sullen, aggressive. Freya shrinks back at the sight of them.

'Don't worry,' says Detective Cohen, as if reading her mind. 'This is one-way glass. They can't see you.'

But their expressions tell a different story. She can feel the hate searing into her. She once trusted that nobody could see her phone, her emails, the inane daily circle she made to work and back every day, but now she is not so sure.

She gulps. Folds her arms.

'The one in the middle,' she says quietly.

'What is that?' says Detective Cohen.

She would recognize him from anywhere. The nice-guy smile, the too-tight sports gear. His breathing, quick and hot against her face. Out of the other offenders he stands out, like a mistake, or a false accusation. 'It's him,' she says, louder and surer. 'The one in the middle – number three.'

Detective Cohen murmurs something to the officer, and the men are led away. Together, they walk to his office.

'Well, I have good news,' he says. 'The man you identified matched the prints on the gift delivered to your office.

He already has a record for stalking and harassing three separate women. Thanks to your testimony, we will be able to sentence him to all charges.'

Freya sighs. It's almost too good to be true. 'I don't know what to say.'

'Well, I would like to thank you for backing yourself, and reporting this. Thanks to you, many other women won't go through the same trauma you did.'

Does she ask the question hot on her lips? Does she want to know?

'Has he told you why? Why me?'

Detective Cohen says, 'From what I can gather from our questioning so far, it was completely random. He happened to be browsing Spark.com when your advert was posted, and something about your profile, and the words written, captured his imagination. All his victims match a similar profile. Medium height, brown hair, brown eyes. Every time, he has targeted a woman through online dating.'

Freya waits for the relief to hit her, but it never does. All these weeks of fear seem so pointless, especially now that they've been linked to a fluke in circumstance. It also doesn't explain who posted the advert in the first place, and why.

Detective Cohen sees her out. 'By the way, what happened to your eye?'

She freezes. She's had enough of the cold, forbidding interior of the police station. She's had enough of expanding on every detail in a testimony. Under it all, there is an insistent, irrational fear that he will react to her allegations the same way Ruth and Julian did.

'It's silly,' she lies, 'I tripped over a weight at gym and fell flat on my face.'

'You lift? I'm impressed.' He shakes her hand. 'Take care, Freya. And if anything else comes up, you have my number.'

Standing in the harsh midday sun, Freya is not sure what to do next. The only thing she can think of is to check her phone. One unread message. Probably Julian or Ruth, checking where she is, or Jasmin, reminding her of the midwife appointment she has scheduled for her. But it is a number she doesn't know.

No, she whispers.

No, no, no.

The message: *You're not as safe as you think you are.*

Chapter 90

Freya
Six and a half weeks after the murder

Jasmin holds Freya's hand as they cross the street.

'He's coming to get me,' Freya says, breathing heavily, 'I see him in the faces of all men, all the time.'

'Darling, no! That message is probably one left over from before that man was arrested.'

But what if the person who posted that advert wants to hurt her, too? Simon has sent Freya a report on their progress so far on identifying the origin of the message. 'We are dealing with Internet service providers and the support team at Spark to try to find the information we'd need to identify the harasser, but this takes time, unfortunately. There is a lot of red tape. Some other members of my team are also looking into classified information which may hold clues as to who created your fake profile, and when.'

This isn't helpful on days like today, when Freya keeps turning and looking over her shoulder, convinced someone is about to attack her.

Jasmin opens a granola bar and offers her a bite. 'What about Jay?'

'You mean, what if he was behind the messages?'

'He could be. We already know he was comfortable doing the same thing to Nicole, and look how he lashed out at you! And he is a coder like you, and a hacker too. It would be easy for him, surely?'

'It can't be. Aggressive as he was the last time he saw me, I just can't imagine it. He made me swear not to tell anyone about our prank, and wanted to distance himself from that night as much as possible. Why would he do the same thing again?'

Freya's mind had started to loop over the idea of another source of the original message – Julian. He could access Freya's computer if he wanted to, posted anything as her, and then have the technological skill to erase his tracks. Now that she has begun to see the darker, controlling side to him, she can imagine him doing it without a trace of guilt. But she doesn't dare accuse him of this, not now, not yet.

'Well, I am here for you no matter what, and now I am excited to support you and your baby!'

Over the past few years, Jasmin has quietly unwound further and further into her true hippy self. She is a qualified kundalini yoga teacher, a part-time reiki practitioner and a doula, who has already helped over a dozen women give birth. Freya didn't think to ask Jasmin the details of her job in the moments where she used to return to their house share in the early hours of the morning, exhausted and fragrant with essential oils, but now she is grateful.

Jasmin is making this new world of motherhood feel a little less alien to her.

Freya pumps with adrenaline but Jasmin is surprisingly calm. 'The birth of a child is a beautiful thing.' And, as if reading Freya's mind, she adds, 'There is never a right time for it. You are strong, capable and you want to be a mother right now, so you will make a plan.'

Jasmin's acceptance forms a stark contrast to the reactions of Hattie and Kate.

'I told you what Ruth said. A pregnancy could be the end of my career. Everyone knows the rumors. On paper, tech firms are supposed to be all-inclusive and accepting of everyone but they find ways to kick you out, loopholes.' The pain spasms in Freya's side again, and she flinches.

'There is still a lot to be grateful for,' says Jasmin. 'Some of the poorer women I have worked with get fired on the spot, because they're involved in physical work, like packing. You have some room to work around this, and stand your ground. You need to be prepared to fight, Freya.'

Her mind returns to the evening in the bar with Melanie. She's been so focused on her immediate problems with Jay that she hasn't figured out how to act on the explosive information she uncovered that night. She thinks of all the strong, intelligent women at Atypical, going about their day-to-day work, ignoring their own discomfort, dismissing their experiences with their CEO. She needs to speak up soon because, if she doesn't, she fears that nobody will.

It's not just about fighting the harassment of strangers anymore. Thanks to changing her number and Detective Cohen's efforts, her stalker will be charged and nobody who saw that advert will ever contact her again. She swallows as she thinks of the other message, the one that shocked her as she left the station. The only explanation is that the harassment is closer to home than she first imagined.

Talking about the potential life with her baby hurts, and Freya begins to wonder if her decision is the right one after all. It's been like this the past week, and growing in intensity, this pendulum swinging from one future to another. 'And what if they keep me on, then what? All the meeting rooms at Atypical are made of glass – there would be nowhere for me to pump breastmilk. And who would I leave her with?'

Jasmin nods quietly, taking it all in. 'You're so sure it's a girl.'

It wasn't conscious, but she did see the baby as a girl – a tough little fighter, here against all odds. 'I just *feel* it.'

They arrive at the home office of the midwife. Jasmin has assured her she is the best in the business, and used to the anxieties of almost-mothers. Her name is Sheryl, and she stands in the doorway, tall, gray-haired, and formidable. She brings to mind the tender pragmatism found in the social workers of her youth.

There are posters on the wall. A cross-section of a uterus with a baby within it. A step-by-step guide on how best to latch a baby to the breast. Massage techniques for when the baby has colic. She sees her mother differently now – small, scared, the type of academic who is uneasy in big crowds. She imagines her doing these checkups, shamed and alone, in a world very different to the one she lives in today. Did she cry every time? Did she look at the posters on the wall and wonder, once or twice, maybe I could take a shot at this?

Sheryl hands her a registration form with the kind of overly personal questions unique to this situation. Are her nipples inverted? She peers inside her shirt to check.

'Have you thought about your birth plan?'

Freya looks to Jasmin. 'Uh, a natural birth?'

Sheryl and Jasmin exchange a look. 'No, it's about a bit more than that. You can choose some birth affirmations to stick up on the wall, light some candles, choose a playlist and decide who you want in the room during the delivery.'

Jasmin seems so confident and relaxed about this, and Freya is filled with pride at her friend. But the idea that there is going to be a birth, a moment where this idea becomes real is both terrifying and lonely. It will be just her, the midwife and Jasmin in the room. No partner holding her hand and wiping her brow like she always imagined. The journey back home will be just the two of them, mom and baby, embarking on their life together, alone.

'But we don't need to go into those details yet, do we, Sheryl? All we're saying is that you can choose how your birth unfolds. You don't have to feel pressured, scared or alone,' Jasmin tells her.

Freya nods, feeling stronger. Maybe I'm a hero, Freya thinks. Maybe I can transform the mess of my life into something beautiful too.

As Freya lies back on the bed, her heart starts to beat faster. What if hers is the only heartbeat? What if there is something wrong? The past few months have been fraught with the fear directed at people outside of her, she never thought to worry about this.

'Just lie back and relax.' Sheryl lifts up her shirt and places a Doppler device on the slight swell of her belly. 'This will feel a little bit cold. Remember, you are very early on in your pregnancy, so it may be too soon to hear a heartbeat.'

But then it fills the room. Like one thousand galloping horses. Like the crashing of waves on a stormy coastline. Again and again, unmistakable.

'Jasmin!' She clutches her friend's hand. Tears fall down her cheeks. 'That's my baby! Hello, my baby, hello, my love!' There she is, unmistakably alive, furiously vital, untouched by the chaos around her.

When the scan is over, Freya stands on the sidewalk outside for a minute, dazed. Jasmin holds her tight, without saying a word. Nothing could express the beauty, the glory of it.

'You know,' Jasmin says, 'this doesn't have to be the end of anything. Have you ever considered the idea that Ruth may be wrong? That they are prejudiced against you because you are a woman? You have every right to want a family.'

Perhaps it is possible to imagine an alternate future, one in which she is valued and her pregnancy is celebrated.

She and Jasmin make their way home, arm in arm, as the clouds in the sky turn pink.

Chapter 91

Isla
Six and a half weeks after the murder

'Come on, people, I know my way inside the damn station!' Two cops, stony-faced, pay Isla no attention. They silently lead her to a small room for questioning.

During her first year as a crime reporter, entering the station was like stepping into a cathedral. The enforced silence, the severe sense of discipline. In the beginning she would walk through the cold, gray corridors holding her breath, afraid to make a wrong move. Today she is defiant. The men and women she has worked with so closely over the years pretend they don't know her. They ignore the fact that one of them is to blame for bringing her over here in the first place.

Simon. So-called friend, co-conspirator and the person who must have ratted her out. What a snake. She sees him as she paces through the office, standing in the kitchen clutching one of the brie and rocket sandwiches he insists on making each day to save himself money. She should confront him, but she is far too hurt.

Isla recognizes the officer from her disciplinary hearing. He is as unmoved as during that afternoon. Her body is one ragged, rapid heartbeat. It's the ones with the poker faces that are the best at questioning. They are the ones that will interrogate you until you snap and admit to something you didn't even do.

Come on, Isla, she thinks to herself, remember what Bernard said. They are out to get you for a reason that has nothing to do with you. A few pink, glittery stickers sparkle on the officer's wrist. A father of little girls. Always look at the person behind the story, even when that person is coming for you.

'You have not been one hundred percent objective in your research for this case,' he says. 'You have gone out of your way to pursue persons of interest and obtain classified information, even though a journalist of your experience should know better.' He looks up at her. 'The only question is *why*? What were your intentions for this information and your reportage of this case?'

How can she explain that Nicole's murder took her back to the night that changed the course of her life? That getting justice and understanding the motives of every person around her feels like a form of redemption?

He drums his fingers on the table, the shining stickers catching the light above. 'Do you know something we don't?'

For a moment she sees the officer's guard slip. He is a father, a person. She tries to look at him with compassion, and reframe his hardness as crystallized fear.

She braces herself, remembers what Bernard said. 'According to US media law, it is my legal right as a journalist to possess classified information, if it is deemed to be in the public interest. Nicole was murdered in a dense block of apartments situated in a highly urbanized part of San Francisco, just a street away from a school. I believed that the documents were a significant part of the case, and I shared them with my source in order to secure her trust.'

It's cocky, but Isla did her research. She knows her rights now. They can try and frighten her all they like, but today they can't arrest her.

Suddenly, the questioning is over. Isla stands outside the station for a moment, allowing the bright sun to soothe her trembling body. For someone who chose to be a crime reporter, police stations are revered places that, when she least expects it, bring up aching memories of feeling small, scared and unheard.

She sits on the brick wall, waiting to feel more grounded. Isla is tired, so very tired. She doesn't even have the energy to move away when she sees Simon approaching her.

He lights a cigarette. 'You mind if I smoke?'

'I mind that you're here next to me.'

Simon looks hurt. 'You haven't been answering my calls, Isla.'

Of course she hasn't. Every time she has seen his number on her phone, she has ignored it.

She can't hold it in any longer. 'You could have just said no when I asked you for those documents. You didn't have to go and tell your boss. You know how tough things have been for me lately.' As she utters that statement, she realizes how much she has shared with him while nursing steaming paper cups on the edges of police tape, she thinks back to that evening, laughing at the band in the park. Their closeness has come on incrementally, organically. That's why his betrayal hurts so much. She let him get too close. For the first time in a decade, she let her guard down.

'What do you mean?' Only then does Isla notice the plaid shirt and jeans he is wearing, and the small box of valuables in his hands. 'I got hauled over the coals for this as much as you did. Haven't you listened to any of my voice messages?'

He starts laughing then. Isla doesn't hear him laugh often. It's gruff, infectious and lights up his whole face. 'You were ignoring me, weren't you! I'm sorry, Isla, this whole situation is just the pits.'

'Wait, so you're fired over this?' The understanding hits her all at once, and she feels terrible. Of course Simon – sweet, sensitive, and kind – didn't say anything. To use his turn of phrase, he is a real mensch, a nice guy who would never put a foot wrong. Now she's got him fired, all because of her obsession with this case.

'I'm suspended until further notice, but it's making me think, you know? Maybe I am a bit too soft for this job. I just can't seem to grow that protective shield everyone else has.'

Isla feels like she is the opposite. She scrubs her protective shield until it shines. Well, that was until Nicole's story came and made a big crack across the middle.

She shifts a little on the wall and Simon sits next to her. There is something about this moment – the glow of the sunshine, her newfound freedom – that makes Isla feel good.

'What do you think you will do, then?'

'I think I may become a pastry chef.'

'Seriously?'

'Seriously. I make a mean loaf of bread, and my chocolate brownies are stronger than any interrogation tactics.'

'That sounds like a slogan to me.'

'Well, the police puns are rather tempting. Maybe I should open a fried chicken and waffle food truck called, Fowl Play?'

'Or a burger bar called Burger in the First Degree?'

They laugh, so close to one another that she can smell the cigarette smoke on his shirt. She's always loved the smell of second-hand smoke. It reminds her of standing up front at a concert, thrashing to the sounds of an underground band. It touches a young, wild part of her that she still feels sometimes when she plays music loud.

'I just don't get it, Simon . . . if you didn't hand me in, who did?'

He is about to respond, but then falls silent. A rough, muscular man walks past them, and greets Simon with a vague grunt. Isla knows his face, in the uncertain way she knows many faces. She could have interviewed him on one of hundreds of cases. If she's honest, all officers start to look similarly hardened.

But there is a shadow of ill feeling when she meets his eyes. He looks at her blankly, and is almost affronted when she attempts to greet him. There is something amiss.

Then, it comes back to her. That morning in the restaurant, when her friend Kirsty rattled on and Isla picked at her eggs benedict, sweating at the thought of the bill. Julian and Kenneth, talking like old friends and conspirators, and then this man, the third, who made them look around the room with narrowed eyes when he entered.

'Who is that?' she asks Simon.

'That guy? He's the Deputy Chief of Police.'

Chapter 92

Isla
Seven weeks after the murder

All the freshness around her makes Isla's eyes water. Ripe tomatoes glisten in the early morning sunlight alongside emerald green bunches of spinach, still speckled with dew. Everywhere she turns there are people filling wicker baskets with fresh produce.

'What is wrong with meeting at a simple coffee shop?' she mutters. Still, looking around at the stalls selling hot sourdough bread and trays of perfect figs, Simon would like this place. She remembers him saying he has a thing for collecting preserves. She contemplates picking up something for his baking, then stops herself.

She spots Freya from a distance. She is wearing a flowing, bohemian dress and her hair is loose. Isla was surprised when Freya called her out of the blue, asking to meet again. And although she has been burned by this story, Isla still has a need to prove herself, and make things right. She turns toward Freya. There is something different about her, an ease in her body that Isla hadn't noticed before.

'Interesting choice of venue. This isn't usually my kind of joint – I've been known to subsist on coffee and dark chocolate.'

Freya laughs. 'Well, the coffee stand might interest you – it's right over there.'

'That's definitely my first stop.' Isla looks over at the bulging tote bag she is carrying. 'You find anything good?'

'Yeah, I'm trying to look after myself a bit more, get my vitamins in.' Freya looks at Isla, places her hand over her belly pointedly, then performs the action again.

It takes Isla a while to click, 'Oh my god, you're pregnant? Congratulations!'

Then. 'Shit. It's Jay's, isn't it?'

'Yes . . .'

'And you're going to keep it?'

Freya looks away then. 'Why does everybody ask me that? I am. It feels right.'

'It's a baby, not a dress at Macy's that you can return if you grow tired of it.'

'Isla, do you want to talk or not?' Freya may be prickly, but Isla can tell by the way she obsesses over finding the perfect quiet spot and buying them coffee that she is desperate to talk. 'Listen, I'm sorry I snapped at you. And I'm sorry I ignored your calls and messages. I was . . .'

'You don't have to explain. I get it. What did you want to talk about?'

'Remember that conversation we had about Julian? And the sexual harassment stuff? Well, you were right. Mel confirmed it, but I just got too tied up with Jay to follow it through. But I'm ready now.' She takes a shallow, nervous breath. 'Julian has behaved inappropriately with several women in our company. What's more, they're ready to talk.'

'Dammit, I knew it!' Isla recalls the flourish of articles in the paper singing Julian's praises. It is a stock-standard pre-emptive PR offensive. He expects these stories to come out, and soon.

Freya looks anxious. There's more. 'Detective Cohen arrested the man stalking me. Turns out he has a history of finding women online and doing the same thing, but the evidence I provided was enough to incriminate him.'

'That's a good thing!'

Freya is silent.

'Isn't it?'

'They still don't know who posted the advert, and I got this message the other day . . .' She hands Isla the phone, looking tearful.

'Nobody else has my number! Nobody except my friends, of course, and my colleagues. I think the person threatening me is the same person who posted the advert in the first place. I'm starting to believe the person doing this is closer to me than I thought.'

'Jay? Or Julian even?'

'I don't know what to think, but I know for sure that Julian isn't as spotless as he'd like us all to believe. There is a side to him that scares me. He could do anything. I know Jay was in bed with me the night Nicole was murdered, but Julian's only alibi is a Facebook video, something he could have easily edited.'

'Are you going to talk to the police about your suspicions? People need to know if he is a sexual predator, and if there is a possibility that he was behind your harassment, you deserve to get to the bottom of it.'

'If I do that, I lose everything, my job, my security. Most importantly, these allegations will destroy Atypical and thousands of underprivileged women won't benefit from the services I have worked so hard on.'

'It's still the right thing to do.'

'Is it? Atypical's work is going to help so many new mothers survive childbirth and give them access to the care they desperately need. I can't imagine being in pain and fearing for mine and my baby's life, knowing that there is no help on the way. It's not fair!'

Isla persists. 'You know, I saw Julian a few weekends ago meeting with my editor, who has consistently tried to squash this story. A strange man was with them. Then, I saw the same guy when I went to the station for questioning. He's the Deputy Chief of Police! We are on to something big, Freya. We now just have to have the faith that if we expose Julian's misdemeanors, justice will follow.'

She clutches Freya's hands, excitement hammering in her chest. 'I will help you, OK? Get me the stories of these women, and I will help publicize your project. An investor is bound to see the story and pick it up.'

'What if it's nothing? What if I am just being paranoid, about Julian's role that night, and even the sexual harassment?'

In Isla's mind, the pieces begin to fall seamlessly together. A long-neglected hurt is resolved.

'I pretended that my own sexual assault was nothing for too long, Freya, and it ate me alive. No matter how "small" you think the action is, no matter how implicated you feel, you need to speak up. You have to free yourself before silence imprisons you for good. I believe you and I are on to something big.'

'Why are you so sure about this?' she says, depleted.

'Because the truth stands firm. And if reporting has taught me anything, it's that if you tug at one strand of evil, the entire illusion unravels.'

Chapter 93

Isla
Seven weeks after the murder

Isla drives through Fisherman's Wharf, System of a Down blaring. It is the first clear day in weeks and she can follow the azure ocean, all the way to the horizon. Finally, everything is coming together. Tomorrow, she will meet with Freya again, who will have gathered the women prepared to speak out against Julian. Bernard has put her in touch with an editor at the *New York Times*, who has already expressed some interest in the story without her even uttering Julian's name.

There's a bit more traffic than usual, but not even that can bring her down. All her hard work is finally adding up. Best of all, her job as a journalist means something again. This is what she is passionate about: exposing the truth about those that profit from lying. She edges forward, inch by inch, her ankle cramping from riding the clutch.

A sound on her passenger window, a dull thud. At first she thinks she's knocked her side mirror on something, but then the glass shatters, and she sees the sharp object jutting through it.

'What the fuck?' she screams, in a voice far removed from her own, a voice she hasn't heard in years.

A man in a balaclava grabs her by the scruff of her shirt, and holds a knife to her neck. He growls unintelligibly but she knows the drill. She hands over everything, from her dad's old watch to all the cash in her wallet and puts her hands up in the air.

'That's it! That's all I fucking have!'

His hand, and the knife quivering in it, retreats. As suddenly as he appeared, he is gone. Isla is left alone, with tiny shards of glass sprayed over her body like snow.

Instead of pulling over, she keeps driving, until she reaches the safety of the police station. Another crime to report. Another statement to make.

Once parked, Isla scrambles to find her state ID and her driver's license, then remembers that both are gone. She stumbles out of the car and trips, her bloodied hands scraping against the gravel of the parking lot. Something inside her unravels, something that she has kept bottled up for far too long.

It's just a smash and grab. Material items that can be replaced. Her car will be repaired, but Isla can't stop crying. She lets out a scream that draws a handful of officers outside. The endless coffee, the days living on only a rush of adrenaline, the nightmares, the asthma. They were all signs that she was trying to ignore. It is time to finally admit that she has been suffering for a very long time. Now, she has to make a change, and do something to heal.

Chapter 94

Freya
Two months after the murder

Freya's heart is in her throat as she walks through the red and green doors of Café Trieste. The place is fuller than she'd like, but most of the patrons are self-enclosed freelancer types tapping away on MacBook Airs, or local North Beach Italians.

She loves the rich smell of espresso in the air, and the fleeting strains of Italian conversation. It reminds her of carrying bowl after bowl of freshly made pasta through the restaurant years before. Funny how those days seemed so grueling, but in hindsight, they shaped her into who she is today. She picks a booth at the back, and busies herself looking at the pictures of famous people who have visited in the past. It's a poor distraction. What if she is the only one who pitches up? What if Julian has gotten wind of her plans? Isla's phone has been off for the past day – what if she has chickened out over the story and this has all been for nothing?

Mel strides in, turning heads in a Sophia Loren-style red polka dot dress and blown-out dark waves.

'An espresso with a shot of Baileys please.' She turns to Freya, 'I need to take the edge off.'

'Tell me about it. Every time I look at the door, my stomach does somersaults.' They try and talk about superficial things, like the quirky stores where Mel buys her clothes, where Freya sources her sewing patterns, and the latest Apple OS update. They have more in common than she realized. Freya wishes she'd had this closeness from the start, it feels so good.

Isla runs in, looking even more wired than usual. 'Hi, Freya, sorry I haven't been in touch. I had a smash-and-grab incident yesterday and my cellphone was stolen.'

She extends a hand towards Mel. 'You must be Nicole's friend, Melanie. I'm so sorry for your loss.' There is a colony of tiny cuts all over Isla's hands.

'Are you OK?' Freya asks.

'Not at all, but I will be one day soon and no, I don't want to talk about it. Let's focus on the story at hand. Do you think people will come today?'

Freya and Mel have relied on word of mouth to get the message out there. As far as possible, they tried to leave no digital footprint. Freya didn't want to believe that they were being tracked, but she had her suspicions, especially after seeing Jay's note in his apartment.

Ten minutes pass, then twenty minutes. They order some pastries to justify more time at their table during peak hour. The custard Danish Freya orders is buttery and soft, but she can barely taste a thing. This was a stupid idea – nobody is coming because they see it for what it is. Career suicide.

Thirty minutes in, the door opens. It's Penny, the ball-busting head of sales at Atypical. 'I'm here for the crucifixion of Julian Cox – is this the right place?'

Soon, she is followed by one woman, and then another. On and on it goes, the women marching in. Soon their booth is filled, then the extra chairs are not enough. Eight women armed with varying allegations of sexual harassment from Julian Cox.

Chapter 95

Isla
Seven and a half weeks after the murder

Julian Cox. Digital maverick. Industry leader. Sexual offender.

Isla flicks through her notes breathlessly. In her hands, she has a number of women who have chosen to speak out against Julian Cox. Some have even agreed to have their names and pictures published alongside the story.

Good, strong, powerful women, all survivors of harassment in a place where they thought they were safe. No matter what the infringement, every woman said the same thing. They thought they were crazy, and that nobody would believe them. In every instance, he found a hook, a way to make them feel guilty, and implied their jobs were on the line. He was always too close for comfort, and knew too much about their habits, their greatest weaknesses.

Not anymore. The second this story drops, every woman will feel vindicated. Julian will receive the outrage he deserves. The combined power of their stories will be impossible to ignore.

She calls Bernard using Freya's personal phone. 'OK, I checked your edits and have been through the story three more times . . . is this really it?'

'It's a great story, Isla: factual, emotive and with a big chunk of your own soul glistening between the lines. The editor is waiting, you know what to do.'

Isla takes a deep breath, and has a sip of cold coffee. In writing this story, she has made sense of herself. She has let go of some of her guilt, enough to feel compassion for the broken shards of her heart, and her aching, strangled voice. If only she could solve the mystery of Nicole's murder too.

She takes a deep breath, presses send, throws on her coat, and races out the door. Now, for another pressing priority – herself.

Chapter 96

Freya
Two months after the murder

It's a funny thing, biding one's time, working up to a big move. Freya is acutely aware that the office that has become her home will soon be closed off to her once more. As soon as the story hits the papers, she will be out of a job, they all will. Her heart aches when she thinks of the women who are waiting for their technology on the other side of the world. Freya hopes that Isla is right, and that she is able to help them one day.

She tries to take in the small moments she loves the most: making herself a cup of tea with a view over the city, the baby stirring the moment the sugar hits. This place was meant to be her answer, and for a while it felt like it could be. On days like today, when the work is interesting and the atmosphere in the office is light, she wishes she could stay like this forever, drawing a salary, contributing to a pension, living a comfortable life. All she had to do was tread gently, and not scratch the surface to reveal the dirt below.

Ruth sidles up next to her. 'Freya, can Julian and I see you for a minute?'

The forced joviality is gone from her voice. Her tone is cold. Have they already found out what she has done?

Julian is already waiting in his office. He's had a haircut – short back and sides cut close to the skull. It highlights the arch of his cheekbones. For Freya, it unmasks the silent aggression he has previously kept so well hidden.

'Freya, we cannot ignore any longer that your focus is not entirely on your work. We think it's time you take a little break.'

'Wait, what?'

'We will cover everything, and your salary will continue to be paid, but we think you need some time away from the office right now.'

'But I have almost completed the project!' She doesn't want to be away when the shit hits the fan. She wants to be here, in the office, when Julian is led away in handcuffs.

'This isn't a debate.' Julian clenches his teeth, his voice firm. 'We will book you into a sanctuary to take some rest. You are exhausted and unfit to work right now.'

It makes no sense. In the past week, she has solved several complex problems, which has had even the most misogynistic of techies hovering around her desk to see how she did it.

As much as she wants to sustain the fantasy of what she wanted Atypical to be, her bosses have shattered it for her. They are as rigid-minded as any corporate executives, a pair of gray suits trussed up in T-shirts and bright sneakers.

'I don't agree with this,' she explodes.

'Take care,' says Ruth saccharinely.

She storms to the balcony and tries to allow the fresh air to calm her. This degree of anger can't be good for the baby. A strange wind has picked up, and it tousles her hair. A rustle behind her, it's Mel.

'You OK?'

'They're kicking me out. Shit, I can't fucking believe it. I've given so much to this company already and now they have decided that I'm a bit fragile, they want to ship me off to some retreat center to relax.'

'I'm so sorry. Do you think that someone chickened out and told him what we're up to?'

'Yes, it began when I spoke to HR about Julian. They're probably hoping that a few months in the countryside will keep me quiet.'

Mel lowers her voice. 'This is exactly what they did with Nicole. One minute she was the company star, the next she was sent off when she started getting out of line.'

Everything starts to fall into place. Nicole was abused, belittled, her fragile mental health ignored. When her feelings became inconvenient, she was sent away.

And then she was murdered.

'Maybe Nicole became such an inconvenience that Julian decided to take care of her, once and for all. Maybe Jay finished the job off for him,' she whispers to Mel.

'Now that I think about it, the whole situation did seem strange at the time. They sent her to a retreat center in Napa Valley. The rich go there to recalibrate among the orchards.

It's lush, beautiful and the perfect place to go if you are struggling with mental illness . . .'

Melanie pauses for a moment and looks around her, leaning in closer. 'I suppose it's harder to believe sexual allegations against a CEO when the accuser is holed up in a treatment facility.'

Freya remembers those early days when she tried to get to know Nicole. She tried to assert her power over Freya, but her edges were frayed, threads of sanity were breaking free, refusing to be contained. She was a woman on the edge.

'It does something to you,' says Melanie, 'when someone continually tells you that you're lying. You start to hate the world you're trying to live in, you start to rage against it. Sometimes, I wonder what Nicole knew that we didn't.'

There is some activity inside. Freya can see Ruth and Julian stirring in his office, looking their way, pushing back their chairs. There isn't much time.

'It was more than the harassment claims and her relationship with Jay that did it in the end,' says Mel. 'A few weeks before she died, she told me she had stumbled on to something shocking that was being done at the Atypical offices, something that would ruin its reputation for good. I think that in order to save the company, they needed to paint her as a woman driven mad by jealousy, by love. Unfortunately, towards the end, she started living up to their expectations.'

Ruth and Julian pace side by side to the balcony. Julian's eyes lock onto Freya's with a contempt she didn't realize was possible.

On her way out of the office, she is stopped by Virginie.

'Where are you off to in such a hurry?'

'Julian and Ruth want me to take some time off. They don't think I'm performing at my best.'

She steps back, aghast. 'That is complete rubbish! You're the best we have!'

Freya hugs her friend tightly. 'Thank you for standing by me from the very beginning. During the months of Nicole bullying me, and the shock of Jay, I don't know what I would have done without you. All those hot chocolates and chats in the kitchen meant so much to me. You were the only person in this company that I could trust.'

Virginie's body trembles within Freya's arms. She pushes away. 'Shit! I can't bear to keep this in any longer. Freya, please believe me when I say I love you as a friend and don't want to lose you.'

Freya's jaw clenches. Not another liar. She can't bear it. Her voice sounds like someone else's – cold. 'What did you do, Virginie?'

'I didn't do anything, it's about what Jay did! I wanted to tell you early on, I really did, but you seemed so happy and in love with him. I thought that maybe things between you and him were different.'

It was hard enough imagining Jay's hands all over her worst enemy, but her trusted friend, too? 'You slept together. Just say it.'

Virginie shakes her head emphatically. The sound of her earrings jangling rings in the silence. 'No, but Jay did hit on me. It was a few days after I joined Atypical. He found me in the kitchen and asked me out for a hot chocolate.'

A terrible instinct resounds in Freya's mind. Hot chocolate. How did Jay know?

'Go on . . .'

'I wasn't interested. I prefer the quiet, geeky type. He was just too . . . excitable for my liking. But he persisted. He knew details about my life, ones that I didn't remember sharing, like where I grew up in France. Then one day he made a comment about a Godard film that just happens to be my favorite. I wrote it off as a coincidence but now, after everything that has happened, I'm not so sure.'

'You think Jay researched you online before you joined the company?'

'Yes, but more than that. His and Julian's behavior is making me feel uneasy. Something is going on in this company. There is more than meets the eye.'

Freya nods. She squeezes her friend's hand, a quiet assurance that everything is fine between them. Something sinister is definitely going on behind the scenes at Atypical, and she intends to find out exactly what it is. Tonight.

Chapter 97

Isla
Two months after the murder

It's a different sort of adrenaline, this. It is not the urgent, distracting excitement of chasing a news story but more direct, uncomfortable. Isla can't pretend it is fun or thrilling. The truth is, she's just plain nervous.

She follows a winding cobbled path, which leads to a small cottage that has almost been swallowed by ivy. A tiny woman with thick, curly hair and glasses smiles from the doorway.

'You must be Isla! I'm Sadie!'

Isla warms to the room immediately. There are so many fascinating books on the bookshelf, and bright scatter cushions decorate the couches. There is no conspicuous tissue box resting on the table, like in most psychologists' offices.

Sadie's voice has a heavy Israeli accent and charming abrasiveness to it, as if it has grown ragged from too many late dinner parties, soaked in laughter.

'What can I help you with today?'

'It's a long story.'

She laughs. 'It just about always is.'

'I was attacked last week in a smash and grab. This, and a story I have been working on have brought up an incident that happened to me a long time ago. It must be over ten years now. For some reason, I can't seem to move past it.'

'That is a long time to wait to talk about something,' Sadie says thoughtfully.

It hurts to say it out loud. 'Sometimes I wasn't sure what happened to me was a big enough deal for me to officially see someone? This smash-and-grab incident is a recognized crime so a visit to you seems more appropriate, if you know what I mean?'

'You can't take the guilt anymore. And the flashbacks.'

She's hit the nail on the head. The memory has not faded, but increased in weight and size. It feels like she is about to burst. Then there are the nightmares, the constant feeling of guilt, the pumping adrenaline and the will to keep running.

'The case I was assigned. The woman who was hurt has brought up some of my own memories.'

'How come?'

'She was hurt by someone who knew her. She trusted someone and they betrayed that trust. I think that's what started this.'

The silence folds around them. 'You're a writer. You are used to telling stories, both to others and to yourself. You say you're not sure if you experienced a real crime? Tell me what happened to you, free from your own judgment of whether it is valid or not.'

There is a lump in Isla's throat. Dammit, she promised she wouldn't cry the moment she got into therapy.

'How?'

'Focus on telling me how you felt, not what actually happened.'

Isla closes her eyes, and the words begin to spill out of her.

She remembers the night, it was uncharacteristically hot. Getting ready in her bedroom, pulling on a short tartan skirt, fishnet tights, Doc Martens and a band T-shirt. Messed-up hair – just the right amount of undone to make it look like she didn't care. She'd bought some chewing gum and cigarettes at a service station, and that delicious feeling that she needed it, she was going to kiss someone that night. Not just anyone, but the guy on stage, shirtless, thrashing the drums.

Full moon, something in the air, like something big was going to happen. She drank the intensity of it away with one tequila shot after another. Her body flowed to the music, the crowd pushed her against the stage, bruising her ribs.

She waited in the crowd for him, when he descended sweaty and resplendent. Her boyfriend, her man, hers. Hyped up on the beat, he smashed his mouth into hers in a kiss. He drew blood but she liked that he felt so passionate, that everyone saw who she was kissing.

Going home, she swayed in his arms, realizing only then how drunk she was, how out of control. She wanted to grab a pizza slice and cuddle up at home, but he took her back with the band. A bunch of guys and one girl, all doing shots. She wanted him, she only wanted him.

White powder, arranged in a line. The air smelled bitter then, like chlorine. The conversation soured with aggression. It started as a joke, as the guitarist moved in to kiss her, and then the singer. She expected him to say something, to say no before her lips could form the word herself. But he stood back, and then he joined them.

Nobody heard her say no. Nobody ran after her when she was spat out on the street, barefoot and broken. She stumbled on shattered glass, cutting the soles of her feet. The way she cried that night was singular – animal-like – stripped down and raw. Anguish ripped its way through her body. Nobody could comfort her, especially not those who should have helped.

Later, they said she asked for it, when the bruises on her wrists had safely faded. Groupies do crazy shit. They denied forcing anything. The drummer was her boyfriend, after all.

Isla has never slept the same since that night. The guilt keeps her awake, the perennial question of whether she was complicit in her own pain. The prospect of facing them in court made her sick, so she dropped the case and tried to forget. She only realized the full scale of the crime when Simon came along. And even when she took the case to court in the end, resolution didn't come in the form she'd hoped. All she felt was hollow.

When Isla is done, she feels both soiled and cleansed. Reliving the memory hurt, but not as much as keeping it festering inside.

Sadie hands her a cup of tea and offers a tin of biscuits. 'Here, have some sugar, it will take the edge off.'

Isla smiles. Her kind of therapist.

'Can you see how something so big could hold you back,' Sadie asks, 'and do you see how your obsession with this case is simply a way of trying to get justice for yourself?'

'Yes, I see that. There's another story I have ended up writing as part of this investigation, which reveals a serial sexual offender. It should be on newsstands tomorrow morning.'

'So everything is coming together then. You have used your pain to help others. Look after yourself, Isla, and come see me again. You also deserve justice and to move forward in your own life.'

Isla leaves the sanctuary of the room. The air feels clearer and her heart isn't pounding as hard as before. She has no job, she is a person of interest in a an unsolved murder case, she has an inflammatory story that will make her more enemies, and a day that stretches ahead of her, empty. Yet somehow, it feels like her life is only just beginning.

Chapter 98

Freya
Two months after the murder

The office she was so proud of has been packed up. It is clean, blank, waiting for the next star to decorate its bare walls. When Freya left earlier that day, she 'forgot' to drop off her access card with Mathilda at HR. Now, she uses it to enter the offices one last time.

She won't be here tomorrow when the police walk in to see Julian. She won't be present when their stock crashes and the investors, inevitably, pull out one by one, and go searching for a cleaner company to attach their names to.

The space, emptied of people and activity, only adds to her melancholy. This place was once so filled with potential, she could feel it. She knows Nicole felt it too. They all wanted to be a part of the fantasy. She thought she had found her dream career, and her true love. Soon, all the dreams and memories will be replaced by another business, a new group of people heady with anticipation that they might change the world.

It's getting late. She doesn't like being out too long. For the baby's sake. Freya pulls her jacket close, instinctively protective. There are too many threats out there after dark.

She types her password into her computer, holding her breath in the hope that IT hasn't removed her account off the system yet. A few seconds pass, then the familiar home screen appears before her. Yes! She's in! If Nicole was able to stumble on inconvenient company information, then she should be able to as well. All staff has the same privileges when it came to accessing data.

Data. That was the only other project both women were working on. In addition to their East African project, Freya had helped Nicole design an algorithm to sort through random data. However, neither knew what the algorithm was being applied to.

She opens the file, not sure what she is looking for. Then she sees it, an innocuous folder called 'Project Pilot'. Inside are three PDF documents. Freya's pulse shoots up as she opens the first.

It's a complex trend map of random words. Travel. Music. Sewing. Rare fabric. Vintage pattern-making. Hacking. Science fiction. Ted Chiang. Cortado. Indian food. Her eyes water, as she zooms in and looks closer. She recognizes these words, and the subjects feel familiar to her.

Then, with a jolt, she understands why. She is looking at the summary of her own Internet search history over the past six months. The algorithm that *she* designed has coolly sorted the information into trends and themes. Seeing such a clear footprint of her life online is the worst exposure of all. She looks over her shoulder, saves the document onto a flash drive, then opens another one. Hot chocolate, Godard, Bordeaux. Virginie. Heart pumping, hands sweating, she opens the third PDF. An algorithm can sort through information and find trends, but it can never recreate this feeling. Of the jigsaw falling into place. Of pure dread.

Her suspicions are confirmed. The words Chanel, Scandi minimalism, and home gardening. When she reads the words 'Poison perfume, Dior' she knows it is a map for Nicole.

The familiar 'ping' of the elevator.

The heavy doors sliding open.

The office, suddenly flooded in bright fluorescent light. Shit.

Footsteps. Heavy, thudding steps that reveal the person behind them.

You walk like the Incredible Hulk, you know that?

A flashback to a happier time, when she knew the inside of his bed, his mind, his mouth. Or thought she knew.

The steps quicken, she sees his silhouette moving towards her door. There isn't much time. She types a message, sends it to Isla and Detective Cohen. Isla, because she knows the truth about Jay, and Detective Cohen because he can protect her.

'At the office. Jay here. Am afraid. Please help.'

The 4G signal isn't good, which she always found ironic given the nature of Atypical's business, so she is not sure if the message sends. She slides the phone into her handbag just as Jay walks into her office.

'Hello, Freya – bit of a surprise to see you here, although nothing should surprise me anymore,' he says, coolly.

'I'm surprised you're here too,' she says. Her heart is hammering but she tries to keep her tone level. The longer she can stall him, the more likely that Simon will arrive in time.

'Call it a hunch,' he smirks.

Suddenly, he is behind her, staring at the screen, his hands resting on her shoulders. 'Well, it looks like it was more like an infringement of my privacy, than a hunch,' Freya says.

'Clever, isn't it?' Jay smiles.

'You were tracking what Nicole and I did online, and Virginie too . . .' It seems so obvious now. The targeted gifts when she joined the company, the way Julian always seemed to know her interests before she told him.

'Atypical was. I wasn't that interested in you three. You're all far too much work.'

Freya sits very still. Jay's hands move from her shoulders and tighten around her neck, not quite strangling her but the potential is there, pulsing in his fingers. She feels for something close to her, her pepper spray, her keys, but she can't reach down to her bag without alerting, and infuriating Jay. She needs to act slowly, carefully. God, she hopes that message sent.

'Virginie told me what you did. Nicole is gone, but the rest of us know now, and we're not going to let you get away with it,' Freya says. Jay must know that the women have started to assemble, and become a force of their own.

'So,' he says, contempt coating his words, 'if you're such a clever girl – can you tell me what we did with the information?'

She thinks for a moment. Come on, Freya, solve the problem! The algorithm was built to analyze the information and organize it into themes. Her thoughts return to the crudely handwritten list she found at Jay's flat.

Then, it hits her, like a slap across the face. The thread running between all women – Jay's attention. His love for Freya was contrived, an act.

'You used that information to make both Nicole and I fall in love with you.'

'Genius, right? Julian and I wanted to test what interests we would have to reflect back at a person to gain their trust. We were going to sell this information to corporations to help with their digital marketing.'

Her thoughts spin. Of course. Every corporation wants people to care about them enough to influence their decisions. The flipside of love is money.

'You invented a mind game to make people spend money?'

'You got it. We secured pre-emptive investment from fast-food corporations, banks, global clothing brands and even political parties looking to canvass voters. It's not enough to simply sell products to people anymore, we need to find a way to make people fall in love with them. We are on to something here, and Atypical will make billions from this. Those little pro-bono projects in Africa that Julian talks about in the press don't pay the bills, you know.'

Freya's heart is thudding now, loud in her ears. This feels dangerous. Will help come in time?

'Everything you ever said to me was fake, even the clothes you were wearing the day I met you.'

He sniggers darkly. 'You women are so superficial when it comes down to it. Just mention a few of your favorite bands and you think we're soul mates. We meant nothing, babe. And I proved my theory right by getting you to date me again, even after everything that had happened. At least with Nicole we had *some* sexual chemistry . . .'

What a waste. All those starry-eyed days spent thinking they had something special. All those awkward evenings spent selling him to her friends. She can already hear Kate's 'I told you so' ringing in her ears. If he hadn't smiled at her across the room that first day, if she hadn't smiled back, then everything would be different. She would be sleeping soundly at night, her life still blissfully simple.

'Why do you hate me?' she whispers.

'Excuse me?'

'Why do you hate me? Actually, why do you hate women so much? Why test this out on us?'

He stares at her for a moment, face contorted with rage. He looks like a different person.

'No matter how smart or accomplished I was when I was younger, women would never look at me. I was always the best friend, the person who had to listen to all their stories of first dates, first kisses and first times having sex. I'm an analytical guy, so I started to look for a pattern. The men that women went for always reflected an aspect of them.

They weren't looking for someone smart and challenging like me, they wanted a reflection of themselves. Once I saw it, I couldn't get over how fucking pathetic it was, how easy.

'So I changed. I began to mirror my female friends, and the women I met in bars. I gave them what I thought they wanted. God, I was good at it. It was only after running this theory past Julian one drunken night that we realized that it could make us money.'

'That's disgusting, you know that, right?'

'It's the truth. Relationships are superficial, a sham. I got into your head by hacking into your email, and your Facebook account. First, I used the information to make you fall for me, and then when I grew bored, to torture you. Everything you thought we shared was actually *nothing*.' He laughs, long and low.

Freya can't hold it in any longer. 'Well, *babe*, we may have meant nothing but that nothing has now created a baby. And believe me when I say that I am going to take you for every cent you have.'

His face twists. 'A. What?'

'You heard right. A baby, and I'm keeping it.'

Jay has scared her before, but she has never seen him this angry. His hand sweeps across the desks as he charges towards her. Old notepads and stationery items clatter to the floor.

'You conniving bitch!'

Freya frantically scrambles backwards. She needs to protect herself, and her baby. He came so close to hurting her last time.

He moves forward. 'You did it on purpose!'

Fearful as she is, she can't hold in her feelings any longer. She wanted to believe Jay was perfect for her but all this time he was selfish, weak, a coward.

'It takes two to have unprotected sex, you idiot.'

She slams backward into her desk. She is trapped in a corner, helpless. Please, please be awake, Isla! Please be on duty, Detective Cohen!

'*I'm sorry*,' she whispers, not to Jay, but to Nicole. It seems insane now that they both fought over someone so violent, that they convinced themselves that someone so empty was capable of love.

As Jay pushes her to the ground, as he looms above her, one sneakered foot in the air poised to strike, she hears the sound of running, then the door to her office slamming open.

'Freya! Freya? Jay Singh, get your hands off her!'

Detective Cohen, thank God, throws himself at Jay and pins him down, forehead slamming into the desk. 'You are under arrest for the assault of Freya Matthews.'

Isla follows close behind him and pulls Freya up and into a hug.

'We're here now,' she whispers. 'Everything is going to be OK.'

Chapter 99

Isla
Ten years ago

The Blackberry rings, shattering the silence. The sound is shrill and alarming. Nobody calls Isla anymore, not since she came to her mother's house to lick her wounds. Apart from Lizzie, and occasionally Kirsty, the friends with whom she used to share cigarettes, shots and clothes have cleared out. Old discarded flotsam from the night before that has washed away. The party is over now.

It's not vindictive, she knows that. People just freeze when it comes to what to say. Their party must go on. The dancefloor fills up, night after night. The beat pulls them in, there is no room for someone sitting broken at the bar, someone fragile holding them back.

Nobody has directly asked her what happened. The news reports took care of that. The other information was passed on through whispers in the cold, joints being shared around a circle, and over coffee dates that she wasn't invited to. Life flows past her, an ongoing river of nights out, drunken stories and love affairs. She stays paralyzed with the guilt that it was all her fault. Nobody has explicitly said that it wasn't, so she assumes it was. She was so drunk that night, after all.

She doesn't recognize the number. Usually she wouldn't pick up and would sit in silence, imagining who was mocking her on the other end. But she's feeling a bit stronger today, so she leans forward and grasps the phone.

'Hello?'

'Hi there,' – the voice is of a young man, gruff and a little unsure – 'am I speaking to Ms Isla Davis?'

'Yes . . . is this a sales call? Now is not really a good time.' She bites her lip at the easy lie. All she has is time. She is made of time. It lies before her unused, all the time in the world.

He is quiet for so long, she thinks he has hung up. 'No, no. My name is Officer Simon Cohen, and I'm currently following up on cold cases from the past five years. I see you reported a rape last year?'

The phone shakes beneath Isla's trembling hands. 'I did, but you don't need to bother following up. I dropped the case. It's fine, I'm fine.'

'I can see that you dropped it. Do you mind telling me why?' His tone is so diligent and formal, as if he is following up on the customer service at a car dealership. Where does she begin? With the repeated flashbacks that make her stomach turn? Or the nightmares of her ex-boyfriend watching as she was assaulted? Can she sum up the angst, guilt and rage holding her hostage in a sentence, delivered to a polite young man over the phone?

'I didn't think it would go anywhere.'

'The trial?' He sounds shocked. Isla imagines him over the phone, trussed up in a new uniform that doesn't fit quite right, filled with pride, intent on believing that there is such a thing as justice.

'You're new to this, aren't you?' she says, sounding a lot wearier than her twenty-two years. 'They've got away with it, and there is nothing anyone can do about it. Now what else do you need from this call so I can get back to my life.'

Her life, which is currently in a state of inertia. All she does all day is eat plates of dry chicken nuggets and oven chips in front of home décor shows. She had plans to continue the journalism degree she dropped out of after the attack, to get a job, but she cannot seem to leave the confines of her mother's house. The world outside is too terrifying.

The line has gone quiet. She thinks he has hung up, petrified by her bitterness. Instead his voice lowers to a whisper.

'Ma'am, I'm not supposed to say these things, but I need to say this. What happened to you was wrong, it was a goddam tragedy. You deserved better, from the cops, from the media, and from the men who hurt you.'

The compassion is so refreshing, it awakens something in Isla, something she hasn't felt in months. 'Thank you, I needed to hear that.'

'Now if I were you, I would reopen the case. Then I would get out and do something that turns your pain into something useful. We all have the power to make the world a better place. I am determined to believe that, no matter how many times life tries to prove me wrong.'

Isla turns a chicken nugget in her hand, slides it through the ketchup pooled at the side of her plate. 'Thank you, Officer Cohen, you've given me a lot to think about.'

'It's a pleasure ma'am, have a lovely day.'

And although the afternoon passes the way it usually does, something shifts in Isla. The next day she gets up, washes her hair, finds a working pen, dusts off her college applications and decides to become a journalist.

Chapter 100

Freya
Two and a half months after the murder

In one day, everything changes. Simon brings Jay into the station for assault, and the story about Julian hits the papers, unleashing a second wave of accusations. Freya, Hattie, Jasmin and even Kate are glued to the news.

'It's finally over,' says Kate, hugging Freya. 'The nightmare is finally over.'

'Well, not quite,' reminds Hattie, the resident crime buff. 'They haven't caught Nicole's murderer yet.'

Jasmin is incredulous. 'It's obviously Jay. Look at how violent he was to Freya! Or it could even be Julian. Why do you think he willingly turned himself in to the police? I'm sure it will all come out soon enough. One crime leads to another and he is practically dripping with motive.'

Her mobile phone rings, and Freya steps into her bedroom, away from the excitement. It's Ruth.

'I hope you don't mind me calling you, Freya. I just wanted to apologize. You tried to reach out to me, and you tried to tell me about what Julian had done to you and I ignored it, just like I did with everyone else. He and I have been friends for years, and it was easier in a way to pretend that you were simply young and emotionally immature.'

'It's OK, Ruth.' She doesn't really mean it. Rage stirs within her. Ruth was Freya's mentor, and she should have protected her.

'But I feel so guilty. If I had let myself read the signs I could have prevented so much from happening.'

Freya feels a little sad for her, but won't let her off that easily. Ruth had the power to do something, power that none of them had. She signed the HR documents that dismissed Freya for an emotional sabbatical. She believed Julian's lies about her being crazy.

'Why call me now? Do you only feel sorry now that we have all been brave enough to tell our stories? We needed you, Ruth.'

'I know. And I feel your pain.' She pauses, and Freya thinks she hears a sniffing sound on the other end of the phone. Her boss – all-powerful, formidable and severe – is crying. 'I'm also going to the police station this afternoon.'

'Why?' Freya's mind races. Did Ruth *kill* Nicole in order to protect Julian? Would she go that far?

'I know where Julian was the night of Nicole's murder, and unfortunately what I have to say will prove his innocence.'

'What?'

'Because I witnessed Julian, in his drunken state, trying to force himself on one of the interns. When I tried to pull him off her, he threatened me. I hate to say it but it wasn't the first time I'd witnessed something like that. I tried to dismiss it, and act like it didn't matter, but

I think it's time I stand up for other women for a change, don't you?'

Freya can't believe Julian got away with it for so long, and that someone as powerful as Ruth was too intimidated to speak out.

'You did the best you could,' she says, and then adds quietly, more to herself than to Ruth, 'If Julian didn't kill Nicole, the police will have to reconsider that it was Jay.'

Chapter 101

Nicole
The night of the murder

Nicole sits on the sofa in her dressing gown, twirling her fork through a bowl of pasta. She sprinkles parmesan with a heavy hand, and adds a dash of chili. Comfort food, and hell, has she earned a little bit of comfort tonight. First, there was the strange incident of someone trying to place a dating advert in her name and then there was her hookup with Jay.

She thought she would feel a little better seeing him in her bed, naked and wanting her. For the minutes building up to the sex, and a few seconds after, she almost did. It was the victory she had been after for so long. All those days seeing him with *her* made her sick. Freya didn't deserve him, she didn't know how to love him the way she did. But he didn't hold her when they were done, or play with her hair like he used to. He simply stood up, put his clothes back on and gruffly excused himself. It would have hurt less if he had made an excuse, or took the time to conjure up a lie, but he didn't meet her eye, not once. She heard him tapping on his phone after cleaning himself up in the bathroom. Minutes after that, he was out the door.

She turns on the television and pours another glass of wine. Tonight cemented Freya as Atypical's new It girl. She is smart, beautiful, easygoing. Nicole, on the other hand, is difficult, messy and dark. Her intelligence has a dangerous edge, like a sharpened blade. She says things that people – Julian in particular – don't want to hear. Nobody likes an inconvenient woman. Even as Jay shifted, as he touched her body, she knew that he wasn't doing it out of desire. Nicole was a liability, a pot boiling over the edge. She'd had enough of Atypical's boys' club tendencies, Julian's come-ons and some of their dishonest business practices. She'd been threatening to blow the lid for some time, which earned her a stint at a high-end retreat supposedly to treat her bipolar disorder. The more she grieved for Jay and what they had, and the more he paraded his new relationship in front of her, the angrier she became. Jay knew that Nicole had nothing to lose, and he was trying to keep her quiet.

It was never meant to be like this. She is a good person, kind, loving. *She* was supposed to be the shining star, dangling on Jay's arm like the Rolex he used to sport before that vintage embarrassment he now wears. *She* used to receive all the praise for a job well done. But bad things have happened, so she lashed out.

A firm knock on the door. Her heart leaps. Maybe it's Jay, returning to apologize for how wrong he's been. Maybe he will share her pasta like old times. They will curl up together, and he will wake up in the right woman's bed after all.

She adjusts her gown so it slips and reveals her left shoulder. Jay always loved her collarbones. He called them elegant.

The knocking again, more urgent this time.

'OK, OK I'm coming!'

She opens the door, already smiling in anticipation. It doesn't have to be a bad night after all. It could be the kind of night that turns everything around.

'Oh,' she says, uncertainty fraying at the edges of her grin, a nervous laugh escaping her lips. 'I wasn't expecting *you.*'

Chapter 102

Isla
Two and a half months after the murder

It's been so long since Isla has rushed across town, arms laden with flowers and a box of chocolates for the host, on her way to a party. But she and Freya agreed that after the tension of the past few months, everyone deserves a celebration.

Julian submitted himself to the police and will stand trial for eight instances of sexual assault. Jay has agreed to pay Freya a monthly stipend for her child, and is under investigation for illegally accessing both Nicole and Freya's personal data. Nothing has reached the press just yet, but Simon has shared with her that they have brought in Kenneth and the Deputy Chief of Police for questioning. Together, the three men have been sharing and selling personal data retrieved through Atypical's data mining, in conjunction with police records, and have been actively squashing the story in the press.

She listens to a voice message from Lizzie. 'Isla! That case you've been obsessed with has hit London. Everyone is talking about what a smart, fascinating woman Nicole was.'

'Thank God.'

'It's all because of your hard work, really.'

'I don't know. I never even figured out who the murderer was in the end.'

'But you tried, and challenged the perception of Nicole as a victim who deserved her fate. I think that's more than enough.'

Isla reaches the apartment, where Freya opens the door, looking more at ease than she has in weeks. Her loose sweater still doesn't reveal a bump, but there is a visible glow to her. Isla dumps the flowers and chocolates in the kitchen and joins the party that is already in full swing. Mel is there, along with the rest of Nicole's friends. Freya's roommates laugh raucously in the kitchen, while trying and failing to fry stuffed jalapeno pepper appetizers. Even Simon is here, in the corner, looking earnestly formal in a checked collared shirt and generous lashings of aftershave.

The air has a vicious chill to it. Even the roaring fire can't take the edge off it.

'Freya, can I borrow your jacket? I didn't dress well enough for this weather at all!'

'Sure! It's in my—'

'Actually, I think it's in my bedroom,' Kate interjects. 'Remember, Freya, I borrowed it yesterday? You can go through – it's hanging in the closet. My bedroom is the first door on the right.'

Kate's room is a chaos of French notes, makeup products and the multiple outfits of a woman who couldn't decide on what she wanted to wear that night.

She peers into the cupboard, searching for the familiar leather jacket Freya loves so dearly. As she pulls it from the hanger, a glint of something catches her eye. It's a gold necklace, tucked away in a clear bag amid the tangle of hats and shoes. Maybe it's the location, maybe it's the item's obvious value, but something urges her to pick it up. It's one of those name necklaces, popular since the days of *Sex and the City*. Isla casts her eyes over the letters, her gut clenching further with each one. The necklace is identical to the one listed as missing in the case report. The necklace spells out a name. Nicole.

She digs deeper in the cupboard. There, buried under more shoes is a scrunched-up piece of lace. She remembers the detail of it from the first time she met Freya, the way it contrasted with the black leather of her jacket. Now, the antique cream color has been stained brown with blood.

She leaves the offending items in place, to avoid sullying them with her fingerprints, and runs across the small apartment to where Simon is standing, awkwardly nursing a beer.

'Isla, hi! You look lovely.'

She blushes, then remembers why she approached him in the first place. 'Uh, thanks. You too. Listen, am I right when I say that a gold necklace was noted as missing in the case file?'

'Yes. As far as I remember, it was one of the items Nicole had recently insured. It was solid gold, burned into the shape of her name.'

It makes no sense, but it's a clue, a trail leading to an unexpected answer. 'Come, I need to show you something.'

They run to the bedroom. Kate's eyes catch them, and she and Freya follow them into the room.

'Everything OK here?' says Freya, looking nervously between Simon and her friend.

Simon is poker-faced. 'Kate, would you mind showing us a couple of things in your closet, please, a necklace and piece of lace, specifically?'

Kate's face crumbles as she leans forward, and they all stand staring at the incriminating name glinting in her hand.

'I can explain.' She looks desperately to Freya, whose face is contorted in horror.

'She was so fucking awful to Freya, she made her life a misery . . .' She backs towards the door. Simon is shifting from foot to foot, ready to move if he has to.

'I didn't ask you to do anything,' Freya says softly.

Kate is sobbing now. 'Freya mentioned that Nicole was learning French at Alliance Française, so I joined the same class as her. At first I tried to be her friend. I wanted to protect Freya, just like I always have. I needed to know why she hated her so much.' In a barely audible whisper, she turns to Freya. 'You're so special. Nobody should hate you.'

Freya cries, 'Kate . . .'

'I didn't mean to kill her,' she cries. 'I befriended her, I started to get how her mind worked. But that night Freya came home from the office party so upset and I knew I needed to teach her a lesson. I just wanted to scare her, but she wasn't even sorry for everything she did. She was wild, crazy, and she lashed out at me. I feared for my life.'

'No, Kate, no, no, no—'

'I needed to protect myself. She was drunk and raging, coming at me with that statue. But I was stronger than her ... you have to believe me when I say it was self-defense. I regretted it the moment I'd done it. She was such an unhappy person.'

'She doesn't need prison, she needs psychological help,' Freya says softly, looking desperately at Simon. 'I hope a judge can see that.'

Hattie, Jasmin and Isla hold Freya tightly while Simon moves forward. Kate doesn't resist.

'Kate Jones, you are under arrest for the murder of Nicole Whittington.'

Chapter 103

Freya
Six months later

'You ready?'

Ruth unveils a bright pink neon sign.

Freya's mouth hangs open, 'Oh my God, it's beautiful.'

'Isn't it just?'

After the dust settled, Ruth decided to relaunch Atypical as an NGO, dedicated to using technology to help women all over the world. She apologized to Freya for being so small-minded about her pregnancy and offered her a job as Head of Technology and Innovation. Together, they decided to rebrand the business *Malkia*, meaning 'queen' in Swahili.

They have designed a new business, one that supports women at all stages of their lives, including motherhood. Freya is much bigger now. She, Hattie and Jasmin have started converting Kate's old room into a nursery. A recent gender identification scan confirmed what she knew all along – the baby is a little girl, Freya's own tiny queen. Just two days ago, she laid out the tiniest piece of fabric and smallest pattern she has ever cut, and started making her baby's first outfit.

'Freya – your phone!' says Mel. 'Wait – don't even think about running to answer it.'

She dashes across the room and returns, looking serious. 'It's Detective Cohen. He says he has news . . .'

At first she thinks it is to do with Kate. Dear Kate, so misguidedly loyal. Some nights, when her back aches and the baby's kicking wakes her, she cannot shake the guilt that she should have done something to help her.

'Detective Cohen? How's everything going?'

He takes a deep breath. 'Kate's case has been scheduled for trial. She is pleading temporary insanity and self-defense, which I hope will hold with a judge. However, the time and effort Kate made befriending Nicole and gaining her trust doesn't look good. It suggests a premeditated crime.'

'All those nights Kate came home after French class, telling me about her new friends. I was so stupid, I didn't suspect a thing!'

'How were you to know? We think we know our friends . . . but often we don't. But that's not what I am calling you about. Our technology unit did a forensic audit on all the laptops possessed by Atypical the night Nicole was murdered. We found a dating advert, written in your name.'

Freya sits down slowly, palms sweating. The stress and fear of those messages still grips her when she least expects it. She still feels a rush of anxiety every time her phone lights up, still looks behind her twice when walking down the street.

'It was someone from work?'

He laughs over the phone. Inappropriately, Freya thinks.

'It was Nicole. She must have known about the prank you pulled that night and decided to get you back.'

Freya can't help but laugh herself. She can imagine Nicole receiving a message that night, asking her to approve the advert, and in her drunken state, writing one for Freya in retaliation. She may have had her good points, but when it came to Freya, Nicole was determined to terrorize her to the very end.

'But how did she get it approved?'

'We're not sure, but my guess is she somehow used her technical knowledge to override it.'

Freya wracks her brain – dammit, it's possible, if you try hard enough. 'She obviously really wanted to get back at me.' Then, she remembers. 'But it wasn't just an advert. Someone was engaging with these men, sending them private photographs of me that were taken long ago but still stored in my Google Drive. I don't understand how that person accessed them.'

Simon is quiet. Freya says, voice shaking, 'Oh shit, it was Jay, wasn't it?'

'Yes. As he confessed, Jay hacked into your Facebook account, and your personal email.'

Freya thinks back to the moment she changed her number, and the email sent to her account notifying her of the change.

'That's why, when I changed my phone number, he was still able to harass me! Him and the man who stalked me were two different people.'

'Correct.'

'You can prove that, right? As part of his data infringement case?'

'We're sure as hell going to try. For now, the advert is down, both Jay and your stalker are in custody, so nobody will bother you anymore.' The relief is so great, she begins to cry, despite herself. For so long she has lived her life looking over her shoulder. She needs to move on.

'I suspect you won't be hearing from me again. Keep well, Freya.'

'You too, Detective Cohen.'

Freya hangs up the phone and sits for a minute on her own, letting the news sink in. A shriek of laughter bellows across the offices – Mel and Ruth are joking around again. For all their complicated history, Freya wishes that Nicole hadn't died, and that she was here to see this, an office alive with smart women, all working together instead of being pitted against each other.

She carefully stands up. This body, once a source of fear, once a threat to her livelihood, is stronger than ever before. This life, that she spent so much effort trying to define, now leads her down a path more wonderful and rewarding than she ever expected. This is the new life she has been waiting for.

Chapter 104

Isla
Six months later

She should wear a dress, Isla thinks. Sadie, her psychologist, has encouraged her to go shopping more, and find items that celebrate her body. No more hiding her sexuality behind androgynous, baggy clothes. She throws on a floral tea dress she found at a vintage store during a shopping trip with Freya. It's cobalt blue and brings out her eyes. But it's a little *too* sweet.

'Fuck it,' she says, scratching in the chaos of her cupboard. Finally she finds them – her pair of Doc Martens, dusty and untouched since that fateful night ten years ago. Isla wipes the dirt off. Pulls them on. Now, she feels herself again.

Her hands brush against her new notebook as she prepares to leave. A brand-new Moleskine, embossed with her name, a gift from Bernard to celebrate her new job. Her exposé on Julian spread across the media like wildfire, and her photographs of Kenneth, Julian and the Deputy Chief of Police together assisted in outing their media coverup. Turns out that several women had tried to go to the press and the police with the story before, but their stories were squashed every time.

She had received job offers to work at *The New Yorker*, *The Atlantic*, even *Buzzfeed*, but Isla wanted to do something more meaningful with her time. With a generous investment from Ruth, she plans to start her own online magazine, filled with stories about women, written in their own words. Just thinking about it makes her feel lighter. She's been eating regular meals for over a month now, and, while she can't quite give up coffee, she has cut down to only two cups a day. All of this feels easier, now that she has found her voice.

A soft knock on the door. A new future lies on the other side, the most daunting future of all. Isla grabs her purse and runs down the hallway, just another girl about to go on a date, ready to love again.

'Hello, Isla,' he says.

Isla's heart swells in her chest. She can't control the smile that beams across her face.

'Hello, Simon.'

Epilogue
The night of the murder

'This is a bad idea, Kate,' Freya says. In the dead of night, the city is imposing, their footsteps echo, loud as gunshots.

Kate paces ahead of her, determined. 'I know Nicole now, we're friends. She is an angel to everybody but you. We need to find out why, tonight.'

'Jay won't be happy that we're doing this,' Freya mutters. Her thoughts are woozy, grabbing at random moments. What if someone else shows up at Nicole's door, someone that she and Jay have summoned through their prank? But her feet lead them to the apartment building, their memory stronger than her fear. Her hand raps abruptly at the door.

Nicole answers in a kimono, and Freya catches a glimpse of a dark nipple beneath the lush fabric. The smooth, tanned skin on her shoulder is exposed. The idea of Jay's hands on her body makes Freya queasy.

'Oh. I wasn't expecting *you* . . .'

'Hello, Nicole,' Kate says calmly, but Freya can sense the aggression in her voice.

'You two know each other?'

'I'm her best friend, bitch.'

Nicole tries to push the door shut. 'It's two in the morning, you're both insane.'

Kate is stronger, she is always stronger. She overpowers Nicole and pushes her out the way.

'You're a bully!'

Nicole starts to laugh, a deep, petrifying laugh. 'Well, that is rich coming from the both of you.'

Freya speaks up now. 'It's not my fault that Jay loves me more than he ever loved you. It's about time you got over him and left us alone.'

There's a wild look in Nicole's eyes. Her laughing grows louder, hooting and out of control. 'Jay loves you *more*. Jay loves *you* more. Oh please, tell me another joke, I'm all ears.'

That's when she smells it. The scent of Jay's aftershave, mixed with Nicole's perfume. She sees his leather jacket carelessly thrown over her sofa. Nicole's naked, sun-kissed chest. It all makes sickening sense.

'You are just a game to him, Freya. Nothing more.'

The laughter is too much, it unravels something in Freya's mind. She is sick of people telling her she is not good enough, that she is not worthy of love, success or a seat at the table. Everybody laughed when she said she wanted to study software engineering, they laughed when she said she wanted to come top of her class. People underestimate her at every turn. A decades-old rage is stoked. She picks up the object nearest to her, a statue, and hits Nicole, her blood soaking into the intricate lace of her leather jacket.

'*Freya!*' Kate shouts.

'Stop laughing at me,' Freya whispers, bringing the statue down over and over again.

'*Stop. Fucking. Laughing.*'

By the time Kate pulls her off, it is too late. Nicole is dead. The two women lug Nicole's body into the bathroom and prop it up in the shower, knocking over her perfume bottles in the process.

They walk quickly, quietly through the silent corridors of Nicole's apartment building. Outside, in the street, they can't stop shivering. It is more than the chill of snow in the air. It is something else.

Kate pulls off their woolen gloves, now soaked through with blood. She stuffs them in her handbag, along with Nicole's necklace that had fallen off during the struggle.

'Run, Freya, we've got to run now!' Her friend, usually so strong, and so self-assured, is shaking.

They sprint through the backstreets, as the sky begins to lighten ahead of them.

'I didn't mean to do it,' Freya says softly, shock coursing through her veins and tears streaming down her face.

'You did it to protect yourself. Shit. You have too much ahead of you, with no safety net to fall back on. This can't ruin that. I will protect you. I owe you so much. My parents are rich, and we have great lawyers. I'll plead insanity, or self-defense. If the police come for you, blame me, OK? I can take it.'

'I'm sorry, Kate. I was so angry. I lost it. I'm so sorry. I'm so sorry. I'm so sorry. I can't let you take the blame for this. What will I do? Tell me what I should do!' She can't stop crying. Every time she takes a breath, more tears flow, hysteria building.

'It's OK, we'll get through this,' Kate tells her. 'We always do, we just need to forget it. I know you didn't mean to do it.' She repeats this, as they walk home, arms interlinked. 'You didn't mean to do it.' But her voice sounds as if she is trying to convince herself.

Acknowledgements

The Pact is a special novel for me, in part because it reflects aspects of my own experiences, and those of the generous experts and people I interviewed.

Thank you to Katherine Armstrong, for seeing the heart of this book from its early drafts. From our first communication on the book, right till the end, you recognized my vision, and applied your incredible editing skills (and intense crime scene knowledge) to help me get out my own way and make the book the best it could be. Thank you to Jennie Rothwell for devising the perfect title for the book, as well as for your razor-sharp editorial insight. I'm also so appreciative of Alex Allden's creative interpretation of the book into a truly striking cover.

I am grateful to the Zaffre team for their assistance in getting *The Pact* out there, and into the hands of readers. A special thanks to Stephen Dumughn, Felice McKeown and Sahina Bibi from marketing; Nico Poilblanc, Angie Willocks, Vincent Kelleher from the sales team; and Francesca Russell, Clare Kelly and Ellen Turner from publicity.

As always, thank you to Sarah Hornsley who is a consistent source of support and guidance. I am so grateful to have you as my agent and so proud to be represented by The Bent Agency. Thank you to Jenny Bent for believing in my writing voice in the first instance. Without you, none of this would have been possible.

I consulted a wide range of sources in the writing of this book. Thank you to Michelle Craig for introducing me to the right journalistic contacts, and to Barry Bateman for your insights and anecdotes on investigative journalism. When it comes to the tech industry Luana Jordaan and Anna Vaulina are two of the most talented women out there – thank you for sharing your experiences with me, and Lu, thank you for our philosophical and entertaining discussions on Silicon Valley. Blaize, thank you for your excitement and encouragement from the start, and for helping me create the perfect tattoo for Freya.

The following people, and their honesty, played a great role in the authenticity of this novel: Lyndal Stuart, Mayleen Vincent, Leanne Renken, Kate Remas, Gail Schimmel, Sarah Anderson Wilson, Hayley Alfers and Dominique Le Grange.

I am grateful to Liesl Sadie and Pamela Power for not only reading the earliest drafts of this novel, but giving such important and relevant editorial feedback. Liesl, all our years of friendship mean the world to me, and it gives me the greatest joy to know that you see parts of me, and of us, in this story.

Thank you to Simon Pridmore and Josh Mason for being my first American readers, and checking that none of my rogue South African phrases and words made it onto the page.

This book was written on very little sleep, during the first year of Zach's life, in stolen moments at the coffee shop down the road. I am so grateful to Kate and Anna at Love Books for your kind words, bookish chats and encouragement, as well as the assurance that I would one day sleep again. Thank you to my family, Rosie, Mom and Dad, for being so supportive, and to my friends. Emma, your daily voice notes/podcasts were a constant source of humour and strength.

Zach, thank you for splitting my heart open, so that suddenly love stories and happy (ish) endings are weaving their way into my previously dark fiction. And finally Rhys, my love, what would I do without you! Thank you for teaching me what true love is, looking after me when I forget, and reminding me to take my vitamins.

And finally, I am grateful to every reader who picks this up, who engages with the characters and discusses this book with a friend. Your imagination brings my characters to life, and your support keeps me writing.

A Conversation with
Amy Heydenrych

What was your inspiration for *The Pact*?

When I was much younger, in fact, in my first job, I was bullied at work. As a result, I made a silly mistake, something that I regret, even to this day. It wasn't a mistake nearly as severe as Freya's but the experience always lived with me, this possibility that a person can be innately good, but crack under pressure and do the wrong thing.

Why do you think office bullying is such an important issue?

When I asked for stories about office bullying on social media, I was sent a deluge of stories. People that I saw as strong and successful told me stories about their ongoing harassment, pain and anxiety as a result of someone at work.

Office bullying, no matter how small or petty it may seem, is an epidemic that affects everybody. And in a changing economic climate where dream jobs are scarce, people sometimes feel forced to put up with unhealthy relationships and unfair treatment. What came up time and time again is that this conversation goes beyond #MeToo, but extends to woman-on-woman emotional abuse as well.

Why was the theme of female friendship so important in writing this book?

I wanted to capture the intense loyalty and complexity of female relationships. Most of the time, this fierce loyalty is a beautiful thing and results in women lifting one another up and protecting each other. However, this intensity can have a dark side, in which women see each other as competition. In the context of the #MeToo discussion, internalized misogyny and how it plays out in female friendships and office relationships is an important part of dismantling the patriarchy.

How does *The Pact* relate to your previous novel, *Shame on You*?

In *Shame on You*, I looked at what happens when someone in the spotlight makes a grave mistake online. With *The Pact*, I wanted to explore what happens when someone like you or I shares the wrong information online and the consequences we may suffer. I think it's a fear for everyone at the moment – share the wrong thing and it lives online forever.

What is your writing process like?

I start off each novel with a broad idea of the plot, and a lot of room for the characters and the story to breathe.

I then get the first draft down as quickly as possible so I can really see what the story is about. As many writers will mention, it is the editing process where the magic happens, as difficult as that can be. In this book, the editing not only allowed me to explore important aspects of the story, but showed me who the actual murderer was!

What are you reading at the moment?

I'm reading *The Doll Factory* by Elizabeth MacNeal, and everything I can get my hands on by Shaun Tan.

What advice do you have for aspiring writers?

Write the best book you can write, and don't rush the process. Everything you write, if it is true and has been edited with care, will find a home when it is meant to. And when your writing is ready, let it go. It is no longer yours but exists in the imaginations of those who read it.

Reading group discussion points
for *The Pact*

1. Nicole is found murdered in her apartment, and her neighbors heard nothing but laughter and a single loud noise. What was your first instinct as to what happened?
2. Freya thinks that she has started her dream job. What signs are there that her dream job will turn into a nightmare?
3. How much would you tolerate to stay in your dream job? If you were Freya, when would you have left?
4. Isla is frustrated with the way female victims of crime are portrayed in the media, as she believes they are objectified. Have you seen examples of this in actual media coverage?
5. Julian is open about researching Freya online. Do you think it is flattering or unsettling when employers look up job applicants on social media before they are hired?
6. Early on, we meet Freya's close friends. Throughout the novel, we find out the history of their friendship. Do you trust all of them?
7. Nicole seems intent on bullying Freya from day one. Why do you think this is?

8. It is clear from the outset that Isla and Simon share a history. When in the novel did you suspect that Isla's interest in Simon went beyond friendship?

9. Which of Freya's friends is your favorite, and why?

10. Nicole and Freya are more similar than they think. What similarities did you notice?

11. What was your first impression of Freya and Jay's relationship? How did that impression change during the course of the novel?

12. We learn that Isla initially didn't want to report her sexual assault. Why do you think women hesitate to report sexual assault?

13. How does the novel capture the feeling of the modern workplace in the wake of the global economic recession? Do you think that the cutthroat tension between Freya and Nicole is emblematic of today's working environments?

14. As you read more about Nicole's history and her struggle with her mental health, do you feel more empathy for her?

15. After months of office bullying, Freya acts out and plays a prank on Nicole. Do you think she was justified in doing this?

16. Isla has her guard up against love. Why do you think this is?

17. Freya's pregnancy is a source of tension in her personal and working life. She believes that it has the potential

to ruin her career. What impact do you think mother-hood has on a mother's career, and is that impact equal to that experienced by the father?

18. Later in the novel, we discover the dark side of Julian when a group of women come forward to report their experiences of sexual harassment. How does this reflect the reality of the #MeToo movement?

19. Discuss the narrative strategy of telling the story through the eyes of Freya and Isla? Why do you think the author chose these two characters? How does it add to the novel when, at the end of the book, there is one chapter written in Nicole's perspective?

20. Were you satisfied with the ending of the novel?